D0010422

A Wedding in Apple Grove

C.H. ADMIRAND

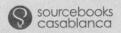
sourcebooks
casablanca

Copyright © 2012 by C.H. Admirand
Cover and internal design © 2012 by Sourcebooks, Inc.
Cover illustration by Tom Hallman

Sourcebooks and the colophon are registered trademarks of Sourcebooks, Inc.

All rights reserved. No part of this book may be reproduced in any form
or by any electronic or mechanical means including information storage
and retrieval systems—except in the case of brief quotations embodied in
critical articles or reviews—without permission in writing from its pub-
lisher, Sourcebooks, Inc.

The characters and events portrayed in this book are fictitious or are used
fictitiously. Any similarity to real persons, living or dead, is purely coin-
cidental and not intended by the author.

Published by Sourcebooks Casablanca, an imprint of Sourcebooks, Inc.
P.O. Box 4410, Naperville, Illinois 60567-4410
(630) 961-3900
FAX: (630) 961-2168
www.sourcebooks.com

Printed and bound in Canada
WC 10 9 8 7 6 5 4 3 2 1

This book is dedicated to three
very important people in my writing life:
my wonderful editor, Deb Werksman;
my fabulous agent, Eric Ruben;
and my dear friend, Anne Elizabeth,
without whom there would be no book.

Thank you all for believing in me and
allowing me to keep pursuing my dream.

Grandma Eagan's Buttered Pecan Pie

This is a wonderful twist to the traditional pecan pie, using roasted pecans for a unique flavor.

¾ cup (½ stick) unsalted butter
¾ cup heavy cream
1 cup firmly packed light brown sugar
¼ teaspoon salt
½ cup light corn syrup
1 teaspoon vanilla
3 eggs
1½ cups toasted pecan halves (toast pecans at 375
degrees for five to ten minutes, stirring three times
while baking)
Your favorite pie crust recipe

Preheat oven to 375 degrees. Heat butter in medium saucepan over low until a golden brown: DO NOT BURN. Immediately pour cream into butter to stop cooking. Pour into mixing bowl and blend in brown sugar, salt, corn syrup, and vanilla. Beat in eggs by hand until well blended.

Stir in pecans. Pour into pastry-lined nine-inch pie pan. Bake forty-five minutes or until filling is set.

© 2002 C.H. Admirand

Apple Grove, Ohio: Population 597

Apple Grove has always boasted that it's a small town with big-town amenities. Some of the local hot spots are:

Honey's Hair Salon—Owned by Honey B. Harrington, who has weekly specials from cuts to coloring and likes to advertise the weekly special by changing her hair color every week. (She's been trying to snag Sheriff Wallace's attention for the last fifteen years, but he's holding firmly on to his bachelorhood.)

The Apple Grove Diner—Owned by Peggy and Katie McCormack, featuring Peggy's Pastries.

Bob's Gas and Gears—Owned by Robert Stuart, former stock car driver who doubles as the mechanic.

Murphy's Market—Owned by the lovely widow Mary Murphy (who has her eye on Joseph Mulcahy—and he has his on her), where you can buy anything from soup to nuts—the metal kind—but it's her free-range chickens that lay the best eggs in Licking County and have people driving for miles to buy them.

Trudi's Garden Center—Owned by eighty-year-old Trudi Philo, who likes to wear khaki jodhpurs and

Wellingtons everywhere; she specializes in perennials and heirloom vegetables and flowers, and has been planting and caring for the flowers in the town square since she was in grade school, taking the job over from her grandmother Phoebe Philo when she passed the business on to her fifty years ago.

The Apple Grove Public Library—Run by Beatrice Wallace, the sheriff's sister—open three days a week!

The Knitting Room—A thriving Internet business run by Apple Grove resident Melanie Culpepper, who had to close up her shop when she became pregnant with twins.

Slater's Mill—Built circa 1850, this converted mill and historic site is a favorite among locals both young and old. Famous for its charcoal-broiled burgers and crispy fries served in the first-floor family restaurant, it's also been a favorite place for the younger set to congregate at the mile-long bar on the second floor.

Chapter 1

THE SWEET SCENT OF WILD ROSES FILLED THE AIR AS the late morning sun warmed the blossoms spilling over the arbor. Blackbirds trilled across the meadow as the bride walked toward her husband-to-be, careful not to trip on the long, white satin runner—the path reaching from her past to her future.

Folding chairs fanned out on both sides of the bride's backyard, enormous white tulle bows adorning every other one. When she passed by Megan Mulcahy, the bride reached for Meg's hand and squeezed it before continuing. Tears filled Meg's eyes as Edie reached the end of the satin walkway and turned so her father could lift the veil covering Edie's face and press his lips to his daughter's cheek before putting her hand in that of the man she would marry.

Who would have thought Meg would be one of the last of her friends still single? If her life had followed her youthful plans, her name would have been the one up on Apple Grove's water tower, Jimmy Van Orden would have been the man doing the asking, and she wouldn't be sitting here wondering how different her life could have been.

But life is full of twists and turns. Her mind drifted toward the last time Jimmy had come home for a couple of days. He'd wined and dined her and she'd been so sure that he was going to ask her to marry him—this time. But they'd had the discussion a long time ago; he wanted out of Apple Grove, and she didn't want to live anywhere else. After replaying that horrible argument multiple times, they'd just let it drop and tried to enjoy each other's company. She kept hoping that on one of his trips back he would change his mind and see how wonderful life here could be. When would she learn?

Reverend Smith's words rang out, "I now pronounce you husband and wife." He paused to smile at the friends and family gathered to celebrate, and then at the couple. "You may kiss the bride."

Bill Stanton tilted Edie's chin up and gently pressed his lips to hers.

A collective sigh whispered through the crowd witnessing the loving touch between the bride and groom. Meg's stomach ached, but she fought not to show it; her friend deserved all of the happiness she could get. This was Edie's day, and Meg wouldn't do anything to ruin it for her.

"Did you ever see such a lovely bride?"

Megan smiled at Mrs. Winter. "It's been a long time since we had a wedding in Apple Grove."

The older woman patted Meg's hand and soothed, "Never you mind about that Van Orden boy, Meg. The perfect man is waiting for you. Don't give up hope."

Meg laughed. "I haven't thought that way about Jimmy in years." *Liar*. "I hear he's doing well playing for the Bengals."

As expected, Mrs. Winter tut-tutted and patted Meg's hand again. "Your eyes say far more than you realize."

Before Meg could contradict her, the woman moved on to speak to the McCormack sisters.

"There now, Meg," her father's deep voice soothed the ache in her belly. "It's time you forgot about Jimmy—"

"I wasn't thinking about him," she insisted. A rumble in the distance made her heart freeze in her breast. She looked up at the lone cloud floating above her and then over at Reverend Smith. The Lord didn't like it when Megan lied. "OK," she admitted. "I might have been thinking about him."

Joseph Mulcahy pulled her close and kissed her forehead. "He isn't the right man for you, even though I should probably thank him."

"Whatever for?" Meg asked.

"He left, but you stayed and helped me keep the family business going. I don't know that I could have done it if you had married him and moved away."

"I love you, Pop."

"I love you back, Meggie." She loved the gruff sound of his voice and leaned into him as he put his arm around her. "Let's pay our respects to the newlyweds, then go find your sisters and dig into the potluck buffet. I'm hoping for some of Slim's barbecued ribs."

"You'll get sauce on your tie," she warned, smiling up at him.

"That's OK." He grinned and pulled her toward the receiving line. "I hate ties."

Meg had to work hard to keep from laughing at the way her father was staring at the food-laden tables just behind the beaming couple. "Congratulations, Bill," Meg said. "You do realize that you married the finest woman in Apple Grove, don't you?"

He smiled and pressed his lips to his wife's cheek. "I'm a lucky man."

Edie laughed and pulled Meg in for a hug. "I'll miss you most."

The words were like a hug she hadn't realized she needed. "I still don't understand why Bill couldn't keep on working at the farm with his father."

"I'm not handy like you, Meg," Bill said. "Besides," he leaned close and asked, "do you really want me to drop my pants in front of God and everyone here just to show you—that wicked scar from my dad's combine again?"

"Oh," her sister, Caitlin, cooed, moving to stand beside their father.

"Can I see?" Grace, the youngest Mulcahy sister, asked, squeezing in next to Meg.

Meg looked over at them and shook her head. "Bill is a newly married man and will not be mooning anyone but his lovely bride from here on in."

"Too bad." Miss Trudi Philo shook her head as she waited in line to congratulate the newlyweds. "I was hoping for a peek, seeing as how I missed out on that particular harvest mooning."

Meg could not help but join in the good-natured laughter the sassy eighty-year-old's comment incited.

"Now, Miss Trudi," Bill soothed. "I don't want to make my wife jealous today of all days."

She agreed. "I expect to see your first offspring nine months from today, so you'd best get to it; I'm not getting any younger."

Meg looked around for her father and noticed Edie's mother walking toward him. Mrs. Parrish linked her arm through Joe's. "You poor man, don't be shy," she said as she led him toward the tables. "Just grab one of those plates and help yourself."

Meg and her sisters stood side by side watching as the Widow Murphy joined her father at the food table. The two had their heads together, looking awfully chummy, making Meg wonder if there was something going on between them. "Hey, guys... I think Mrs. Murphy's flirting with Pop."

Cait and Grace turned as one to stare at their father and the dark-haired widow. Caitlin was the first to speak. "Maybe he's placing an order for supplies; you know she takes pride in the fact that she carries everything from soup to nuts... the metal kind."

Meg frowned up at her sister. "Are you being facetious or just naive?"

Caitlin shrugged. "Just giving Pop the benefit of the doubt."

"Besides," Grace said, "I like seeing him smile."

Cait hooked her arm through Meg's on one side, while Grace did the same on the other. "Give it a rest," Caitlin said. "Pop deserves a little flirtation, just the same as you do."

Looking up at her willowy sisters, Meg wished that she too could have been born with just a smidge more of their father's height. Knowing it was useless to wish for what you didn't have, she sighed and said, "Yeah, but I'm not interested in a little flirtation." Thunder rumbled in the distance and Meg fought the urge to make the sign of the cross as she looked up at that one cloud still hanging above them in the clear blue sky. "Maybe I could be interested, but not right now."

Her sisters were laughing as the three joined their father and Mrs. Murphy by the main dish table. "Check it out," Grace said. "Mrs. Winter's chicken marsala. Don't you just love the way it melts in your mouth?"

Caitlin nodded. "Her chicken is always so tender, but

what about Mrs. Hawkins's firehouse chili?" she asked as she handed plates to her sisters. "I love the way it heats up as it makes it way down to your stomach."

"Fire in the hole," Meg quipped. She perused the dazzling array of food spread out before them, all the while keeping a discrete eye on their father... just in case he needed saving. Women were always trying to tempt Joe Mulcahy with their feminine wiles. "Jeez," she whispered, leaning close to Caitlin. "The way she's hanging on Pop, he's gonna drip barbecue sauce all over his shirt and tie!"

Caitlin reached across the table to grab a buttermilk biscuit and glanced at the couple. "I think Pop can handle her," she said as she broke it open and slathered butter on both sides.

Grace scooped up macaroni, tomato, and cheese casserole and wrinkled her nose. "We'll just make sure to use a little bleach on his shirt and hang it outside tomorrow."

Meg smiled. "Mom always said the sun and a healthy dose of bleach helped get stubborn stains out." Remembering tidbits of their mother's advice always made her feel as if their mom were still close by.

"Here," Grace said, plopping a huge spoonful of the macaroni casserole onto Meg's plate. "Your plate's still empty."

"I was going to have the ribs first," Meg grumbled. "I guess I can come back for seconds."

"Hello, girls."

The three looked up in time to see Joe and the Widow Murphy walking toward them from the other end of the table. "Hi, Mrs. Murphy," the sisters said. "Hey, Pop."

As if he knew they were up to something, he stared at Meg first, then Cait, then Grace. "My three darling girls," he said at last. "Don't overeat; you want to save room for the cake the McCormack sisters baked."

Meg glanced at the dessert table and the three-tiered ivory confection covered with pink wild roses and agreed. "Did Peggy say if it was chocolate or vanilla? Edie wouldn't tell me, said it was going to be a surprise."

Joe's chuckle had them all smiling. "I can't spill the beans," he said with a glance at the Widow Murphy. "But it's not vanilla and it's not chocolate."

"What other kind of cake is there?" Meg asked.

The widow laughed and Meg noticed the way her father was staring at Mrs. Murphy, as if he'd only just noticed something important. Meg shook her head; she'd have to sort through how she felt about that later.

"It's green," Mrs. Murphy told her.

Meg nodded. "Well, at least we know the color will be a surprise to the other guests."

Joe took another bite of his ribs and licked sauce from his thumb. "Jeez, Pop," Grace said, handing him a napkin. "You're not supposed to lick your fingers in public."

He smiled at his youngest daughter. "So it's OK to lick them at home?"

Grace flushed a bright pink and Meg felt sorry for her. Moving to stand beside her sister, she frowned at their father. "Now, Pop. Don't tease; you know Grace means well."

He agreed. "I know she does. Sorry, Gracie." He and Mary Murphy moved off to wait for the cake to be sliced.

"Come on," Cait urged. "Let's go see if we can get Peggy to tell us what flavor cake they baked." She paused when Meg didn't immediately follow along behind. "You coming, Meg?"

Meg shook her head; she was watching the way Edie leaned into her husband. Cait and Grace headed to where the McCormack sisters were chatting with a group of young people. When her friend wrapped her arms around her new husband and kissed him, Meg looked away. "I guess I'll never see my name on the water tower," Meg whispered. "Or wear my mother's wedding dress or kiss my new husband beneath swags of daisy chains and wild roses."

"Never you mind about that Van Orden boy," Miss Trudi soothed, coming to stand beside her. "I happen to know of a very eligible bachelor who just moved to Apple Grove."

Meg didn't want to be interested, but Miss Trudi had a way of speaking that drew you in. Just to be on the safe side, she grumbled, "I'm not interested."

Miss Trudi shook her finger in Meg's face. "You're too young to give up on men. There's just something about making whoopee out under the stars that keeps a heart young, a mind sharp, and"—she leaned close to whisper in Meg's ear—"your coochie ready to do the hoochie!"

Meg nearly swallowed her tongue, trying not to picture the eighty-year-old in her birthday suit. "I'll, uh... keep that in mind."

"You do that," Miss Trudi told her. "And remember, you aren't dead yet. There's still time to snag your man."

"I don't need a man," Meg insisted. "And I don't want to get married."

Miss Trudi's eyes gleamed. "You are going to eat those words when you meet him."

Meg didn't want to admit to the nerves jangling

inside of her. She waited a beat until they settled back down and said, "I don't think so."

"I'll take that bet." Miss Trudi stuck out her hand and Meg knew then that she'd been reeled in, hook, line, and sinker. A firm believer in playing fair, Meg shook hands, but had a funny feeling that Miss Trudi had an ace up her sleeve.

Needing a few moments to herself, she sought out her dad to tell him she was going for a short walk and would be right back. She was relieved that the widow wasn't with him. Mary Murphy was very observant and might pick up on what was really bothering Meg.

But if her father suspected she was brooding, he didn't let on. "I'll save you a slice of cake," he promised.

"Thanks, Pop."

—⁓—

Daniel Eagan downshifted then accelerated through the curve in the road leading him toward his new home—his new life in Ohio. Weeping hemlocks and spruce trees grew side by side with oak and maple trees. The sheer size and number of the trees were daunting.

The shades of green melded into a blur as he picked up speed on the straightaway. "No sidewalks." He knew he was getting closer to the town of Apple Grove but still hadn't seen more than a handful of homes along Route 70. Up ahead, there was a break in the trees; he slowed down to see if it was a driveway or the street he'd been looking for: Eden Church Road.

It was a pond just a few feet from the edge of the road. The weathered split-rail fence by the road was covered with vines. He couldn't guess what it was—he'd have to wait until spring. He checked his watch and saw that he'd made good time and could slow down and admire his surroundings. What he saw made him smile. There was a brightly colored, inflatable, kid-sized canoe on the other side of the pond next to a beat-up rowboat, with a fence just beyond. Seeing the horses grazing on the other side of the fence, he wondered if the owners competed in equestrian events, like his friends back home in Sussex County, New Jersey. He'd have to find out later; he wanted to get to his destination before late afternoon.

He'd started to wonder if he'd missed his turn when all at once he noticed the bright yellow water tower looming ahead and knew he was almost there. He drove past a cornfield with a ship's mast and crow's nest and had to pull over, grab his cell phone, and snap a picture out the window to send to his cousin back home. As he approached the water tower, he noticed writing on the side of it; in bold green letters it read: *Marry me, Edie, Love Bill*. He wasn't sure if it was the John Deere color scheme or the fact that someone would write a marriage proposal on the side of a water tower that tipped him off to the fact that he wasn't back East anymore—life was definitely different in the Midwest. He only hoped he'd fit in. He couldn't go back; he could only go forward.

A few miles later, he saw the sign for Eden Church Road and slowed down to make the turn. He smiled. The county name at the top of the street sign—Licking County—just added to the charm. The road ahead wound through gently rolling hills. Ten minutes down the road he noticed a farmer's wall—stones piled a few feet high and deep—outlining the property he could see up ahead. A huge barn, corral, and freshly painted white, two-story farmhouse, complete with the requisite wraparound porch and rocking chairs, were off to the left. As he drove past, he saw a crowd of people gathered out on the lawn. He slowed down and took it all in—the women dressed in myriad colors standing amid the background of grays and dark blues of the men in jackets and ties. There were long tables clothed in white and folding chairs sporting ridiculously large bows. Everyone seemed to be talking, laughing, and having a wonderful time. A wedding—he wondered if it was Edie and Bill from the water tower.

As he drove past, he saw a figure up ahead and laughed. "Must be my perspective." A few more feet and he saw he wasn't hallucinating; there was a young woman walking along the top of the fence as if it were a balance beam!

His heart stuttered as the figure windmilled her arms to keep from falling, barely regaining her balance. Swerving to the shoulder, he threw the gearshift into park, cut the engine, and ran toward her as she lost her balance a second time. This time she pitched backward off the fence and into his waiting arms.

She weighed more than he'd thought she would, but that wasn't as much of a problem as the warning bells going off in his head as her curves brought his libido roaring to life. He opened his mouth to speak as she turned her head, and he nearly lost himself in the endless blue of her eyes. The sprinkling of freckles across the bridge of her nose captivated him, and they both laughed suddenly, for no apparent reason. He gently set her on her feet and noticed the bright green polish on her bare toes. It somehow fit the intriguing young woman.

Irritation tangled with thoughts he had no business thinking. "You could have been seriously injured," he ground out. "What were you thinking, pulling a stunt like that?"

The imp's head was even with his shoulder. She tilted back to look up at him. "I didn't ask you to stop—"

"You could have broken an arm or leg." It was his "coach" voice, he realized with some chagrin. He was here for a new teaching job, and he was used to being the boss. Kids, and their parents, respected his authority. Why was this disconcerting new acquaintance giving him a problem?

She put her hands on her hips, giving him a measuring look, and he began to wonder if she was older than he'd first thought. He took in the swirl of pale green silk— but then remembered that some of the teenagers he'd taught dressed as if they were in their thirties. Looking for other clues as to her age, he focused on her face. The freckles hinted at youth, but he just wasn't sure. He shook his head and demanded, "Does your mother know you walk on fences?"

Her smiled slipped and tears filled her eyes. "She used to."

Now he'd gone and done it. It was obvious she'd lost her mother recently. "Can I call someone to pick you up?" He was reaching in his pocket for his phone when she brushed a strand of fiery silk out of her eyes. Damn him for noticing the color and texture of her hair. If she was a minor, the local law would be taking him out behind the first available barn and shooting him for harboring the kind of thoughts he was having.

He had to put some distance between them. "Here,"

he handed her his phone, but she shook her head, declining his offer.

"I'm just taking a walk and I'll be heading back to my friend's wedding." She tilted her head to one side and asked, "Are you driving through Apple Grove or staying on?"

"Moving here. I'm Dan Eagan," he said, holding out his hand, "your new phys ed teacher."

At her lilting laughter, he withdrew his hand and balled it into a tight fist. He didn't like to be laughed at. While he searched for the diplomatic words to put her in her place, she crossed her arms beneath the breasts he was trying his best to ignore and said, "Well, Dan Eagan, you would have been a welcome addition to the teaching staff a dozen years ago when I was there. Mr. Creed didn't have the high school girls' hearts all aflutter, like I am sure they will be when you walk into class."

She smiled and he noticed the fine lines around her eyes and the maturity that comes with living life. He narrowed his eyes. "You're not one of my students." Relief speared through him.

This time, she held out her hand. "No," she agreed. "I'm Meg Mulcahy. Welcome to Apple Grove."

He clasped her hand in his and realized she'd known all along what he was thinking—and she seemed to enjoy the fact that he'd been caught off guard. In his book, he owed her... and payback was a bitch.

He held her hand captive. "Well, Meg," he said, "I'm glad you're not one of my students."

"Oh?" She seemed surprised by his comment. "And why's that?"

Encouraged by the catch in her voice and interest in her gaze, he drew her even closer. When she tumbled against him, he felt the jolt of energy all the way to his soul.

Her eyes said yes, but her body tensed as if she wanted to say no. He waited a heartbeat for her to make up her mind. The instant she relaxed against him, he lowered his mouth until it was a breath from hers. "What is it about you?" he asked. "I don't even know if you have a boyfriend waiting over at that reception, or a husband, and I still want to kiss you."

She slowly smiled. "No boyfriend, no husband."

Right answer, but still he hesitated, asking, "If I kiss you now, will you hold it against me?"

"If you don't, I just might."

Unable to resist her sassy mouth, he brushed his lips against hers. She might have expected heat, but it was their first kiss—a kiss that shouldn't even be happening—so instead of heat, he gave her softness and the promise of more to come.

Then, unable to resist, he pressed his lips to the freckles on her nose and eased her out of his arms, wondering what had possessed him.

Indecision filled her gaze for a heartbeat before she grinned and launched herself at him. "That wasn't a kiss—" She wrapped her arms around him and used his shock to her advantage, tangling her tongue with his.

He groaned and would later swear that he'd lost his mind on the side of Eden Church Road.

When she finally slipped out of his arms, she rasped, "That's a kiss."

He had to agree. "Are all of the female residents of Apple Grove this friendly?"

She frowned. "They better not be."

Before he could think of a reply, she was walking away from him, searching the side of the road for something. "What did you lose?"

He could have sworn she said *her mind*, but when he asked her again, she called out over her shoulder, "My sandals—I dropped them when I fell."

Dan found himself following her—he just couldn't seem to keep his distance. He reminded himself that he wasn't ready for a relationship, and given what he'd been told about the size of Apple Grove, if he started an affair with the winsome Meg, one of their 597 residents would be sure to find out. Was he ready for that?

"Welcome to Apple Grove," he mumbled beneath his breath, finding one of her shoes. "This yours?"

"Thanks." She reached for the strappy sandal, put her hand on his shoulder, and slipped it on.

"You'll break your neck, walking around on one heel," he muttered.

"Not if you find the other one for me."

He was right; she was going to be trouble.

—◊◊◊—

Meg watched Dan's eyes change from a soft, clear gray to the color of winter storm clouds and she wondered if he was angry or aroused. He turned toward her and she got distracted by his strong jaw and the deep cleft in his chin. The temptation to touch it with the tip of her tongue had her staring at him, mesmerized... she couldn't look away. He was built like a linebacker, but moved with the grace of a dancer. But the last thing she needed in this life was to get involved with another football player—a reminder of a past that would never be her future.

She used to have a weakness for broad shoulders and muscular biceps. When she'd fallen against Dan, tingles of awareness set off sparks of desire wherever their bodies had touched. He was a big man—the only part of her that hadn't brushed against him were the soles of her feet. She shivered at the thought; the reawakening of her libido was acutely painful.

That was the only explanation she could think of for why she'd been tempted beyond reason to kiss him—really kiss him: she'd lost her mind. Maybe it was the celebratory atmosphere of Dan and Edie's wedding… maybe it was seeing yet one more proposal on the water tower. Whatever the trigger had been, she'd acted on the impulse and had been rewarded. Although he'd been a perfect stranger, there was something perfectly wonderful about Dan Eagan, something she intended to explore—later.

"Here it is."

The sound of his deep voice broke through her wandering thoughts. When Dan handed her the other sandal, she drew in a calming breath. It had been years since a man had affected her. It felt as if she'd been reawakened to sights, sounds, scents, and touch after years of moving through everyday life without feeling anything.

"Are you all right, Meg?"

"Uh, yes," she said. "I was just thinking."

His eyes sparkled and she could tell he was trying not to smile. "About that kiss?"

She laughed as she stopped to slip into her other shoe. "Yeah," she confessed. "And boy, do you pack a wallop."

When she straightened up, he reached for her hand, entranced by her refreshing honesty. "I'd like to get to know you better, Meg," he said, squeezing her hand briefly before letting it go. "And I could use a friend in Apple Grove. I'm a long way from home."

The plaintive note in his voice tugged at her heartstrings. She may have jumped the gun by tangling tongues with Dan before she got to know the man, but there was no use regretting a kiss that she would be replaying in her mind for days to come. Deciding to go with her gut, she said, "Town's closed up on account of Edie and Bill's wedding, but I know where we could get a good cup of coffee—my treat—and I could introduce you to some people."

When Dan smiled, laugh lines formed around his eyes. It was nice to be attracted to a man who she hadn't known since grade school. This was a first for her and she felt giddy. There was an air of mystery about him, his personality a puzzle to be figured out—she couldn't wait to get started. "I could really use some caffeine," he told her. "Is it far from here?"

She laughed and felt the years fall away. "Nothing is that far away in Apple Grove." She fell into step beside him as they walked to his car. Easy in his company, she marveled that the day had done a complete one-eighty. Nothing like a little gut-burning passion to put a spring in your step and a smile on your face.

Thoughts of Miss Trudi's prediction occurred to her and she asked, "Are you a betting man, Dan Eagan?"

He shrugged. "I used to be."

That was a loaded statement—she'd have to find out what was behind that comment. As he moved to open the passenger side door for her, she stepped back and shook her head. A sidelong glance in Dan's direction had her mouth drying up. She swallowed—it was either that or drool. She knew she wouldn't be waiting long before she'd be following up that heart-pumping kiss with another. Good Lord, she needed to talk to Honey B. She smiled up at him, took his hand, and led him away from the car and toward the boisterous crowd still gathered in Edie Parrish's backyard.

Trudi Philo looked up from where she sat beneath the hundred-year-old oak tree and slowly smiled. "Why, Meg dear," she crooned. "I see you didn't waste any time finding a man."

Meg couldn't help but laugh. With a shake of her head, she grinned. "Miss Trudi Philo, meet Mr. Dan Eagan."

Trudi's smile was wide and welcoming. "Welcome to Apple Grove, Daniel."

He leaned close so he could gently grasp her hand. "It seems like forever since you've visited, Aunt Trudi."

Aunt? "I thought you didn't have any family left, Miss Trudi." Meg was confused. "I thought you were the last Philo in the great state of Ohio."

Like the crafty old dear that she was, Miss Trudi patted Dan's hand and drew him into the empty chair beside her. "I am dear, but my grandnephew Dan, here, is from my mother's side of the family: the Eagans."

"No wonder you gave him such a glowing recommendation to the Board of Ed." Meg looked at Dan in a new light; he wouldn't be as much of a mystery as she'd thought—she actually did know his family. Small world.

Miss Trudi's eyes flashed a split-second warning that Meg was wise enough to heed. "Daniel's a wonderful teacher and a fine man. Our familial relationship had absolutely no bearing on the decision. Everyone on the Board knows of our connection, but they wanted Daniel because of his résumé."

Meg stared at Dan and noticed the tinge of pink on his cheeks. *Was he embarrassed?* It made him all the more human in her eyes. Unable to help herself, she gave in to the overwhelming need to tease. "I have a feeling he'll get on famously with his students—especially the troublesome female ones. Won't you, Dan?"

The sidelong look he cast her way had her fighting to hold back a bubble of laughter. Fifteen minutes in the man's company and she felt more alive than she had in months. Deciding to give the poor man a break, she urged, "Why don't you tell your aunt how we met? I'm sure she'd find it humorous."

Dan's jaw clenched, and Meg wondered if she'd gone too far. Once she started to tease, it was hard to stop.

He drew in a deep breath and rumbled, "Meg was walking on top of the fence and was about to fall off when I came along. I caught her."

Miss Trudi turned toward Meg. "Really? How providential. Did you get hurt?"

"Not a scratch." Dan frowned and flicked a glance at Meg. "But if I'd gotten there just a few seconds later, she would have done a header off the fence and knocked herself unconscious."

It was Meg's turn to frown. "I wouldn't have fallen if he hadn't scared the crap out of me."

"Watch your language around Miss Trudi," came a gruff voice from behind them.

Damn, she'd done it again, and after she'd been

doing so well lately. It would have to be Sheriff Wallace catching her backsliding into her old habits. Sometimes the eight-year difference in their ages felt like two... and other times... "Sorry, Mitch," she answered without missing a beat. She'd been on the wrong side of the man more than once growing up. The last time had been her wake-up call that she wasn't immortal.

The memory of having been caught and, worse— having to be rescued a third time—made her face burn with embarrassment. The sheriff had seemed like a god to her youthful imagination the time he'd climbed up the water tower and reached out his broad-palmed hand to grasp hers, pulling her to safety. She owed the man her life. Since she hadn't come up with a way to repay the favor, the very least she could do was listen to him.

"Sorry, Miss Trudi." And she was. She liked Miss Philo; she just got carried away every once in awhile and forgot about her colorful language. In her defense, she'd learned most of it working alongside her father.

"Mitch," Meg said, "this is Dan Eagan, he just moved to Apple Grove."

"He'll be coaching our soccer team and teaching physical education," Miss Trudi added.

The sheriff held out his hand while she continued, "Dan, I'd like you to meet Sheriff Mitch Wallace," she said with a nod in the lawman's direction as he joined their little group. "He's been the law around here for..." Searching her brain, she couldn't exactly remember when he hadn't been sheriff. "How long has it been, Sheriff?"

He chuckled. "You mean you really don't remember?"

She could tell by the teasing tone of his voice that he

wasn't bothered by the fact that she didn't. "You're part of the fiber of this town, Mitch. I can't remember when you weren't."

"How old were you when I plucked you off the water tower railing?"

He would have to bring that up. She felt her cheeks flush with heat and answered, "Fourteen."

"How old were you when you climbed up on Weatherbee's barn roof and got stuck?"

She felt her face growing even hotter. *She'd almost forgotten about that time.* "Thirteen."

"What about the time you decided to climb the ship's mast to get in the crow's nest over at the McCormack farm?"

"Our Meg has an affinity for climbing to high places," Miss Trudi confided to Dan, "but once she gets there, remembers she doesn't like heights."

Dan's face was alight with amused interest as her childhood high jinks were being recounted. "Well? Aren't you going to answer?"

She sighed. "Eleven."

"Your poor momma was fraught with worry that time," Trudi said. "Caitlin and Grace were just four and three at the time and were starting to follow you everywhere."

Meg cleared her throat. She didn't want to dredge up any more of her past history. That was enough for one night. Although she enjoyed the odd moments when memories of her mother came flooding back, she didn't like to dwell on them because they always reminded her of mother's untimely death.

As if he sensed the direction of her thoughts, Mitch chuckled, drawing her attention back to him. "Climbing up that ship's mast was my first official juvenile delinquent rescue."

"Hey. I wasn't a delinquent."

"Close enough," he said with a grin. "Every year on the first day of spring, you climbed something."

She blew out a breath and said, "I didn't get stuck every year." Her gaze met Dan's and she warned him, "If you stay here for any length of time, the entire town will know your deepest, darkest secrets and will happily pass them along over a cup of coffee at the Apple Grove Diner."

"Aunt Trudi highly recommended their pecan pie," Dan said.

If being the subject of morning gossip over coffee at the local diner didn't bother him, maybe he'd fit right in. The points in his favor were rapidly adding up.

"So, Mitch," Dan said, bringing her attention back to what he was saying, "you never mentioned how long you've been keeping the peace—and Meg out of trouble." When Dan turned toward her, she added the first check to the negative column. When he started to chuckle, she had the overwhelming urge to stick her tongue out at him. It was a struggle, but she managed to control the urge.

Mitch didn't miss a beat or seem to notice the byplay between Dan and Meg. "Fourteen years. I came back to town with my criminal justice degree and old Sheriff Stuart hired me as one of his deputies on the spot... just like he'd promised."

"Smartest decision he ever made," said a familiar female voice.

Meg smiled. "Dan, I'd like you to meet Honey B.

Harrington. She owns Honey's Hair Salon over on Main Street, catty-corner to the sheriff's office." She didn't add that Honey was one year older than her and had been trying to get the sheriff's attention since that night he'd rescued Meg from the water tower railing, while Honey looked on from the ground. Honey had gone for help and lost her heart to the heroic deputy Mitch Wallace that night.

When Dan looked at Honey and smiled, Meg added, "Dan Eagan is our new phys ed teacher at the high school."

"And their varsity soccer coach," Miss Trudi said with a smile. "He played on the varsity team in college."

"Really?" a deep voice called out, joining them. "I like watching soccer almost as much as racing. Can't always find a game on TV, though."

Dan smiled as Meg introduced him to the latest newcomer. "Dan Eagan, meet Robert Stuart. He owns Bob's Gas and Gears and is the man you want to know if you've got car trouble. He can fix anything under the hood."

"Nice to meet you, Robert." Dan grasped the other man's hand and shook it.

"Call me Bob."

"Bob used to race stock cars, had a winning season back in '81," Sheriff Wallace told him.

"My dad's a huge NASCAR fan," Dan said. "I grew up beneath the hood of his '65 Corvette. In my spare time, I like to tinker with engines."

Bob's eyes narrowed as if he were concentrating. "Big block... carbureted or fuel-injected?"

Dan grinned and Meg's belly did that fluttery thing again. There was something so boy-like about Dan's open smile, as if he hadn't a care in the world and was ready to experience everything all at once. Her dad got that way about cars too.

"My grandfather never liked a fuel-injected engine," Dan answered. "He preferred carbureted engines; dad still does."

"Fully restored?" Bob asked.

"Cherry condition," Dan answered.

"Car talk," Meg said to Honey B. and Miss Trudi. "Good thing my dad's not here or else we'd never talk about anything else."

The ladies laughed and made room as the McCormack sisters joined them. "Dan, I hate to interrupt your manly discussion," Meg said, "but I'd like you to meet Peggy and Katie McCormack."

He nodded to the sisters. "Owners of the Apple Grove Diner?"

When they smiled, he confided, "I'm real partial to pecan pie."

Peggy's smile was friendly and flirtatious, a combination that baffled Meg. She herself could never manage to pull off that particular look; Meg was either friendly or she was flirtatious. "I'm sure we can save you a slice if you want to stop by the diner later," Peggy said.

"We're going to be open later than normal," Katie added, "on account of closing up for Bill and Edie's wedding."

Dan smiled at the sisters. "It's good to know there's a place to eat nearby."

"People come from miles around for a piece of pie and our biscuits and gravy," Peggy told him.

"But they come back because of Apple Grove," Katie added. "There's just something about Apple Grove. Even if you've only been here a few years, you feel as if you've always lived here. People care about each other here—always have, always will."

Dan hung on every word and was quick to agree. "I can see why people would be tempted to stay." He glanced at Meg and added, "I've met some intriguing people so far."

Warmth spread from her belly to her heart. It felt good to have Dan pay her a compliment—intriguing wasn't quite what she hoped for, but it was still good, wasn't it? Before she could decide, Sheriff Wallace's sister Beatrice walked over to say hello. "Beatrice runs the library. It's open three days a week," Miss Trudi proudly proclaimed.

Meg nodded. "We have a huge selection of classics and a first-class reference section."

"That's right," Beatrice agreed. "If the book you want isn't on our shelves, we're connected to three other libraries in Licking County and have an extensive online catalogue. We can have the book you need sent over from any of the libraries in our group."

Dan's brow was furrowed when he asked, "Do you have cookbook and automotive sections?"

His question surprised Meg, but she was encouraged that he was interested in their library.

"Do you want to learn to cook?" Beatrice asked Dan.

He shook his head. "My mom taught me when I was a kid, but I didn't actually start to put those lessons to good use until I was at college and hungry all the time. I'm always looking for new recipes to try out."

It was nice that he wanted to know more about the library. His interest in her town, added to the fact that he could apparently cook, gave him major points in Meg's

book. The way Dan interacted with Apple Grove's
townsfolk only added to his appeal. He was relaxed,
open, and friendly. She could see that he'd be an asset
to their community and had a feeling that the kids at the
high school would respond well to Dan. Time would
tell, and the gossip chain would keep everyone in town
up-to-date on his progress.

When her father and the Widow Murphy walked
over, she introduced them. "Dan, I'd like you to meet
my dad, Joseph Mulcahy, and Mary Murphy. She owns
Murphy's Market in town." She stumbled over the in-
troduction, unused to seeing her father with a woman.

Mary Murphy was polite as always, and even though
Meg wasn't sure how she felt about her father spending
time with Mrs. Murphy, she had to admit the woman
had a way of making everyone feel comfortable in her
presence. "Lovely to meet you, Dan."

"Nice to meet you, Dan." Her father took Dan's
measure in three seconds flat. She'd have to ask him
later what he thought. Of all the folks gathered in Edie's
backyard, her father and Sheriff Wallace would have
Dan's character defined and dissected most accurately
and ready for public consumption by the time the wedding guests dispersed.

"Joseph owns Mulcahy's," Miss Trudi informed Dan.

"What's Mulcahy's?" he asked.

Meg smiled. "It's our family-run handyman business."

"You have brothers?" Dan actually scanned the
crowd to look for likely candidates.

She frowned up at him. "Two younger sisters, why?"

"Do you have male cousins?"

Was the man trying to irritate her? "No, is there a

reason that you think my sisters and I cannot work for my father?"

He looked at her father and then back at her. "I, uh…" His voice trailed off and he stared down at her. "You look like you're about to open up on me with both barrels."

Her dad smiled. "Megan inherited my temper. It's always best to know about it before she works on your house."

"I don't need any work done on the house"—he pauscd—"that I know of."

Her dad smiled at Dan. "If you bought the Saunders place, and don't plan to keep on top of the daily maintenance on a house that old, you'll be calling me sooner than you think."

Dan fell silent, digesting what he'd just been told. Meg took that as a good sign that he was at least willing to listen.

She caught herself staring. In her defense, the man was gorgeous—and damn him for waking up those particular thoughts after all these years. She'd been comfortable in her rut… er, routine… working hard all day six days a week, grabbing a cold one when she got home from work, and then watching TV with her dad. If Jimmy was in town, she would spend all of her free time with him until he left town again. Lately her dad went off by himself. She'd heard through the grapevine that he was visiting the widow but she hadn't come right out and asked him yet. It wasn't easy to give her dad the third degree, the way he had done to her and her sisters for so many years. Besides, it wasn't really any of her business, was it?

She glanced over at her dad and watched the

proprietary way he slid his hand to the widow's waist. The signs were there for a blind woman to see, so how had she missed that particular fact? In a moment of clarity, she realized it was because she'd been so wrapped up in her own little world, merely existing in between Jimmy's visits, that she'd kept her emotions hidden— like sorrow and pain—but the downside was she also didn't experience happiness or joy. Face it: up until today, she'd been a workaholic with an empty life. She had walked a straight path and kept her emotions in check most of the time—except for her temper. She had a hair-trigger temper. She had a feeling that was all about to change.

When she looked over at Dan, her gaze collided with his and she sensed that he'd been watching her. There was no doubt in her mind that they had a definite spark that could lead to something amazing. She wouldn't see her on-again, off-again boyfriend for a few more months and, not for the first time, wondered what he did—and who took her place in Jimmy's life back in the city— during those long months they spent apart. Her stomach clenched as the cold truth slithered into her belly. Maybe it was time she started living. She definitely wanted to get to know Dan Eagan better.

"Melanie Culpepper has the most adorable twin toddlers," Miss Trudi was saying when Meg dragged her gaze from Dan's.

"Boys," Mitch added with a glance in Honey B.'s direction.

Meg wondered if she was the only one who saw the longing in Honey B.'s eyes or the fire burning in the sheriff's. Why was the man so hardheaded about courting Honey B.? It was clear to everyone in town that they were perfect for one another. "Melanie owns the Knitting Room," Meg added. "Our local Internet café. She had to close up her shop when the twins were born, but she's thinking of starting up a knitting circle during the day and keeping the Internet café going at night."

Dan looked skeptical. "My grandmother knits, but my mom doesn't. Is it that popular around here?"

He was looking at Meg when he asked, so she answered, "You'd be surprised. There are women everywhere who like to knit or crochet."

He shrugged. "I don't know of any."

"But you're a guy," Meg said, as if that explained it all.

Dan's smile was like a magnet, and a few of the unattached females in town wandered over until they were surrounded by women, the men having stepped back to make room for the swirl of skirts and waft of perfume. She introduced him to women between the ages of eighteen and eighty and stood back and watched the way he chatted and smiled with everyone.

"Small towns are a lot different than the suburban area where I grew up."

"I'd love to hear all about it," Peggy said, tugging on Dan's arm to draw him away from Meg and toward the empty chairs.

He didn't resist, and to Meg's dismay, she felt the green monster of envy rear her ugly head. She'd just met the man, and although he'd been the one to make the first move, she'd taken it up a notch. But that didn't explain the feelings swirling around inside of her, other than the fact that so many of her emotions had been bottled up for too long, waiting for a promise from Jimmy that was never coming. It was easier to accept than the reality that she'd fallen hard and fast the moment their eyes met.

"Quite a catch, isn't he?" Miss Trudi hooked her arm with Meg's. "Daniel's a hard worker and honest to the core," the older woman continued. "You can trust him to keep his word."

Meg nodded and said, "He seems to be enjoying himself, getting to know the good people of Apple Grove."

Joe Mulcahy walked over carrying a plate with a slice of green cake and cream-colored icing. Meg was laughing as she held out her hand. "Thanks, Pop... it really is green!"

He shook his head. "Apparently Edie's favorite kind of cake is pistachio pudding cake."

Miss Trudi joined in their laughter and added, "Mrs. Parrish had the devil of a time convincing Peggy and Katie to create the wedding cake of Edie's dreams when they found out the recipe came off the back of a pudding box."

Meg held the plate close and sniffed at it. "Smells OK." She cut off a tiny bite with the side of her fork and put it in her mouth. "I wasn't expecting the pistachio flavor, but it is delicious." She was polishing off the last bite when Dan walked back over.

"Was that cake?" Dan asked.

His aunt patted his arm before hooking her arm through his. "Why don't we go on over to the dessert table and I'll get you a slice."

He looked over his shoulder at Meg and called out, "Don't leave without me!"

Meg felt the heat of her dad's gaze on her. When she

lifted her eyes, he was waiting to speak. "Why would he say something like that?"

Meg could either tell the truth or fib… and five minutes later her dad would call her out on it. She looked over at the table and the rapidly shrinking cake and sighed. "We uh… that is… when he caught me, I… uh."

Her dad crossed her arms and stared down at her. Not a good sign. Time to fess up. "He kissed me."

"Really? I might have to change my opinion of him." Her father's stare turned to a glare. She'd swear she saw steam coming out of his ears. Rather than get into it with her dad at her friend's wedding, she backed away declaring, "Would you look at the time? Gotta go, Pop. See you at home!"

She waved in Dan's direction, but she wasn't sure if he saw her leaving. Self-preservation had her hotfooting it down the road; no way was she going to sit next to her dad on the ride home and listen to him asking what a woman her age was thinking throwing herself at a man, a complete stranger. But after five minutes of walking, she had to stop to take her sandals off and walk the rest of the way barefoot. She smiled at the emerald green toe polish, her sisters' handiwork and not her normal plain-Jane look.

The ache in her arches had her feeling sorry for her poor feet, which were not used to high heels. Her normal footwear consisted of three different pairs of work boots… all of them worn down at the heels. Funny thing, until she'd met Dan, she'd been starting to feel the way her boot heels looked.

She heard the sound of a car coming up fast behind her. Figuring it was one of her neighbors, she didn't bother to look over her shoulder. When the car pulled up alongside of her, she glanced over and was surprised to see that it was Dan behind the wheel.

"I thought you were going to wait for me."

She couldn't decipher what emotions were hiding behind those dark gray eyes. "I'm sorry, I kind of told my dad about you kissing me and then he got that look on his face."

Dan nodded. "The 'what were you thinking' look?"

She brushed her hair out of her eyes and heaved a sigh of relief. "Exactly."

"It's a dad thing," he agreed. "So… do you want a ride home?"

She grinned and reached for the door handle. "Sure," she said, climbing inside. "Thanks, Dan."

He smiled at her and a shiver raced up her spine. "You cold?"

"No," she insisted. "It's warm for this time of year—feels like summer."

"So where to?" he asked. "Is it far?"

She laughed, and it felt good. "Didn't I tell you that nothing is that far away in Apple Grove?"

He smiled. "Yes," he said. "You did. But exactly how much farther?"

"About two miles ahead on the left, you'll want to turn onto Goose Pond Road, then right onto Cherry Valley Lane."

"OK, so you live on Cherry Valley?"

"We live on Peat Moss Road."

"Seriously?"

"Yes, why?"

He shook his head. "No reason."

He glanced down at his gauges and then up ahead. "Goose Pond?"

"Uh-huh. Left turn up there." She pointed to a spot in the distance and he signaled, although why, she had no idea; there wasn't anyone on the road behind them.

Dan turned and started looking for their right-hand turn. She fell silent, not really sure how to get back to the earlier camaraderie. He stopped to look at her before making the turn onto her street. "I thought you were kidding."

"What's so strange about the name of my road?"

"Uh, nothing. It's just so rural."

She laughed. "More than half of Licking County is farmland."

"Yeah," he agreed. "I saw that on the drive in."

Meg shrugged. "I suppose the street names in your city were all named after important people."

"Dead presidents."

She couldn't think of anything more boring than naming your town's streets after former presidents.

"That's our house—last one on the left."

Dan pulled into the driveway of an old farmhouse and noticed the barn out back as they were getting out. "You wouldn't happen to have an old clunker just waiting for someone to restore her in that barn, would you?"

Every single hair on the back of her neck stood on end. "How did you know?"

He stopped dead in his tracks. "You're serious?"

She smiled. "My great-grandfather's 1929 Model A pickup."

His entire demeanor changed; gone was the responsible mature man she'd met when he kept her from falling, and in his place was the eight-year-old who couldn't wait for Christmas morning to unwrap his presents. "I have got to see it."

"Dad never had time to work on it; he was too busy keeping the business going, and then after mom…"

"What?"

She shook her head; she hadn't meant to say anything, so she glossed over it and motioned for him to follow. He followed, as eager as a puppy. "What kind of shape is it in?"

"Not bad, considering its age and the fact that my great-grandfather drove it every day until he parked it in the barn, where it's been ever since. It needed a lot of work and with the nature of our family business, we don't have a lot of spare time."

"I'm sure you heard back there that I love cars—it's in the blood."

"You should talk to my dad; he's car-crazy."

Meg slid the side door open and flipped on the light. The soft glow of the incandescent bulbs hanging from the rafters shone down on the black-tarped mound off to the side. Waiting until Dan was standing beside her, she grabbed the closest corner and pulled on the tarp.

Dan's low whistle of appreciation gave her a warm, fuzzy feeling inside. He was a lot like her dad in his love for classic and antique cars. The way he looked over his shoulder at her, waiting for her nod of permission to touch, just added to the positives that were making it hard to ignore her fascination with the man.

"This could be a beauty."

"My dad has pictures of it when it was new. My great-grandfather bought it in 1933, so he wasn't the original owner, but he had it all his life. My dad got to ride in it, but it was off the road a long time before he got his license. It's one of his dreams to restore it and get it back on the road."

"I don't blame him," Dan said, his look solemn. "This would be an amazing project to get my hands on."

She nodded to the tarp and he grabbed the opposite corner and helped her cover the pickup. "Why don't you ask him if you can help?"

"I might just do that."

Walking to the house, she said, "I know you got to have a piece of cake, but did you ever get that cup of coffee? I got so caught up introducing you around… and then when Mitch started telling you about my misspent youth, I forgot all about it."

He nodded. "I did have a cup, but that was awhile ago."

"Come on inside. I'll make some."

While she brewed coffee, he made himself at home at the scarred oak farm table. "Do you think he'll be back soon?"

"He would have to take the Widow Murphy home first."

"Why do you call her that?"

Meg shrugged and wiped her hands on a flour sack dish towel that was so thin it didn't really dry much, but her mom had bought them, and she couldn't bring herself to consign them to the rag bag yet. She opened the antique copper cookie jar that had stood on the counter since her great-grandmother Molly had set it there. Reaching in, she selected two kinds of cookies— chocolate chip and peanut butter, nothing but the best— and put them on a plate. "Because she is."

"A widow?"

"Well, yeah."

"Why don't you call her Mary?"

She shrugged. "As far back as I can remember, folks in town called her that. The name just sort of stuck."

"Once you make a name for yourself in Apple Grove—good or bad—can you ever change it?"

Meg took the time to think about it and tried to answer honestly, sensing that what she said would be important to Dan's understanding and expectations of the town. "Not that I've ever heard of, but hey, it could happen. One small whisper could start a roar—especially if Miss Trudi is behind it."

As she'd hoped, he smiled at the mention of his great-aunt. "She really loves getting into the thick of things."

It was Meg's turn to smile as she set out the plate of cookies and steaming mugs. "Real milk or two percent?"

"Real if you have it."

"Sugar?"

"Great, thanks." As he prepared his coffee, she noted that he used two heaping spoons of sugar and two drops of milk. She noticed things like that—always had, always would.

She watched him bring the blue enamel cup close enough to blow across the surface to cool it. He sipped, closed his eyes, and sighed. "That's the best cup of coffee I've had in days."

"Thanks." She pushed the yellow-ware plate closer. "Have a cookie. Grandma's recipes can't be beat."

—✺—

Dan noticed the way Megan bit her bottom lip when she was deep in thought. Megan Mulcahy had thrown him for a loop from the moment she'd fallen off the fence into his arms. The image of her cradled against his heart filled him. *Mine*, his heart whispered. *Whoa!* his head shouted. Don't get carried away... isn't that what happened the last time? But nothing about Meg reminded him of his ex—they were light years apart in temperament, stature, looks, and personality. He had no worries in that regard; why not follow his heart? He could still pull back if things got too hot too quickly. With Meg, he had a feeling they might.

As Meg quietly talked about cookie recipes, he noticed the competent way she held herself, comfortable in her own skin. He admired that in others, but in Meg it was tempting as well as attractive. And it wasn't just the fact that she had a Model A pickup in her barn. Smiling, he bit into a second cookie. "I'm glad I uh... caught you today."

She set her mug down. "I don't remember if I thanked you properly and for that I'm sorry. I should have done that right off."

"You were distracted at the time," he said slowly, watching the hue of her blue eyes darken to sapphire. "So was I."

"That's no excuse. My parents taught me better than that."

"And you're a dutiful daughter?" He could get behind that; he'd been raised the same way.

She nodded and a couple of hairpins pinged on the tabletop. He glanced up in time to see a long, silky strand caress the side of her face. Without thought, he reached out to smooth it behind her ear.

The back door slammed as a deep voice called out, "I didn't think I'd see you again so soon."

Dan nearly jumped out of his skin and knocked over his coffee. Meg was out of her seat like a shot and snagged the paper towels, mopping up the mess. She bent forward to reach across the table and his mind went blank as the scooped neckline of her dress let him glimpse the lacy edge of her flesh-toned bra. He didn't think she realized that she'd flashed him. The no-nonsense way she cleaned up the mess and smiled at her father spoke volumes.

Joe cleared his throat and Dan's brain kicked back into gear. "I saw Meg walking alongside the road, so I offered her a ride."

He needed to go slowly and lay the proper foundation for a relationship this time, because he sensed that there was something special about Meg and he didn't want to make the same mistakes he had with his ex.

"Meg's stubborn," her dad said. "I'm surprised she agreed."

Dan shrugged. "Meg seems reasonable to me; besides, I think it was the thought of walking home in those heels—or barefoot—that had her accepting my offer of a ride home."

Joe's frown turned around and Dan noticed one side of the man's mouth twitching. Was he trying not to smile? Deciding to deflect and protect Meg from her father's grumbling, he said, "Meg showed me the Model A in the barn. I'm handy with engines and would be happy to give you a hand sometime."

Her dad was watching him. Was he thinking about Dan's offer? Needing to sway the man, he said, "I was telling Sheriff Wallace about my Dad's 1965 Corvette—"

Joe stepped closer to the table. "Coupe or convertible?"

"Coupe."

"Big block or fuel-injected?"

"396 Turbo-jet—"

"425 HP." Joe nodded and sighed deeply. "I'd love to get under the hood; any chance of your dad driving it out to Apple Grove?"

Dan shook his head. "He drives it locally in sunny weather, mostly to the Tuesday night car meets where he shows it off. Guys come from miles around to drool."

"Restored?"

"Cherry," he answered with a grin. "I've got a picture in my wallet."

Her father stepped around Meg, pulled a chair over, sat down, and waited for Dan to show him the picture.

"Dad likes cars almost as much as baseball," Megan said with a smile.

Dan handed over the snapshot and looked up. "Really?" Turning toward Joe he asked the name of his favorite team.

Joe smiled at him and said, "The Cleveland Indians. Yours?"

"Diehard, third generation Yankee fan."

Meg's father snickered. "Figures."

"Really?"

"Well, you are from back East," Joe said. "Now if you had that '65 'Vette with the fuel-injected 327…"

Dan laughed good-naturedly. "Carbs—you either love 'em or hate 'em."

They were both laughing by the time Meg had poured Dan another cup of coffee and offered one to her dad. Instead of sitting down, her dad nodded toward the barn. "Want to go look under the hood?"

Dan's heart skipped a beat. "Now?"

Joe nodded and Dan knew then he'd follow the man anywhere as long as he got a good look underneath the hood of that pickup. He did a double take as he stepped outside and saw the pristine, glossy black 1950 Ford F1 pickup gleaming in the late afternoon sun. "You are one lucky man, Mr. Mulcahy."

Joe grinned. "I've worked hard for what I've got."

"I understand," Dan said, distracted by the pickup in the driveway and the antique in the barn. "I intend to work even harder so that I can buy back a rookie base-ball card I pawned..." his voice trailed off. *Damn. If he'd been paying attention to what he was saying, that last part wouldn't have come out.*

Joe was watching him intently. "What year?"

Dan hesitated before deciding that it really didn't matter if Meg's dad knew about the damned card. At least he hadn't been shocked about pawning it. "1952."

Joe's look intensified. "Holy shit. Don't tell me it was Mickey Mantle's!"

Dan's shoulders slumped. "Yeah. Long story. Family and a couple of exes involved—ends badly."

The older man regarded him for a moment, glanced over his shoulder at the house, and then asked, "You coming?"

Dan grinned, glad that he'd dodged that particular bullet. "Yeah!"

Their mutual love for classic and antique cars led them to the barn first; they had plenty of time to check out the F1 later—if he didn't wear out his welcome or forget and slip up and talk about things best left unsaid. His gut told him he'd better get to his new home before it got dark, but he was car crazy and had two stellar Fords to check out, inside and out, first. Whatever problems waited for him would still be there when he arrived later.

Two hours later, he followed Joe back inside to find the kitchen empty and their coffee ice cold.

"Do you want me to brew a fresh pot?" Joe offered.

Dan hesitated; he'd love to spend more time talking cars, but knew he had to check things out and make sure he had everything he needed for the first day of his new job at Apple Grove High. "I'd like to take a rain check on the coffee. Thanks, Joe."

"Come on back and talk cars anytime, Dan."

They shook hands on it.

"Thanks, Joe."

"No problem. Will we see you tomorrow at church?"

Dan paused in the doorway. "I hadn't really thought about it. I haven't even begun to unpack."

"Service is at ten o'clock. Reverend Smith was the minister you met at the Parrish's farm. He welcomes all newcomers."

"I'll think about it."

"Your aunt has her special spot in the front pew opposite the pulpit."

Dan knew then he'd better go. "All right then. See you in the morning." He paused on the threshold. "Would you please say good-bye to Meg for me?"

"Will do."

Instead of pausing for one last look at the gorgeous pickup in the driveway, he turned and looked up at the farmhouse to see which window had a light on. Second story, third window from the front. He caught himself staring and forced his thoughts back to square one and the plan he'd already begun outlining in his mind: get to know Meg better before he gave in to the overwhelming need to talk her into bed. Even though he would have liked a little more time to plan his strategy, tomorrow at church would be the perfect place to start.

Chapter 2

DAN FOLLOWED HIS AUNT'S DIRECTIONS, TURNING LEFT at the end of Main Street and onto Apple Grove Road to pick her up. The sign outside made him smile. *Trudi's Garden Center* was painted in bright purple on a soft yellow sign.

Dan chuckled. "A true attention-getter."

The building was low and long and not particularly attractive; his aunt was big on functional. There were double doors that looked like they could be left open to invite customers inside the building during warm weather.

He pulled around the back of the building and was surprised to see a vine-covered Victorian-style home and his aunt waiting by the foot of the steps to the front porch. He got out and opened the door for her.

She smiled as she patted his cheek and slid onto the passenger's seat. "It's such a treat to have family to go to church with this morning."

"I, uh... haven't been in awhile," he admitted. He lost one chunk of faith after his ex flushed her engagement ring and another one when he found out she'd been having a fling with his ex–best friend.

As they drove, she caught him up on the former coach's recovery. Dan was glad Coach Creed was on the mend. Dan would make sure he did everything in his power to do right by the coach's former team, now Dan's team.

"It's just up ahead," his aunt told him. "Across the railroad tracks on the right."

He pulled up in front of the white clapboard church with a bold sign declaring it to be the Apple Grove United Methodist Church.

He helped his aunt out of the car and into the church, where heads turned as they walked arm in arm to the front row.

Reverend Smith walked up the aisle a few minutes later and stood in front of the congregation with his arms raised, greeting his flock. When he asked if anyone was visiting or new to the congregation, his gaze settled on Dan, and the reverend motioned for Dan to stand and tell everyone his name.

Dan hesitated, but his aunt was waiting expectantly, so he stood up and smiled. "Hi, I'm Dan Eagan. I'm the new phys ed teacher at the high school. I'm taking over for Coach Creed, who I hear is on the road to recovery, thank goodness for that."

Reverend Smith's amen was echoed by the entire church.

When the service was over, Aunt Trudi leaned toward him and said, "I'm serving during coffee hour. I hope you don't mind staying."

He had hoped to have a minute to speak to Meg after church, not get roped into staying for the entire coffee hour, but he wasn't going to put a damper on things for his aunt. She'd gone to so much trouble helping him find and land the job in Apple Grove. He owed her a great deal and would make sure he did all he could for her, even if he had to stick around and make small talk when he could be unpacking the rest of his boxes.

Drawing in a deep breath, he followed Aunt Trudi

down the aisle and into the wide room at the back of the church. There were two long folding tables, one set up with the coffee urn, milk, sugar, and mugs, and the other with sweets: donuts, coffee cake, and, his favorite, a sugar-glazed pecan ring. Everything appeared to be homemade—too bad; he really loved Entenmann's cakes. He hoped they carried his favorite brand in Apple Grove.

"Come on over here and help pass out the coffee, Daniel."

Thus summoned, he made his way to the coffee urn and started passing out the mugs his aunt filled with fresh, hot, fragrant coffee. Dan recognized a few faces from the wedding.

"Hi, Bob." He passed a steaming mug to Bob Stuart. "What time is the race on today?"

Bob grinned. "It's an early one, since it's on the East Coast. Things are heating up with the chase in full gear."

Dan agreed. "I can't believe there are only a handful of races left."

"Sounds like you're a fan."

"I used to watch the race with my dad, but now it'll have to wait until I go back home for a visit during the school break in the spring."

"You're welcome to come on over and watch the race with me anytime."

"Thanks, Bob. I didn't get much unpacking done yesterday, so I'm going to have to get it all done today. How about a rain check?"

"No problem."

"Dan Eagan," Mrs. Parrish smiled warmly.

It was easy to return her warm smile as he handed her a cup of coffee. "How are you today?"

"Missing our Edie," Mr. Parrish said as Dan handed him the cup his aunt just poured.

"You have your children with you for so many years," Mrs. Parrish said. "Sometimes they drive you crazy and you can't wait for them to grow up and move out—and then they do!"

Dan's mom had said something along those lines when he'd told them of his plans to move to Ohio. Even though he'd moved out of his family home a few years back, this was much farther away. "My mom was sorry to see me move out here but understood that it was important to me to make the leap."

"Parents will do just about anything for their kids," Joe Mulcahy said, walking over with Mrs. Murphy close to his side.

"Good morning, Joe, Mrs. Murphy."

The widow smiled. "Please, call me Mary."

He handed her a mug. "Mary. Beautiful day, isn't it?"

Mary Murphy looked up at Joe and smiled, a soft sweet smile that had Dan suspecting they were a couple, even though no one seemed to refer to them as such. "It surely is. How was your first night in your new home?"

"I still need to unpack, but I really love the house. There's just something about it… it's hard to describe… it's like it has a character all its own."

"I believe that houses absorb the personalities of those who have lived in it. The older the house, the more interesting it is."

Dan looked at his aunt and nodded. "That's it exactly, Aunt Trudi."

She smiled and poured another cup. "Well, hello, Megan dear."

"Hi, Miss Trudi."

Megan was every bit as entrancing as she'd been the day before. Her auburn hair was loose today and fell in a silky curtain past her shoulders.

"Hi, Dan." Meg's smile lit her face. She scrunched her nose so that he had no choice but to notice her freckles.

He cleared his throat and returned the greeting. "How are you today?"

"I'm great. The sun is shining, the wind is soft, and there's a hint of fall in the air." Their fingers brushed and the zing of electricity had his gaze locking on hers. He knew she'd felt the sparking sensation too.

She licked her lips, stared at his mouth, and said, "Thanks, Dan."

———

Meg's skin tingled from the tips of her fingers to the soles of her feet and all because of that brief brush of skin to skin. Her stomach had an odd fluttering and she felt light-headed. Who knew that his hands would cause her body to go haywire?

"Did you sleep well?" *Now why did she ask him something like that?*

His gorgeous gray eyes focused on hers. "Not really—strange house and so quiet."

She wondered if he realized that he was staring at her mouth. Storm-gray eyes filled with emotions she recognized because they were sprinting through her own system—interest, desire, and need.

"Give it a couple of days and you'll feel right at home."

It was hard not to be captivated by the cleft in his chin and the strong line of his jaw, but she focused on his face and not his mouth, his smile and not his lips. It wasn't easy. She finally asked as casually as she could, "What are you going to be doing the rest of today?"

He handed out one of the last few mugs of coffee and brushed his hands on the thighs of his jeans.

"I was hoping he'd be staying for lunch after church," Aunt Trudi said.

"Oh, well I…" Dan looked down at his aunt and then back at Meg, and Meg could see the wheels turning inside his head and knew he'd be accepting his aunt's invitation, no matter what else he had planned today.

"That would be great. Let me help clean up and I'll drive you home."

A warmth spread from the vicinity of Meg's heart all the way down to her toes. "I'm sure I'll be seeing you around town, Dan."

"Meg, wait—"

She felt the heat from Dan's hand as it enveloped hers. Staring down, she noticed his was twice the size of hers and shades darker, as if he spent a lot of time outside. Because of the way she made her living, working for her family's handyman company, hands were important. Her father, grandfather, and great-grandfather all had wide-palmed, long-fingered hands that could finesse just about everything.

"Can I see you later tonight?"

Her throat went dry and her tongue got stuck to the roof of her mouth. Finally, she summoned up enough spit to loosen her tongue. "I'm not sure—"

Peggy McCormack chose that moment to join their conversation. "Hey, Meg, are you still coming to take a look at the backup stove at the diner?"

"Yeah," Katie said, coming to stand beside her sister. "We're worried that we won't be able to handle all of the baking for the diner without it."

Dan released her hand, and she sighed and looked at the McCormacks. "Sorry, I had forgotten, but I won't let you down. I'll be there and see what we can do to keep you running at full speed. Aside from Sunday afternoons, Monday's your busiest day."

"You're the best, Meg!" Peggy said.

Meg wished she didn't feel so guilty about wanting to forego the repair and head on over to Dan's house to distract him with another heart-pumping lip-lock... maybe a make-out session. Jeez, now she was thinking like a hormonal teenager.

Dan put his hands in his front pockets and the regret in his gaze was echoed in hers. "Well, maybe I'll catch up to you tomorrow."

"Sounds great, Dan." Meg looked from one sister to the other. "See you."

"Are you coming, Daniel?"

He grinned down at Meg and called out, "Right behind you, Aunt Trudi."

Monday morning at half past seven, Meg and her sisters were already at the shop. When the phone rang, Meg glanced at the clock, put it on speaker, and answered it. "Mulcahy's Funeral Home, you plug 'em, we plant 'em." Meg smiled, held the phone away from her ear, and waited for the fireworks.

"Megan Maureen Mulcahy!" her father shouted into the phone. "I told you no shenanigans when answering the telephone! Besides," he grumbled, not quite as loudly, "it's bad for business."

She smiled at her sisters, who were both trying not to laugh—their dad would hear them and reprimand them for acting like hooligans. With the press of a button, she turned the speaker off so she didn't get her sisters in trouble. She looked from one to the other and felt a burst of familial pride fill her.

Caitlin was dressed for another day at Mulcahy's in jeans and a black polo shirt with their logo on the breast pocket. Her sister wore her jeans snug at the hip and thigh. Meg preferred the looser fit of carpenter jeans and had taken to wearing a chambray work shirt a size larger than she needed; that way she could move without feeling restricted when she worked.

Grace, on the other hand, looked like a picture out of a fashion magazine in taupe slacks and silky blouse the color of a summer sky. Meg couldn't help but wonder how much longer they'd be able to convince the youngest of the bunch to stay on in Apple Grove. The big city beckoned to Grace in a way it never had to Meg.

"Are you listening, Megan?"

"Uh... yes, Pop." While he listed all the reasons why she shouldn't fool around on the phone, she rolled her eyes.

Caitlin shook her head and walked past their father's massive oak desk, giving Meg a thumbs up. Before she made it to the door marked "employees only" at the back of their hole-in-the-wall office, Grace passed her a steaming mug of fresh-brewed coffee. Caitlin smiled and sipped from her mug before opening the door and heading to the storage area at the back of their shop.

Meg knew her sister was going to be gathering the tools she'd need for the day. Meg would be doing the same thing as soon as she could get her dad to stop talking.

When Grace handed Meg her cup, Meg mouthed to please pick up the phone, but it was her sister's turn to roll her eyes. It had been their silent way of communicating whenever one of them was on the phone with their father, who would undoubtedly be telling them what to do, when, and how.

Grace held up her hands and walked through the same door Caitlin had. Their office on Main Street was set up shotgun style with the office at the front and their tiny kitchen behind the door at the back. Passing through the kitchen there was another door leading to the nuts and bolts of the shop, their storage area, and the parking lot.

Meg listened as her father continued to remind her of their family's reputation in Apple Grove until Meg had a chance to tell him, "I'm sorry, Pop, I just can't seem to help myself."

His sigh of acceptance was loud and low, "Why did the Lord decide to bless me with daughters? I could have had strong, strapping sons and handed the business your great-grandfather toiled to build with his own two hands over to someone who would appreciate what they'd been given."

Alone in the office, Meg waited a moment before speaking; she wanted to make sure her father was finished with his morning lecture. Ever since he'd retired six months ago, he called at the same time every morning, and she answered the phone the same way, every morning. It never failed to rile him or have her smiling when she went off to the first call of the day. "Now, Pop, you know we love you and have worked just as hard as any angel of a brother would."

As if he sensed that she needed it, Joseph Mulcahy soothed, "I know, Meggie, it's my temper talking. A father couldn't have asked for better than my three darling girls."

"I'll be heading over to Miss Trudi's today. Grace said that she called and left a message on our machine about the sump pump in her basement again."

"You might need to replace the switch again; that half-horse motor should be good for another couple of years."

"But, Pop, it's the third switch this year."

"Those pumps are workhorses; they just can't seem to build a switch that'll last as long. Mark my words, there's still life in that motor."

"Yes, Pop. I'll talk to you later. Bye." She always listened to her father. No one knew as well as he did how to keep things running long after a sane person would have given up. Joseph Mulcahy would magically coax just a bit more life out of whatever he was working on, whether it be an aging refrigerator or a finicky sump pump. He had passed on his gift to his daughters: Meg had inherited his way with plumbing, Caitlin his carpentry skills, and Grace his innate charm and good business sense.

Together the sisters had been keeping the family business going, despite Grace's daily grumbling that she was being wasted working in Apple Grove, Ohio, when she could have gone off to Columbus and landed a job as an executive assistant. Caitlin insisted that she really wanted to build things, not repair them, but at least Cait hadn't talked about moving away. Meg loved every minute spent working in their town to rebuild, and when that wasn't possible, replace, whatever the good citizens of Apple Grove needed to keep their lives moving forward.

She had never doubted that she and her sisters would grow up and learn how to be handymen. Gender had nothing to do with it; they were Mulcahys, and in their small town, their name had always been associated with the family business their great-grandfather had built and kept going through good times and bad.

They didn't always receive payment in monetary form; there were a few customers who bartered whatever they could, and the Mulcahys always accepted trade in exchange for whatever repair work was needed. Meg's personal favorite was Mrs. Winter's home-baked cherry pie. She'd gladly continue to sweat the pipes or crawl through spiderwebs in the basement of Mrs. Winter's house in exchange for the pie. Caitlin was fond of Mr. Weatherbee's wind chimes. He used bits of metal and glass to create musical whimsies that her sister treasured and accepted in trade for replacing his linoleum floor.

The phone rang, startling Meg back to the present and the fact that the clock was ticking. "Mulcahy's," she answered, "no job is too small, Meg speaking."

"Hi, I need help," a familiar deep voice rumbled. "The power just went off in my house, I can't find the circuit breaker, I'm late for work, and it's the first day of my new job."

Meg listened to the frustration building in the baritone on the other end of the line and couldn't hold back her smile. The image of the man who'd brought a spark back to her life filled her mind and then her heart. "Well, Dan, let's see what we can do for you."

The heartfelt sigh had her fighting the urge to chuckle. It was definitely a challenge; just the idea of not knowing where your circuit breakers were located was too funny.

"How did you know it was—did you say Meg?"

"Yes," she laughed. "This is Meg. I recognized your voice first of all," Meg told him, "and then the clue about the first day of your new job, unfamiliar house, blah, blah, blah."

"So you probably know where I live too, don't you?"

"Yep: 32 Elm Street, the old Saunders place."

There had been a lot of talk in town about the new phys ed teacher and high school varsity soccer coach. A few people had seen him when he came to town for the interview a few weeks ago. According to Honey B. Harrington, head of gossip central at Honey's Hair Salon, he had a physique to die for—or in Honey's younger sister's words, he was a "hottie!" After meeting him Saturday and then seeing him again yesterday at church, Meg could testify to the fact that he more than lived up to the gossip. He was totally hot.

"You don't have a circuit breaker box, just fuse panels."

"I know where to locate the fuses under the dashboard of a car, but heck if I'd know what to do with one in a house. Don't all homes have circuit breakers for power these days?"

"Depends on the age of the house and whether or not you have 120 or 220 volts of power coming in off the pole."

"I... uh... listen, I'd love to learn more, but right

now I'm seriously going to be late and I've only got one chance to make a good first impression."

She knew exactly what he meant. Her heart went out to him and had her shifting her schedule around. "Tell you what, why don't you head on out to work and I'll squeeze you in between Miss Trudi's sump pump and Mr. Weatherbee's broken back door latch."

"But I won't be home."

Taken aback, Meg didn't know what to say. It wasn't as if they were strangers. He'd met her dad and had been to their home. Growing up in Apple Grove meant that you took care of your neighbors, no matter how irascible they might be. Trust was second nature here. Everyone knew everyone else, or knew someone who did. Apple Grove was a close-knit town—like a page out of the past.

She blew out a breath and said, "Since you've just moved to Apple Grove, you're a neighbor. Neighbors help each other out here." When he didn't say anything, she added, "Technically we aren't strangers since we met at Edie and Bill's wedding, but I can have one of Sheriff Wallace's deputies accompany me if you're worried."

"I'm sorry. I'm just not used to such a friendly, open environment. Where I'm from, we lock our doors and have security systems."

Meg paused to let that foreign concept sink in. "I guess Apple Grove is a world away from that."

"I guess it is. My aunt doesn't lock her doors and that makes me crazy."

Meg sighed. "I can squeeze you in around three o'clock."

"Great. Thanks!"

A little while later, she had just finished coaxing life back into a thirty-year-old furnace when her cell phone rang. Since she was at a stopping point, she answered.

"Oh my God, Meg!" her sister Grace squealed into the phone.

Switching to speaker, Meg set her phone down on the top of the battered toolbox that had been her great-grandfather's. "What now? Did Caitlin put a dead mouse next to your keyboard again?" Their middle sister was the family prankster and had the strangest sense of humor.

"Don't remind me and don't get me sidetracked," her sister said. "You have got to swing by the high school on your way back to the shop."

"Get real, Grace." There were times when Meg felt so much older than the youngest of their Mulcahy brood.

"Would you just shut up and listen?"

Stunned that the normally calm one of the trio was getting agitated, she did.

"I'm talking about the new soccer coach. He's the first real eligible bachelor to hit town in three whole years! How could you not be paying attention? What is wrong with you, Megan?"

"Jeez, Gracie, you sound just like Pop. Besides, I already met him."

"When?"

"At the wedding. You and Caitlin were busy flirting with Deputy Jones over by the cake."

Her sister laughed and said, "You know we just can't resist a man in uniform."

"You two were all over the poor guy." Meg remembered watching her sisters flirting and feeling every bit of the seven-year age difference between herself and Grace.

"You could have called us over."

"And interrupt when you and Cait were on a roll? No thanks. I've been on the receiving end of Cait's sharp tongue enough to know she'd have left me bleeding if I did."

"I'm worried about you, Sis," Grace confided. "You work all the time and have no social life. I can't remember the last time you wore a dress and went out on a date."

"I wore a dress yesterday to church and Saturday to the wedding. Besides, I don't like dresses, and what does one have to do with the other?" Meg asked.

"Yeah, I know. You prefer your battered carpenter jeans, but, Meggie, you've got great legs."

Meg laughed. "Standing next to you and Cait, who'd notice, since both of you have legs up to your eyeballs?"

"Hey, until senior year in high school it really sucked being taller than all of the boys in school."

It was an old argument and neither one would ever win. They both had valid points. "Being short is worse," Meg said, just to get under her sister's skin so Grace would hang up and let her get back to work.

"Give me a break, Meg."

"OK, look, I've got to get going. My next stop is to replace a blown fuse at Dan's house; he doesn't have any power."

"Oh," Grace breathed. "That's excellent."

Meg snorted. "Actually, it's a problem not having power."

"You know that's not what I meant."

"Look, Gracie, if you hang up now, maybe I'll let you

talk me into another pedicure—my choice of color this time. But if I'm gonna make it to Dan's house and still get to all of the other calls you've scheduled for me, I've got to go now."

"Oh, all right… Talk to you later, Sis."

———

Dan couldn't believe he'd started the day without power. No power in his new home meant no water—good thing he'd showered the night before, or else he would have made a really bad first impression on the staff at Apple Grove High. He already had half of the Board of Education wondering if he'd last to the Christmas break. You'd think they'd never hired anyone from out of town before. Thank goodness his great-aunt had swayed the board to focus on his résumé and not where he came from.

He headed toward the locker room to change for practice. He had a team to get to know and a physical routine guaranteed to have the guys groaning before he sent them to the showers.

"All right," he rumbled, standing in the middle of the field, looking at the eager faces surrounding him. "Line up on the end line in the order I call your names. Doyle, Hawkins, Weatherbee, Winter, and McCormack—are you related to the sisters who own the Apple Grove Diner?"

McCormack nodded and said, "First cousins."

He took note of who was who on his clipboard so he would remember who they were by sight tomorrow. Scanning the rest of the group of, he called out, "The rest of you line up behind them so we can get started."

"Doing what, Coach?"

He looked up from his clipboard and noticed it was the captain, Charlie Doyle, asking. Doyle was the tallest of the bunch with a lean runner's build and coal-black hair. He hoped there was speed to match the boy's build.

"Trips." He chuckled at the sea of blank faces before him. "It was my coach's favorite drill. Now when I blow the whistle the first five run to the six-yard line—the edge of the goal box—bend down and touch it, turn around and run back. Then run to the eighteen-yard line—the edge of the penalty box—touch it, and run back. Then run to center field, touch the line, and run back. Finally, I want you to run to the other end line, touch it, and then run like you've got the ball and winning States depends on how fast you can go."

"We can't go that fast if we have to keep bending down to the touch the lines." This time it was Hawkins, who was as fair as Doyle was dark, but built like a football player. He hoped the kid could run. The way Hawkins and Doyle stood beside one another had him thinking the two were close friends. He'd find out soon enough.

Dan nodded. "That's true, but you'll be working on your abs and footwork." Seeing that he had everyone's attention, he added, "A soccer player depends on the strength in his legs, ankles, and feet. Offensive players also count on the power of their lungs and their ability to keep running."

"But Coach Creed—" one of the players began.

"Is recovering from a heart attack and I know you all wish him a speedy recovery, so let's make Coach Creed proud and see how fast on your feet you really are."

The challenge had been thrown down, and from the

eager expressions on the faces of the players lined up on the end line, they'd reacted the way he'd hoped. They were ready to show off for the new coach.

He blew the whistle and watched the first five off the line. Weatherbee and Winter were about the same height and equally matched, keeping pace with one another, but he'd remember who Winter was without taking notes—the kid had freckles and bright red hair that reminded him of Meg.

Focusing his thoughts on the team and getting to know the players, he watched them, evaluating as they performed the exercise. They weren't too bad, a little slow to start, but the short distances inside the penalty box and beyond were a definite challenge; once they got to sprint to center field, they started to show off.

As the first group made it to the other end line, he shouted, "The States are within reach and Apple Grove High will be the champs. If you want it, run for it."

The group charged toward where he stood waiting. Every single face had a look of concentrated determination. He couldn't be more proud. As they crossed the line, he blew the whistle and the next group repeated the drill.

When everyone had gone at least once, he gathered them in a circle. "We've got our work cut out for us if we're going to beat Newark High on Friday."

"We did last year," Doyle said.

Dan nodded. "But they will be expecting our team to be unorganized with Coach Creed gone and an unknown coach stepping in."

One look at the determined scowls on the players' faces convinced Dan they all wanted the same thing: to win. Apple Grove's varsity team wasn't that different from the last team he coached in north Jersey. "What is the most important skill a soccer player has?"

He waited a beat, staring at their faces, until someone called out, "Ball handling?"

He shook his head. Someone else called out, "Kicking?"

With a glance at his watch, he knew he didn't have time to waste, so he told them, "Running. You have to be fast, you have to think on your feet, and you have to be able to dribble the ball in a perfect three-sixty."

Now that he had their attention, he nodded. "So starting today, one quarter of our practice time will be devoted to running; everyone needs to work on their cardio. Any questions?"

"When do we scrimmage?"

Dan paused for a moment then said, "When I'm confident I have players who can run their hearts out for the entire eighty minutes."

"Not everyone gets to play the whole game," McCormack said.

"But we'll be ready." He was pleased to see that there weren't any dissenters in the group; that was a plus because the next drill was a guaranteed killer. "OK, our last drill before scrimmaging is the hardest. Everyone line up behind Doyle and me—"

"You're gonna run with us?"

"Every day," Dan said. "When I blow the whistle, the last man in line will sprint to the front." Now they looked worried. "Let's see who can keep up."

Four laps around the field later, he was satisfied that every player had given it his best shot. Some of the defenders didn't have the wind for sprinting by the third lap around the field, but they would by the end of the week.

He blew the whistle. "Great job, guys. Who's ready to play?"

The resounding cheer was music to his ears. Teenagers were not that different out here in Ohio. "Since I couldn't find any pinnies, we'll have to play skins and shirts. Line up and count-off by twos. The ones will be skins, and the twos will be shirts."

After a few minutes, he called out, "All right, guys. Let's change it up." Moving players around, he watched them play for another ten minutes before calling an end to practice.

"Great job. Hit the showers."

After the boys left, he showered, changed, and drove home. He had a date to cook for. A glance at his watch reminded him that he really had to work quickly if everything was going to be ready to eat when she got there.

—⁓—

The soufflé was rising and turning a golden brown. He already knew it would taste delectable; it was one of his foolproof recipes and guaranteed to impress a woman.

The apple tart he'd baked the night before was sitting on the center island awaiting the whipped topping he thought he'd experiment with. Glancing at the clock on the wall, he was pleased to note that everything was going according to schedule. He believed that timing was everything in life and had in fact led him to Apple Grove. Fifteen minutes more for the soufflé. Once that was out of the oven, he'd begin to sauté the garlic in sweet cream butter for the scampi.

His mom had told him that his great-aunt loved shrimp and he was determined to do everything he could to ensure he delivered a first-class meal for a first-class lady. He could have said thank you in a more conventional way, but he enjoyed cooking. To him, preparing a meal was akin to a science experiment. The outcome depended on the precision of his measurements, technique, and the timing, which had to be perfect.

With a sigh of satisfaction, he grinned and turned to double-check the table and decided the single red rose that he'd placed across her plate was just the right touch. A whole bouquet would have been overdoing it. He wanted her to feel special, not embarrassed. And while he'd done his part yesterday during coffee hour, he had a feeling this special meal would make her the talk of the town. "Why not, she deserves the attention."

Checking the time, he turned on the coffeemaker and pressed the button on the food processor to whip the topping—and the lights went out.

———

Meg groaned as her cell phone played "Urgent" by Foreigner. It was her father's sense of humor that decided they'd use that song for emergencies. She was so tired her eyeballs hurt; it had been a really long day. She'd just finished a foray into Mr. Sweeney's barn to help him gather a dozen eggs as payment for replacing his burned out floodlights. "What's up, Grace?"

The youngest Mulcahy sister got right to the point. "We have an emergency call from Dan Eagan. His power just went out again."

"I changed out the blown fuse this afternoon." There

had only been one; she'd checked. "I just finished up at Sweeney's—"

"I'd ask Caitlin," Grace interrupted, "but she's on the other side of Licking County."

Meg knew she'd have to answer the emergency call; their family business had been built on their reputation of being on-call twenty-four/seven—no job was too small. Four generations of Mulcahys have lived, worked, and died in Apple Grove. The townsfolk had come to count on them to keep their furnaces heating, their washing machines agitating, and their roofs watertight.

"Meg?"

Her sister's voice snapped her back to the present. "Call him back and tell him I'm on my way."

She set the basket of eggs on the floor and wedged her sweatshirt and lunch pail against it so it wouldn't move and she'd get them home in one piece. On the drive over to Elm Street, Meg relaxed and started to feel just a bit more energized knowing she was going to be seeing Dan again. It was exciting having someone new move into town—especially someone like Dan. He'd definitely made a great first impression and had been on her mind most of the day.

She wondered how long it would take for Miss Trudi and her cohorts to find out what was behind Dan's move to Ohio. Not that there was anything wrong with Apple Grove. She loved the rolling farmland dotted with Victorian-style homes and the more traditional farmhouses you expected to see with wide front porches and a barn out back. But it wasn't just the pretty scenery that kept her rooted to Apple Grove; it was her own family's history.

Her great-grandparents, Joseph and Molly Mulcahy, had settled in town in the early twenties, fresh off the boat from County Cork, and with their work ethic and eagerness to lend a helping hand, one thing led to another, and Mulcahy's handyman business had been born. Oh, some of her friends had moved to Cincinnati and some had even moved out of Ohio, but she liked living in a town where generations of her family had left their mark. She intended to do the same.

Smiling, she drove past the handful of houses dotting the street. Most of them had rocking chairs on their porches, inviting you to sit a spell and share a tidbit of gossip. She knew that if she pulled into any one of those driveways, she'd be greeted with a welcoming smile and cup of hot tea or coffee. Any other night, she just might think about it, but she had one more stop to make before quitting time.

The Saunders place was the last house on the dead end. Since half the homes in Apple Grove were built around the turn of the century, most still used the standard fuse panels with six screw-in type fuses. Meg kept spare fuses in the back of her truck. Mulcahys were always prepared for any emergency call.

She grabbed her flashlight and three fuses, stuffing them in her pockets as she closed the door. Looking out over the open fields behind the old house, she knew it wouldn't be long before the days would be getting shorter and colder. The hay bales were rolled up and ready to be stored for the winter. Mrs. Saunders had sold off a good part of her land years ago with the stipulation that it be used for farming, same as her grandparents had done. The next field over had a different crop every other year; pumpkins one year and corn the next. She didn't know much about rotating crops, but whatever grew there always looked healthy and good enough to eat.

She drew in a breath and smiled. She loved autumn, the way the leaves changed color, the beautiful reds and oranges of the sugar maples against the backdrop of the brown oak leaves. The smell of wet leaves on a rainy fall day never failed to have her craving a long walk through the fields and woods surrounding her home.

She didn't like when the temperature fell below twenty degrees. Her sisters loved winter and were always getting a group of friends together to go ice-skating or cross-country skiing. Meg never really got the hang of balancing on those thin blades or the long, thin skis her sisters used when they headed off across the snowy fields behind their home. Give her a toasty fire, her grandmother's quilt, a good book, and cup of cocoa over winter sports any day. Come early spring, Meg would be tromping through the mud and rain checking for signs that the trees would soon sprout leaves and the early bulbs in her garden would bloom.

If it were dark, she knew she'd hear the owl hooting in the pines behind the house. A pair of great horned owls hunted in the fields behind their barn, but she'd never seen the one that kept Mrs. Saunders company at night—could be a barn owl. She'd have to see if Dan was interested in finding out; it could be something they shared: bird watching. Smiling, she lifted her face to the crisp breeze rustling through the leaves. The moon was barely visible low in the sky, just shy of full. In a few hours it would light up the sky.

The door swung open and her breath snagged in her lungs; eyes the color of the wintry ice on the horse pond in February stared down at her. The longer she stared up at him the harder her heart pounded. Her body's reaction to him would have scared her spit-less a few days ago, but she'd slowly begun her journey back to the living, where deep-seated emotions and feelings weren't quite so scary.

He rumbled, "I'm so glad you're here. I'm in a bind."

"I was on my way home after a really long day…" Her words trailed off as her gaze met his.

He didn't say anything, just continued to look at her. She shifted from foot to foot, knowing there was probably more than one streak of dirt on her face. Meg didn't mind getting covered with grease, dirt, or what-have-you, as long as she got the job done—besides, that's what soap was for. But compared to the man in the doorway, impeccably dressed in a pale blue, fitted button-down shirt and charcoal pleated pants, she felt like a scrubby street urchin.

Why didn't he say anything? Was he going to apologize for kissing her?

Deciding to take the bull by the horns, she spoke up as she scooted around him. "I can't imagine what happened. I changed out the blown fuse earlier. There might have been another one going. I'll have a look and have the power back on in a few minutes."

"That would be wonderful," his deep baritone rumbled. "But it's not just the power that's out. I have no water."

She paused just inside the kitchen. She knew he wasn't from around here; he must have lived in a city before coming to Apple Grove. Everyone in Apple

Grove had a well. "Your well pump is operated by electricity, that's why you don't have any water."

He frowned at her. "I'm used to city water. The only time we didn't have water was if a water main broke or we didn't pay the water bill."

"We've got a deep well at our house. I'm pretty sure you have one here too. It only gets tricky if the power goes out and the well pump can't work. But a generator would take care of that."

"I guess there's a lot I'll have to get used to out here."

"It's not like it's another country—just a few states west of where you come from."

She scooted around him and across the kitchen. As she passed the oven, a heavenly smell wafted toward her. Whatever he had been cooking before the power went out had her stomach rumbling and her mouth watering. It had been a long day, and at that moment, she couldn't remember if, let alone what, she'd eaten for lunch.

At least her stomach distracted her from her reaction to the man. She reacted to him on an emotional and physical level. That hadn't happened in a long time. Not many men in her acquaintance dressed up, unless someone was getting married or buried. An uneasy feeling roiled in her belly—did he have a date?

She wondered if it was someone from the wedding or someone he'd met at church yesterday. The overwhelming need to find out had her panties in a twist. Normally Grace was the one who wheedled whatever she wanted to know out of people, but her sister wasn't here and Meg had a vested interest in Daniel Eagan. Maybe she would be able to finesse some information out of him.

She paused in the doorway to the cellar and asked, "Do you have an evening meeting with the Board of Ed?"

He shook his head. "No. Why?"

"No reason," she said, turning on her flashlight. She'd need it to find her way down the stairs. She wished she could think of another question to ask that might make him give away the name of his date. She didn't always have company while she worked, but when she did, she treated it like background music if the job she had to do was intense and required her full concentration; otherwise, she enjoyed chatting with whomever she was working for. Replacing a few screw-type fuses wasn't difficult, so when she heard Dan's footsteps on the stairs behind her, she wracked her brain to think of something to say—and another way to ask him without flat out asking who he was cooking for.

"Did you meet anyone special yesterday?"

"I saw someone special yesterday."

The caress in his voice had her fumbling with the flashlight. "Really?" her voice squeaked.

"I'm not sure she realizes it yet, though."

Did he mean her? She couldn't just ask, could she?

Her hands were shaking as she located the fuse panel. It took all of her willpower to steady them in order to shine the light on the fuses. "Here's the trouble," she told him, trying to tamp down on the crazy feeling in her stomach. "Two more fuses must have been going; they've burned out." Reaching in her pockets, she pulled out the replacements, screwed them in, and the power came back on. "You're back in business."

"Thanks, Meg. I don't know what I'd do without you."

Those sinful gray eyes, with a cauldron of emotions

bubbling below his surface calm, had her insides doing a slow burn. All thoughts of trying to find out who he was dressed up for flew out of her head; she couldn't think when he looked at her like that.

—⁓—

Dan's gut clenched before tying itself in one big knot. What the hell was wrong with him, anyway? He'd moved to Apple Grove to start over—after his fiancée flushed the engagement ring he'd pawned his prized 1952 Mickey Mantle rookie card to buy—not to get tied up by a pretty little bit of a thing with an engaging smile and freckles he was dying to taste again.

Meg brushed a lock of hair out of her eyes and the movement pulled her boxy shirt snug against her curves. He swallowed and reminded himself that women were not to be trusted—well, the ones his age weren't. Ones like Miss Trudi and his grandmother, they were honest to the core and the best of friends.

"I guess I'll just be going then," she said as she flicked off her flashlight and headed for the stairs.

He caught up to her at the top.

She was staring at the table he'd set for two and the rose he'd placed across one plate. "So, who are you cooking dinner for?"

He wanted to pump his fist in the air; the little lady wanted to know who he was cooking for. That meant she was definitely interested. She looked as if she were ready to bolt and he wanted to keep her there just a moment longer.

Before he could answer, she spun around and started past the center island and noticed the dessert. Her gaze met his again. "Whoever it is must have made quite an impression for you to go to all of this trouble." She stood there with dirt smudged across her cheek, her shirtsleeves rolled up to her elbows, staring up at him.

She blew out a breath and asked, "Is it Peggy or Katie McCormack?"

The insecurity in her eyes tugged at his heart.

"Uh… neither. I'm cooking for my aunt."

When she didn't react, he wondered if she'd been paying attention and heard what he'd said.

"Look, I've got to go." She didn't hang around for him to say any more. He almost wished she would; he liked seeing her in his kitchen. He thought about calling her back, but that would have been selfish when she'd already told him what a long day she'd had.

"Thanks, Meg. I really appreciate that you made the extra stop for me."

She smiled and waved on her way out the door. He chuckled softly watching her go, flattered that she'd been trying to get him to tell her who he was making dinner for. Was it possible she'd been jealous, or was he imagining things? He scrubbed his hands over his face and admitted he hadn't been able to figure women out since his ex. He had a lot on his plate right now, but it would be well worth it to get to the heart of Megan Mulcahy.

His parents had warned him that people would be different out here and not like folks from back home. He heard an engine roar to life and thought about going out to catch her and ask her to have dinner with him tomorrow night. With a glance at the clock, he factored in the time spent in the basement and knew Miss Trudi would arrive any time now. He set all thoughts of the mercurial Megan aside; he had a woman to impress and a dinner to rescue—hopefully his soufflé wasn't ruined. But as he opened the oven door, his thoughts drifted back to the prickly redhead, and he knew he'd be seeing her again—soon.

Megan was beat when she opened the door and slid onto the driver's seat. It felt good to be this tired, because it meant that she'd gotten to every job on her list—and the ones not on her list. She wished she'd been able to get Dan to tell her who he was preparing that mouth-watering meal for. Maybe she could find out through Miss Trudi; right now, she needed to get home, eat, and crash. Exhausted as she was, she still made it a point to make sure she didn't lean against the truck door or let the flashlight in her back pocket accidently scratch the paint. Pop would have her hide if she scratched or dented his baby. He'd inherited his father's black 1950 Ford F1 pickup with the understanding that he would continue to drive the truck every day. Her grandfather had insisted that the people in Apple Grove always knew the Mulcahys were on the job when they saw his black truck with the gold lettering proclaiming *Mulcahy's—No Job is Too Small* driving through town.

Feathering the gas, she engaged the clutch and shifted into reverse. She didn't have far to drive, but it was just enough time to replay what had happened in her mind. Analyzing everything usually helped her resolve whatever was bothering her. By the time she'd driven home, she had realized what worried her most wasn't her physical reaction to the man; it was the feeling that they were meant to be together whether she was ready to accept it or not.

The last time she'd felt like this she'd been sixteen years old and so in love with Jimmy Van Orden that nothing anyone could say would convince her that he wasn't coming back after college. He was on the fast track to achieving his goal of playing pro football, and he would leave Apple Grove, Ohio, and Megan Mulcahy in the dust. Except for his twice-yearly visits, when he picked up where they'd left off, she'd be pinning her hopes on her childhood sweetheart popping the question for years—but so far it hadn't happened.

Growing up, she'd learned there were two types of people who lived in the sleepy Midwest town of Apple Grove: those who loved it and those who hated it. The ones who loved it still lived there, and those who hated it, well, they worked hard to earn scholastic or sports scholarships to colleges that would take them away to the bright lights and big city. Columbus wasn't that far away, and Ohio State had one of the best football teams in the nation. When Jimmy played for the Buckeyes, they'd been number one. Last year, they'd been in twelfth place—decent, but not in the top ten. She still followed college football, but she also enjoyed watching NASCAR and her favorite driver.

Thinking about Jimmy lifted the lid she'd put on her feelings back then. It had been a point of pride with her that she had been right; he did come back, often, but he'd yet to stay or ask her that all-important question. She'd been living in a time warp, keeping her nose to the grindstone, doing what had to be done for her sisters before and after school, burying her heart in the work that kept the family business afloat—living for the times when Jimmy would blow into town, take her out, and then shatter her heart with his excuses about why he just had to leave again. That is, until her wake-up call the other day at Edie and Bill's wedding when she'd encountered Dan Eagan.

It should have been a nick to her pride that that handsome, fair-haired phys ed teacher had gotten beneath her guard and under her skin, but the way he'd reawakened feelings she never thought she'd experience again had her wanting to thank him. The heat in his gaze had beckoned to her, tempting her, twice now. The first time, she'd gone with the overwhelming need to kiss him back and look how that worked out. He was dressed to kill and preparing a delicious-smelling dinner for someone—who she was, Meg hadn't been able to find out—but she did wonder if it was one of the McCormack sisters. They were blonde, tall, and simply gorgeous. Nice too, damn it. It would be hard to stay mad at them when they were so likable. If not the McCormacks, then who?

Since the resurgence of interest in the opposite sex wasn't something she was ready to deal with tonight, she'd chill out, talk to her dad, and have that beer.

For the first time in a dozen years, she wondered why she had never moved out of her parents' home. It wasn't that she hadn't felt the need to have a place of her own—she had, more than once, but she just hadn't done anything about it. It required energy she usually didn't have after a long day.

While Meg loved her sisters, there were times when they could be a pain, but she knew they felt the same way about her, saying she was too much of a mother hen. If they sensed there was something going on in her love life, they'd badger her until she confessed, and she wasn't sure she was ready to talk about the way the new teacher in town made her heart jump and her skin tingle. Oh, she knew they'd promise not to tell anyone, but she also knew they'd tell one of their gossipy friends, who'd tell two friends, who would eventually tell Honey B., and by nightfall their half of Licking County would know.

"Maybe I should call Susie Sanders." Her friend owned Sanders Real Estate and would know who had an available apartment to rent. Thinking about moving was exciting and the possibilities were endless.

Partway home, she wondered why she'd waited, then a heartbeat later wondered why she wanted to move. "Conflicted much?" She laughed at herself and felt better. It was a big move to make without having second thoughts.

She needed more privacy than their family home afforded. Her sisters were long past the point where either of them needed her guidance or advice on anything. They basically lived and worked in each other's pockets, but after meeting Dan, she suddenly felt as if she were being confined and needed to spread her wings.

Without thinking, she'd taken the long way home, detouring past the water tower. One of her favorite spots in town was the Apple Grove water tower. Not because of its construction or historical significance; it was *the* equivalent of their local billboard, announcing everything from who was going steady or breaking up to who had just graduated from Ohio State or the Air Force Institute of Technology.

She looked up and grinned; sure enough, there was

a new message today. Chuckling, she shook her head. "Well, now everyone's going to know that Rod and Susie are dating." She ignored the twinge she felt every time a new name appeared up there that wasn't hers and she pulled over. Reaching for her phone, she sent a text to Rhonda Beaudine, letting her know the message on the water tower had changed. Rhonda replied right away that she'd do a drive-by and get a picture for the *Apple Grove Gazette*.

Knowing that she'd done her small part to keep the gossip flowing and the town moving forward, she grinned as the floodlights came on, illuminating the ladder leading to the catwalk that circled the tower. Sheriff Wallace had quit trying to keep kids from climbing up and painting their news, knowing he couldn't be there twenty-four/seven, so he did the next best thing and had floodlights installed so that no one would ever be climbing in the dark. Smart man, Mitch Wallace... except for not figuring out that Honey B. Harrington had been in love with him for the last fifteen years.

Then again, he probably did know but was hanging on to bachelorhood with both hands. As far as Meg was concerned, Honey had been wasting her time waiting for that man to wake up and smell the coffee.

Shaking her head, wondering what made men's minds work the way they do, she decided she'd waited long enough to do something with her life. Dialing Susie's number, she took the first step toward making an overdue change in her life.

Once she'd made up her mind and placed that phone call, she had set things in motion. Excitement tingled to the tips of her fingers. Anticipation filled her as she pulled into the driveway. She wondered what kind of a reaction waited for her.

Energized, ready to tackle life head on, she parked the truck, hefted her toolbox, and walked to the back door. It opened and her father stood beneath the back door light, frowning. Meg couldn't believe that he'd already heard that she'd called Sanders Real Estate. His stance, feet apart, hands loose at his sides—just like a gunslinger from the old west—and his words confirmed her suspicions. "Why didn't you tell me you weren't happy?"

"What?"

"Mary Murphy just called. Mrs. Graves was picking up a few groceries when Susie Sanders called her about renting her garage apartment to you." He paused and drew in a deep breath. "You don't have to move out, Meg." He reached for the heavy toolbox she carried. "I can convert the barn loft to an apartment for you if you're dead set on having a place of your own."

She let go of the toolbox handle and turned and walked back to the truck.

"Wait!" he called out following her. "Mulcahys talk things through; you can't just leave without telling me what happened."

She opened the passenger door and softly smiled. "I'm not," she said, reaching in the truck once more.

"Then why are you moving out?"

She handed him the basket of eggs and stared up at the face that was more familiar than her own. "Pop," she said. "I'm twenty-nine years old. Don't you think it's way past time for me to live on my own?"

His big frame relaxed as he took the basket from her and asked, "Sweeney's payment?"

"Yep. I think his arthritis is acting up again. He was having a hard time collecting them, so I helped."

Putting his arm around her shoulders, he hugged her to his side. "How about a cold one? We can talk about what furniture you'll need to take with you."

Meg blinked back tears. "Thanks for understanding, Pop."

"I knew it was coming, but why now? Why today?"

She shrugged. "I'm not sure. I was driving past the water tower and it hit me."

He pressed his lips to the top of her head. "I hear Rod'll have to marry Susie."

Meg smiled and reached for the door. "He loves her."

He nodded and held the door for her. "Your sisters might not be ready to let you move out, but I think they'll come around."

"You aren't mad?"

"Not a bit, Meggie, everyone has to spread their wings sometime." Their eyes met. "Seems that now is your time."

"I love you, Pop."

"I love you more."

Chapter 3

"YOU'VE GONE TO SUCH TROUBLE, AND ALL FOR AN old biddy like me."

"Aunt Trudi, you're worth every effort. How's the scampi?"

"Perfect... and my favorite." She narrowed her gaze at him. "Did you call your mother to ask what I'd like to eat?"

"Of course. How else would I know?"

They ate companionably for a few minutes before he asked, "What do you make of Megan Mulcahy?"

His great-aunt slowly smiled as she lifted another forkful to her lips. Finishing the bite, she sighed. "You are a wonderful cook, Daniel. Did you know that some women couldn't cook if their lives depended upon it?"

He shrugged. "Hunger is a great motivator." He looked over at her and grinned. "I really love to eat."

They were laughing when he got up to clear their places. "I'm trying out a new topping for the apple tart. I'd like your honest opinion about it."

"Of course. Now, getting back to Megan, she's the hardest working of the three girls."

"She looked like she'd been inside that furnace she said she repaired earlier today." He remembered wanting to brush the smudge of dirt off her nose. "I thought she was much younger when I caught her."

"Caught her doing what?" Trudi leaned across the table toward him to hear better.

"Falling off the fence. Remember?"

"Hmmm… yes," she answered. "Of course I do. I was just thinking."

"You've got that look in your eye, Aunt Trudi."

"Megan hasn't dated, except for when that young man who left to play football for Ohio State comes back to town."

Dan really didn't think he wanted to know but needed to ask. "And how long ago was that?"

"A dozen or so years ago."

He stopped midpour and set the coffee carafe down. "You have to be kidding me."

Trudi shook her head. "I wish I was. That Van Orden boy broke Meg's heart. But what I don't understand is why she settles for a week or two of happiness out of fifty-two. He is keeping Meg right where he wants her—here in Apple Grove, waiting for his call." She paused to draw in a breath before continuing. "A year or so after he left for college, Meg's mother died, and Meg retreated from everything but taking care of her sisters and working at Mulcahy's with her father."

At his aunt's encouraging, he picked up the coffee and started pouring again.

"Let me help you with that, Daniel dear."

They worked together and had dessert served and coffee poured before they got back to the subject of Megan. "Maybe she really loves the guy."

"I think not dating anyone when he's not around has become habit," Trudi said before sipping from her cup. "You can bet a man like Van Orden has a bevy of beauties at his beck and call back there in the city."

He couldn't help himself; he laughed. "You haven't lost your flair for embellishing the facts. You could give grandma a run for her money."

"She learned everything she knows from me. I am the big sister, you know."

They were laughing again when he leaned over to squeeze her hand in his. "It's great to be here. Thanks for putting in a good word for me."

"Your résumé spoke for itself. All I did was make sure it was added it to those applying for the job. Every one of the applicants had the same consideration from the board, in case you were wondering."

"I wasn't, but it's good to know. In case anyone asks, I'll be prepared."

"Oh, there will be a few making comments, after all, this is Apple Grove and everyone knows everyone else's business. If one person is in favor of something, there are two more who are against it."

"Should I be worried about anyone in particular?"

"No one except Meg for the moment."

"It was funny, she kept trying to get me to tell her who I was making dinner for without coming right out and asking me, but I don't think she heard me tell her I was cooking for you."

"And how did that make you feel?" his aunt pressed.

He didn't even have to think about it; he knew. "Flattered. It was interesting, but she mentioned Peggy McCormack. Why do you think that was? I didn't really pay the woman any more attention than anyone else I met at Bill and Edie's wedding."

His aunt nodded. "Meg's always been a bit touchy about the fact that her sisters inherited their father's height and she her mother's diminutive stature. Peggy and Katie are both tall, like the younger Mulcahy sisters."

"That's crazy. Who thinks of things like that?"

Trudi wrinkled her nose as she set her coffee down. "Women are fragile creatures sometimes, Daniel. Best you remember that."

He cleared away the last of the dirty dishes and asked, "Are you ready for me to take you home?"

"Yes, thank you, dear. Dinner was such a treat… and I did enjoy dessert. It's not often a handsome man goes to such trouble for me."

He studied her as he waited for her to rise. "Are the eligible bachelors all blind here in Apple Grove?"

She patted her hair and laughed. "Lord love you, Daniel. It's good to have you here."

"It's good to be here and to know I'm not all alone… I have family."

"There are times when it seems like friends desert you, but family will always be there," she said as he held the back door open and ushered her through. Arm in arm, she let Daniel lead the way outside to his car.

On their way through town, Aunt Trudi happily chatted about what was new over at her garden shop and the various plants she'd be "putting to bed" for the coming winter.

"Mom still rakes the leaves into her gardens for the same reason," Dan told her.

When they passed the town square, she said, "I'll be putting in mums and ornamental cabbages here in the morning."

"Do you plant them all by yourself?" Dan asked.

His aunt drew herself up in the seat next to him and huffed out a breath. "I am perfectly capable, young man."

"Yes, Aunt Trudi," he agreed, smiling at the eccentric picture she made sitting there wearing her khaki jodhpurs; a white, button-down, collared men's shirt; and her Wellingtons. "But that's not the point—"

"Thank you for agreeing." She waited a few minutes before adding, "Robert Stuart usually stops by to help on his way in to the Gas and Gears."

Dan felt better; he was worried that his eighty-year-old aunt would try to do the work all alone. "That's good because I don't have a moment to spare until after practice tomorrow."

"I could use a hand over at the shop Saturday morning if you're free."

"I'll be there," he promised. A glint of chrome glistened in the moonlight off to the left. "Aunt Trudi, what's over there?"

She looked out the window and answered, "The back side of the cemetery. Oh," she sighed.

He recognized the sleek black pickup before he noticed the compact curvy form of the woman who intrigued him. "Meg?"

"She must be troubled," Trudi lowered her voice to just above a whisper. "She always visits her mother when she is."

"Do you think we should—"

"Leave her be," his aunt said. "Some things are best done alone. She's a strong young woman who has been carrying too heavy a burden, but doesn't always let it show."

"I thought she lived at home and worked in the family business?" *How could that be a burden?*

Trudi shook her head. "Some of the strongest people I know work for family. It's never easy; you can't just up and quit if you don't like the way you're being treated or if the business isn't bringing in enough money. Families stick together, weather storms together and all of life's trials."

"Is that what it was like working for your grandmother?"

She smiled. "I loved working with her. Grandmother Phoebe knew I'd have to be tough to keep her business flourishing after she turned it over to me. I'm grateful for every day that I had working and learning alongside her."

He thought she'd finished and was about to speak when she softly added, "Hard to believe she's been gone close to thirty years now."

Dan wanted their dinner date to end on a positive note, so he changed the subject. "My granddad still isn't speaking to me. It's been three years."

"I heard from your grandmother that he was softening in his attitude once he discovered that you hadn't sold the card outright, just pawned it. Too bad that the pawnbroker sold your Mickey Mantle card right out from under your nose."

"Yeah." He didn't often think about his ex–best friend and was surprised that it wasn't quite as raw a feeling as it had been the last time he had. "She knew I was a diehard Yankee fan. How could she not see it was a symbol of how much I loved her?"

His aunt patted the back of his hand. "So you pawned the card, but didn't sell it? You were planning on buying the card back?"

"That was the plan, but my ex-friend and ex-fiancée changed that."

"I'm truly sorry, Daniel," his aunt soothed. "But things have a way of working out the way they're supposed to."

Dan cleared his throat and confessed, "She flushed the diamond ring I gave her."

The sharply indrawn breath had him feeling a tiny bit better. He'd shocked his aunt, which meant she agreed with what he hadn't even had a chance to say.

"Bitch."

Shock had him slowing down, putting on the brake, and turning to look at her. "What did you say?"

"You heard what I said, young man."

He swallowed his laughter; he didn't want to get his aunt riled this late in the evening. He'd save it for Saturday morning when he planned to be at her shop. Needing to distract her, he said, "I heard that since they got married, he's in debt up to his eyeballs."

His aunt sniffed and nodded. "Serves him right. He bought her love, Daniel. Don't you forget that she willingly sold it to the highest bidder."

He had no response to that. His great-aunt was whip-smart and had hit the nail on the head. "Thanks, Aunt Trudi."

She smiled as he helped her from the car and into the house that sat behind the garden center she lived and breathed for. "Thank you for a lovely evening."

"You're welcome. It's a rush to watch someone eating my food with such gusto and enjoyment."

She tilted her head to one side and pushed a loose hairpin back into the bun on the top of her head. "In that case, you should know that I'm partial to lasagna."

He laughed and hugged her tight. "How about Saturday after we finish up doing whatever is it you need help with?"

"I'm expecting a delivery of hay bales midmorning on Saturday, but need to make room."

"Could you use a couple of extra hands?"

"The more the merrier. Who did you have in mind?"

"Maybe a couple of the guys from the team."

She patted him on the shoulder so he could lean down and she could reach his cheek. She kissed it, then patted the side of his face. "You're a good boy, Daniel. Don't wait until Saturday to visit."

He grinned down at her. "How early are you up in the morning?"

"I have my first cup of tea at four thirty—"

He laughed, surprised at how good it had felt. "That's too early, even for me, but Wednesday morning the kids have an assembly and I don't have to attend. I have the first period free."

Her smile lit up her face. "I'll see you then."

After dropping his aunt off at her house, Dan drove through town. "Where is everyone?" From the way the street was deserted, he wondered if they rolled it up after nine o'clock only to unroll it again around five or six in the morning.

Just when he thought he was all alone, he saw headlights coming toward him. A black Ford F1 passed by him without slowing down. "Meg." He wished he could follow her and make sure she was all right, but his aunt had known Meg far longer than he had. It would be best to follow Aunt Trudi's advice. There were some things he wanted to say to her but wasn't quite sure if he was pushing too hard too soon. She needed to know that he wasn't chasing after Peggy or any other woman in town. He was a one-woman man and even though he hadn't planned on it yet—wasn't ready yet—he was looking for a one-man woman. Dan had a feeling that Meg was that woman.

When she turned off onto Goose Pond Road, he didn't follow along behind. He'd wait until tomorrow to plan out their next meeting. By then, he should have figured out what move to make.

—◆◆—

Meg felt better having gone to talk to her mom. Oh, she knew her mother's spirit wasn't in the cold, hard ground of Apple Grove Cemetery, but she needed something tangible to look at when she unburdened her troubles. The headstone with the words "beloved wife, loving mother" grounded her and had borne witness to more than one outpouring of Meg's heart over the years.

She passed a car on the way back through town. Squinting, she tried to make out who was out at this hour, but all she could see was a dark car; she couldn't make out the driver. Uneasy at the thought of a stranger driving through town from the direction of Miss Trudi's home, she picked up her cell phone and dialed, but no one answered.

"She'll be in bed by now." Meg knew the woman got up with the birds just before dawn. But once the feeling started to unfurl inside of her, it wouldn't go away. She'd had Sheriff Wallace on speed dial ever since the scare last year when she thought her dad had had a heart attack. She hit the number.

"Wallace."

The deep rumbling voice of the man who'd been there through most of the disasters in her life reassured her that all would be well just by answering the phone. "Hey, Mitch, it's me, Meg."

"Everything all right?"

"I don't know. I've got a hinky feeling. I just passed a dark-colored car on my way through town."

"Where were you headed?"

She sighed. It's not like he didn't know about her visits and would think she was crazy. Everyone in town knew she talked to her mom. "Just heading back home from the cemetery."

"The car could have been coming from Miss Trudi's place."

"That's what's got me worried. I tried to call, but she didn't answer, and you know how upset she'd be if I showed up on her doorstep, checking up on her."

The sheriff agreed and asked, "Can you remember anything about the car? Could you see inside of it?"

She wished she could. "It was dark, and I wasn't paying that much attention until the car had already passed me."

"No problem," he reassured her. "You head on home and I'll drive on over and check things out. Miss Trudi has a soft spot for me."

Relief swept through her, leaving a feeling of well-being, knowing he would handle things. He always would. "Thanks, Mitch."

"Drive safe, you hear?"

She laughed. "I will."

Lighter of heart, Meg headed home to the house she would be moving out of. In just a few short days, she'd be renting an apartment. What a concept! A place of her own.

With the worry of Miss Trudi in the sheriff's capable hands, she drove the rest of the way home, formulating a plan for packing and how she was going to arrange her new space.

Meg wandered through the house in the dark, saying good-bye to her childhood memories. With a hand skimming the wall to guide her, she made her way down the back staircase from the second floor to the kitchen. It was really dark at the bottom, but she'd snuck up and down this staircase so many times as a kid, she'd have known the way blindfolded.

The staircase opened up into the back of the kitchen near the pantry, where her dad used to stash his supply of potato chips and Funny Bones. Meg had a weakness for potato chips but had a bad habit of forgetting to close the bag tight, so her dad always knew when she'd been snacking on them; they weren't as crisp the next day. But it was the chocolate-covered, peanut butter cream-filled snack cakes that got her into the most trouble. Just like the chips, she couldn't eat just one and they had been her mom's favorite too. Lord help the Mulcahy sisters if their mother found out they'd been in her chocolate stash—they'd be scrubbing toilets for a week!

Reaching above her head, she pulled the chain and the pantry was illuminated by the soft incandescent glow of the bare lightbulb hanging overhead. "Damn it, Grace, where did you hide them this time?"

Craning her neck to see, she caught a glimpse of the box of chocolaty goodness on the top shelf. Her sisters didn't hide them on the top shelf to be cruel; it was just to keep Meg from eating the whole box, which she had done on more than one occasion. Knowing the shelves wouldn't hold her weight now as they had as a child, she turned around and got a kitchen chair and carried it into the pantry to stand on.

Coveted box in hand, she sat down on the chair, opened the cellophane package, and gobbled the first cake in three bites. Once she'd satisfied the chocolate monster living inside of her, she put the box back on the shelf and the chair where it belonged. But she wasn't ready to go back upstairs, so she nuked a mug of milk and carried it and the other cake out to the porch.

The autumn air was brisk, carrying a chill that would be gone come midmorning, but for now, she folded her legs beneath her and settled down to enjoy her late-night snack. As if on cue, the owl called to her from behind the barn. She smiled, remembering the nights she'd sat on her mother's lap waiting for the owl to talk to them.

"Probably not the same owl," she mumbled before sipping her warm milk.

"Great horned owls have been known to live for more than twenty-eight years, Meggie."

She bobbled her mug and splashed warm milk on her thigh. "Gee thanks, Pop." She got up to wring the milk out of her pant leg. "You could have let me know you were there."

"And spoil your fun, thinking no one would know you'd found the stash of Funny Bones and eaten half of them?"

"Hey," she said. "I only took one package."

"This time." Her father grinned and she couldn't keep from smiling back. "So have you sorted it all out in your head?"

She knew he wanted to ask how the talk had gone

with her mother, but it was a subject they both avoided. He'd made his peace when her mother had died, but Meg still needed that earthly connection in the form of visits to the cemetery.

"I think so. I was just enjoying one last midnight walk through the house and out here on the porch."

"Just because you are moving out doesn't mean that you can't spend the night once in a while."

A lump the size of a grapefruit constricted her throat while tears filled her eyes. But Meg wouldn't cry. She'd already put this off for too long; any longer and she was afraid that she'd never leave. "Thanks, It means a lot that you understand and aren't trying to make me doubt my decision."

"I've been expecting it to happen someday, so I'm more or less prepared. It'll be hard, but anything worthwhile is never easy. Spread your wings, Meg, but know you can always come back to roost if you need to."

"They don't make them like you anymore, Pop."

"You know they broke the mold after me."

They sat side by side for a while listening to the owl calling and another answering. "He'll have found his mate by the sounds of it."

She nodded. "I wonder if they mate for life like some birds."

"You can check out our field guide tomorrow; you'll want to hit the sack soon, or else you won't be able to stay awake long enough to get through the long list of service calls Grace lined up for you."

Meg sighed and got to her feet. "Sounds like a plan. I'll see you in the morning, Pop." She leaned over and kissed his cheek. He ruffled her hair and said good night. Walking away, she wondered if he would miss having someone to sit with in the middle of the night, when their worries were many and the need to talk about them overrode the need for sleep.

She would make sure to ask her sisters to keep an ear out for their father and to take turns sitting up with him. The last thing she wanted to do was send him back into the downward spiral he'd descended into when their mother died.

With that new plan forming in her tired brain, Meg rinsed out her milky sweatpants and hung them over the shower rod to dry. Exhausted beyond belief, she slid between the sheets and was asleep before she could say her prayers.

—∿∿—

"Do you need help moving into your new apartment?"

Meg paused and looked over her shoulder at her friend Melanie. "Are you offering your back or Jim's?"

Melanie laughed and handed two cookies to Timmy and two to Tommy. "One for each hand, you rascals."

They laughed and said something Meg didn't even try to decipher. "They've grown so fast."

"Babies do," her friend answered. "But to answer your question, I was offering to help with whatever you need. If it's a strong back, Jim's is definitely stronger. But if it's a little organization and unpacking, them I'm your woman."

Touched, Meg nodded and continued to screw the hinge into the door frame. "I just might take you up on your offer. This should hold for at least one more season."

"Good, because we just don't have the extra funds to replace that storm door; it has to last."

Meg tested the hinge and said, "This will hold, even though that last storm took a chunk of wood with it when it ripped the door off the hinges. I added a little extra wood glue to the block of wood and a few extra screws. It will definitely hold."

"Can you stay for a cup of coffee?"

Meg looked at the kitchen clock and shook her head. "Grace has me on a really tight schedule today, but I'll take a rain check."

Stowing her toolbox in the pickup, she marveled at the speed with which good and bad news travels. This was her third stop today and so far everyone knew that she'd shaken hands with Mrs. Graves and rented the apartment on top of her three-car garage. Good thing she'd been saving her pennies since she'd started working; she had a nice cushion that would take care of the utilities and a few odds and ends that she would need starting out in her life as a single woman supporting herself.

Just saying it was exciting. She could watch whatever she wanted on TV, once she could afford to buy one, and she could eat meals standing up over the sink without her dad telling her to sit down or she'd ruin her digestion. But the biggest change that she'd be making was that she would have to answer to no one but herself if the dishes weren't done or the bed not made.

The enormity of the change hit her between the eyes and she had to pull over so she could catch her breath. "I'll be on my own—all alone—just me." She tilted her head back and let it all out. "Woohoo!"

"From now on, it'll be all about me—just me." Her hands were shaking when she gripped the steering wheel to slip back onto the road. Who knew that it would be so liberating to move out? She sure as heck hadn't.

"OK, next stop on my list is… crap. Where'd I leave my list of appointments?" Damn, she'd have to call Grace.

She hit the number three on speed dial and Grace answered on the first ring. "Hey, Gracie, I lost my list. Where am I supposed to be after the Culpeppers'?"

Grace sighed. "Again? That's three times in the last two weeks, Meg."

"Oh, you know I don't do it on purpose. I'm just better with fixing things than I am scheduling things. You're the whiz at that, Gracie."

As expected, her sister laughed. "When you're right, you're right. Your next stop is the Hawkins's, to change out the frozen lock mechanism on their back door, then Doyle's to see if you can trace out a faulty wire in their kitchen that keeps tripping their circuit breakers and cutting their power."

"OK, but isn't there one more stop after Doyle's?"

"Yes," Grace said slowly. "Mrs. Winter—"

"Hot damn and hallelujah!" Meg crowed. "I'm getting a cherry pie and I don't have to share it."

"Yes," Grace said. "You do. Payment is payment, whether it be a dozen eggs, one cherry pie, cash, check, or credit card. Besides, you know how mad Pop got the last time you brought home half a pie."

Meg sighed theatrically. "And here I thought I could just bring the pie back to my apartment and no one would be the wiser."

Grace chuckled. "Except for the little fact that I schedule the repair visits and know that you would be due to receive said pie."

"I guess I can't pull the wool over your eyes anymore."

Grace snickered. "You haven't been able to in years. Just be sure to bring the whole pie home."

"Yeah, yeah," Meg said. "I'll bring home the whole damn pie."

"And no swearing on the job, Sis."

"I'm not on the job yet, Grace. I'll be there in a few. Talk to you later." She disconnected and wondered if there was a way to finagle a piece of pie from Mrs. Winter in addition to the pie she'd give Meg as payment for whatever job she needed Meg to do. Of all the residents in Apple Grove, she always loved chatting with Mrs. Winter while she worked.

The widow was pushing seventy—not quite as old as Miss Trudi and definitely not as spry as the owner of their local garden center. Maybe it had to do with the fact that Amelia had broken her leg in three places a few years back. She never really did bounce back from that.

She made short work of the next two jobs on her list, grateful that today's job list was all in town. Not that she minded driving to one of the farms on the outskirts of Apple Grove; she enjoyed the chance to drive on Route 70. She always put the pedal to the metal and cleared out the carbs; she couldn't do that inside the town limits. It wasn't safe.

Pulling up in front of the Winters' two-story farmhouse, she took the time to admire the way the leaves were changing color. Tall maples with golden leaves stood beside oaks turning a rich reddish-brown, and the Virginia Creeper hanging on to the oak tree by the barn added just the right touch in all its crimson glory.

The planters on either side of the front steps were

colorful no matter what season. Right now, her friend had a mix of bold chrysanthemums: rust, orange, yellow, and gold. It wouldn't be long before they too would die off and the planters would be empty until spring.

Meg noticed that some of the white paint had started to check, cracking and lifting, on the left side of the screen door. Once that happened, there wasn't much else to do but scrape it off, check for water damage, prime, and paint.

"She should start using her front door more." She shook her head, knowing that the widow wouldn't. Mrs. Winter insisted that the front door was for company, and since most of her visitors were friends and friends were an extension of family, well then, they'd use the back door like her family.

Meg turned around and, before walking down the steps, paused, and noticed the dried honeysuckle vine clinging to the lattice at one end of the porch. Meg wished it was spring; she loved when the pretty little yellow blossoms were in bloom—it not only shaded that end of the porch, but it's light, sweet scent filled the air around Mrs. Winter's home. "Maybe someday, I'll have my own house with honeysuckle vines, sweet peas, and morning glories growing all over the front and back porches."

She shook her head at the fanciful thought. "I guess it'll have to wait until I can see if I can pay the rent for Mrs. Graves's apartment first."

Drawing in a deep breath, she tucked those thoughts away for another day when she had time to dally. Walking around the back, she wondered how Jimmy could leave Apple Grove behind. He hadn't been able to wait to blow the dust of their little town off his shoes. Funny, but his need to leave town because he didn't love it as much as she did hurt more than his need to leave to play football.

She opened the wood screen door, knocked on the back door, and waited for Mrs. Winter to answer. When the door opened, she breathed in the welcoming smell of freshly baked cherry pie. "I will do whatever you need me to, as long as there's a piece of that pie in my future."

"Land sakes, Megan," Mrs. Winter said. "You surely do love your sweets."

Meg laughed. "It's a good thing I work hard every day, or else I'd probably be as big as a house."

The older woman shook her head and motioned for Meg to come in. Happy to follow her nose toward the pies cooling on the Formica countertop, she stepped inside. Mrs. Winter's kitchen always made Meg miss her mom. Maureen Mulcahy used to bake up a storm on Tuesdays. It was something Meg's grandmother had always done too—have a day dedicated to a certain chore. Mondays were for laundry, Tuesdays baking.

Knowing that Mrs. Winter thrived on routine, Meg set her toolbox down on the left side of the back door and walked over to sniff the pies. "What do you need me to do today? I lost my list—"

"Again?"

Meg paused with her hands on the countertop, poised to breathe in the tempting scent of cherries through the slits in the top of the pie. Mrs. Winter knew her too well. "Yeah, so I don't know what needs fixing."

Mrs. Winter tut-tutted, but Meg was so close to paradise, she leaned close and got a good whiff of the flakiest pie crust in Licking County. Forget the McCormack sister's pie—they didn't use butter in their crust like Mrs. Winter did.

Now that she'd gotten a nose-full of the fabulous scent, it would hold her until she'd repaired whatever needed fixing. "So, what needs my attention today?"

The woman held out both her hands, took Meg's right hand in hers, and patted the back of it. "I do. I haven't seen you in a while and woke up wanting to bake a cherry pie."

Meg tried hard not to tear up, but she couldn't help it. Mrs. Winter had a way of getting to the heart of any matter... no matter how small. "I need to fix something if I'm going to earn that pie."

Amelia released Meg's hand and looked around the kitchen. "Everything's still working from the last time you were here, but the igniter on my stovetop is acting finicky and doesn't always light."

With a nod of understanding, Meg focused on the ten-year-old stove and set about unclogging the tiny holes at the bottom of the sealed gas burners and tried lighting the burners a few times before she was satisfied that all of them were in working order. "All fixed. Anything else?"

"How is that handsome father of yours, Meg? Is he happy with your move?"

She opened her mouth to speak but nothing came out. "I guess you were talking to—"

"I had my hair done at Honey B.'s this morning." Mrs. Winter patted the back of her short bob and asked, "What do you think of the color? It's more silver than my usual gray."

"Gorgeous. Honey B. has a way with color." Knowing what was expected, she asked, "So what's the shade of the week?"

Mrs. Winter smiled. "Honey B.'s dyed her hair a lovely rich auburn—a lot like your color. I wished my skin tone hadn't faded quite so much, because if I was just ten years younger, I would have insisted Honey B. dye mine the same color. Smartest thing that young woman ever did was to change her hair color every week to advertise the latest shades in her shop."

"Has she been outside to sweep the sidewalk in front of her shop yet?"

Mrs. Winter's eyes practically danced as she clapped her hands in front of her face. "You'd think with the way it sits catty corner across from the sheriff's office, he'd take a look out his own window once in a while."

"He is a busy man; keeping the law around here is more than a full-time job."

Mrs. Winter agreed. "Such a handsome man. Why does he have to be so set in his ways? Honey B. is just perfect for that hardheaded bachelor."

"The whole town knows it—and so does he," Meg agreed. "I think he's just scared to make the commitment. Not everyone wants a relationship, you know."

"Isn't it time you let the past go and focused on someone new?"

Crafty old woman caught her by surprise, changing the subject like that. Meg started to answer, but Mrs. Winter cut her off. "I hear from Trudi Philo that her grandnephew is a very handsome young man, who has a steady job and just bought his first house."

"Er… thanks for the info, Mrs. Winter."

She beamed. "Now, why don't we sit down and have a bit of tea with our pie, then you can take home the second one I baked this morning?"

Meg knew then that if she lived to be a hundred, she'd never find anywhere in the world like Apple Grove. Friendly but nosy; small in population but big in heart. "I'd love to."

"Now," Mrs. Winter said, sitting across from Meg, "why don't you tell me what prompted your move and why you didn't do this years ago?"

Meg smiled. It was a small payment, in addition to fixing whatever needed it; she always shared news in exchange for her favorite dessert. "Well, it all started at Edie and Bill's wedding." As she told her friend about the wedding and falling off the fence into Dan's arms, she knew that if she didn't run into him in town, she'd make a point to seek him out. Whether they'd intended to or not, they'd begun something on the side of the road that they would have to take the time to see where it was headed.

Mrs. Winter's eyes were misty as she sipped the last of her tea. "I'm sorry I wasn't able to be there for Edie and Bill. I dropped off a batch of chicken marsala before I left to visit my daughter and brand new grandson at the hospital in Toledo. It sounds like it was a wonderful wedding."

Meg agreed. "It was."

"What are you waiting for?"

Meg set down her tea and looked over at her friend. "Excuse me?"

Mrs. Winter got up and wrapped the other pie with tinfoil and then a Turkish towel and set it down in front of Meg. "Edie is the second to last of the young women your age to marry. When are you going to start living again? You're missing out on life when you spend all of it working—and waiting."

"Honey B.'s still single—"

"She's a year older than you, dear."

Sly fox that she was, Amelia Winter had Meg in her crosshairs and wasn't about to let her go free. "When I called Bill's mother to hear about the wedding, she mentioned that her younger son, Jack, saw you flirting with Dan Eagan before you brought him over to meet everyone."

Meg could have fibbed, but the truth always seemed to come out. Whether you wanted it to or not, someone was always ready to share news. The only downside to living in a small town; whether you wanted folks to or not, if they thought what you were doing was newsworthy, it'd be all over town. "Busted."

Mrs. Winter's smile was hard to ignore, but Meg didn't want to have to spill the rest of the beans and tell her about the emergency call to Dan's house and the amazing-smelling dinner that he'd cooked for his date, because she still didn't know who he'd cooked it for and that was an important part of spreading the news. So she dangled an irresistible tidbit of gossip out, hoping to distract the woman. "Cindy Harrington said that they received an emergency call through the sheriff's dispatch this morning."

She had the other woman's full attention. Nothing like news from the local law office to attract and distract. "Really? Who was it?"

"Apparently, a couple of the boys from the football

team decided to leave their mark on the school by putting tires on the flagpole—"

"That's not news," Mrs. Winter interrupted. "Every decade or so they do that."

Meg agreed. "Well, this year's crop of seniors aren't as smart as they think they are, because one of them decided he'd climb the tires, so they could make a video and put it up on the Internet. Halfway up, Joey realized that he was afraid of heights."

"Sounds familiar."

Meg felt her cheeks getting red, but she'd rather be embarrassed about something she'd done as a kid than to have to talk about Dan.

"What happened?"

"One of Joey's friends called 911 and our intrepid sheriff had to climb up and rescue Joey." She was grinning when she added, "The video rescue went viral ten minutes later."

"About time Sheriff Wallace made the news. How many times has he had to rescue someone from the water tower?"

Meg sighed. "Thirteen." She'd been the third.

"How many times has he had to climb up that ship's mast at the McCormacks' farm?"

"Only five." She'd been his first official rescue on the job.

"No wonder he doesn't want to get involved with Honey B."

Meg was shaking her head when she asked, "How do you figure that?"

"Honey B. has always been vocal about wanting to raise a family—a big one with at least six kids. Can you imagine how tough Mitch Wallace's life would become not only taking care of every kid in town but six of his own?"

Meg's jaw dropped open; she'd never thought of it that way. But she shouldn't have been surprised; Honey B. had always been the first choice of babysitters when they'd been in school. The kids always loved having Honey B. sit for them. Meg never seemed to have the time, spending so much of her teen years watching her younger sisters when she wasn't on the job with her dad.

"Maybe it's time that Honey B. took the bull by the horns," Meg admitted, "and let the sheriff know that she's tired of waiting and is going to start looking on the Internet for a man who will fits the bill and fulfills all her needs."

The devilish look in Mrs. Winter's eyes had Meg wishing she'd kept her thoughts to herself. When the older woman got up to get a pad of paper and a pen, Meg was looking for an excuse to leave. But Mrs. Winter wasn't having any of it. "Now then, Megan, I need the names of several reputable Internet dating sites."

"Oh no." Meg stood and held her hands out in front of her as if that could stop Amelia when she was on a roll. "I can't do that to Honey B."

"She'll thank you once she's got Mitch's ring on her hand."

Would she? Meg wasn't so sure. Out of all the women around their age, they were still single after all these years, and the men they'd loved hadn't had enough sense or money to buy a clue where Honey B. and Meg were concerned.

"What if it doesn't work?" Meg asked.

Mrs. Winter nodded. "What if she finds out that she and Mitch aren't meant to be and that there is another man out there who will love her and cherish her just because of who she is?"

Meg finally acquiesced and wrote down three names for Mrs. Winter. "These are the ones I've heard about and read about, but I can't guarantee anything because I've never used any of them."

Mrs. Winter nodded. "Agreed. I'll just see about doing a little research, shall I?"

Fifteen minutes later, Meg was in the truck, her precious pie in the basket she kept on hand for valuables received as payment for work, and wondering if she'd just gotten involved where she shouldn't have. "Won't be the first time," she said with a sigh.

Driving past Honey's Hair Salon, she no longer thought she was doing the right thing. What if someone decided they wanted to help Meg with her love life? She groaned in frustration. She would not like it. Pulling around the corner, she parked, got out, and walked to Honey's shop.

"Well, hi there, Meg." Honey's smile was as sweet as her name. It was one reason Meg decided they'd be friends all those years ago. Meg looked around at the empty shop, with its three hair dryers lined up like soldiers at attention on the left and the pair of sinks across the narrow shop on the right. Three antique barber chairs sat in front of vintage mirrors in need of silvering, but patrons didn't notice the age or the wear on the interior of Honey B.'s shop; they noticed the warmth. It was just like the shop's owner, Honey B. Harrington.

Encouraged by her friend's warm and welcoming smile, Meg unloaded and told Honey B. the whole plan.

Honey's face didn't give away what she was think-ing, so Meg was surprised when Honey finally nodded. "I'm tired of chasing after that man."

"But, Honey—"

"I have loved that man for half my life." She sat down and motioned for Meg to do the same. Sitting there in front of the hair dryers, Honey confided, "I didn't want to believe that he didn't return the feelings that were so huge inside of me I thought they would consume me."

Meg felt a lump forming in her throat, but she ig-nored it and said, "I know what you mean. I guess I only recently realized that I'd been hanging on to the false hope that Jimmy would ask me to marry him—and stay. I guess it didn't occur to me that maybe what I thought was love had morphed into an obsession."

"What happened?"

"I didn't say—"

"You didn't have to," Honey B. said. "I know you."

"Busted." Meg didn't want to talk about her reac-tion to Dan, but once she got started, she realized that deep down, she needed to bounce what she was feeling off a trusted friend who would understand and help her to cope with the rejection that she felt was sure to follow.

"What makes you think he's dating Peggy?"

"She's the complete opposite of me."

"What's wrong with you?" Honey B. asked.

"I saw the reaction on his face when the McCormack sisters strolled over to meet him… all that blonde hair and those mile-long legs are hard to ignore. Just like my sisters—"

"Oh, give it up, Meg," Honey B. grumbled. "And get

over it. Your sisters take after your dad in height; you take after your mom. Embrace who you are, damn it!"

Meg's ire started to bubble to the surface. "Like you have?"

Honey's eyes widened and then her gaze narrowed as she frowned at Meg. "That's right. I decided long ago that if I couldn't catch Mitch's eye as a blonde, then I would try a different hair color every week until I could." She waited a beat before adding, "I didn't just step aside and let another woman usurp my rightful place."

"But you didn't get your man," Meg said quietly.

"Then it's about time I woke up and smelled the coffee, 'cause right now it's boiling over." When Meg looked down at her feet, Honey B. reached over and touched her on the arm. "It sounds like this man could be someone special if he jarred you back to reality with just one innocent kiss."

Meg tried to keep from smiling, but in the end she gave in. "Well, it wasn't exactly the kiss that did it."

"Well?" Honey asked, and then threatened, "Don't make me hurt you to get you to fess up."

"It was when I lost my balance and fell into his arms." She drew in a long slow breath and let it go. "Being held in his arms only added to the sparks and tingles…" She paused to inhale a deep breath. "And then I looked up into his clear gray eyes… and got lost."

"Girl, you've got it bad." Honey got up and started to pace. "I'll make a deal with you, Meg."

She paid attention, because when Honey called her that, her friend meant business. "I'm listening."

"Good. Because I'm going to call Mrs. Winter and give her a free haircut and color if she'll keep quiet about those dating sites until I'm ready to let it leak out to a certain someone that I'm giving up on the sheriff."

Meg bounced to her feet. "All right, Honey B.!"

"But," Honey added, "only if you agree to go after Dan Eagan with every bit of fire you possess." Honey held out her hand. "Deal?"

Meg didn't even hesitate; she put out her hand and they shook on it. "Deal."

"You'd better call Amelia right away; she's bound to have told Miss Trudi by now."

Meg pulled out her cell phone and dialed. "Mrs. Winter? Hey it's Meg. There's been a slight change in plans." She looked at her friend and smiled. "Honey B.'s in on it."

Chapter 4

DAN CONCENTRATED ON THE PAPERWORK PILED ON HIS desk. He was grateful to be busy; it kept him from replaying last night and Meg's confusing response. She didn't exactly run hot and cold, but she did withdraw at moments just when he thought they were getting closer.

"Coach, did you hear about the Smolinsky brothers?"

Dan looked up from the player evaluations he was working on and noticed the excited expression on Doyle's pale, thin face. "Yes. It's sad; there are some pranks that are just not meant to be repeated."

Doyle nodded and a lock of black hair fell into his eyes. He brushed it out of the way and was grinning when he said, "The guys are all talking about it, and we just have one question." Dan pushed back in his chair and waited. Doyle rubbed his palms on his jean-clad thighs. "How come the soccer team never gets into trouble like that?"

Dan grinned, grateful that the question had been an easy one. "We have to be smarter and faster."

Doyle was nodding as Dan added, "Soccer players will always have great core strength, can run all day long, and have the smarts to outwit defenders on the opposite team because it's the nature of the game."

Doyle grinned and said, "So we're smarter, faster, and never get caught."

Dan laughed out loud. "Exactly."

Doyle spun around and was about to leave when Dan stopped him. "That doesn't mean that you should go out and plan something idiotic to one-up the varsity football team."

It was Doyle's turn to grin. "No sir, Coach!"

Watching him leave, Dan wondered if he'd gotten through to the young man or if he'd inadvertently managed to fire up the kid's imagination. Maybe it was time to lay a little groundwork—do some preemptive damage control—and get to know the sheriff better.

He had five minutes before his free period, the last class of the day, was over, time enough to place a phone call. He punched in the numbers and waited to be connected.

"Wallace."

"Hi, Sheriff, it's Dan Eagan. We met—"

"Save your breath, Dan, and call me Mitch—you're making me feel old," the sheriff drawled. "What's on your mind?"

"I heard there was a little mishap outside the school early this morning."

"News always travels fast," Sheriff Wallace said, "good and bad."

"I heard no one was injured."

"You heard right, but I'm sure you didn't call just to verify that statement."

The sheriff spoke at a slower pace than Dan was used to back home, but he wasn't a pushover; the man was shark-smart. "I might need your help with Doyle and Hawkins."

The other man chuckled. "Smart boys. I went to school with their folks."

"Doyle was in here asking about the Smolinsky brothers and when he left he reassured me he and the other guys on the team wouldn't be pulling any pranks, but now I'm not sure."

"Why?"

"When he asked me why the soccer team never got into trouble like that, I told him that's because soccer players have to be smarter and faster."

There was a slight pause before the sheriff finally spoke. "So you're thinking, in Doyle's teenaged mind, it was a challenge of sorts?"

"I didn't mean it that way, but I can't help but wonder if it is." Dan wished he'd thought it through more carefully before speaking, but he'd been reliving his college soccer years and really missed the camaraderie of the team—and the hell they'd raised.

"You think they'll try something?"

"Couldn't hurt to be on guard," Dan admitted. "Was there ever a prank that the soccer players played that the kids might try to reenact?"

"Let me think on it," Sheriff Wallace said. "You know where to find me if you need me."

"I do. Thanks, Mitch." Dan was surprised that he really meant it. He was relieved.

The bell rang, startling him back to reality and the last class of the day. "Time for some three-on-three drills."

It had been a long day and a great practice. Dan was feeling more at ease with his new job and position as coach. He liked the kids and was really encouraged by their excitement about playing hard and advancing to the States. It didn't bother him that the main motive for the guys was their former coach. He hoped one day to have the team feel that way about him, but in the meantime was happy to be a part of the team and helping them achieve their goal of a winning season.

Who knows, maybe the kids would come to appreciate Dan for who he was—the same as he was beginning to appreciate the little differences in a town the size of Apple Grove.

He'd had the opportunity to repay his great-aunt's generosity by helping her at coffee hour at church and planned to help out at her garden center. He had an open invitation to taste the pie at the Apple Grove Diner— which he would have to do soon, fix (make that drool over) Joe Mulcahy's Model A pickup, talk fast cars and watch racing on TV with Bob Stuart, and then there was the mystery that was Meg…

As he walked to his car, lost in thought, he didn't notice the tall, blonde woman leaning against the driver's door until he was nearly there. "Ms. McCormack," he said by way of greeting. "What a surprise." He wasn't exactly afraid to talk to the woman that Meg seemed to be jealous of, but it wouldn't hurt to keep his tone neutral so that he didn't give her the wrong impression. A few of the women he'd dated before his ex had mistaken open friendliness for interest. "How are you?"

Her smile made him uneasy, but he tamped down the feeling and maintained his friendly attitude. He was interested in a petite redhead with a sprinkling of freckles across the bridge of her nose. Even though he hadn't seen Meg in a day or so, he couldn't stop thinking about her.

"Now that you're here, I'm better," she said, pushing off the car and walking toward him. "Much better."

Why did women pick the worst possible moments to come on to a guy? He wanted to laugh but didn't want to hurt Peggy's feelings. Damn. He didn't have time for this right now. "Good to hear," he said, neatly blocking her advance and stepping around her. "Have a nice day." Before she could regroup, he was in the car, revving the engine and backing out of his parking space.

"Women," he mumbled, tilting his rearview mirror, watching to see what she'd do. His sigh of relief echoed in the car. She'd been right behind him, but then she turned left when he turned right. He couldn't help but wonder if there was something he'd said or done that had encouraged the woman—or if she was just taking charge of the situation and making her move. He'd have to think about it later; right now the sheriff had asked him to stop by his office after practice. Dan guessed the man had come up with a few thoughts to keep Dan's team from doing something stupid. A short ride from the high school, he parallel parked and got out. He couldn't tell how old the brick building was, but he smiled at the fresh coat of bright green paint on the front door and wondered... it looked a lot like the color on the water tower. He'd have to ask the sheriff if he'd noticed any of his paint missing lately.

"Hi, Dan," the brunette behind the desk greeted him by name. He knew he'd never met her before, but she did look familiar...

"Hi, I'm meeting with—"

The brunette smiled. "Sheriff Wallace, he's expecting you. First door on the left."

Dan hesitated and asked, "Did we meet at Bill and Edie's wedding?"

She shook her head. "You met my sister, Honey B."

The woman's name was familiar, but he couldn't quite place her face; he'd been bowled over by Megan Mulcahy that day and had yet to recover his balance.

The woman behind the desk smiled and stretched out her hand. "I'm Cindy Harrington, my sister Honey B. owns Honey's Hair Salon."

He took her hand and shook it. "Pleasure to meet you, Cindy."

She smiled up at him and he felt the welcome down to his toes. "I hear the kids on the soccer team are working hard to impress their new coach. They needed someone to lift their spirits after Coach Creed had his heart attack. I hear that you were the top-scoring forward on the Rensselaer college team."

He was momentarily at a loss for words before his brain kicked in and he started to laugh. "Has Aunt Trudi been talking about me behind my back?"

Cindy's laugh was infectious. "She's talking about you every chance she gets. She's very proud of you."

"Um… thanks. I think I'll go talk to the sheriff now." He walked down the hallway and knocked on the door frame since the door to the sheriff's office was open.

The man himself was seated behind a beat-up oak desk. "Eagan," the lawman said, rising to his feet. "Glad you're here. Sit down."

Dan took the seat across from the sheriff and leaned forward. "Well?"

"I have been going through the records and have found a couple of pranks that were memorable that should not be repeated." The older man sighed. "To tell you the truth, I'm not sure that the kids are going to do something stupid, but I'm a cautious man."

"It didn't hit me right away, but after Doyle left, I had this really bad feeling."

Sheriff Wallace snorted. "Happens more times that I'd like… when I feel like that, I roll with it and put out feelers all over town."

"I'm sure you've seen it all over the years."

The sheriff smiled. "In a town the size of Apple Grove, not much that goes on gets forgotten. There's always a group of knuckleheads who think they can outdo their predecessors, and safety never crosses their minds. As you know, we've had kids climbing the water tower and the ship's mast, and there's the railroad trestle bridge some fool tries to jump off of and invariably breaks something important… and then there's the quarry." The sheriff's gaze met his. "Worst day of my life, dredging the quarry for those bodies."

An eerie cold seeped into Dan's gut and lay there. Would Doyle and Hawkins try something like that? He needed to know what he was up against. "What's the challenge over at the quarry?"

"Deep pool, couple hundred feet deep, and the ledge on the far side of it is just perfect for diving off of."

The hair raised on the back of Dan's neck. "When did you drag the quarry?"

The sheriff looked out the window and then back at Dan. "Ten years back. Some things just stick, no matter how hard you try to forget them."

"Would any of the kids in the high school think to try something like that now?"

The lawman got up and paced in front of the window. "I don't know. It's been long enough that the high school juniors and seniors were just little kids and might not remember."

"Can't you fence off the property?"

Sheriff Wallace laughed. "And here I thought today would be routine. Hell, you think we didn't have a fence? Even when the quarry was in full operation, there was a chain-link fence topped with barbed wire surrounding the grounds." He hooked his thumbs in his gun belt. "Didn't stop 'em. You know what the hardest lesson teenagers have to learn in life?"

Dan could think of a few, but one in particular came to mind. "That they aren't all ten feet tall and bulletproof?"

"Bingo."

"I'll have a talk with Doyle and Hawkins," Dan said quietly. "Will you talk with their folks?"

The sheriff walked over to his desk and picked up the phone. "I'm on it." When Dan started to leave, the sheriff called out, "Keep me posted."

"Will do."

As he drove away, Dan was having trouble sorting through what was troubling him most—how to convince his two star players that they couldn't leap buildings in a single bound or stop a freight train. Dan pulled over and called Sheriff Wallace. When the man answered, he blurted out, "Did you say there's a train trestle bridge nearby?" He wasn't sure why that image stuck in his head; he'd worry about that later, right now he had to go with his gut instincts and track down Doyle and Hawkins.

"Yes, why?"

Dan answered his question with a question. "Can you

give me directions to the bridge? Oh, and what did their parents say?"

"Not much. The boys aren't home."

When the lawman rattled off the directions to the trestle bridge, Dan asked him one more question. "Can you send someone up to the quarry? I'm hoping they are together, at either the bridge or the quarry, but it's best not to try to outthink a teenager."

The sheriff agreed and disconnected. Dan pushed the speed limit all the way to the railroad bridge; when he saw it looming up ahead, he cursed under his breath. There were two figures standing on the edge, right over the water—one tall and lean and one shorter and stocky.

He pulled out his cell and dialed. "They're here at the bridge." Without waiting for a reply, he disconnected and broke into a run. "Doyle, wait!" he called, running full out, leaping over the rocks lined up at the edge of the road to keep people from parking there.

Dan didn't stop until he was on the bridge and yelling at them. "What the hell do you think you're doing?"

The two looked guilty, and Doyle shrugged in answer.

"Did you just say 'hell'?" Hawkins asked.

Dan was fighting to control his temper, and it took all of his concentration not to lash out at the boys now that he had them in his sights and they had taken a step back from the edge. "Yeah, I said 'hell,'" he answered, walking along the rail toward where they stood. "And you still haven't answered me. What is wrong with you two?"

The boys looked at one another and then at Dan. This time they both shrugged.

Dan felt the vibration in his feet before he connected the dots and realized what was happening.

"Jump!" a familiar deep voice yelled as a diesel engine's whistle blasted—too close for comfort.

Dan didn't hesitate; he grabbed hold of Doyle with his left hand and Hawkins with his right and jumped, pulling them with him. For a moment, he wondered if this was how Butch and Sundance felt when they jumped into the river, but then they hit the water and it was all he could do to swim to the surface and make sure the boys did too.

If the roar of the freight train moving at killing speed didn't keep him up nights for the rest of his life, Doyle's next words would. "Coach, help! Hawkins can't swim."

Dan wiped the water from his eyes and struck out toward Doyle who was trying to reach his friend. He swam past Doyle and dove under the surface, reaching and praying. *God help me save this boy.*

The water was clear and he saw Hawkins a few feet away. Adrenaline pumping through his system, he reached Hawkins, yanked him to the surface, and swam for the shoreline, never once breaking the silent chant in his head praying for help.

He dragged Hawkins out of the water and turned him on his stomach, pushing on his back to force the water out of his lungs.

"I've got it from here." Sheriff Wallace took over while Dan stood up and started back toward the water.

"You all right, Doyle?"

"Yeah," Doyle said, wiping his hands over his eyes. "I couldn't swim fast enough." Their gazes met and Dan saw the tears pooling in the boy's eyes. "I thought he was gonna drown."

Dan shook his head. "Sheriff Wallace is coaxing the river water out of his lungs."

Doyle sat down on a rock next to his friend and shook like a wet dog. Dan let the boy watch in silence. These two had a very important lesson to learn. If Doyle thought Hawkins still might die, it might shake them up enough to face some hard truths—the biggest one being friends don't let friends talk them into diving off a railroad trestle bridge.

The wail of a siren was getting louder, but Dan didn't look away; he concentrated on willing every ounce of strength left in his body into that of the Hawkins boy. Drained, he didn't notice at first when Hawkins moaned, but he did when the boy puked up every bit of river water he'd swallowed.

Sheriff Wallace sat back and wiped his forearm across his forehead. "Hang on, help is on its way."

The scene was soon swarming with emergency vehicles. The EMTs had pulled up right behind one of the deputies. When the boys were bundled up and tucked in the back of the ambulance, Mitch walked over to where Dan stood looking out over the water.

"You saved their lives, Dan."

"But did I put the idea in their heads in the first place?"

"Did you know we had a railroad bridge spanning the river?"

He shook his head. "But I can't help but feel—"

"Relief. Say a prayer of thanks for God's help rescuing those two and quit blaming yourself."

Dan's voice was thick with emotion; he cleared his throat and asked, "Does it always feel this way?"

"Hell no," the sheriff answered. "The outcome's not always this positive. Brace yourself, Dan."

Dan grabbed the hem of his T-shirt and started to wring some of the water out of it. "For what?"

"The onslaught—heroes are not forgotten in Apple Grove."

—⁓—

"Mulcahy's, Meg speaking."

"Oh my God, Meg! Did you hear?"

Meg took a moment to stretch her back; working bent over was almost as hard as working over her head for any length of time. "No, what's up, Gracie?"

"Cindy just called—it's all over town!"

Meg was ready for a break after replacing gnawed-on wire, so she sat down on the Smiths' attic floor and waited for her sister to get around to telling her. "What is?"

"Daniel Eagan is a hero!"

Meg's heart stuttered in her breast. She didn't want to appear too eager, but she definitely wanted to know what her sister was talking about. "What happened?"

Gracie relayed the tale of Dan's driving out to the railroad trestle bridge and then pulling Charlie Doyle and Tommy Hawkins out of harm's way. Before Meg could process the news, her sister added, "He saved Tommy from drowning."

It was a good thing Meg was sitting down, because that last comment knocked the wind right out of her.

"Meg? Are you still there?"

"Um, yeah, yes. I'm here." She paused for a moment and then had to ask, "Gracie, do you swear you and Cindy didn't cook this up?"

"On a stack of Bibles, Sis."

The impact of the news was a little scary. "What were the three of them doing out at the bridge anyway?"

"Cindy didn't know. I'm going to call Peggy and Katie in a minute, but I had to tell you first."

"Thanks, Gracie. See what you can find out and call me back. I just finished up here and am headed back to the shop."

"In case you were wondering, there's an impromptu get together at Slater's Mill in about an hour."

Meg sighed; she was really tired and had been looking forward to heading home to a hot shower and a cold beer.

"Dan's a real hero. Are you seriously thinking of not going?"

Meg's tired brain cleared.

"I'm not sure what time I'll get there, but I will definitely be there. Thanks for telling me, Grace."

"What are sisters for? Hey, that's Peggy calling right now. Gotta go!"

Meg pulled into the parking lot behind the shop and her driver's side door swung open. Honey B. Harrington was working up to a full head of steam. Before Meg could protest, Honey reached in, pulled her from the truck, and spun her around and then started to pat her back as if searching for something. "Girl, I thought you had a backbone. Where the heck did it go?"

Meg burst out laughing. "Only you would dare to ask me that, Honey B."

"You are so getting in the shower right now and going over to Slater's Mill with me. You got that?"

Meg wanted to tell Honey B. that she'd already decided she was going but knew better than to open her mouth when Honey B. was getting ready to kick ass and take names. She nodded.

"I'm picking you up at the house in twenty minutes," her friend told her. "So be ready." Meg had her toolbox in hand and was opening the back door to the shop when Honey B. called out, "You are going wear something other than a ratty old T-shirt and your farmer jeans tonight!"

"It would serve you right if I showed up in a pair of my dad's jeans."

Honey narrowed her eyes at Meg and crossed her arms beneath her breasts. "You are going to wear whatever I bring with me."

"We haven't shared clothes since high school."

"Don't worry. By the time I get done dressing you up, you'll look great."

When she spun around on her heel and walked away, Meg just shook her head. "That woman is bossier than me."

"You know it, Sis," Caitlin said as she held the door open for Meg.

"I'd hate to be on her bad side," Grace said.

Meg sighed. "I hope she brings a cotton T-shirt for me to wear."

Her sisters grinned and ushered her into the shop. "I'll put away your tools," Caitlin offered.

Twenty minutes later, right on the dot, Honey B. honked the horn as she pulled into the driveway at the Mulcahy house. Meg answered the door in her bib overalls and ripped Guinness T-shirt. "Well, Honey B., what a surprise."

Her friend smiled and tossed a pair of jeans and a silky shirt at her. "Get dressed. We don't want to be late."

Meg grumbled, "Can't we be fashionably late so I can catch a catnap?"

Honey pushed Meg toward the bathroom door and sympathized. "I'm tired too, but we don't want to miss out on our first chance to plant the seeds of doubt in Mitch Wallace's pea-brain."

"I thought we were going to support Dan."

"We are," Honey B., told her. "It's a side benefit that I can get underneath Mitch's skin at the same time."

Meg wiggled into the jeans and sucked in a breath in order to zip them. "I don't think I can breathe in these."

"Doesn't matter as long as you look good. Besides, we used to wear the same size. I'm guessing you just started wearing a bigger size when you started working for your Dad full-time—not that you needed to."

Meg frowned at her reflection; the jeans definitely looked different. She wasn't used to such a snug fit. "I'm not sure, Honey B."

"I'm coming in."

Meg let her in and shook her head. "I don't think I'll be sitting down tonight, either."

"Put this on, and for heaven's sake, take your hair out of that ponytail."

Meg shimmied into the figure-flattering silky shirt and was surprised at how it changed her appearance. The fabric clung to her figure and flattered her shape, rather than hiding it. "I don't look like myself."

"And that, my dear friend," Honey B. said, "is the point. Are you ready to kick some butt?"

"I thought the point was to cheer for our new local hero."

"We will, and he deserves all of the attention he'll be

getting tonight. Besides, it's high time somebody else did something heroic, other than our intrepid sheriff."

"You sure about this?"

"Dead sure."

"All right, I'm ready."

Honey shook her head and reached for the elastic band holding Meg's hair away from her face. "Now bend over and shake out your hair."

Meg did as she was told and had the shock of her life when her hair fell softly against her neck. The woman looking back at her had flushed cheeks and tousled hair—it definitely looked like she'd just climbed out of the backseat of some guy's car. "I look—"

"Totally hot, my friend," Honey said, taking Meg's hand. "Let's go."

"See you at the shop, Pop!"

"You look lovely, Megan."

She frowned and her father's smile widened. "The image of your mother."

"Except for the hair," she grumbled, knowing he was only trying to make her feel better.

He bent down and pressed his lips to the top of her head. "Try to have a nice time and don't get home too late."

"Pop, I'll be going back to my apartment, remember?"

His frown was fierce, but his words gentle. "See if Wallace will escort you home."

"Pop!"

"Never mind. I'll call him myself."

"He never changes."

Honey B.'s smile was wistful. "I wish my father were here to worry about me like that."

"Are you going to visit your folks this year?"

Her friend shook her head. "I can't afford the time away from the salon. Maybe in a year or two."

"They really like living in Florida, don't they?"

"Yeah." Honey B. grinned. "Who would have thought it was possible?"

"Not me," Meg answered as they walked to Honey's car.

———

Meg felt Honey B.'s hand in the middle of her back as she stood in the doorway to Slater's Mill. She'd always loved this place. The knotty pine paneling on the walls, the tables scattered across the wide expanse of the old mill, and especially the mile-long bar on the second floor kept the younger crowd from going out of town to find places to congregate. She'd spent time upstairs and knew it would be busy later on tonight.

She inhaled and sighed. "Charcoal broiled burger with cheese, hold the onions, and pile on the cheesy fries!"

Honey B. was laughing when they heard someone calling to them.

"Honey B.! Meg!" an elderly voice called out. "Over here."

Meg saw Miss Trudi and Mrs. Winter at a table in the corner and started walking, avoiding the crowd at the center of the room. "Hello, ladies. How are you tonight?"

The two were positively vibrating with excitement. "Have you heard?" Mrs. Winter asked.

"Can you believe it?" Miss Trudi added. "Only in town a few days and already my grandnephew is a hero!" She fanned herself with a paper napkin embossed with an etching of the mill in its earlier days, and motioned for Meg and Honey B. to join them.

Meg pulled over a chair from another table and sat down. "I've heard bits and pieces of the story, but not the why of it. What were those boys and Dan doing on that bridge?"

Miss Trudi's eyes were so bright, for a moment Meg wondered if the older woman was feverish.

"I hear tell," Miss Trudi began, "that the boys were discussing those idiotic Smolinsky brothers from the football team who borrowed Ned's cherry picker and stacked the tires on the school's flagpole—"

"And then tried to climb it and had to be rescued!" Mrs. Winter finished for her.

"What is it with boys that they are always trying to outdo one another?" Miss Trudi asked.

Meg shook her head. "I only have sisters."

Honey B. tapped her on the arm and pointed toward the crowd surrounding a table in the middle of the room.

There were a bunch of bruisers from the football team, the entire soccer team, and their dads in the group—as well as a few women. "Men," Meg said. "Probably telling tales like the one about the large-mouthed bass that got away."

Miss Trudi patted Meg on the hand. "Now, dear, you know they love stories of derring-do."

Mrs. Winter nodded in agreement. "Dan's rescue is such a dashing tale."

Meg nodded. "It is. Too bad about the other night—"

"What night?" Miss Trudi asked.

Meg felt her cheeks growing warm as she tried to backpedal and keep from confessing that she was turned inside out with frustration not knowing who Dan had been cooking for the other night.

"Don't just sit there like you swallowed a mouthful of castor oil," Mrs. Winter said. "Tell us."

Meg looked at Honey B., who was smiling like the cat that ate the canary. She sighed and gave in. "Dan was cooking a special meal for someone the other night. Whatever he'd put in the oven smelled delicious," she admitted, "but it was the single red rose he'd laid across the plate that's been keeping me up nights."

Miss Trudi and Mrs. Winter shared a knowing look. Meg didn't want to know what that might mean—well, she did, but she wouldn't admit it. Honey B. distracted her again when she tapped her arm a second time. Meg looked over in time to watch the McCormack sisters, Cindy Harrington, and Beatrice Wallace working their way through the growing crowd.

"I happen to know who Dan invited over that night." Mrs. Winter was waiting for Meg to turn back around. "Would you like to know who it was?"

Meg shuddered. She wanted to know but hesitated to ask. What if her suspicions were correct and it was one of the McCormack sisters? Then her initial feelings for Dan would be crushed out like a smoldering cigarette that someone had finished with and then discarded. "I guess if it was any of my business, which it isn't, Dan would have mentioned it."

"When?" Honey B. asked. "You're always working. When you're not working, you're ordering and restocking the supply room at Mulcahy's."

"That leaves just enough time for getting a good night's sleep." Miss Trudi was watching her intently, so Meg nodded, agreeing with the woman.

"You're too young to spend your nights sleeping," Mrs. Winter said.

"But I—"

"I've got a fresh-baked cherry pie sitting on my counter that says you're too busy to walk over there and ask Dan Eagan out to dinner."

Meg practically salivated at the thought of another cherry pie with her name on it. "Now why would I want to do that?"

Miss Trudi leaned forward and whispered, "It's called a date, dear. It's been so long, you might not remember what it's like."

Meg bit her tongue to keep the caustic reply to herself, while Honey B. started to laugh.

"Not so fast, missy," Mrs. Winter cautioned Honey B., leaning in close. "We have some work to do tonight. I want to put your profile up on at least three dating sites tonight. Melanie said that she'd let me in after hours, so no one else knows what we're doing."

Meg was grateful that she was no longer the center of attention. She wanted to tease her friend but didn't want the older ladies to start harping on her again. Besides, it gave her a chance to see if the crowd had shifted and she could see Dan. If she were sixteen again, she'd have to admit to having a crush on him. But she wasn't—she was pushing thirty and women her age didn't develop crushes; they had affairs with men who interested them. At least that's what she'd been told. She'd spent too much of her late teens and most of her twenties burying herself in her work and had missed out on that particular part of life. Was it too late to catch up and start living it to the fullest, starting with a certain broad-shouldered hunk who was a bona fide chick magnet?

Maybe that was why she had been so tempted when Dan had caught her in his arms. Meg noticed that Dan was still surrounded by well-wishers congratulating him on his heroic feat.

"Meg!"

"Hmmm? What?" She turned around and a strand of hair got caught on her eyelashes. She tucked it behind her ear and wondered why she listened to Honey B. She liked her hair in a ponytail—it stayed put. She rarely wore it down.

Three faces were staring at her and she knew right away that something was up. "Are you plotting against me?"

Miss Trudi shook her head. "We're plotting for you, Megan dear."

That took the wind out of Meg's sails. "I guess I'd better hear it now instead of tomorrow when I'm trying to wrestle Mr. Ainsley's ancient plumbing into submission."

Her friends smiled. "Well then," Mrs. Winter said. "As I said, I have that cherry pie just waiting for someone brave enough to walk on over to that crowd and push her way through to save Dan."

"From what I've heard, he's a hero," Meg insisted. "What would I be saving him from?"

"He really doesn't like crowds," Miss Trudi said quietly.

Meg processed that particular tidbit that Miss Trudi provided and knew then that she was hooked. For all of his size and obvious strength, Dan Eagan had a human weakness after all. Her gaze met Miss Trudi's and she gave in. "All right, I'll do it, but you

ladies don't fight fair using my weakness for pie
against me."

They were giddy with excitement by the time Meg
pushed to her feet and brushed her damp hands on her
thighs. With a glance over her shoulder, she received
the encouragement she needed when the group gave her
the thumbs up.

Digging deep for the strength to not just turn and
walk out the door, Meg walked over to the group surrounding Dan and tapped the first of a dozen men on
their shoulders.

Before she could get to the middle of the crowd a
wolf whistle sounded nearby. Meg huffed, crossed her
arms, and looked around for the source.

"I haven't seen you in tight-fitting jeans since we
were in high school."

She glared at the man brave enough to bring that
up—Jimmy's cousin Clint. "That's because it's hard to
get beneath a sink wearing clothes like this."

"I'd forgotten just how pretty you are."

She felt her face go hot at Clint's comment. The last
thing she needed was a reminder of her past. She shook
her head. "Well, tomorrow when I get to the third job on
my list, you won't even recognize me," she promised.
"I'll be invisible again." Clint shook his head as if he
didn't believe it.

"What's up, Meg?" Peggy asked, sliding through the
mass of people to stand beside her.

She was about to answer when Katie joined her sister,
saying, "You look great, Meg."

"Thanks."

Dan had that deer-in-the-headlights look on his

face as people moved closer to shake his hand and congratulate him. There were folks she hadn't seen in a while gathering around the reason they made a special trip to town. Meg realized his aunt had been right. He was uncomfortable and did need saving. "Miss Trudi wanted to ask you something if you have a minute, Dan."

His look of gratitude warmed her.

Dan glanced at the crowd and said, "I've... uh... got to go. My aunt needs me."

Meg's heart picked up the beat when Dan placed a protective hand to the small of her back and leaned close. "You are a lifesaver," he whispered. "I'm not used to being the center of attention like that."

Mrs. Winter and Miss Trudi were smiling up at them when the returned. Miss Trudi said, "Daniel, do you still think you'll be able to help out Saturday morning?"

He pulled out a chair for Meg. When she sat, he walked over to stand by his aunt. "With everything that happened today, I forgot that I was going to ask Doyle and Hawkins to help. Maybe a few other team members would be interested in helping."

"How about if I promise fresh cinnamon rolls and coffee for when we're finished?"

"That sounds great. I'll ask tomorrow at practice."

"Wonderful," Miss Trudi said, patting him on the hand he'd rested on the back of Meg's chair. "Oh, by the way, did I thank you for that wonderful meal you cooked for me the other night?" She turned toward Meg and said, "The night your power went out."

Meg felt as if she'd had the wind knocked out of her. She couldn't draw in a breath or let one go. *He'd prepared that wonderful meal for his aunt?* When she messed up, she messed up big time.

As if sensing her dilemma, Honey B. leaned close and whispered, "Just breathe." Her friend slowly stroked a hand up and down Meg's spine to help her relax. When she had her breathing under control, she glanced over at Dan and his aunt and knew she owed the man an apology.

A quick look at Miss Trudi confirmed that the crafty old woman knew all about Meg's hint of jealousy where her grandnephew was concerned. She wondered if she were that transparent and that everyone knew what she was thinking. Mrs. Winter took her hand and squeezed it. "Isn't that sweet? Instead of unpacking boxes, he was making dinner for his aunt."

"Yes," Meg answered. "It is." She lifted her gaze to his. "I, uh… thought—"

His solemn look bothered her, but she couldn't apologize with an audience. "You thought…" he prompted.

Damn. She owed him that apology now. "I'm sorry, Dan," she blurted out. "I thought your emergency that night was that you had a hot date and it ticked me off that I was tired and wanted to go home to relax but had to drive to your place to fix whatever the problem was so you could make dinner for Peggy."

The look on his face was priceless. "But I told you it was for my aunt."

She felt like a fool but worse, acted like one. "I didn't hear you."

"Now, Daniel," his aunt interrupted, snagging his attention. "Why don't you drive Meg home. Honey B. is driving Amelia Winter and me over to meet with Melanie, and Meg looks dead on her feet."

Meg knew a plot when she heard one. "No thanks. I can walk." He hadn't accepted her apology, and it had scraped her guts raw just getting up the courage to say she was sorry only to find out she'd wasted energy being angry for no reason. She had to leave now before her Irish was up. If her temper bubbled any closer to the surface, the lid was bound to blow off.

She made it outside and breathed a sigh of relief. It was a nice night, warm for October. The walk to her apartment might just help her clear her mind. Five minutes down the road, she realized just how dark it was with the moon hiding behind the clouds. "Should have noticed that before you let your temper do the talking."

The sound of an engine coming closer had her focusing on the road ahead; the last thing she needed to do was stumble and fall into the path of a car. Careful not to misstep, she didn't notice that the car had slowed down until she heard her name being called. "Let me drive you home, Meg."

Dan. It figured. "No thanks. I'm good."

"It's pitch black out here—I can't let you walk home. If you don't trip and break your neck, some car won't see you until it's too late and you're roadkill."

She had to stop because she was laughing so hard. "Roadkill? You really know the way to get a woman's attention."

He'd parked the car and was walking toward her. "Got yours," he said, reaching for her hand. "Come on, Meg." He sounded tired. "I really don't need any more guilt piled on top of the shit storm my day turned out to be."

Wondering if this was the real Dan talking to her now or the stressed-out Dan who'd saved two of his student's from being run over by a freight train, nearly causing one of them to drown in the process, she decided she wanted to find out and took his hand. "It sounds like you need a friend to talk to."

He squeezed her hand, but didn't let go until he opened the passenger door for her. "I can't decide if I'm the cause of their brush with disaster or their savior."

The turmoil inside of Dan called to her. She could almost feel the knots tightening around him. "I'm not trying to come on to you, Dan, but I could brew a pot of coffee or make you a cup of tea if you want to talk—as friends."

He nodded and shut her door. When he was in the driver's seat, she gave him directions to her new apartment. "It's kind of empty right now, but I'm saving up to buy a small sofa."

His deep chuckle eased the knots forming at the base of her neck. "Sounds like my house," he admitted. "I'm hoping to be able to buy a sleeper sofa by Thanksgiving." Dan pulled into the long driveway and parked in front of the garage. "Don't you have a car?"

She shrugged. "I haven't needed one. I drive my dad's truck during the day." Her eyes met his. "I don't go out at night."

"So tonight's special?" he asked, reaching to tuck a strand of auburn behind her ear.

His touch had her skin tingling. Meg had to clear her throat to speak. "Yes. It's not every day that someone rescues two teenagers from disaster."

He shook his head. "I'm still not sure about that."

She wanted to tell him how proud of him she was, that she'd have been scared spit-less if she had been in his shoes. But what she wanted to say was getting tangled up with what she needed—to be touched by him, kissed by him—and that was a problem because she'd already promised that she'd invited him up as a friend.

His fingertip traced the line of her jaw and tapped against her bottom lip. "You look different with your hair down... softer."

Her mouth went dry at his touch. "Maybe I wouldn't be much help tonight." The reality of him being so close in the dark had her belly fluttering and parts of her anticipating what she had no business even thinking about!

"So you're not going to make me a cup of tea?"

He sounded so forlorn that, against her better judgment, she caved. "Well, maybe one cup." She got out of the car and warned him, "But that's all—just a cup of tea and some friendly conversation. Deal?"

He got out of the car and walked to where she stood. "Meg," he rasped. "Is that all you want from me?"

Her heart skidded to a stop as his arms banded around her. When their lips were a breath apart, he brushed his lightly across hers. "Tell me I'm reading you wrong and that you don't want me to kiss you again."

She melted against him. "I can't."

He captured her lips in a tongue-tangling, heart-pumping kiss. Meg got caught up in the rapture of his mouth molded to hers and distracted by the strength of his hands as he slowly traced the line of her spine from the back of her neck to the top of her backside.

He paused for air and urged, "Ask me inside, Meg."

"My apartment?"

He groaned. "That'll do for starters."

She knew what he was asking, and at this moment,

standing in the dark, locked in his arms, she knew she wanted more—she wanted it all. "Come upstairs with me, Dan."

Chapter 5

DAN COULDN'T SEEM TO HANG ON TO ANY THOUGHT save one: he wanted Meg—needed her more than his next breath. He'd been waging a silent battle with himself to take things at a slower pace. Fast and furious had only ended in disaster. But Meg had been on his mind and in his heart since the first moment he saw her walking on that fence. Today had pushed him to the limits of his endurance. He'd never been so scared in his life. He was trembling on the inside and using every ounce of strength not to let it show.

He needed to channel the emotions rioting inside of him before they consumed him. Gathering Meg in his arms to soothe the ragged remains of what could have been a devastating disaster was all he could think to do. Where it led from there might just be the balm he needed to soothe the adrenaline beast inside of him.

When she closed the door behind him, he crushed her against him and dug deep for honesty. "I'm not thirsty for tea."

Her groan nearly sent him to his knees; he'd been right. She wanted him too. Nuzzling her neck, he gave in to desire and pressed his lips to the tendon beneath her ear, flicking the tip of his tongue across it, tasting the sweetness of her skin. "Do you taste this good all over, Meg?" *Would she let him find out?*

"I, uh—"

He was too impatient to let her finish. Lifting her up higher, he let his lips savor the salty sweetness of her collarbone and used his teeth to tug the neck of her shirt and bare her shoulder. He nipped it, then soothed it with his lips. "God, Meg. This isn't me—I'm not like this." His hands started shaking. "But I've been dreaming of making love with you since you fell off that fence and into my arms. I wanted to wait and take things at a slower pace."

"Don't," she rasped, moaning his name as he set her back on her feet and stripped her shirt up and over her head. Drawing her in close, he pressed his palms to the middle of her back so he could let his mouth and tongue sample the creamy, smooth skin he'd bared. He found the hook to her bra and flipped it open. Her breasts spilled into his hands and he knew then he wouldn't be waiting to get to know her before he made love to her.

"Tell me to stop now, Meg. I'm not strong enough to resist you tonight."

She stroked her hands up and over his shoulders and drew his head down to her breasts. "It's been a long time for me, so don't expect too much."

He clamped his jaw shut and breathed in through his nose. "Don't expect too little." Lifting her into his arms, he drew her breast into his mouth and suckled, drowning in the taste of her, reveling in the gift she was giving him—her sweetly curved body.

He let his tongue torment her left breast until she was squirming against him, then he let go of it and sucked her other breast into his mouth. She had a delicate build but packed a lethal punch. "Tell me what you want, Meg. I need to give it to you."

She buried her head against his chest. "Equal time, Dan. I want to drive you over the edge."

His chuckle sounded rusty. Before she could ask, he started walking. "Where's the nearest bed?"

Her laughter bubbled up from deep inside of her. "First door on the left."

He opened it with his hip and closed it with his foot, but surprised her when he gently laid her out on the bed. She'd almost expected him to toss her on it. The sweet edge to his passion was her undoing. She was a grown woman with needs she'd been ignoring for way too long.

Dan had been the one to unlock the torrent of passion raging inside of her, and he would be the one she would share it with. She lifted her arms to him, and he paused to unbutton his shirt. The raw beauty of the man standing at the side of her bed had every ounce of moisture in her body coming to the surface. She'd reason out the whys later. Life was too short—it was time she indulged her passionate side.

Instead of stripping out of his jeans, he crawled up the bed until she was beneath him, looking up into the depths of his stormy gray eyes. She confessed, "Your eyes were one of the first things I noticed."

He pressed his lips to the end of her nose. "Really?" He braced himself on one elbow and tilted her chin up with his free hand.

"Yes," she breathed out the word, and every other thought evaporated as his lips touched hers and his tongue swirled along the rim of her mouth. Her body ached to feel him skin-to-skin; her core wept for him.

"I want to feel you touching me," she rasped.

He lifted himself off of her but froze in place above her at the broken sound she made. "Did I hurt you?"

A sweetness filled her. He cared whether or not he pleased her or hurt her. For tonight it would be enough. "Not unless you decide you're finished," she teased. It was freeing to confess what was in her heart.

"Brace yourself, Megan," he promised. "I won't be finished until daylight."

He knelt on the bed, unbuttoned her jeans, and tugged them off, but left her panties on. "You're so delicate."

She disagreed. "I'm strong from years of working with my hands," she told him. "Why don't you let me show you?"

The look in his eyes told her he was tempted to let her. "Not just yet. I'm not finished warming you up."

"I'm not cold."

He laughed, a rich sound that reverberated from deep within his broad chest. "Think of it as priming the pump."

She felt her cheeks filling with heat, but she ignored it. She could be embarrassed later; right now she had a devastatingly sexy man in her bed, wanting to make love with her. Who was she to quibble?

"That flicking thing you did with your tongue before had all of my cylinders firing."

"God, I love a woman who can talk cars."

He bent his head and kissed her until her toes curled. "Dan, I—" She wanted to tell him that she didn't do this sort of thing with just any man, but the words got lost in her mind as callused hands swept up her sides and began to knead her breasts. Her thoughts scattered like dandelion seeds on the wind.

He was watching her intently, and she knew from the

way he was touching her that he would find the places that hadn't been caressed in more years than she'd admit to. "Do you like that?" he asked as he cupped and stroked her breasts before smoothing his hands up and over her shoulders.

He was relaxing her and exciting her at the same time—talented man.

"Mmmm."

"Then you're going to love this." His mouth replaced his hands and she gasped for air.

"Daniel—I—don't make me wait!" She moaned as his tongue flicked in the hollow at the base of her throat. Who knew that her neck would be so sensitive to his touch?

"You're like fire in my arms." He nestled his face against her breasts and held her for one achingly sweet moment. When he lifted his head, he was grinning. "Let me see if you're really ready."

His hand swept down her belly and tested the moisture that had been building inside of her with each flick of his tongue, each press of his lips, and brush of his fingertips. He rested his forehead against hers. "God you're so wet!"

"What are you waiting for?" she urged.

He eased up off of her and the bed, and shucked his jeans. She should have been afraid by the sheer size of him. Clothed, Dan was impressive; naked and fully aroused, he stole her breath. Taking her silence for agreement, he reached into his pocket and pulled out a foil three-pack. Gripping it with his teeth, he ripped the first one open and slipped it on.

Settling between her thighs, he captured her lips

and gently slid into her welcoming warmth. "I don't share, Meg."

She lifted her gaze to meet his. The emotion swirling beneath the dark and desperate desire he was controlling for her sake reached out and grabbed her by the heart. It wasn't a promise of forever, but it was close enough for right now.

She lifted her hips and took him deep inside of her. "I won't either."

His groan echoed in the room around them as he plunged into her again and again. Spreading her legs to draw him in closer, Meg felt her body taking over and her mind stepping back to let it. It had been so long since she'd made love that she wasn't prepared for the heart-stopping orgasm that whipped through her, bringing tears of sheer joy to her eyes.

"Meg," he growled. "Tell me I haven't hurt you."

She couldn't speak. The sensation of falling, only to be pinned beneath the formidable strength of the man connected to her physically, opened her heart to the possibility that this was the man she wanted in her bed and in her life for more than one night. Without words, she lifted her hips and urged him to make love to her faster... deeper.

He bent down and took her breast in his mouth. The swirl of his tongue and thrust of his body sent her up and over the edge, free falling into the madness that embraced her and took her under.

~~

She woke when he shifted and his erection throbbed beneath her backside. "Mmmm." She turned over so they were face-to-face. "I've never…" She didn't know what to say that wouldn't make her sound pathetic.

"You pack a lethal punch, Megan Mulcahy." He pressed his lips to her forehead and settled her against him. "I think I should warn you that I'm keeping you."

She chuckled. "Shouldn't you ask me first? It's not like I followed you home."

It was his turn to laugh. "True," he said. "But I thought you should know to give you time to decide if beginning a relationship with me would be worth the gossip it's sure to cause."

She pushed against his shoulder and he rolled onto his back. She sighed as she stacked her hands on his chest and rested her chin on them. "What makes you think we'd be gossip-worthy?"

"I may not have been living in Apple Grove long, but long enough to know that if Mrs. Winter's cat crossed the road, it would be gossip worthy."

Dan's eyes crinkled at the corners and she lost a little piece of her heart just then. Unsure if she should let any more of it go, she shifted away from him.

"Having second thoughts?" he asked, watching her closely.

"No." And she wasn't; she just didn't know what to do now. She didn't have much experience with what to do after making love with the man who'd just turned her ordered existence upside down.

"Good," he said. "Me either." She still hadn't moved back into his arms, so he asked, "Are you kicking me out already?"

She shook her head. "Of course not." The devil in her prompted her to add, "I haven't made your tea yet."

Dan didn't wait for her to come back to him; he reached out, snagged her arm, and pulled her beneath him. "Ah," he groaned. "Much better."

When he pulsed against her, her gaze flew up to meet his. "You aren't seriously ready to make love to me again? Are you?"

His eyes were thundercloud gray as he reached for the second foil packet, covered himself from tip to base, and rolled her onto her back. "Ready or not," he rasped as he filled her to the core.

She lifted her hips and joyfully let him fill her—all the way to her heart. "Ready."

———∿∿∿———

Meg woke to the sound of rhythmic snoring. She had a man in her bed… she, Megan Maureen Mulcahy, had a to die for, sexy as all get out man in her bed… and they'd just made love not once, but twice!

She'd never experienced multiple orgasms before. Daniel Eagan had changed all of that in a few magical hours. She reached out to trace the strong line of his jaw, the cleft in his chin, and fullness of his bottom lip. He shifted onto his back, freeing her from his embrace.

She scooted off the bed and reached for his shirt. Buttoning it up, she tiptoed out of her bedroom and into the kitchen. She was ravenous and planned to cook a late-night breakfast to go with the promised cup of tea.

"Here you are." He walked into her kitchen, looking all rumpled and manly with his jeans barely zipped, like he'd just pulled them on and zipped them high enough so they wouldn't fall off. He was staring at her as if he expected her to vanish into thin air.

"Are you all right?" she asked. "Were you dreaming about what happened earlier today?"

He shook his head. "Not yet, but I probably will later," he admitted. "I got cold and was beginning to wonder if I'd dreamed you into existence." He slipped his arms around her waist and pulled her back against him.

"You're real," he breathed against her neck before he brushed his lips to the sensitive skin there.

"Very," she said, twisting in his arms until she could wrap her arms around his neck. "I don't know what's going to happen next, Dan."

He grinned. "I'm going to kiss you, Meg."

They were both laughing when their lips met, but their laughter died as he kissed the breath out of her.

When she had it back, she looked up at him and confessed, "Seriously. I don't get out much and have a relationship that is hard to explain."

"You said you didn't have a husband or boyfriend."

"I don't—except for a few days a year when..."

"Van Orden comes back to town... I heard." Dan paused for a moment then asked, "Does he have a girl-friend in the city?"

Meg felt deflated. "Probably—yes—maybe one or two. You see, I don't want to live in the city, and he doesn't want to live here."

"So you're what to him?"

She shook her head. "I have no idea... convenient?"

He nodded as if he understood.

She busied herself with frying the bacon. After making love with Dan, she had something to compare what she and Jimmy shared to... and what they had had paled in comparison to the lush tastes, textures, and emotions Dan had shared with her all in one night!

He sighed and wrapped himself around her again and she set the fork down. "I'm feeling out of my element here and to be honest, I don't want to mess up the most amazing night of my life. This was a huge step for me."

He laid his cheek on the top of her head. "I'm getting that, Meg."

His lips met hers as he backed her toward the stove, deepening the kiss, reaching behind her, and shutting off the burner. "I have this great idea." He slipped his hands beneath her backside and lifted her up. "Wrap your legs around me." When she did, he walked toward the sink and set her down next to it. "Open wide, Meg."

She opened her mouth and he cracked up. "Are you always this literal?"

She tried to hang on to being mad at him but couldn't quite pull it off as what he said and how she reacted began to sink in. "Maybe," she admitted.

"OK. Now that I know that, let me rephrase the question." He nibbled on her earlobe and rasped, "Open your legs wide, Meg."

When she did, he stepped between them and reached into his back pocket.

"What have got in there, Dan?"

He whipped out the last of his three-pack of condoms and opened it. She tugged on his zipper and freed him. Once he was sheathed, he reached for her. "Hang on, baby, this ride's about to get wild."

She took him at his word and wrapped her arms and legs tightly around him. It wasn't easy to hang on once he entered her and began to move in and out of her. Her hands were slipping, so he grabbed her butt cheeks and held on to her as he plunged deep and slid free.

"Oh God," she screamed as she came apart in his arms.

Dan thrust in so far she felt him touching her womb, but when he exploded in her arms, she lost all track of time, space, and reality, giving in to the wonder of Dan's lovemaking.

"I can't feel my legs."

He grabbed a hold of her ankles and asked, "Can you feel them now?"

She giggled and buried her head against his neck. "Mmmm."

He slid his hands from her ankles to the backs of her knees. "How about now?"

"Oh…" she breathed.

Then he slipped his hands from her knees to the tops of her thighs and cupped her backside and squeezed. "Now?"

"Ahhh," she rasped. "I was wrong," she admitted, pressing her lips to his jaw. "I felt it all."

When Dan tilted her head up, their gazes locked and he admitted, "So did I."

"Are you hungry?" she asked, when he set her back on her feet.

"I'm out of protection."

"I was thinking of your stomach, not your, um—"

"Cat got your tongue?"

"No." She swatted at him. "Maybe I'm just not used to talking about body parts."

"Any body parts in particular?" he teased, brushing the hair out of her eyes.

"Yes," she giggled. "Yours."

"I can see we have a lot of work to do if we're going to be able to communicate effectively."

"Oh, I think you've got communication down pat."

He grinned. "Maybe so, but you need a little work." Dan held her in a hug that warmed her heart. "I could eat," he admitted.

"Give me a few minutes to scramble some eggs."

"I'll pour the tea."

Sitting across the bistro-sized table from Dan, she couldn't help but wonder how her life had changed so drastically, from semi-spinster to lover. Could she have stopped the attraction once it started—should she have thought to?

"A penny for your thoughts."

"I was thinking about things."

He grumbled, bit into a slice of buttered toast, chewed, and swallowed. "Which things?"

"The you and me kind."

"Ah," he said, lifting a forkful of eggs to his lips.

She watched while he chewed. "Do you do everything with such gusto?"

He set his fork down. "Is it a problem?"

She reached out to take hold of his hand. "Not from where I'm sitting. I just wondered."

"Is this where I'm supposed to tell you about my past lovers?" He winced when he asked.

She shook her head. "Nope. And for the record, I'm not going to either."

He shrugged. "OK."

Meg stared at him until he lifted his head and looked at her... really looked at her. When she had his undivided attention, she smiled and agreed, "OK."

He smiled and she couldn't help but smile with him.

"I didn't intend to invite you up tonight for more than a cup of tea."

"Then we'd better start drinking in case anyone asks what we were doing together tonight."

She laughed and nearly spilled her cup. "Do you think anyone suspects that we're not just drinking tea?"

"Besides anyone in town with half a brain?"

"That many?" she asked, setting her cup down. "Was I that obvious?"

"No," he told her. "I was."

"Not to me; I thought you were hung up on somebody else."

He shook his head at her. "You'd be wrong about that."

"Good thing," she told him, "because I'm definitely the jealous type."

He watched her as he lifted his cup to his lips and sipped. "I wouldn't have thought that about you."

She shrugged. "I don't have to have sex with someone to be jealous of the attention he's paying someone other than me."

"That's so convoluted, I'm not even going to try to figure out what you meant by that."

"Let me explain," she began.

He silenced her with the tips of his fingers pressed to her lips. "I need to talk about something serious, Meg."

She folded her hands in front of her. "The bridge?"

"Yeah," he said. "It's going to keep me up nights if I don't."

"So tell me all about it, and then I'll keep you up for the rest of the night." She knew he needed to purge his mind; he'd already purged the pent-up adrenaline from his system. She hoped now that the edge was off he'd still want to be with her. She wasn't sure her heart could take the fall if he didn't.

"But I don't have any more protection with me—"

The imp in her asked, "How about at your house?"

Their gazes locked and he nodded. "How fast can you get dressed?"

She laughed. "Faster than you."

He stood up and looked down at his jeans. "I'm half dressed already."

She laughed harder. "I'm dressed all the way."

"Are you wearing any underwear?"

She threw her arms around his neck and whispered, "A gentleman would never ask such a question."

His grin was positively wicked as he pulled her into his arms and slid his hands to the curve of her backside. "Who said I was a gentleman?"

She melted against him and sighed. "I hear being a gentleman is highly overrated."

He slipped his hands higher on her back and then swept around to cup her breasts, teasing her nipples with the flick of his fingers. "I prefer being a man."

She tilted her head back, parted her lips, and sighed. "Works for me."

The bulge behind his zipper brought her back to reality and the fact that they were still in her kitchen without condoms. "Right," she said, pushing out of his arms. "I'll put on underwear if you put on a shirt."

"But you're wearing my shirt." He reached to undo the buttons. When he had them open he lifted his gaze to hers. "God, you're beautiful." He pressed his lips to her heart and set her away from him. "No more until we get back to my house."

She nodded, slipped out of his shirt, and ran down the hallway to her bedroom, reaching for her discarded clothes. They were both dressed in record time and didn't speak the whole ride over to his house, whether by silent agreement or because neither one wanted to break the magic spell that had descended upon them when he'd kissed her under the dark night sky. They were in his bedroom when he told her, "I've never felt this way before, Meg." Her eyes met his and he nodded as if to enforce what he'd just said. "It scares the crap out of me."

She was relieved that he was the first to admit to the feelings similar to the ones running amok inside of her. But she didn't let him flounder for long before telling him, "Then that makes two of us."

He had a wicked gleam in his eyes when he unbuttoned his shirt and shrugged out of it, asking, "How about a power nap and then three more rounds?"

She flipped her hair over her shoulder and tried to pretend she was thinking about it. He grabbed her around the waist and tossed her on the bed. She pulled her shirt off and was smiling when he unbuttoned his jeans and stepped out of them. He knelt on the bed, unfastened her jeans, slipped his hands beneath her bottom, and tugged her pants off.

"Maybe one more bout of lovemaking—then a power nap."

Her laughter died as his lips unerringly found her breast and suckled until she agreed with him.

———

"Morning, Meg." The deep rumbling voice came from behind her, and for one moment, her brain couldn't process the fact that there was a deep voice in her bed. The breath she drew in froze in her lungs while her vision grayed due to lack of air. Then warm, firm lips kissed her shoulder and powerful arms wrapped around her, pulling her back against him.

"Dan." His name came out as a sigh. Memories of last night and the lovemaking they'd indulged in filled her. She'd never spent the night doing such decadent things—ever. Before she got lost thinking how sad that was, she realized it would be a better use of her time rejoicing in the fact that she now had someone special in her life.

He kissed the top of her head and tightened his hold on her, as if he wasn't going to ever let her go. She liked that.

"I hope you don't think I'm being naive," she said.

His breathing was slow and rhythmic; his heartbeat strong and sure, giving her the courage to tell him, "I thought I knew what making love and being in love was all about until last night."

"I don't want to rush into anything, especially when everything inside of me is screaming that what we have between us will only get better," he said, "but I wasn't kidding last night—what I'm feeling for you scares the crap out of me."

There was a tiny corner of Meg's heart that ached, the corner she'd exposed after a decade or more of keeping it to herself. "I understand."

"How can you when I don't understand myself?"

She shifted and slipped out his arms and his bed. "So," she said, looking for her clothes, "I guess I should leave."

He was out of bed and had her in his arms before

she could process the fact that he'd moved. "No. Don't leave. Let me make you breakfast and we can talk."

Her heart was bruised by his comment about being scared of his feelings for her. What she felt for Dan was so new and so huge that it threatened to consume her. She ached for what might not be and strove to hide what she was feeling. She agreed. "Can I use your shower while you cook?"

He tilted her chin up and pressed his mouth to hers. "If I didn't have to be at school early, I'd join you."

She smiled. This was the Dan she'd come to know last night, the man with the broad hands and giving heart. "I'll take a quick one."

Standing beneath the hot spray, she couldn't believe she'd spent the better part of last night making love to Dan. That wasn't like her; she didn't jump in and out of bed with a man just because she was attracted to him. OK, she reasoned, she'd sped way past attraction when she'd fallen against him and looked up into his eyes.

She turned the spigot to just shy of scalding and let the hot water ease some of the ache in her lower back. She turned her face to the water, unable to believe all the positions they'd tried out. Lord she ached in places she hadn't known she had. She grinned; the aches were sweet because they reminded her of the places they'd kissed, they'd touched, and they'd loved. She was a babe in the woods compared to the knowledge and technique Dan shared with her last night.

"So you spent the most amazing night of your life in bed with the hottest man on the face of the Earth," she said as she toweled dry. "You've got a schedule of repairs today that will keep you busy until five o'clock and he has a full day of classes to teach and a team to coach." *Time to get back to reality.*

Getting dressed she wondered when they'd have a chance to spend more time together. She was surprised that the yearning to learn more about the man and what was in his heart was equal to the need to make love with him again.

"I'm in trouble."

Chapter 6

DAN GLANCED UP AT THE CLOCK. HE HAD JUST ENOUGH time to make their first breakfast together special — Nantucket French toast special. He gathered the ingredients and had the thick slices of Italian bread drying in the toaster oven while he whipped up the egg and heavy cream mixture, adding his secret ingredient — a splash of pure vanilla. He planned to knock her socks off with his favorite breakfast.

The coffee was brewed and he was pouring a cup when Meg walked into the kitchen. She looked so tiny and fragile in the pale morning light. He couldn't believe the positions he had convinced her to try, and the way she'd happily accommodated him, bending and stretching while he sampled, savored, and had taken all that she had offered, hoping what he gave in return would convince her that she was special.

Last night was special.

"Smells good." She smiled and his brain simply shut down as parts of him stood at attention, ready, willing, and able to please again.

Oblivious to his condition, she walked over to the coffee pot. "I'd give my right arm for a cup of hot coffee."

He grinned. "You're in luck this morning. I thought you might want hot tea, but I made a big pot of coffee — just in case."

"I thought tea was in order last night, in case you'd

had too many beers while braving the onslaught of Apple Grove's townsfolk and their best intentions."

He really needed to talk to someone about yesterday and had hoped to have that conversation last night. "Meg. About last night…"

She had been about to take a drink from her cup but immediately set it down on the counter. "Which part of last night?"

He turned off the burner, divided the French toast between two plates, and carried it over to the table. "A couple of things happened that normally would not have."

Dan watched her face to gauge her reaction and didn't like seeing the closed expression settle on her pixie face. "Before you go jumping to conclusions, I wouldn't change any of it," he told her. "But I might need to take a step back until I get my head around what's filling my heart this morning."

Meg's cup still sat on the counter and she hadn't touched her breakfast. After last night, he'd been convinced that it had been awhile since she'd been involved in a relationship; her words and explosive reactions only added to that conviction. How did she feel about Van Orden? Was she telling the truth when she said she didn't share? It would be wrong to jump into bed with Meg again not knowing where they were going. He liked her—craved the fiery passion she shared with him—and wanted more, but couldn't get past the fact that he'd followed his dick and not his head, jumping into bed last night. He'd made that mistake with his ex and that had been a disaster of epic proportions. What he felt for Meg already eclipsed what he'd felt for his ex.

A tiny piece of his battered heart called out that it

had been more than his dick that kept him in bed with Meg long after the initial adrenaline had worn itself out. He'd been accused of being hardheaded more than once growing up, but he had to make sure this wasn't just sex—for him and for Meg.

A woman like Meg deserved far more than just a romp in tangled, sweaty sheets. She deserved something he didn't know if he was capable of giving to her—the love he once had in his heart.

"I think the coffee hit my empty stomach too hard," she said, pushing back from the table. "Breakfast looks great," she rasped, "but I've got to get going or I'll be late."

"Damn it, Meg!" His chair hit the floor as he shot to his feet. "Wait! You don't understand…"

Her face was drawn and her eyes pale blue—every ounce of the vibrant woman he'd made love to last night had vanished. The shell of the woman standing before him was nearly unrecognizable. "I understand far more than you know. Good-bye, Dan."

He reached for her, but she slipped out of his grasp and out of his house. Watching her walk away, he realized that it was a really long walk to town; she wouldn't really leave without asking for a ride. Would she?

She never once slowed down or turned around. He knew; he watched from the doorway to his empty home. But who could he call to give her a ride, because he knew she wouldn't accept one from him.

"I'm such an idiot!" He checked the stove, unplugged the coffeemaker, and sprinted to his car. He caught up to her a half mile down the road. This was getting to be a habit. He sighed and slowed down so he could talk while she walked. He called out, "Get in the car, Meg."

She pretended she didn't hear him.

Keeping up with her wasn't easy, because of the manual transmission, but he rode the clutch to keep the car going at the same speed she was walking. "Please, get in the car, Meg."

The third time he asked, she finally turned to glare at him. "Don't need a ride, don't want one from you."

"Look, I'm sorry, but you didn't let me finish."

This time she stopped, put her hands on her hips, and lashed out at him. "What's there to say? We spent the night tangling up the sheets on my bed and then yours. This morning, you realized you made a mistake. It's not a new version, just the end of this story."

His stomach turned upside down. "You don't know anything about me or why I'm taking a step back from us."

She was back to staring straight ahead and not acknowledging him.

Enough was enough; he gassed it, cut her off, and got out of his car. "This is my chance to start over, damn it, in a new state, a new town. I'm not going to mess this chance up because I can't keep my hands off you, Meg. I need to think. I can't do that when you are around. I made a huge mistake yesterday, speaking without thinking, that could have caused two teenagers their lives. How the hell do you think I'm going to deal with that if my fucking brain is stuck in my fucking pants?"

She crossed her arms beneath her breasts and glared at him.

He glared back. What else could he say without telling her about his ex and the fool she and his ex–best friend had made him out to be?

Her lips twitched and she smiled. "Well. I can see that when you're angry your eloquent way of speaking goes by the wayside."

Relief cloaked the icy chill in his churning gut. "Sorry. When I get mad, I, uh—"

"Curse?"

She was still smiling when she walked to his car, opened the door, and got in. She waited until he did the same before saying, "I'll take that ride, but only because I don't want my family to wonder what happened to me if I don't show up at the shop on time."

He nodded and drove toward town. "Can we continue this conversation later? You aren't going to just pretend this never happened—we never happened—are you?"

She turned to look at him. "I don't know yet. I'm feeling pretty bruised right now. A few years ago, I wouldn't have been able to say that or admit to how I felt." She shrugged. "I guess I'm making progress."

"He didn't deserve you, Meg."

"And you do?"

He gripped the steering wheel tighter and shook his head. "I don't know, but I'm hoping you'll give me the chance to start over so we can find out."

"Hell," she grumbled. "I don't want to start over. I want to jump your bones right now."

He nearly swallowed his tongue. "I, uh…"

"You think on that, Dan, and while you do, I'll be thinking that maybe I wasted a good part of my life waiting for someone who doesn't love me when I could have been out kicking up my heels, enjoying life. You showed me a part of myself last night that I'd forgotten existed… the passionate part."

He knew he wouldn't like what she was going to say next and braced for it.

"I enjoyed being with you. I loved making love with you—but maybe I'd enjoy it just as much with someone else." She was staring out the window when she added, "I once thought there would only ever be one man for me. I was wrong—you blew that theory right out of the water last night."

"So you're not going to wait for me to get my head on straight?"

"I'm not sure."

"You're going to go out looking for someone else?"

"I'm not the one who's putting the brakes on here, Dan. And frankly, since you don't want to stake your claim, why should I sit around and wait? Life's too short to spend it brooding over past mistakes. I learned that lesson well." She reached out and touched his hand. "I had an excellent teacher."

He didn't know what to do or say. He was so sure that he had to start over slowly with Meg, to get to know her better before they jumped back into bed. His heart couldn't take another blow like the one his ex had delivered. That's why he'd quit his job and moved to Ohio, to get far enough away that he could think straight and get his life back on track.

But he kept his thoughts to himself; he didn't know if he was ready to trust Meg. When he pulled up behind her shop, he stopped the car and would have parked it, but she got out and waved at him. "Thanks for the lift. See you around, Dan."

His gut told him to follow her, but his head said to wait. He'd been hasty before and had ended up losing his prized baseball card, the diamond ring his ex had flushed down the toilet, and his best friend.

The thought of letting Meg go ripped his guts to shreds, but he couldn't see any other way to get back the control he'd lost when she'd come apart in his arms. As he drove back home, he wondered if he was the biggest fool in the world or the smartest man in town.

He showered and dressed quickly, ignoring the mess in the kitchen. It would still be there when he got home after practice. Driving to the school, he knew one thing: he'd reawakened the passionate woman inside of Meg— and he wasn't sharing.

Whether she liked it or not, she was his!

———

Halfway through the first job of the day, Meg's stomach started to complain. She needed to grab a quick bite to eat between jobs or she'd never make it until lunchtime without keeling over.

Thoughts of Dan had plagued her ever since she'd walked away from him. He'd asked for her understanding, but he hadn't explained why he needed it. He'd asked her to start over but refused to tell her why. So when he'd asked her for time, she refused to give it to him.

"He either wants me or he doesn't," she grumbled, tightening the hinges on Mrs. Green's barn door. Taking a step back, she double-checked to make sure that she'd hung it properly. She opened it and watched as it swung closed. "Mulcahy's strikes again."

Why couldn't she be as successful in her love life as she was on the job, repairing things that were broken? She'd been broken, and Dan had put her heart back together. But when she tried to give it to him, why had he stepped back so quickly?

The part of her brain that had been fuzzy since last night suddenly kicked into high gear. "Did he take this job to recover from a broken heart or broken career?" Neither thought sat well with her. Maybe instead of prowling Apple Grove or heading into Cincinnati's bright lights looking for a little action, she should wait it out and see if she couldn't convince Dan that she was the woman he needed in his life.

Hell, she already knew she wanted to get to know everything about him. Why was she so ready to throw in the towel? "Knee-jerk reaction," she mumbled, putting away her tools.

Her stomach growled again and she knew it was past time to feed it. Digging her phone out of her pocket, she hit speed dial and waited for someone to answer.

"Mulcahy's, Grace speaking."

"Hey, Sis, can you call Mr. Peters and tell him I'm running ten minutes late?"

There was a slight pause before her sister asked, "Do you need me to call Pop and have him drive on over to help you hang Mrs. Green's doors?"

"Nope," she answered. "All done."

"Well then, you're right on schedule."

"I need to take a quick break and get something to eat."

"Does this have anything to do with the fact that you were seen leaving Slater's Mill with Dan Eagan last night?"

Meg cheerfully wished her sister would develop a case of laryngitis, so she'd quit asking questions. "No."

"Hmmm," Grace said. "I hear that the two of you

didn't show up again and that his car was parked at your apartment until really early this morning."

"You shouldn't listen to gossip, Sis," Meg told her. "More than half of it isn't true."

Grace laughed. "Which half: the part where you didn't go back to Slater's or the part where his car was parked at your apartment?"

"I'm hanging up now, Gracie. Gotta eat."

"Have a heart, Meg—"

Meg disconnected and shook her head. "Sisters." She didn't have time to talk if she was going to grab a hard roll and coffee—her plans to eat died as she realized she couldn't go to the Apple Grove Diner. Peggy might not be feeling neighborly toward her since Meg had left with Dan last night, but she'd get over it in a few days.

"Now what?" She brooded as she stowed her tools in the truck and drove back through town. The sign for Honey's Hair Salon was like a beacon in the dark. She knew Honey would be waiting to hear all about last night. Meg just wasn't sure how much to tell her friend. It was early yet for Honey to be open, but she pulled up out front and walked around to the back and knocked.

"Hey there, Meg." Honey B. seemed pleased to see her. "You've been on my mind since last night. Come on in." When Meg followed her inside, her friend asked, "I've got some coffee brewing. Want some?"

"I was wondering if I was going to have to beg for a cup this morning."

"Really?" Honey B. glanced over her shoulder as she added milk and sugar to Meg's cup. "I'll even add a couple of Katie McCormack's sweet rolls if you sit down and tell me what I'm dying to know."

Bolstered by the feminine company, she started to feel more like herself. Meg sighed. "I'm so hungry, I could gnaw off my right arm."

Her friend laughed. "How long have you got before your next stop?"

Meg stretched and said, "Ten minutes, but you can talk while I eat, and then maybe I'll have the strength to talk."

"OK," Honey B. said, putting her hands on her hips. "Now you're just bragging."

Meg didn't argue with her; she was too busy letting the wonders of coffee—hot, light, and sweet—work its magic on her beleaguered brain. When the plate of sweet rolls appeared before her, Meg wolfed down the first one before she realized Honey B. was talking.

"Sorry. I wasn't listening. What did you just say?"

Her friend frowned. "Pay attention, I'm only going to repeat myself once, because you're obviously famished and I'm dying to find out why."

"OK," Meg mumbled, her mouth full of gooey, sweet carbs.

"Melanie was waiting for us last night. Between Mrs. Winter, Miss Trudi, and I, we came up with a bio that I think will attract someone interesting."

Meg nodded. "You're a fabulous person," she said. "What's not to like?"

Honey B. shook her head. "I used to wonder why I couldn't catch the sheriff's eye. I've been in love with that man for so long, I'm starting to think maybe it was just a habit I'd gotten into."

"And now?"

"I'm still not sure, but I feel good about doing

something instead of sitting around and waiting for him to notice me beyond the fact that my sister is his dispatcher."

"Mitch Wallace is a busy man, but even he can't help but notice someone like you, Honey B."

Meg got up and poured herself another cup of coffee and held up the pot. "You want some?"

Honey nodded. "Thanks."

When Meg handed it to her black, just the way Honey B. liked it, Honey sipped and set it back down. "All right, now start talking."

That was all the urging Meg needed as she unburdened her soul to her friend. They'd shared so many years of broken dreams, it was time they shared some happy news. "I was going to let him go and start looking for someone else, now that I've realized what I have with Jimmy isn't worth keeping."

"But?" Honey B. prompted.

"Now I'm wondering if maybe I'm not the only one who has a past and maybe I should be reasonable and try it Dan's way for a little while."

"Is that what you want?"

"No," Meg admitted. "But it's what I'm willing to do as long as I get what I want in the end."

Honey B. smiled. "And what is that?"

Meg grinned. "Dan in my bed every night."

"Is that all you want from the man?"

Meg laughed, a deep sultry sound that surprised even her. "For starters. I'm hoping that we have a few more things in common other than we like classic cars and burn each other up in bed."

Honey B. took a long, slow sip. "I'm willing to bet

that you do. Otherwise, your heart wouldn't have let you anywhere near that man last night."

"You think so?" Meg wasn't so sure but was hopeful.

"I do. Now, do you want to know how we're going to leak the information about my online dating?"

Meg glanced at her wristwatch and grinned. "I've got three minutes. Spill."

"I'm going to use the Apple Grove Diner as my meeting place and make sure that the McCormack sisters know why."

"But what good will that do?"

"My sister Cindy's in on my plans and has convinced me that I just might meet someone who is more suited to me than Mitch, and you know what a hotbed of gossip the diner is."

Meg digested that thought and waited for Honey B. to continue.

"Cindy's in the perfect spot to relay information as I feed it to her, and she's told me more than once that he has the ears of a cat, so I plan to give him something really interesting to hear."

"But you will be careful, won't you?"

Her friend sighed. "I'm not stupid."

"I never said you were. I just don't want you to get hurt or your heart to get broken."

"Like yours?"

Meg rubbed her hand over her heart. "Mine's not really broken… bruised, but on the mend."

"Can you stop by later?" Honey B. asked, getting up to clear the tiny table in the back of her shop.

"I've got a busy day but sure. What time did you have in mind?"

"Right around closing time, that way you can be in on the first call to Apple Grove's dispatcher."

"You really think you'll have some responses by then?"

Her friend's smile was just this side of wicked. "I've got twenty messages in my inbox right now."

"That must be some bio you came up with."

Honey B. laughed. "I may have tweaked it a bit too much."

Meg looked at the time and swore. "I've got to go, but I'll be back."

Honey B. pulled her in for a quick hug and was pushing Meg out the door. "Get going so you can hurry back."

"I'll keep you posted if I hear any scuttlebutt about Dan the man."

Meg was laughing when she got back into her truck. Recharged and lighter of heart, she was ready to tackle the rest of her day. "Maybe I'll let Dan stew a little first before I tell him I've decided to let him start over."

Chapter 7

DAN WONDERED IF HE WAS GOING TO MAKE IT THROUGH the day without losing his temper. He had to talk to Meg to make her understand, but he also needed to speak to Doyle and Hawkins to make sure that they hadn't gone out onto that bridge because of something that he had said. When they showed up early for his first period phys ed class, he did a double take. "What are you two doing here?"

They looked at one another and then at him. Doyle grinned. "Taking class?"

Hawkins started to laugh and Dan knew then that he must have lost his mind sometime during the night. If he had, he knew right where to place the blame—it was his own fault.

"Do you have a doctor's note?"

Doyle and Hawkins both shrugged. "We weren't sick."

He turned to Hawkins and rasped, "But you almost drowned."

"Heck, Coach," Hawkins said, "everybody knows that almost doesn't count except for in hand grenades and horseshoes."

Dan shook his head at the two of them and motioned for them to go over to the bleachers and have a seat. "I need to talk to you two."

"We wanted to say something to you too, Coach." Doyle's voice was quiet as he and Hawkins sat down.

"I need to ask: what were you doing on the bridge?" He'd hoped that he'd been making progress and getting the boys on the team in particular to open up and trust him. Thin beads of sweat trickled from his temples. "Well?"

They finally looked back at him and Doyle told him, "We've been walking on that bridge since we were kids. It's our thinking place."

"Why?"

They stared at him for the longest time before Hawkins suggested, "Because we can?"

"But it's dangerous!" Dan was incensed. How could he have given these two the benefit of the doubt that they were marginally intelligent and compared them to the football players who had pulled a stunt that was far less dangerous? He had to ask, "Couldn't you think of another way to amuse yourselves?"

"We didn't feel like cow tipping and the Smolinsky brothers had already pulled one prank at the school, so we wanted to think up something better."

Dan shook his head. At least he knew it wasn't because of him that they'd been on that bridge yesterday. "But why would you walk there if Hawkins can't swim?"

Doyle and Hawkins looked at each other again. "It's never been a problem before."

"Well, what the heck do you do when the train starts coming?"

Doyle grinned. "We usually slip underneath and wait until it's gone, then we climb back up."

Dan shook his head. "So it *is* my fault that you nearly drowned. I'm sorry."

"No problem, Coach. My mom's been telling me for

years I've got to learn to swim. After yesterday, I understand why and I'm gonna take lessons."

"Is there a local pool?"

Doyle laughed. "I'm going to teach him down at the lake."

"There's a lake nearby?"

The boys looked at one another and then back at him. Doyle told him, "On the other side of town."

"Great bass and trout fishing," Hawkins told him. "Not too many weeds by the shore."

"Take another one of your friends with you."

"Why?" Doyle asked.

"One of you can be with Hawkins teaching him and the other can be ready to call for help. Swimming where it's weedy is dangerous. You can get tangled up fast." He rubbed at the ache in his forehead. "Isn't there a swimming pool nearby?"

"Not indoor," Hawkins told him.

"Then make sure you go with someone else—safety in numbers. Maybe you should wait until spring; it's too cold to go swimming."

The boys were still chuckling when the rest of the kids started to wander in to class. "Are you two busy Saturday morning?"

Doyle shook his head. "My mom always makes me do my homework before the weekend. I'm free."

"Me too," Hawkins said. "What do you have in mind?"

"My great-aunt needs help over at her garden center and I was wondering if anyone wants to help. She promised hot cinnamon rolls and coffee in exchange for an hour or so of our help."

"We'll be there," Doyle said. "What time?"

"Is eight o'clock too early?"

They looked as if they were about to say no when Weatherbee and McCormack walked over to join in their conversation. "Too early for what?"

"We're gonna help the coach over at Miss Trudi's Saturday morning," Doyle said.

"Wanna come too?" Hawkins asked.

"Sure."

"My aunt's promised cinnamon rolls and coffee—"

"I'm in! Your aunt makes awesome cinnamon rolls," Weatherbee said.

"Yeah," McCormack added. "She makes them for the church's rummage sale in the spring and then again in the fall."

At his first break, he called his aunt and told her the good news that four of his team members would be joining him Saturday morning. Somehow Dan made it through the rest of the day without trying to second-guess all that the boys had told him. He'd made a mistake, but in his defense, the sheriff had urged him to grab the boys and jump. He'd acted quickly, and in the end no one had been seriously injured. Life was funny that way—sometimes bad things had to happen to prevent something even worse from occurring.

If he was going to put this behind him, he had to talk to Sheriff Wallace too.

After practice, he drove to the Sheriff's office and walked into bedlam.

"What in the hell do you mean, she's put herself up on a dating site?"

The sheriff was a formidable man when he wasn't riled. Angry, the man resembled a bear, and even a suburbanite like Dan knew better than to poke a wild animal.

"I don't see what the problem is, Sheriff," his dispatcher said quietly, glancing behind the sheriff at Dan. "Besides, what's done is done and you've got someone waiting to see you."

"I don't care who the hell—"

Dan decided he'd better distract the man before he took his temper out on Cindy. "Thought I'd come back and fill you in on what Doyle and Hawkins had to say today."

The sheriff's anger evaporated. Dan admired the man's ironclad control. "So they showed up for school today?"

"I figured they'd be out for a couple of days," Dan said, "all things considered."

"Well, they weren't sick."

Dan bit back what he wanted to say. He was still the new guy in town and didn't want to give anyone the wrong impression of him... but then again, maybe it was better if he leveled with the sheriff from the start. "Did you know that the bridge is their *thinking place*?"

Mitch was watching Dan closely, which made him wonder if maybe he shouldn't have brought it up. Had he just told the man something he didn't need to know?

"Hell, I've known that for years. Those boys pretty much hang out there and climb like monkeys... you, on the other hand, were an unknown yesterday. I figured by telling you to jump that you'd pull them in with you. I couldn't count on the fact that you could clamber down under the trestle bridge and wait for the train to pass overhead."

"What if I didn't think to grab those boys and

pull them into the water with me? What would have happened then?"

"I'm a pretty good judge of character. Besides, it's best not to think about the what-ifs in life." Mitch turned to listen to what Cindy was saying and bent down to place his huge hands on the front of her desk when he answered her. "You tell your sister that I'll be over there later to discuss her putting herself out there where all kinds of psychos, wackos, and weirdos are bound to prey on her."

Cindy nodded. "I agree, but you know Honey B. She's turning thirty in a few months and... well"—Cindy leaned close to confide—"her biological clock's ticking."

"Damn fool woman," the sheriff grumbled, straightening up and spinning on his boot heel. "Dating site, my ass." He stalked past Dan into his office and slammed the door.

"Well." Cindy dialed the phone and was smiling when she said, "That went far better than we'd hoped."

Dan picked up on the comment and wondered what she'd meant by it, but felt like an idiot asking her outright. Maybe he could find out later.

Walking outside to his car he realized where his train of thought was going and had to laugh at himself. "Not even two weeks in the sticks and you're getting involved in local gossip."

He wondered if he'd started any gossip by staying at Meg's so late last night. He pulled a U-turn and headed toward his aunt's garden center. She'd be his best source of information right now and might be able to help him decide what to do about Meg.

"Daniel," his aunt called out from where she stood at

the front of her shop, holding her watering wand. "I'm just giving these mums some water."

He had to smile. His great-aunt was wearing her signature outfit again—including the rubber boots she referred to as her *Wellies*. He stared at her and the odd extra width of fabric at her hips. Who the heck wore pants like that? Well, aside from his great-aunt and equestrians.

"Everything looks great here."

She smiled at him and then her look turned thoughtful. "Something heavy weighing on your mind, Daniel?"

Was he that transparent or had the gossips been at work?

"I, uh… was just at the sheriff's office."

She nodded and moved to another row of planters. "Those boys were bound to get into trouble one of these days, sitting on that bridge instead of finding somewhere safer to spend their time."

"Does everyone in town know that Doyle and Hawkins spend their time out on that bridge?"

She looked over her shoulder at him and inadvertently sprayed the window of her garden center.

"You're watering your front window, Aunt Trudi."

She harrumphed at him but turned around to watch where she pointed her water wand. "To answer your question, I cannot speak for everyone in town, but their parents, the sheriff, Amelia Winter, and I know that they do. Why do you ask?"

"Shouldn't someone have warned them to stay away from that bridge? Don't they know how dangerous it could be?"

She turned off the water and hung the hose with its attachment on the hook by the big double doors to her shop. "Land sakes, Daniel. I don't know why you're all het up about this. The boys are fine. Besides, you have far more that you *should be* worried about than those boys."

A cold chill chased up his spine, leaving the hair on the back of his neck standing on end. "Do I?" He watched her closely for a clue as to what she meant, but if there was one thing he admired most about his great-aunt Trudi, it was her ability to hide her thoughts behind a truly blank expression.

"Why don't you help me bring those planters inside and I'll make us a nice cup of tea?"

Tea was the last thing he wanted right now. What he wanted was to drive over to Meg's apartment, storm up the stairs, take her in his arms, and—

"Daniel?" His aunt was tugging on his arm.

"Hmmm?" Great, now he was daydreaming about the woman who'd turned him inside out and backward… the one he'd slammed the brakes on the possibility of a relationship with.

She slipped her arm through his and patted his hand. "Come on, dear," she said. "I've got a lovely blend of Darjeeling, so soothing."

"What about the stuff you want me to move?"

"You can move it later."

He let himself be led, not so eager to speak to her now that he knew there was something his aunt thought he needed to know. She puttered around in her kitchen. He offered to help, but she refused, motioning him into one of the chairs surrounding the round oak table by the picture window.

Dan sat and wondered how she managed things all by herself. "Who winterizes your house?"

She paused and set the tea kettle back on the burner. "I do."

"These windows are so old, they can't be double-paned."

She smiled. "I usually put a nice thick plastic on the inside of the windows. Keeps the warm air on the inside."

"What about the plumbing?"

She shook her head and picked up the kettle, pouring hot water into the waiting teapot. When she was finished she carried the pot to the table and placed it on an iron trivet. "You're going to love this tea. We just need to let it sit for a few minutes. While we wait," she said, meeting his gaze, "I'd like to talk to you about Megan."

Damn, she knew! "What about her?"

"There's a lot of history here that you might need to understand before you get involved with her."

An image of Meg perched on the edge of her countertop flashed in his mind, distracting him.

"Daniel!"

"Huh?"

His aunt frowned up at him. "Well. That certainly answers my next question. Don't you think you should have courted the girl first?"

Fishing to see just how thorough the gossip chain in Apple Grove was, he asked, "First before what?"

His aunt got up and started to pace around the kitchen, and he couldn't help but notice that she looked like an indignant fairy, but he wasn't about to tell her that. "Just because there's snow on the roof, doesn't mean there isn't a fire inside, young man."

It took a moment for her words to sink in, and when they did, he was speechless. He had no idea what to say and no desire to discuss sex with his great-aunt. So he did what any red-blooded American man would do when faced with this type of a situation: he changed the subject.

"So Aunt Trudi, I was at the sheriff's office before and noticed he was upset about Honey B. signing up at a dating site. Why would that be?"

She took the bait, hook, line, and sinker. "Was he angry or upset? Upset means she got his attention, angry means he really does care."

He got up and pulled out her chair so she could sit back down. "He wasn't angry to start out, but once he got going, he worked up a full head of steam."

His aunt tut-tutted, shook her head, and gave him another telling look, so he added fuel to the gossip he'd just fed her. "When Cindy mentioned her sister's biological clock ticking, the sheriff stormed into his office and slammed the door."

His aunt got up, put her hands on either side of his face, and planted a noisy kiss on his cheek. "That is the best news I've heard all day. I've got to call Amelia."

"What about Honey B.?"

"Oh, I'm sure her sister already called her by now." She paused with the phone in her hand. "What else did the sheriff have to say?"

"Something about psychos, wackos, and weirdos." If anyone asked what he thought, Dan would have told him that the sheriff had more than a passing interest in Honey B.'s welfare—and dating status.

"It's about time that man showed some interest in that poor girl. She's been in love with him for years."

Dan was halfway to the door when his aunt added, "Which reminds me of Megan." When he turned around, she was standing there with the cordless phone in her hand and a frown on her face. "You're going to want to sit down for this conversation, Daniel Patrick Eagan."

Jeez! All three names—a sure sign that he was in trouble. But how had she found out what he'd been doing... and then it hit him. She didn't know—she was guessing, and as long as he didn't act guilty, she had nothing to go on. *Did she?*

He smiled and slowly walked over to the chair she'd pulled out for him. "Are you sure you should be talking to me about Meg? Isn't that the same as gossiping?"

She stood in front of him and shook her pointer finger at him. "Now you just sit and listen up, Daniel."

Her frown was fierce, so he swallowed the laughter building inside of him. "Yes, ma'am."

"Hmmpfh. That's better. Meg's a good girl," she said slowly. "She's a hard worker, has a kind heart and a gentle soul."

"All redeeming qualities, I'm sure, but weren't you going to call Mrs. Winter?"

She poked him in the shoulder. "Be still," she said, placing the phone on the counter. "And don't change the subject."

He nodded.

"Meg's had a lot on her plate for the last twelve years or so; she could use someone steady in her life."

"She's got a good job from what I hear, working for her family."

His aunt agreed. "But she's been carrying the burden as the oldest sister for too long since their poor mother died."

Curiosity got the better of him. "How long?"

"Ten long years. She's a half a dozen years older than

the middle girl, Caitlin, and seven years older than the baby, Grace."

"What about their father?"

"Joseph is a hard-working man," his aunt confided. "But he just about fell apart when Maureen died. Megan was nineteen at the time and just stepped into the role of mom for her younger sisters. She'd been working with her father full-time since the year before when she graduated from high school."

"So she's been shouldering quite a burden. It couldn't have been easy helping to raise two younger sisters who probably resented the fact that she was trying to step in for their mom."

His aunt nodded. "I knew you'd understand. You're a good man, Daniel, and I know you wouldn't try to break Meg's heart intentionally."

He needed to ask the next question, but it wasn't easy to get the words out. Finally, he asked, "Were they engaged?"

She laid her hand on his shoulder. "Daniel, I know what that girl did to you, and I think it's a sin. I'm just sorry I didn't live closer, or else I'd have taken care of her and that poor excuse for an ex–best friend of yours."

"Thanks, Aunt Trudi."

"And I'm sure your grandfather will come around soon. He can't stay mad at you forever, especially since he knows the whole story—and since you gave him that Murder's Row signed baseball your great-grandfather gave to you."

He grinned.

"That went a long way toward making up for that nasty argument your grandfather had with his father. You just give it some more time and he'll come around. You'll see."

Feeling better about some things but worse about the rest, he asked, "What would you do if you discovered you have feelings for someone that you'd only just met and you'd… acted on those feelings… but then realized that you might have acted too quickly?"

"Depends on your definition of acting on those feelings, Daniel."

Busted. "You might be my only relative in Apple Grove, but there are certain things that I'm not willing to discuss." That certainly sounded prudish to him and from the look on his aunt's face, she thought so too.

"Fine, then. But it's your funeral if you dallied with Meg and have no intention of making an honest woman out of her."

"I just met her. Why would I want to jump into marriage with her?"

His aunt's gaze turned positively lethal. He didn't know she had it in her. "You obviously jumped into bed with her. Is she only good enough for the sex?"

"Jeez, Aunt Trudi!" He covered his face with his hands.

"I knew it!" She danced gleefully around her kitchen and for a moment he thought he'd gone over the edge into madness and he was in alternate universe where fairy tales were the reality and he was watching one of the little people dancing around a fire.

"I thought you knew!" he ground out, getting to his feet.

She stopped long enough to put her hands on her hips and glare up at him. "I figured you had. She's a beautiful woman, passionate—and you're an Eagan."

"What's that supposed to mean?"

"The men in the Eagan family are known to be fabulous lovers."

He put his pointer fingers in his ears and started saying, "La la la la la… I don't want to hear anymore, Aunt Trudi."

She frowned and shook her finger in his face. "You're going to listen anyway."

He dropped his hands to his sides and sighed.

"If you do anything to hurt that girl, there will be a long line of people just waiting to beat the ever-living tar out of you."

He nodded.

"So whatever happened this morning to change your mind from last night, you go fix it."

"Yes, ma'am."

"And start courting that girl!"

He sighed and got to his feet. "Yes, ma'am."

"Oh, Daniel?"

"Yeah?"

"I've got a lovely bunch of late-season day lilies in the fridge in my shop. She'd love them."

How could he refuse? "Anything else?"

"Now that you mention it, Amelia Winter has a fresh-baked cherry pie for Meg. Be a dear and pick it up and deliver it to Meg when you give her the flowers."

He followed her back to her shop, moved the planters she needed taken care of, and swallowed his pride and walked to the back where she was holding up a huge bouquet of day lilies. "How much is this going to cost me?"

She beamed up at him. "Only your heart, Daniel."

He didn't want to admit that his aunt was right, that he'd overreacted this morning. Maybe he could make things right. He'd been acting out of fear—fear of the unknown as far as those two boys were concerned, tangled up with his past.

Meg had to understand.

"You are one in a million," he told his aunt, taking the flowers from her and bending down to wrap her in his arms.

She sighed and patted him on the back. "You're a good man, Daniel. Now go show that side to Meg and make her fall in love with what's inside of you. She's worth it."

He nodded, swallowing to ease the tightness in his throat. "Thanks."

He had already opened the driver's side door when he heard her calling his name. He looked over his shoulder.

She was smiling when she told him, "You are too."

He grinned. It was good to be in a new place, a new town, but it was even better to have family there. "I owe you, Aunt Trudi."

"Don't worry, I'll think of something you can do for me."

He was afraid she'd say that.

Dan was exhausted by the time he parked his car in the driveway. Walking through the doorway, he flicked the light switch and stood on the threshold and stared. His kitchen pretty much summed up how the morning had gone, with the dried-up remnants of the breakfast he'd prepared, hoping to show Meg that she was more than just one night to him. He couldn't quite figure out where he'd gone wrong and when he'd put his foot—up to his kneecap—in his mouth.

If he had to do it over again, he wondered if he'd screw it up again. Given his history—"Yeah," he rasped. "I probably would because there was no way I could keep my hands off of her."

He put the flowers in water and began to straighten

his kitchen and put it to rights. He'd give them to Meg the next time he saw her. When the last of the ruined breakfast had been tossed in the garbage and the sticky plates stacked in the dishwasher, he opened the cabinet over the sink and reached for the bottle of aspirin. Shaking two into his hand, he poured a glass of water and downed the pain reliever.

He rubbed the back of his neck. "I'll call Mrs. Winter about Meg's pie tomorrow."

The lure of a hot shower had him detouring to the bedroom; he could always turn on the TV after he relaxed under the hot spray. Twenty minutes later, he was dressed in his favorite ratty sweatpants and sweatshirt and parked in front of the tube, but he just couldn't get comfortable. His conscience was eating at him.

"You are asking for trouble, Honey B."

"Actually, Mitch," she purred, "I've been practically begging for it for years now and you haven't done one thing about it."

For more than half of Meg's life, Sheriff Mitch Wallace had been the strong, stalwart figure upholding the law in Apple Grove. Watching his mouth open and close with no sound coming out, she realized he was just as vulnerable as any other person. She nearly applauded on the spot because two-thirds of the triumvirate were correct—the man wouldn't like Honey B.'s plans. *Ah,* she thought, *but would he try to stop her?*

"I think it's a great idea," Meg said, watching both of their faces for reactions. Honey's smile was like the cat who'd just finished a bowl of cream, while the sheriff's—well, he looked like he'd just taken a big bite of a rotten apple.

He turned around and glared at her. "If you think you're going to be signing up too," he warned, "you've got another think coming."

Wrong thing to say to a woman whose lady parts were still singing from their late-night marathon doing the hoochie-coochie. "You might be the law around here, but you have no jurisdiction over what happens on the Internet—in my life or Honey B.'s." She crossed her arms and waited for the fireworks.

The sheriff surprised her by keeping a lid on his temper, but his eyes were definitely the window to his soul—they burned like hot molten coals. "I do if I feel it crosses the line into Internet pornography."

Honey B. lunged past Meg, placed her hands in the middle of his chest, and shoved him toward the door. "Get out!" she yelled. "Why, if you were the last man in Apple Grove, and I was the last woman—"

He threw his arms out to keep from falling. Braced in her doorway, he growled—seriously growled at Meg's friend. "You'll want to watch what you threaten, Honey B., or you'll find out that I'm a man who takes what he wants."

Honey B. lifted her chin high in the air. "Obviously it isn't me." She spun on her heel and walked to the back of her shop.

Meg looked over at the sheriff and straightened to her full height. "I've always looked up to you, Mitch. You've saved my sorry butt on more than one occasion, and I know I owe you for that, but you're just plain stupid if you can't see how badly you just hurt Honey B.'s feelings."

When he just stared past her in the direction Honey had gone, she felt her temper bubbling to the surface. "I hope to hell she finds a man worthy of her." That had his gaze snapping back to clash with Meg's. "She deserves better than being ignored."

She swept past him, hurrying after her friend. "Honey B., are you all right?"

Her friend was running water in the kitchenette. "I'm just so mad I could spit nails."

Meg agreed. "I feel like I just found out my best friend ran away with my man."

Honey B. laughed, just as Meg had intended. "I guess it's time that I woke up and smelled the coffee. That man has no interest in me at all. You heard him," she rasped, as tears welled up in her pretty green eyes. "If he was interested, nothing would stop him from pursuing the woman he wanted."

"I'm not so sure about that. There might be more here than meets the eye. The sheriff is a quiet man... maybe you haven't misjudged him. Maybe he does feel more for you than you realize."

When Honey B. glared at her, Meg shrugged again. "Why else would he threaten to interfere, tossing around words like 'Internet pornography'?"

Honey B. sniffed and tossed her glossy mane of hair over her shoulder. "I'm so tired of waiting, and after you took the bull by the horns with Dan, I realized that I'd let life pass me by for too long waiting on that man."

Meg put her arm around her friend and hugged her close. "I think we should stick to the plan you ladies came up with. Besides, wouldn't it just irritate the crap out of Mitch if you had to close the shop early come Friday night because you had a date with a hunky guy from Newark or Cincinnati?"

Honey B.'s eyes glazed over. "Yeah," she whispered. "And instead of meeting here in town, I'll go there—so much better than if it was someone I've known since grade school."

"Just be sure to arrange for the meeting in a public place, and let me know where and when you're going to be meeting him. It would be good to tell a few people," Meg said. "That way, you aren't taking any undue risks—or I could just happen to show up where you're meeting him."

"It's starting to sound better all the time."

"Have you decided who you want to meet first?" Meg figured it would be a good idea to test the waters vicariously through Honey B. That way, she could be a help to her friend and figure out what exactly this whole Internet dating thing was all about, just in case Dan wasn't interested now that he'd purged the bridge incident from his soul.

Her friend shrugged. "There were so many replies, I don't know where to start." She waited a beat before asking, "Want to help me pick out my first three candidates?"

Meg grinned. "I thought you'd never ask."

Chapter 8

MEG POURED ANOTHER GLASS OF WINE FOR HONEY B. and herself. "Mmmm." She licked her lips after taking a long slow sip of the red wine. "I usually don't drink wine," she confided in her friend. "I like beer."

Honey flicked a glance in Meg's direction and grinned. "I know. But now and then it's good to change it up. Try something different." She was staring at the computer screen and was using the mouse to shift from one picture to another. "Take these five guys, for instance."

Meg scooted closer. "I like the fireman from Newark. He sounds dedicated and likes the outdoors—and working with his hands." Meg sighed. "There's just something about a man with callused hands—it feels so—" She stopped before she shared just a bit too much information.

Honey B. sighed. "That's the problem; I'm not a wilderness type of girl. I'm more of the I'll-sit-here-by-the-fire-and-admire-the-wood-you-just-chopped kind of gal."

Their shared laughter felt wonderful. Meg was loose from a long night of loving, and although she wondered if she could convince Dan she was worth the time to get to know, she wasn't worried about it right now. Honey B.'s happiness was on the line, and besides, it was up to Dan to make the first move. *Wasn't it?*

She pointed to the second picture Honey B. brought up. "How about him?"

They both stared at the picture and then each other. "He's a teacher over at the Police Academy."

"So?" Honey B. hadn't looked up from the photo, so she couldn't see the expression on Meg's face.

"You need to stop thinking about Mitch."

Her friend scrunched up her face and looked over her shoulder. "Maybe I happen to like guys who are involved with the law."

Meg snickered into her wineglass. "Just make sure they aren't on the wrong side of the law."

Honey B. started giggling and couldn't stop. "Now I have to pee." She got up and said, "See what you can come up with for me," as she ran down the hall to the bathroom. "I like the Police Academy instructor and the fireman so far, but I'd like at least one more so I can have three dates lined up for the end of this week."

While Honey B. was occupied, Meg quickly scanned the profiles of the most likely candidates, selecting a former air force pilot, who could be tricky—pilots were known for their big egos. But then again, they had a right to feel that way with all of their specialized training.

When her friend walked back into the room, Meg had added a few more men to Honey B.'s list.

"I'm not interested in meeting a rancher or an entrepreneur; I have my own business to worry about. Besides, on the outside chance that things start cooking, I don't want to have to travel too far and get stuck out on somebody's ranch."

"It sounds like you've already made up your mind." Meg always admired that trait in her friend. "I wouldn't know where to begin."

"Once I find a man, I'll help you find one too."

"Gee, Honey B.," Meg said. "You're such a good friend."

"Cross your fingers," she said as she clicked the mouse.

"Crossed," Meg promised.

"Now we wait."

"How about if we plan out what you're going to wear and what you want to do for your dates?"

"I was going to leave that up to my dates."

Meg shook her head. "OK, but these guys are virtual strangers, right?"

Honey B. agreed. "So?"

"Then you should have an idea of where you want to go, so that you'll at least be in comfortable or familiar surroundings."

"I never thought of that."

Meg grinned. "I know. You're too busy wondering what you'll do if one of these stellar guys decides he wants more than a good-night kiss."

"I'm not jumping into bed with anyone I don't know." Honey B. must have realized what she'd said a moment after the words had left her mouth—too late to call them back. "Meg—I'm sorry."

"It's all right," she reassured her. "It was my decision, and it wasn't right after our first meeting—it was a couple of days—and besides, I know his great-aunt."

"I'm not judging you, Meg," Honey B. told her. "I was just making a decision as to what I want and don't want to do."

Meg nodded. "Just be open to the possibility that one of these men might just knock your socks off with a look that will have your panties in a twist—in a good way. You need to be prepared, just in case. At least bring a three-pack."

The look on her friend's face was worth a picture. Honey B. finally agreed, "I guess it's a good idea."

"So what are you going to wear?"

"I've never had a chance to wear this dress I bought two years ago." Honey B. reached into her closet and pulled out a tiny black dress that didn't look like much on the hanger. With a glance at her friend, Meg knew it would look amazing on Honey B.—she wasn't built like a hanger.

"Why don't you try it on to make sure you still love the way it fits and then you can show me the shoes you're going to wear?"

While they played dress up, they heard Honey B.'s inbox receiving mail. "It couldn't be."

Meg shrugged. "Why not? I'd email you back right away. You're a seriously hot chick, my friend." Honey laughed as Meg hoped, and they both took one more look at Honey's form-hugging little black dress and the electric-blue spike heels she pulled out of the back of her closet. "You could be arrested for inciting men to riot."

"That good?" Honey B. asked.

"You know it," Meg reassured her. "Let's see who's trying to email you."

With a few clicks, Honey B.'s inbox was open—and so was her mouth. She closed it and whispered, "Every one of them?"

Meg grinned. "I have a feeling you're going to forget old what's-his-name by the time the weekend is over."

Honey B. tried to give her the stink eye, but it didn't work. "We've been friends too long," Meg told her. "Besides, I'm trying to decide just how much of this information to leak to the sheriff."

"My brain's not working—maybe I've had too much wine."

Meg giggled and upended the bottle, checking to see if they'd finished it off. "Yep, it's ready to recycle." With a glance at her friend who was still staring at the computer screen, she asked, "Coffee to sober up a little, or should I open another bottle?"

"When was the last time you and I spent the night watching old movies and drinking wine?"

That had her pausing to think; when she realized it had been a couple of years, she answered cheerfully, "Too long." Meg grabbed their empty wineglasses. "I'll open another bottle. Meet me in your living room."

An hour later they were halfway through *How Green Was My Valley* and crying buckets. "Whose idea was it to watch this?" Meg demanded.

"Yours." Honey B. held out her hand. "Pass me the tissues."

By the time *Roman Holiday* had finished, they'd wound down and were sipping hot cocoa. "I always wished they'd met again and had a stormy love affair," Honey B. confided. "Gregory Peck just has this way he looks at Audrey Hepburn that makes me want to tell her to toss her crown, kick up her heels, and jump him."

"Yeah," Meg agreed, "but then you'd miss out on all that angst they so obviously felt having to sacrifice their love for who and what she was."

"Did you ever wonder what you'd do if it was you?"

Honey B. hadn't realized how closely the movie mirrored her relationship with the sheriff. Meg wasn't sure she should point that out now when they were still just slightly buzzed from the yummy red wine. But then again, she wasn't sure if her friend would see the similarities between the sheriff's job and Audrey's job as princess. She decided to turn the focus away from Honey B., saying, "No, my story's not quite as angst-filled, just really sad."

"Like Maureen O'Hara," Honey B. said quietly.

Meg didn't want to acknowledge the comparison to the movie they'd watched earlier, so she snipped, "Which movie? She appeared in several." Hating the way her voice sounded, even to hear own ears, she picked up her mug and swallowed a mouthful of cocoa so she wouldn't have to talk.

"The one we just watched. She never gave up loving Walter Pidgeon, ever." After a long pause her friend added, "You really should forget about Jimmy and focus on Dan. I like him."

Meg was about to give her a snippy comeback, then realized that her friend was right, but more, she already had taken the first steps. "I do too. I just wish I knew whether I'm going to get my heart stepped on again or if it will be the beginning of a fabulous love affair."

Honey B. crossed her legs to sit Indian-style and settled in the corner of the couch, mug in hand. "Why can't you be the one to push for what you want? Why does it have to be the guy who makes all of the moves?"

Meg set her mug down. "I can and it doesn't."

"I'm liking this new direction my love life is taking."

Meg agreed. "You're taking control of it and moving in a positive direction. What's not to like?"

Across the street, one of the men in question rolled his shoulders and punched the steering wheel. "Is she going to stay all night?" Sheriff Wallace had been sitting in his truck for the last few hours, waiting for Meg to leave so he could go up and talk some sense into Honey B.

But he couldn't have that particular conversation if the stubborn woman wasn't all alone. "Damn fool women," he grumbled. "Always sticking in pairs." He couldn't say what bothered him more: the prospect of Honey B. looking for love outside of Apple Grove or the worrisome fact that she just might find it.

He shook his head and punched the wheel again. "Shit that hurts." He shook his hand until it stopped aching. Squeezing his hand into a tight fist and then opening it all the way, he satisfied the worry that he had broken bones in it.

"Why would she want to date someone she didn't know?" But he already knew the answer: because she was tired of waiting for him to ask. Lord, that woman had turned him inside out and backward the first time she'd looked at him—and she'd been one hundred percent jailbait at the time.

A lawman to the bone, he could no more encourage her than he could step over that line and taste what she so willingly offered. She'd been fifteen at the time, seven years younger than him. So he'd waited, bided his time, but when she'd turned eighteen, the town had been undergoing some serious growing pains and he'd spent the better part of that year and the next keeping the latest crop of teenagers from breaking their heads—and the law.

She'd turned twenty-one before he had blinked an eye, and that was nine years ago—where had the time gone? Sitting in the cab of his pickup, he shivered. It wasn't the temperature so much as the dampness that chilled him to the bone.

Watching the living room window, he swore. He could tell from the light flickering inside that the two weren't going anywhere tonight. "Another damned movie." He knew she had a stockpile of old movies; he shared a similar passion for the classics, but he preferred the war movies—action and adventure.

Turning the truck on, he let it heat up for a few minutes before turning it back off again. He should just give up and go home, but couldn't as long as there was a chance of Meg leaving in the wee hours of the morning. He could still have that talk with Honey B.—even if he had to wait all night.

The tap on the window woke him. And there she was, smiling and holding up a steaming mug of what he knew would taste like ambrosia. Pride tossed to the wind, he rolled down the window and nodded. "Mornin', Honey B."

"What kept you parked outside my house all night, Sheriff?" From the look on her face, the woman had no clue. Hell, if she'd had a clue she wouldn't be setting herself up for a cyber date of disastrous proportions.

"Official business," he grumbled, then added, "if there is a God—and I truly believe there is—then that cup of coffee is for me."

She smiled and handed it through the window. "Hot, black, and sweet, just how you like it."

He reached for the mug with both hands so he could cup her hand and the mug, and watch her reaction. Her full-body shiver spilled some of the coffee onto the back of his hand. It was hot as hell—just as he'd always imagined Honey B. would be. He sucked in a breath and ignored the burn. He'd have to wait her out and see if he could salvage what could have been a relationship with this woman, but he had to be smart and let her go out on a few damn dates first.

"Thank you," he rasped. He sipped the coffee when what he really wanted was to sip from her lips. He'd had it bad but had put it off, had let his job rule his life, but if he weathered this next little while and could prove to her that he was ready for a relationship, things just might start moving in the direction he'd been dying to take them—to his house and his bed.

She turned to go and he reached for her, keeping her close for just a few minutes more. When he couldn't say all of the things that were in his heart, he warned, "Be careful."

She nodded and walked away.

———※———

"Well, what did he have to say for himself?" Meg demanded when her friend came back inside.

She shrugged and reached for the steaming mug of coffee Meg was holding out to her. "He thanked me and told me to be careful."

Meg shook her head. "He's afraid of you, but he's willing to let you go—for now."

"What makes you say that?"

"How long have you been tossing your feminine wiles in that man's face?" Meg figured it had been close to fifteen years but waited to hear what Honey B. would say.

"Ten years, tops."

Meg laughed. "Liar. You've been stuck on him since you called for help the night we were up on the water tower."

Honey B.'s eyes narrowed. "If I hadn't, you would have lost your grip, fallen on your head, and broken it."

Meg agreed but was smiling as she took another drink of coffee. "Tell me again how his jaw clenched and his eyes got that determined look in them as he got out of his truck and ran past you and started climbing?"

Her friend's eyes got a faraway look in them and Meg knew she was reliving their shared nightmare.

"I got out of his way but followed him over to the tower," she whispered. "He kept mumbling something under his breath, but I couldn't quite hear what he was saying."

"Probably because I'd started yelling for help by then." Meg snickered.

"He almost looked like he dreaded the task," Honey B. said, "but then started climbing and then next thing I knew he had a hold of you and had swung you onto his back and was climbing back down."

"I don't remember much past him telling me I was safe and to take his hand," Meg said quietly. She didn't like to think about that night, partly because she'd been fourteen years old and embarrassed that she'd gotten dizzy when she looked down and scared the crap out of herself when she almost fell. It was the third and last time the sheriff had had to rescue her.

"Well, it all turned out OK," Honey B. said. "Although I can't help but think that if he had dropped you on your hard head, it might have been a good thing—maybe you wouldn't have spent so much time working yourself to the bone trying to forget about Jimmy, all the while waiting for him to show up and have a change of heart about this town."

"That wasn't why I spent all that time working and you know it." Meg didn't want to get angry with her friend, so she buried the resentment deep. She didn't want to talk about losing her mother or the years that just piled one right on top of the other as she eased her grief by keeping her hands busy and her neighbors homes in good working order.

To distract her friend, she asked, "So what's the plan for today?"

Honey B. sipped and then said, "I'm going to color my hair."

Meg snorted the sip of coffee she'd intended to swallow. She took the napkin her friend offered and blew her nose. "That hurt." She wiped her eyes and blew her nose a second time.

"If you weren't so busy laughing at me, you wouldn't have snorted that hot coffee." Their gazes met and Honey's lips twitched up into a smile. "Besides, what's so funny about me coloring my hair?"

"Nothing. I know it's how you advertise… well, at least that's what you say is the reason you do it so often."

"Why else would I?"

Meg paused and set her cup down. "To catch a certain sheriff's eye when you're out in front of your shop sweeping the sidewalk."

"Hmmpf. A lot you know." But her friend was already moving on to the next thought. "Maybe I should go back to my real color."

Meg laughed out loud. "I can't remember that far back."

"Honey blonde."

"Really?" Meg didn't remember.

Honey B. nodded. "It's been years. Hey, don't you have to get to the shop?"

"Yeah."

"Be careful today, Meg."

"Because?"

"We spent the night drinking and watching old movies instead of sleeping. You work with dangerous tools—"

"And you work with dangerous chemicals, so be careful yourself."

"I will if you will," Honey B. challenged.

They agreed and started cleaning up the living room. When they made their way to the kitchen, Meg said, "I just had an idea."

Honey put the last mug in the dishwasher and decided it was full enough to run it. "About Dan?"

Meg shook her head. "No, about your date tonight."

"Are you going to make me pry it from you or are you going to tell me?"

Meg laughed. She really enjoyed her friend's sense of humor—maybe because it was just a bit snarky and a lot like her own. "Instead of just showing up, I think I should go too."

Honey B. put her hands on her hips and glared. "I'm not planning on sharing—"

Meg held up both hands as if to keep her friend from jumping to the wrong conclusion. "Just hear me out. You don't know any of these guys, right?"

"Right."

"And you've only dated men from Apple Grove, from families you've known all of your life right?"

"So."

"So I'd feel better if I went too—separately and got another table on the other side of the restaurant. I could get there first and—"

"You'd go to Newark and go out to dinner all by yourself?"

"No," Meg said quietly. "I'd probably bring someone."

Honey B. crossed her arms beneath her breasts. "Who did you have in mind?"

"I'm not sure. If I can't get who I have in mind, I'll probably drag one of my sisters. Is that OK with you?"

Honey B. finally relaxed and nodded. "You're not trying to horn in on my date, then?"

Meg reached out and smacked her friend in the back of the head. "No, you idiot, I care about what happens to you. These guys are the unknown—"

"A lot like Dan is?"

Meg's stomach clenched and started a slow burn, but she hid the hurt because she knew her friend was just looking out for her welfare as much as she was looking out for Honey B.'s. She dug deep for the words to explain how she felt. "I know you're not going to believe me, but from the moment I looked up into his eyes, something happened inside of me."

Her friend waited for her to continue.

Meg stroked a hand across her stomach. "It wasn't an ache exactly, but it was a really odd feeling, kind of like butterflies. The width of his shoulders distracted me, but it was the sound of his voice reverberating inside his chest that totally had me going."

"In other words, you lusted after him and went for it."

That wasn't entirely true. "No," she insisted. "That's not all it was. I could tell that he was interested, but then he made a comment about me being in one of his classes and I knew he thought I was just a kid. When I set him straight he was still hesitant, despite the fireworks going off inside of the both of us—and then he kissed me. Well, it wasn't a real kiss—more like he brushed his lips across mine."

"Lust," her friend said again.

"No," Meg insisted. "But I did show him what a real kiss was."

"And then?"

"Then he took me home, and I showed him my great-grandfather's truck."

"The Model A in your barn?"

"Yep."

Honey B.'s expression changed. "Then what?"

"My dad came home and they talked cars."

"Does he like baseball?"

Meg laughed. "So you do understand?"

"Yeah," Honey B. told her. "I do, but I still think things got going too quickly between you two."

"That's only because you and the sheriff are moving slower than a snail's pace."

"So we agree to disagree?"

"Only on how quickly to move when you know in your heart that this is the one," Meg said quietly.

"You're still dead set on going with me?"

"No," Meg corrected her friend. "I'm going to the same restaurant as you, that's all. I'll be there if you need me."

"What if I decide that he's the one and want more?"

"Then I'll hang around in the area. You have my cell; make sure you have yours."

Honey B. laughed. "Yes, mom."

Meg's smile was bittersweet. "I've got to go if I'm going to get through my day in time to get cleaned up. I still have to find someone to go with me."

"Are you going to ask Dan?"

"Maybe." Meg wondered what his reaction would be. "I'm not sure he'd go with me."

"He might need a little push."

"I won't be going alone," she reassured her friend. "Just in case your dream man turns out to be a creep—or worse, a psycho."

"I'm so glad you have such a positive vibe about my first date."

Meg laughed, hugged her friend good-bye, and was out the door.

She'd started her day in a far better frame of mind than she would have if she'd spent the night alone and brooding over the way Dan stepped back from her. She was worth fighting for and she thought he was too... Time would tell. She had a full day ahead of her and questions she'd been avoiding from her sisters. Maybe she should try to get in touch with Dan before she got to the shop.

Before she could talk herself out of it, she dialed his number.

Chapter 9

DAN FELT SLUGGISH AND STILL COULDN'T BELIEVE he'd fallen asleep in front of the TV. His neck had a crick in it, but given the way he'd been hunched over in the wooden chair with his feet up on a second one, it was a wonder he could move at all. He made a mental note to start looking for a recliner or a sofa; that way, if he was going to spend the night in front of the TV, he'd at least get a good night's sleep.

His phone vibrated on the counter. Draining the rest of his first cup of coffee, he walked over and picked it up. Surprised—no, relieved—to see the number, he answered. "Megan, hi."

"I was wondering if I could ask a favor." She sounded hesitant, as if she expected him to refuse.

Well, probably because of the way he'd taken a giant step back from what they'd started. He was an idiot. Adrenaline or not, too many months without a woman or not, Megan Mulcahy was special—she might even be the one. Too bad if he wasn't ready to find her, but still, he couldn't just let her walk away.

"Absolutely. What's up?"

"I need you to help me help a friend."

"Sounds complicated."

"Well, it is and it isn't."

He laughed. "Just ask me, Meg. I can't say yes until you do." He hoped his opening would sway her.

He heard her drawing in a breath before saying, "A friend of mine is going on a blind date, up in Newark, and I want to be there too—just in case."

"You don't think too highly of her blind date," he said, "do you?"

There was another pause before Meg said, "I really don't know him."

"So he's a friend of one of her friends then?"

"Not exactly."

She sounded as if there were more to the story that she should be telling him, so he asked, "What aren't you telling me, Meg?"

"OK, the truth is that she met him online—"

Dan worked hard to keep a lid on his temper, still his voice sounded gruff to his own ears when he bit out, "You have to be kidding me! Doesn't she understand how risky that is? Haven't you two paid attention to anything in the news lately?" He couldn't believe they would be that naive.

"Look, Dan. I didn't call for a lecture. I called for your help. If you don't want to, fine. I'll ask someone else."

"Wait, Meg." He didn't want her to ask anyone else. That she'd asked him over any of the other people she knew in town was a surprise. "I'll help you, but I am wondering: why me?"

"At the moment," she drawled, "I have no idea."

He chuckled. "OK, before I kind of lost it just now, why me?" He couldn't say why he needed to know, but he knew deep down that it was important to have her confide in him.

"Can't I tell you later?" She sounded like she was in a hurry.

"Are you late for work?"

She hesitated again and he knew that she just didn't want to tell him... yet.

"You can tell me on the way to Newark. What time do you need me to pick you up?" He heard her audible sigh of relief and grinned.

"Can we leave right after practice?"

"I'm calling practice early today. I don't want the guys to overdo it. We have a big game tomorrow."

"Great, so should I walk to your house?"

He laughed. She was something else. "No. I'll pick you up. Oh and, Meg?"

"Yes?"

"Does Honey B. know what you're up to?"

"How do you know—" She mumbled something beneath her breath that sounded suspiciously like one of his favorite curse words. "You guessed, didn't you?"

He swallowed the laughter filling him. "Yes. I'm sorry, but I don't like being blindsided."

"Neither do I."

He knew she was talking about the other day. "Look Meg, I've done some thinking and I want to talk about the other night."

"If you're going to reiterate what has already been said, don't bother."

"No," he rushed out. "In fact, I think that maybe it wasn't adrenaline pumping through my veins at all... I've never felt like this before, Meg. It happened so fast."

"I know," she sighed. "I keep wondering if I dreamed it all."

He tightened his grip on the phone and told her what thought kept him up most of the night. "I think we need to take it slower but definitely get back to where we were the other night." He prayed she'd give him the chance. "Don't give me your answer right now," he rasped. "Just promise me you'll think about it."

"Since you're coming with me tonight," she told him, "I'll think about it."

He struggled to push the emotions struggling to the surface back where he could control them. "Thanks."

"Hey, Dan?"

"Yeah?"

"Wear a nice shirt."

"Man, I thought you were going to tell me I had to wear a tie."

She laughed, a full rich sound that wrapped itself around his healing heart. "Not this time, but maybe tomorrow night."

"You need me to go out with you again?"

Her sigh was deep. "Look, it's part of what I need to talk to you about on the way to Newark. Can it wait until then?"

A glance at the kitchen clock told him they'd both be late if he didn't hang up the phone. "All right, you can fill me in—but you will tell me everything, right?"

"Maybe."

They were both laughing when they disconnected. "God I hope she gives me the chance to get back to where we were the other night."

You're the one who put the brakes on, his conscience screamed. "Yeah," he grumbled unplugging his coffee-maker. "But I know now that was a stupid thing to do."

Go figure.

"What do you mean she's got an out-of-town date tonight?"

The sheriff didn't mince words and Dan had to respect the guy for his calm when he could see from the way the other man's jaw tightened and the tick that started beneath the sheriff's left eye that he was anything but. "Meg called and asked me to go with her to Newark, that a friend of hers had a blind date and Meg was uneasy about it."

"Did she say it was Honey B.?"

"No, I guessed that it was."

"And she didn't deny it?" The man's big hands were curling into fists.

Dan wondered, *If the sheriff ever let his temper loose would the other guy survive?* "No, she seemed relieved that I guessed. You're not going to like who she's going with."

"Sam Reynolds?" the sheriff asked.

"Uh, no," Dan told him. "It's—"

"Gary Jones?"

"No—I don't know his name. She met him online."

Mitch's hands uncurled and slapped against the desk as he shot to his feet. "Son of a bitch! I didn't think she'd really go through with it."

Dan's suspicions were confirmed. The sheriff had feelings for Honey B. Because of the mistake he'd made with Meg, he had to ask, "Does she know how you feel about her?"

Mitch glared at him before rocking back on his heels. "What does that have to do with anything?"

"She might not be headed for trouble right now if she knew you were interested in her."

"She knows."

"Does she?" Dan wondered because the man avoided eye contact with him.

The sheriff finally sighed and grumbled, "She should."

"I'm taking Meg tonight, but she said something about tomorrow too."

"Damn it. She's going out tomorrow too?"

Dan sensed the other man needed to be reassured. "I think so," he said slowly. "I'll find out and keep you posted."

"You've got my private number?"

"Uh, no."

The sheriff gave Dan the number and waited for him to input the digits into his contacts. "You'll call me if things get out of hand?"

"Just as soon as I sort them out and make sure that Honey B. is out of trouble." He held out his hand and the other man took it, a look of gratitude mixing with the uncertainty he was trying to hide from Dan.

"I'm counting on you."

"I won't let you down."

Fifteen minutes later he pulled into the driveway to Meg's apartment and felt a rush of hopeful anticipation skidding through his veins. He wasn't going to mess this up—if he had to slow down because he'd made a mistake and needed to make it up to Meg, he would, but otherwise, he was going to lock lips with the delectable pixie-sized woman again. She'd offered him a second chance and he was taking it. He'd been thinking of sampling her sweet-tart flavor ever since their phone conversation this morning.

Knocking on the downstairs door, he waited for her

to answer. When she didn't, he walked in and called out, "Meg, are you ready?"

"Almost, come on up."

He grinned and thought, *That way lay dragons*, but he figured he could keep a lid on his libido for tonight. "I stopped off at the sheriff's office."

Her frown was fierce. "Why?"

"I, uh…" He lost his train of thought when he saw the hunter-green formfitting dress she was wearing. "You look beautiful."

She put her hands on her hips and he nearly swallowed his tongue, but she got his attention when she said, "Don't change the subject, Dan."

He grinned down at her. God, she was something when she was annoyed. Her eyes sparkled, like they were lit from within, and her sassy mouth tempted the hell out of him. She appeared to be waiting for him to reply, so he told her what was on his mind. "I thought he should know. He's stuck on Honey B., Meg."

"Maybe, but you should have asked me first." She must have realized how she sounded because she added, "Besides, you only just moved here and don't understand their situation."

"I understand plenty. Did you know that he has feelings for Honey B.?"

Meg's face had an expression of pain that she struggled to hide. Dan wanted to get to the bottom of that and more. She caught his interest when she said, "He's had a lot of years to do something about those feelings but hasn't. How long would you have Honey B. wait?"

What could he say now that wouldn't have her jumping down his throat? That was definitely not the mood he wanted her in tonight. He shrugged and changed the subject. "Can we leave now?"

She shook her head at him. "Fine, but next time, ask me before you go talking to the sheriff about my friend. You could have upset the plans we've set in motion."

He felt like laughing but knew it would be a big mistake. So he agreed with her. "Yes, ma'am." As he followed her down the stairs, he asked, "So how long should it take to get there?"

"Forty-five minutes or so. Depends on traffic and how fast you drive."

He held the passenger door open and waited for her to get inside. "Then let's get this show on the road. Are we following her?"

Meg waited until he'd gotten in the driver's side before answering, "I think that's the best idea. I told her we'd meet her out on County Road 16. That way we might get out of town without everyone knowing something's up."

She seemed edgy, so he reassured her, "I'm going to do everything in my power to make sure that her date goes off without a hitch. If there's trouble, I'm there." He told her, "So try to relax."

She smiled at him. "I'll try. Let's go see if she's waiting for us."

Honey B.'s car was sitting on the shoulder a few miles away. Dan slowed down and waited for her to pull in front of them. She waved in her rearview mirror and Meg finally relaxed beside him.

"I know this might seem a little crazy to you, but a person can only wait so long before they begin to wonder if what happened was all in their mind and the feelings tangling inside of them won't ever be returned."

He kept his eyes on the road and the car in front of him, struggling to keep the unease sprinting through him from showing. "Thinking about the other night is too distracting. Can we talk about it later?" He saw her turn to face him in his peripheral vision. "Right now what's important is keeping your friend safe, and keeping the man who spent the night outside of her house in his truck up to speed on what's happening."

"The sheriff told you about that?"

"He's got bone-deep feelings for her, Meg."

The road ahead wound past farmland that rolled gently on past them. Every so often there was a perpendicular line of trees separating the land, but his favorite were the ponds dotting the landscape, some of them surrounded by trees—like an oasis amid the tilled soil. This wasn't like the farmland he'd driven by on his way through Lancaster County in Pennsylvania. It was much flatter there. "Are these farms owned by different people?"

Meg looked out the window. "The Edwards family owns the next couple hundred acres," she told him.

"But what about the lines of trees separating the fields?"

"Some of those trees are property lines, some for a wind break, and some because a different crop's planted on the other side of the trees."

He digested the information and told her, "When I was a kid, we used to drive into the country to attend the Sussex County Fair and most of the farms we drove past had stone walls separating them and big sections of woods on the back edge of fields—fields where horses, dairy cattle, sheep, and goats would graze."

"So you're not a total stranger to farms and farmers?"

He laughed. "Well, except for one day out of the summer, I pretty much am. Where I grew up, we had sidewalks, streetlights, and houses too close together. I liked taking that drive with my family because it was a chance to see something completely different and to wonder if someday I'd own land and a house with plenty of space on either side—not within spitting distance of my neighbors."

He hadn't thought about going to the fair in years. "The last time I went to the fair they called it the Sussex County Farm and Horse Show, but I heard from some of my cousins who went last year that the fair is even bigger and that it had moved to a permanent location and they changed the name again. Now it's the New Jersey State Fair, but we don't call it that."

She smiled and he knew if he didn't focus on getting them where they had to be, he'd pull over so he could watch the way her features softened as her smile deepened. It hit him then that he had it bad—the inner battle his heart was waging with his mind churned his stomach. He should be on guard, his mind insisted. Remember the scent of her skin and the softness of her sighs, his heart reminded him.

"Some of my best memories are from when I was little."

The wistful sound of her voice filtered through his concentration, and he almost ignored it, but then had to ask, "What's your favorite one?"

"We were in grade school and my momma had us all dressed up—I hated putting on these patent leather dress shoes—because we were going to her friend's wedding." He stole a glance out of the corner of his eye; she was lost in the memory. "My mom and her friend were like sisters and this was a cause for celebration because everybody in town figured she'd be an old maid."

She seemed happy remembering, so he prompted her to stay there just a bit longer. "How old was she?"

Meg grinned, and told him, "Twenty-nine."

That was a surprise. "But isn't that how old you are?"

Her laughter sounded just a bit sad. "Yeah. Out here, folks usually marry young."

"Why?"

"Why not?"

"Well, there's college, finding the right job, and making a living so you can afford a nice house in a nice neighborhood. What else would you have to offer the woman you intend to marry?"

"Is that what happened to you, Dan?"

He shrugged. "I guess that's how it started, but it ended far differently than I'd planned." When she remained silent, he asked, "How do you make a living out here if you don't go to school? How do you afford a home for your family?"

"A lot of the kids I went to high school with graduated and went to the local Ohio State campus—where we're headed in Newark—but just as many went to the big campus on scholarships."

"Well then, why the rush to get married?"

"It's just a part of the lifestyle out here. Some of the people out here marry their childhood sweethearts. Others never marry."

"But what about getting out there and experiencing life?"

"We do," she grumbled. "What do you think we do out here in Apple Grove?"

He shook his head. "After finding out that Doyle and

Hawkins spend their time out on that railroad trestle bridge, I'm afraid to ask."

She didn't say anything more for a while and they drove in silence. He realized that it wasn't one of those awkward silences where you were struggling for something clever to say to keep your date interested. He was almost afraid to use the word, but it fit how he felt perfectly—comfortable.

———

Meg relaxed while Dan drove. It was a good feeling to just be. She wondered if he felt the same way in her company. Was she willing to hear the answer if it wasn't what she'd hoped? Fear of rejection had her reaching for her phone to check her messages. She'd told Grace and Caitlin she was going to Newark this afternoon. They tried to pry the details out of her, but she'd left them wondering. There were three messages from Grace and one from Caitlin. Not ready to read what Grace had to say, she opened Caitlin's first.

It was short, sweet, and to the point—just like the middle Mulcahy sister. *Have fun*. She laughed.

"What?"

Hmmm, he sounded interested. "Nothing, just catching up on my messages." Scrolling through Grace's messages, she decided to answer them later, instead focusing on what lay ahead—Honey B.'s date and the possibility that she just might meet the man of her dreams. Meg was optimistic enough to believe that it was possible that, after all the years Honey B. spent waiting for the sheriff to pay attention to her, her wait was over—and she was about to meet a new man, one who would be a part of her future. Either that or the sheriff would wake up and realize that the best thing that ever happened to him was just waiting for him to walk across the street.

She needed to be on guard and vigilant, sizing up the situation and paying close attention to her friend's body language and that of the man she was meeting. It was a lot of responsibility, but Meg was determined to do her part to keep her friend safe. The tension was giving her a headache. She gave in to the need to confide her thoughts in Dan and said, "We're almost there and I can't decide if I'm scared or excited for Honey B."

His hands eased the death-grip he had on the steering wheel. "I won't let you down."

His fervent words wrapped around her like one of her dad's bear hugs. She hadn't realized how badly she'd needed one. "Thanks."

"You're welcome."

"She's taking the shortcut."

Dan signaled and kept his speed up so he wouldn't lose sight of Honey B.'s car. Meg hadn't realized how intense it would be making sure they followed her friend and not get caught behind traffic. The throbbing that began at the base of her skull was moving up her neck.

"There're a couple of bottles of water behind you."

"Thanks, but I'm not really thirsty."

He mumbled something beneath his breath and told her, "You'll need it to take something for your head."

She turned her head around to stare at him and wished she hadn't. But she ignored the pain and asked, "What makes you think I have a headache?"

He sighed. "You've been tense since you told me

about your plans, Meg. I can see it in the way you're hunching your shoulders."

"I might have a slight headache."

His snort sounded suspiciously like laughter to her. "Are you laughing at me?"

"No, ma'am. There's a bottle of aspirin in the glove box. If you're going to be any help to Honey B. at all, you'll need a clear head. Don't be stubborn, Meg. Grab a bottle of water from the backseat and take the damned aspirin."

"Don't hold back, Coach."

The words were already out of her mouth and couldn't be called back. She sounded snarky and, worse, bitchy.

He laughed. "Just do it, Mulcahy."

The tension building inside of her eased up. She unbuckled her seat belt and reached around behind her, snagging a bottle and opening it before she put her seat belt back on. After she'd taken the pain reliever, she buckled up and let go of the bad feelings she'd been hoarding. It wouldn't do either of them any good if she spent the next few hours in a bad mood.

"Thanks."

"You're welcome."

"Are you always this polite, Dan?"

He grinned. "My momma raised me right."

They passed a few businesses and restaurants before Honey B. signaled and pulled into one. "Bob Evans?"

Meg shrugged. "You can always get good food here," she said. Although it wasn't quite what she'd envisioned, but her friend hadn't told her what the name of the restaurant was and now she knew why—Meg would have questioned what kind of guy would have her friend meet him at a family-style restaurant.

"This could go either way," she told Dan. "He'll either be a really great guy who likes home-cooked food, or he'll be a loser and expecting Honey B. to pay his way."

Dan looked at the building and then back at her. "It looks bright and clean—inside and out—what's wrong with it?"

"Don't they have Bob Evan's restaurants up by you?" The look he gave her was all the answer she needed. "It's a chain of restaurants specializing in home-style food."

"And the problem with that is?"

"If he's trying to impress Honey B., he should have taken her someplace else."

Dan frowned. "You mean more expensive?"

Meg shrugged. Honey B. was worth the extra money her date could have shelled out. "She's getting out; let's give her a head start."

"Do we need a reservation for here?"

Meg shook her head. "Not that kind of place."

"Is the food bad?"

She looked at him and wondered how to explain what was going through her head. Finally, she blurted out, "The food's great, their sausage gravy and biscuits are to-die-for, but it's like having a home-cooked meal."

"And that's bad because?"

She shrugged, ignoring his question.

"Do you cook?"

Busted. But she wasn't going to admit to it. Big on telling the truth, she evaded the question and blurted out, "All of the women in town over the age of twenty-one know that you do."

With that she pushed her door open, got out, and started walking. She didn't want Honey B. to have too much of a head start and she was getting tired of trying to explain what had been a part of her foundation growing up in Apple Grove. Was it really that different wherever Dan was from? "Guess I'll have to ask."

"Ask me what?" the deep voice rumbled from behind her. She should have known he wouldn't let her get too far ahead, especially after giving her his opinion of the whole online-dating scene in general. She huffed out a breath and told him, "I'll ask you later. Come on!"

They'd managed to pick a good time, and the place was fairly empty, so they didn't have to wait for a seat and could sit far enough away from Honey B. to not attract attention, but close enough to eavesdrop if they wanted to.

Once they'd picked their spot, Dan pulled out the chair for her and she sat down. "I can't believe I'm doing this."

"I thought it was your idea."

Her gaze swept the room before settling on the man across from her. He'd worn a royal blue polo shirt—a hue that changed the color of his eyes, as they reflected the warm, deep blue. But it was the way his broad shoulders and deep chest filled out that shirt that had her breath snagging in her lungs as she remembered the way he'd caged her beneath him and gently, with devastating precision, awakened the passion sleeping inside of her before catapulting her to the stars.

"Meg."

"Hmmm? What?" *Crap*. She felt her cheeks heat with the embarrassment she was trying to hide. She didn't want him to know what she'd been thinking about, especially after everything she'd said about being here for Honey B.

He shook his head. "You must have been thinking about something else."

Hoo baby, was she! "I don't get out much," she confessed. And that was all she was going to tell him. Let him draw his own conclusions.

He nodded. "That's why I started teaching myself how to cook more than just scrambled eggs and hamburgers."

"Because you didn't eat out much?"

"Actually, because I love to eat—and then later because I enjoyed experimenting with recipes. It's like chemistry."

She searched his face for a sign that he was pulling her leg but couldn't find one. "You're serious?"

"Hey," he said, "eating is serious business."

His lightning-quick grin had that funny feeling fluttering in her belly again. She gave him a quick smile and then leaned closer, saying, "You need to stop being so distracting. I'm working here."

He started to laugh and then must have seen that she wasn't kidding, so he cleared his throat, took a sip of water, and looked over her shoulder. "Tall, broad, and auburn-haired at twelve o'clock."

She started to turn around and he stopped her with the slight shake of his head and whispered, "He's coming this way. Look at me, Meg."

The depth and urgency in his voice compelled her to look at him. Their gazes connected and something warm and sweet shifted inside of her, catching her off guard with the intensity of the feelings she wasn't quite sure what to do with; they were more cerebral than the passion that swept her away the other night. A warmth in the vicinity of her heart started to spread, sending tingles of heat to the tips of her fingers and end of her nose.

"Whatever you're thinking," Dan rasped, "I want some."

She blinked and asked, "What did you say?"

He looked over at the table where Honey B. and her date were quietly talking and then back at her. His cheeks flushed and she wondered if he regretted what he'd just said or was embarrassed that he'd said it.

"Sorry," he said, "but the look on your face was just short of rapture."

She swallowed to clear her throat and give herself time to figure out just how much to tell him. Finally, she realized that she should go forward the way she'd been living her life since she'd lost her mom and Jimmy left town: being as honest and straightforward as possible.

"When I looked at you just now, I had the feeling come over me—"

He reached for her hand. "Thinking of the other night?"

She shook her head. "No. That's the funny thing. I kind of got lost in your eyes and felt something warm and sort of—" She paused and looked down at her hand cradled in his. "It'll sound silly."

He stroked the back of her hand gently. "If we're going to get to know one another better, shouldn't we start now?"

She marveled that his touch could be so tender, so light, yet move her so deeply. "Sweet," she whispered. "I felt something in here." She placed her hand over her heart. "It wasn't physical… it was almost cerebral, yet ethereal—" She looked away and confessed, "I've never felt anything like that before."

His fingers tightened around hers, and she jolted when his warm, firm lips brushed against the back of her hand. "Thank you for telling me."

"I was afraid you'd laugh." She didn't like being made fun of, and because of her size compared to that of her younger sisters, she'd been the brunt of more than one joke growing up. Kids could be really mean.

He released her hand and sat back. "After the joke my ex-fiancée and ex–best friend played on me, I never laugh at anyone."

Sensing there was a depth of emotion here, both raw and turbulent, she waited for him to say something else. When it was obvious he wasn't going to... yet... she glanced in the direction of the other table and leaned toward Dan. "I'm getting a friendly vibe from Honey B. and her date. What about you?"

His gaze swept the room and then slowly settled on Meg's friend. Up until he'd been dumped, royally flushed—whatever you wanted to call it—he'd thought himself a good judge of character. He'd been hesitant to trust his judgment since then—obviously, or he wouldn't have pushed Meg out the door the other morning. He owed it to Meg and because of her, her friend Honey B., to observe the couple's body language.

From a quick glance, without really hearing the couples' conversation, he had to agree. "I don't think she has anything to worry about tonight. He seems to be keeping a respectful distance and his body is definitely relaxed." He paused to chuckle. "Maybe slouched is a better word. Is she going straight home from here, or does she have something else planned?"

"Just dinner, then home. I'm hungry; why don't we order?"

Despite the fact that he knew his way around a kitchen and liked to try new recipes, Dan wasn't a food snob. He'd eat whatever was put in front of him. "How do you decide? Everything sounds good to me."

"But you're a good cook."

"So? I like to eat. What are you having?"

"A burger."

"Are they good here?"

"Oh yeah." The look on her face actually convinced him to order one too.

While they ate, he kept an eye on Honey B. and her mystery date, but it wasn't as easy as he imagined with Meg sitting across from him licking her lips after taking a big bite of her burger.

"Don't you like it?" She was looking at him expectantly.

He blinked and looked down at his half-eaten hamburger. "It's really great."

She was frowning at him. "Then why aren't you eating?"

"I was watching your friend."

Meg snorted—an inelegant sound coming from such pretty lips. "If you say so."

"Why don't you just say what's on your mind, Mulcahy?"

"Ooooh." Her eyes lit with amusement as she picked up a fry and dipped it into the mayonnaise she'd ordered on the side. "Am I hitting a nerve, Coach?"

He picked up his burger took a big bite and frowned at her. When his mouth was empty, he grumbled. "Don't call me coach."

"Why not?"

He finished the rest of his burger before answering, "It reminds me that you look like you could be one of my students and I look—"

"Amazing."

He shut his mouth and didn't quite know how to

respond to that. He knew he was strong; he worked out on his own and with his team. But he hadn't thought much about his appearance since he'd been dumped.

"Um… thanks."

She leaned across the table and said, "If you hadn't changed your mind about us, I'd be tempted to coerce you into the backseat of your car to pick up where we left off."

Dan's jaw dropped open and for a moment he just stared at Meg then reached across the table to grab her hand and was about to stand when Honey B. and her date approached their table.

Smoothing over what could be a delicate situation, Dan held out his hand. "My name's Dan Eagan. I coach high school soccer in Apple Grove."

The other man grinned. "Small world. My name's Patrick Garahan—Pat. Before I moved out here, I used to play for the FDNY Soccer Club." He looked at Dan and shook his head. "Isn't it funny that my date Honey's from Apple Grove?" He looked over his shoulder at her and then back at Dan and Meg. "From what Honey's told me, Apple Grove is a small town," he said slowly. "You two must know each other."

Meg looked at Honey B., who said, "Pat was curious when he noticed you and Meg watching us more than once, so I told him the truth."

Dan and Meg shared a look and Dan nodded. "I'm glad she told you."

"Can you join us for dessert?" Meg asked. "It'll save Dan from getting a crick in his neck."

When the table had been cleared, coffee poured, and dessert served, Pat glanced from them to Honey and back again. "I'm getting a pretty clear picture. You're Honey's friends and wanted to make sure I wasn't some psycho she'd met on the Internet. That about sum it up?"

Dan grinned. "Pretty much. Thanks for not getting mad."

Pat laughed. "I would have done the same for my sister or one of their friends."

"So, Pat," Meg asked, "how long have you been a firefighter?"

The other man relaxed and started to slouch down in his seat. Dan realized it was because the guy was exhausted, not because he didn't have any manners. Dan'd been wrong about that.

"Since 9/11, I started out in New York City, but moved here a few months ago."

"I'm from New Jersey," Dan told him. "I lost a good friend that day."

Pat looked down at his hands. "I lost two of my best friends," he told them before looking up to meet Dan's gaze. "I'd been trying to decide what to do with my bachelor's degree in English... that day was my wake-up call. And up until the fire last month..."

Dan watched the play of emotions cross the man's face and knew something raw and painful had prompted Pat to move from New York City to Ohio. "Well, I realized a couple of months ago that I needed a change, so here I am."

Honey B. reached out and took hold of his hand. "Thanks for not being mad that my friends were here to watch my back."

Pat looked down at their joined hands and grinned. "It's good to have friends who will do anything for you… it's almost as good as having your brothers here."

Dan picked up on the odd note in his voice. "I've got a sister who is married and living in Connecticut. How many brothers and sisters do you have?"

Pat grinned. "Three brothers and three sisters."

"Are your brothers firefighters too?" Meg wanted to know.

Dan watched as a look that could only be described as pride had the man nodding and shifting higher in his seat. "They're at different firehouses; after the attack, it was mandatory."

Dan started thinking and knew that it wouldn't be a good idea to ask about why Pat had made the move to Ohio. He'd made a life-changing move recently and it was still a touchy subject. An idea popped into his head. "Do the Newark firefighters have a soccer team too?"

"There are a couple of us that get together a couple of times a month and mess around on the field. Why?"

"Maybe I could round up a couple of guys and we could challenge your team to a game."

Pat grinned. "Let me see who's off shift. Between our three firehouses, I know I can get a team together."

While the men were talking to one another, Meg finished her pie, sat back, and smiled. "Did you enjoy dinner?"

Her friend nodded and leaned close. "I had a great time. Pat's a nice guy."

Meg agreed and added, "Does he remind you of anyone you know back home in Apple Grove?"

Honey B. hissed at her. "Shhh—not now, Meg."

Meg rolled her eyes at her friend. It was obvious to her that Honey B. was having a good time with Pat, but it was also obvious that Pat had a similar personality and profession to Mitch. Firefighter versus sheriff. "I bet Mitch would like to meet Pat."

"I need to use the ladies' room, Meg. Don't you?"

Meg started to refuse, but the look in her friend's eyes warned her not to. "We'll be right back."

Dan and Pat nodded but kept talking—they'd moved from soccer to football, and were now talking baseball.

"Men," Meg grumbled, following Honey B. to the ladies room.

"Why are you bringing up Mitch when I'm on a date with Pat?"

"If you can't figure it out, then I'm not telling you."

"Wait," her friend told her. "I've really gotta pee."

Meg washed her hands and tried to think of a way to remind Honey B. that, although Pat seemed like a great guy, he had baggage—just like Mitch. She didn't know if she should warn Mitch or root for Pat. Her heart went out to Mitch, even though he should have paid attention to Honey B. about ten years ago.

Men... so slow sometimes.

Honey B. came out and washed her hands. "We should be getting back."

Meg agreed. "Will you be seeing Pat again?"

Honey B. laughed. "I will if Dan has anything to say about getting together in town for a soccer game."

Meg was laughing as they walked back over to the table.

Dan looked up at her and smiled a warm and friendly smile before turning to the other couple.

The other man smiled and shook hands. "I'll give you a call in a couple of days. I know I can get a group of guys together for a pickup game."

Dan smiled. "Great. Maybe some of the guys from

the varsity soccer team can come and get a different perspective on the game."

They paid the cashier and walked outside. Meg and Dan gave Honey and Pat a chance to say their good-byes.

"I like him," Dan said as he opened the door for Meg.

She slid onto the seat and clipped her seat belt. When Dan got in the other side, she waited until he started the car and fastened his belt. "I do too, but I'm not sure Honey B. should jump into a relationship with him… it sounds like he's got some baggage."

"Don't we all," Dan murmured, watching for Honey to get into her car so he could follow her home. "Maybe he just needs a break and someone to talk to."

"Is that all you need, Dan?"

He waited a moment before he answered. "I thought I knew what I wanted, but it turned out that I was wrong." He put the car in gear and drove out of the lot.

When they'd driven a couple of miles, Meg said, "So was I."

Picking up speed once they were on the highway, Dan finally spoke. "I didn't want to get involved with anyone yet—it wasn't in my plan."

Meg snorted out a laugh. "The last thing I planned on was getting involved with the varsity soccer coach."

"So, if I was a plumber, you'd be interested?"

She laughed a low sultry sound. "Now you're talking, Eagan."

Chapter 10

THE RAIN HITTING THE ROOF WOKE HIM UP, BUT IT WAS thoughts of Meg that kept him awake. The one night they'd spent in one another's arms played over and over in his mind until he'd all but given up on the thought of sleeping. He'd never been so wrapped up and turned inside out by a woman before. This was new—scary. He couldn't stop thinking about her.

He punched his pillow a couple of times and turned over; maybe he could fall back to sleep. Fifteen minutes later, he realized the futility of that plan. The soft sound of the rain had him wishing Meg were with him; he knew he'd fall back to sleep if he could just hold her in his arms. Well, maybe after they tired themselves out—once that thought was in his head, he couldn't shake it loose. If he was going to be honest with himself, he didn't want to.

"Damn." He gave up and sent her a text: Meg, are you awake?

He put his phone on the bedside table. "She's probably sleeping."

His phone beeped, signaling that he'd received a message. Grabbing for the phone, he held his breath, unsure of her response but hopeful.

He chuckled as he read her response. No.

Unsure of how she'd react if he actually called her, he sent her another text. Listening to the rain, wishing I could hold you.

She didn't answer right away. She could have fallen back to sleep. Angry with himself for starting something, backing away from it, and then realizing too late that he shouldn't have, he rolled onto his back and stared at the ceiling.

A cold splat of water hit him in the middle of his chest. "What the hell?" He rubbed at the spot and stared at his hand. Another drop hit him before his brain kicked in and he realized his roof was leaking.

He got up and turned on the light. Sure enough, there was a dark spot on the ceiling right over his bed. "Perfect." He'd never had to deal with a leaky roof before and had no idea what to do. A few drops hit the mattress, leaving a wet spot. "Better move the bed."

A few minutes later, he'd shoved the bed up against the far wall and watched the water drip onto the hardwood floor. "It's gonna ruin the wood." He got a towel from the bathroom and folded it up under the leak and stood there watching it. As the rain intensified outside, the leak dripped faster.

"Damn. I need a pot."

He grumbled all the way down to the kitchen, grabbed his red enamel stockpot, and carried it upstairs. In position to catch the water, he winced when he heard the first few drops hitting the bottom of the empty pan. A few minutes later, the sound changed, as the drops hit water.

Raking a hand through his hair, he sat down on the edge of his bed and wondered why he thought buying a hundred-year-old home would be a good idea. His parents had warned him it would take a lot of maintenance to keep things running, but he ignored their advice, thinking he could handle it all.

"Guess I was wrong about that." Wondering if he'd been wrong about Meg too, he sent her another message, even though she hadn't answered the last one. Changed my mind, he typed, rain sucks, roof's leaking.

He tossed a towel on the wet spot on his bed and climbed back in. Keeping his phone at hand, he laid back down and closed his eyes, ignoring the steady sound of rainwater dripping into the pot.

His phone beeped; he looked at the screen and laughed out loud. Get a damn bucket; I'll check it out in the morning.

No soft words from his Meg... *his*... He let that thought roll around in his brain for a while and decided he liked the way it sounded. His self-deprecating laugh sounded more like a snort.

Sometime around two o'clock the rain stopped and so did the leak. With a sigh of relief, Dan drifted off to sleep.

———

Meg wondered what Dan wanted from her... well, other than to hold her and listen to the rain. She smiled. The thought was really romantic, and she couldn't remember the last time someone had tried to romance her.

He was kind, sexy as hell, and willing to help someone he didn't really know just because Meg had asked him... that and he was car crazy. She would be ten times a fool if she didn't practice a little patience and stick around to find out if she could fan the flames of what they'd started until it flared bright and burned steadily.

Rolling out of bed, she knew it would be a busy day. It had rained heavily during the night, so she

might have a few other calls this morning to do minor
roof repairs. She really didn't like getting up on anyone's roof, but as long as she was careful and didn't
move too quickly, she could usually get the job done
without getting dizzy. For more than a patch job, her
dad usually farmed the work out to a roofer he knew
over in Newark.

"Best to just get a move on and go see what I'm getting into." Before she left her apartment, she checked in
with Grace. "Hey, I got a call this morning. Dan's roof
leaked last night."

"Why didn't he call the shop?"

"He's got my number," Meg told her. "I guess he
figured he'd go right to the source."

"Alright," Grace said, "but that's going to completely
mess up the schedule for the day."

"I'll just work overtime," Meg answered. "I've done
it before. Don't worry, Gracie. I'll get it all done."

Dan was waiting for her when she arrived. His eyes
looked bleary from lack of sleep. But was it from the
leak or from lying awake thinking about her? With the
number of calls she had to make today, now wasn't the
time to ask. Shoving those thoughts aside, she focused
on the work at hand and asked, "Where's the leak?"

He stepped back and to let her in. "Upstairs," he said.
"Over my bed."

She chuckled softly as she walked through the kitchen
to the second floor.

He was right behind her and grabbed a hold of her
elbow, stopping her. "You think that's funny?"

She looked over her shoulder at him and was sorry
that she'd put that hesitant uncertainty in his gray eyes.

"No, sorry. I was just thinking that that explains your last message."

He let go of her elbow and slid his hand to the small of her back. The heat of his wide-palmed hand seeped in through her chambray work shirt. Pinpricks of awareness sprinted from that spot straight to her lady parts—saying, "Pay attention! The man with the magic hands is back!"

When she stumbled over her own feet, he steadied her against his rock-hard chest. Helpless to resist, she sighed and curled against him. His arms wrapped around her and his chin rested on the top of her head.

"I'm so damn glad to see you, Meg."

She cleared her throat. "I didn't sleep much last night," she confessed. "It was the little things I kept remembering that had me tossing and turning."

He buried his face in her hair and asked, "Like what?"

She loved the way his voice rumbled around in his broad chest, the vibrations as tempting as his hot breath on the side of her neck. "Your talented mouth and lethal lips. The calluses on your hands and the way you kept sweeping them along my sides and up to cup my breasts."

Good Lord, she was getting turned on remembering every touch, every taste. His arms tightened around her and he pressed his lips against the underside of her jaw. "Dan, wait!" she urged.

He groaned and molded his mouth to hers and her protests died as his tongue traced the line of her lips and dipped inside to tangle with hers.

His hands were hot, urgent.

Hers were desperate to touch, to take. "I can't," she moaned.

He lifted his lips but didn't back away. Poised to kiss her again, his lips a breath away from hers, he asked, "Why? Because I was stupid and afraid?"

She gave in to need and cupped the side of his face in her hand. "No. It's not that. Grace has me working overtime what with the rain last night."

The desire lingering in his dark gray eyes flared to life. "Then you still want me?"

"Oh yeah," she said, grabbing him by the face and kissing him like it was their last moment on Earth. When she came up for air, she asked, "Does that answer your question?"

He laughed and hugged her tight. "Yes, ma'am. I'd better let you go now, or neither one of us will be going anywhere today."

"Why can't I resist you?" She really wanted to know. He was good-looking, but it was what was inside of Dan that pulled at her.

"Must be my charm," he said with a straight face.

Their laughter diffused the sexual tension surrounding them. "I'd better take a look at that leak." He nodded, and she added, "And you keep your hands to yourself."

He grinned. "Yes, ma'am."

When she looked up at his ceiling, she knew that it wasn't going to be as simple as looking for a hole right above the spot where it had dripped all night.

"So do you think it's a cracked shingle or something?"

"Could be," she said, considering. "I'll know for sure once I get up on your roof."

He bristled. "You're not climbing up there," he said. "I've got to go to work; you'll be all alone here."

She turned around and looked up into his frowning

face. Was he worried about her doing her job? "I've done a number of jobs where the homeowner wasn't there."

"I sure as heck didn't picture you up on my roof today while I'm at school."

"But that's where the leak is," she said slowly.

"You're afraid of heights, Meg."

Oh, she thought, that was at the heart of his worry. "It's an occupational hazard in the home repair business. About one-third of our calls involve patching leaky roofs. You get used to it."

"What about what the sheriff said the other day at Edie and Bill's wedding?"

She shrugged. "I used to be terrified of heights."

"Meg," he said, reaching for her hand.

She let him envelope her hand in his much larger one. A sigh escaped before she could think to hold it in. His hand was strong, his grip firm… a workingman's hand. "What?"

"Don't go up on my roof when I'm not here, OK?"

"I've already adjusted my schedule and made you my first stop today." She squeezed his hand and slipped hers free. "I can't make Gracie go through the list and rearrange everything again. People are counting on me."

"Then let me call in and tell them I'm going to be late for my first period class."

"Dan, don't be stubborn. I go up on roofs all of the time; it's my job." She waited for him to argue.

He stared down at her, fire banked in his stormy eyes. She didn't want to know exactly what he was thinking; it would distract her when she was up on his roof. "Be careful," he warned.

"Always am." She touched his arm briefly before

easing past him and heading downstairs. She had climbed onto the peak and was inspecting the ridge for damage when she heard him backing out of the driveway.

Relieved that he'd left her to do her job, she got down to business tracking the possible locations where the damaged shingle could be. Close inspection proved her first theory that it was near the peak of the roof. "Roofing tar will take care of it on the outside."

Half an hour later she'd finished up and was about to climb down when she heard a car door close. She looked down and sighed as her father got out of his truck. How long had he been here? Dan must have been really worried and called the shop. Pop knew she didn't like heights, but hadn't shadowed her on roofing jobs in a long time.

She made her way down the extension ladder, bucket of tar in one hand and mason's trowel in the other.

"Megan," her father called out. "Take your time."

"I always do, Pop." When she got to the ground, she set the tar down, grabbed a hold of the rope, and unhooked the ladder mechanism. When it was closed, she carted it over to her grandfather's pickup and slid it onto the rack. "How long have you been here?"

He grinned. "Awhile. Nice young man, Dan Eagan." He was watching her like a hawk, and she his prey. "He's going to be stopping by Saturday afternoon to help me work on the Model A, after he helps Miss Trudi at the garden center." He waited a moment before asking, "Did you know that he has four of his team meeting him there to help out?"

She smiled. "No, he didn't mention it, but I'm not surprised."

"He's got a good heart, Meggie."

She agreed. "It's hard not to notice. He's been open and friendly to everyone I've introduced him to."

"Is that all you've noticed?"

She laughed. "Nice try, Pop, but I'm pleading the fifth." She fetched the tar and stowed it along with her toolbox. "I've got to leave Dan a note telling him to let the ceiling dry out for a few days, then I'll take another look at it and see what's to be done. I know I don't have to tell you that you have to be careful with plaster."

He followed her into the house. "He seemed concerned about you being up on his roof." His gaze met hers and he asked, "Is there more here than meets the eye?"

She shook her head. "I've got a long list of calls today. Can we talk later?" She'd scribbled the note and was halfway out the door before her father followed.

"Meg, it's a simple question."

"Pop—" she began and then paused, deciding to give him as honest an answer as she could. "He has my head in a spin and my heart beating double-time."

"Really?" he said. "Then I'll have to make sure I keep an eagle eye on him tomorrow." He opened the driver's side door for her and said, "I told him I wanted to start working on the engine—"

"Checking to see what can be salvaged beneath the hood?"

Her father nodded, watching her intently.

She reached for the door and closed it. Rolling down the window, she smiled up at her father. "Pop, you're so easy to read, but give it up because you know that no matter how I feel about him, if you didn't like him and the way he was salivating over the Model A, you wouldn't have invited him to come over and play under the hood."

He lifted his eyes heavenward. "If only women were are easy to figure out. You surely try my patience, Meggie."

"I'm not trying to. It's just that I'm afraid to hope for too much, too fast. I don't want to jinx things. I really like him."

"Don't wait too long to do something about it." Her father's eyes got that faraway look in them again. When he realized that he'd checked out for a moment, he shrugged and said, "Life's too short."

When she remained silent, he added, "Check in with Grace. I think she's had a cancellation today, something about somebody having the stomach flu."

"No problem," Meg said. "See you later."

He nodded and stepped back.

Meg put the truck in gear and started to roll forward. She put it in neutral, stepped on the brake, and leaned out the window. "Thanks for hanging around while I was on the roof, Pop."

His smile lit his entire face and suddenly Meg's day seemed brighter. Backing out of Dan's driveway she knew she had a long day ahead of her, but if she didn't dawdle between jobs, she just might be able to meet Honey B. and hang around while she met date number two.

She'd found and repaired the leaky pipe in Mrs. Hawkins's basement and had tackled the next two jobs on her agenda before she let herself take a lunch break. She checked her messages and felt all warm and gooey inside. There were three from Dan and every one of them was more insistent than the last that she check in with him. She must have forgotten and left her phone on vibrate again, or else she would have known she had a few calls and checked them sooner.

"He cares," she said, as she shot off a text to him, telling him that she was fine. She remembered to thank him for calling her father and asking him to hang around while she was on Dan's roof.

He answered right away. She laughed when she read his text: I was about to call the sheriff to have him check up on you.

She texted back. What about my dad?

Your dad said you were fine when you left my house.

Finishing up her ham and swiss on rye, she drank the rest of the coffee in her thermos and sent one more text; she had to keep to her time schedule. Got a full schedule. You don't have to worry about me, but I'm glad you do.

His answer was short and sweet. I care, Meg. See you later.

Five hours later, she had a knot between her shoulder blades and her hands ached, but she'd made it to all of her appointments; the one cancellation had rescheduled for Monday.

She was stowing her tools when her sister walked in. "Hey, Caitlin, how was your day?"

Her sister smiled. "Arms are sore from working overhead for the last few hours, but the new ceiling looks great. Just needs to be sanded." She was watching Meg closely when she asked, "So what's this I hear from Pop that Dan was worried about you being on his roof?"

Meg shook her head. "Why is it that the men in our lives worry about us being up on the roof but get insulted when we worry about them being up there?"

Caitlin's eyes gleamed with amusement. "Men think they are the only ones who can fix things—and climb up on the roof. I think it's kind of nice that Dan was worried."

Meg wiped her hands on the rag in her back pocket and finished putting away the extra supplies she'd used that day. "I'm not used to it, but yeah," she said, looking over her shoulder at her sister. "It is nice."

"Meg—"

"Can we talk later, Cait? I've got to go meet Honey B."

Her sister nodded and called out, "My money's on the sheriff."

Meg was laughing when she got to her truck. Her phone rang as she was walking up the stairs to her apartment. "Hey, Honey B., what's up?"

"My date cancelled, so you can relax tonight."

"OK," Meg said. "Are you good with that?"

Honey B. laughed. "Yes, I've had a long day and a few irritating phone calls from the sheriff. I'm about done in."

"Has he confessed his undying love for you yet?"

Honey B. snickered and said, "Not yet, damn him."

"I'm going to hit the showers then," Meg said. "Call me if you need to talk."

"Thanks. Talk to you later."

As they said good-bye, Meg disconnected and changed her mind. "Why shower when there's a perfectly good tub just waiting to be filled with hot water?"

She pulled off her sweatshirt and work shirt and left them at the top of the steps. She bent down and untied her work boots, toed them off, and left them in the kitchen by the tiny bistro table. Two steps later her overalls joined her boots on the kitchen floor. Even though the muscles in her upper back were screaming, she pulled her T-shirt over her head and dropped it in the hallway.

The freedom to leave her clothes wherever she wanted made her giggle like a little girl. She walked into the bathroom and stretched, trying to work the kinks out. The hot water would take care of the aches, and what a good soaking didn't fix… well, there was always aspirin.

She cranked the hot water on, let a trickle of cold keep it from scalding, and added her favorite fragrance beneath the gush of water coming out of the spigot, smiling as it made bubbles on top of bubbles. Slipping out of her black lace bikini bottoms, she unhooked her bra and tossed it on top of her panties.

Dipping her toe in to test the temperature she moaned. "Oh Lord, this feels sinful." Sinking into the hot, fragrant bubbles, she let her worries go while the hot water eased some of the deep-seated ache between her shoulder blades. Her cell phone rang, but she ignored it; whoever it was could call back. She wasn't moving until her fingers were pruney and the water was cold.

The shiver woke her. "I can't believe I fell asleep." Now that she was awake, she realized how cool the water was. She debated draining some of the water and adding hot, but she might fall asleep again and end up right back where she was right now. The rumbling of her empty stomach was the deciding factor.

"Time to get out and rustle up something to eat." Too bad her talents only extended from heating up a can of soup to scrambling eggs. But as long as she had either one in her kitchen, she wouldn't go hungry.

Wrapped in the bath towel, she bent over to pick

up her underwear and heard someone knocking on her door. "Honey B. must have changed her mind and needs to talk." Although why she'd knock and not just come in, she had no idea. "Door's open," she called out.

With one hand holding the towel around her and the other spilling with black lace, she walked down the hallway intending to grab the rest of her clothes and nearly swallowed her tongue. Dan stood in her kitchen with her T-shirt in one hand and her overalls in the other.

"Meg."

The raspy sound of her name had her belly fluttering and her juices flowing. The depth of Dan's voice reminded her of the way his lips had devoured hers just that morning. She wanted to ask him what he was doing here but couldn't quite get her brain to function—it was on sensory overload.

His eyes darkened to charcoal, the promise of passion calling to her. He stared at her clothes for a moment before draping them over the back of a chair. He scrubbed his hands over his face before saying, "You didn't answer your phone," he said. "I was worried."

"I was in the tub." Why would he drive over here just because she didn't pick up her phone? "I don't always pick up my phone, Dan." Her gaze met his and she would later swear she saw something vulnerable flicker in the depths for a moment and then was gone. "Is something wrong? Is it one of the boys on your team?"

He raked a hand through his hair and stared at her. "No."

"Is it your family?"

He shook his head and took a step closer. "You've been on my mind all day and I couldn't get past what the sheriff said about you hating heights. When you didn't answer your phone and I couldn't talk to you, I decided to come see for myself that you weren't suffering from a delayed stress thing."

She stared up at his face and saw the worry he wasn't quick enough to hide. Humbled that he cared and sensing that it went deeper than mere concern for a friend, she told him, "It isn't always easy. Sometimes I don't get dizzy at all if I'm slow and careful. I've been working on the roofs of nearly everyone in Apple Grove for the last decade without a mishap. You didn't have to worry, but I'm awfully glad you did."

He walked toward her and asked, "How did you get over your fear? Most people never do."

She swallowed past the growing lump in her throat and clenched the black lace tight in her hand; the need to grab hold of him and never let go swept up from her toes.

He reached for her and pulled her against the solid warmth of his body. "You're an amazing woman, Meg. I know it wasn't easy for you, but yet you still do what needs to be done without complaint. That's admirable."

The nasty, edgy fear she'd bottled up inside of her all day bubbled slowly to the surface… She didn't know what to do with it there… she was used to keeping it to herself.

His big hands roamed across her back and shoulders, finding the knot of tension that had returned and just wouldn't go away. "You're tense." Without asking, he started to knead the spot and slid his other hand to the base of her spine, pinning her against him.

The tight knot opened and slowly gave way under his ministrations. Meg sighed and snuggled closer. "You have amazing hands." The memory of where those powerful hands had caressed and how he'd gentled his touch, tuning it to correspond with her sighs, filled her until she couldn't stop herself from asking, "Are you here to just check up on me, or are you planning on spending the night?"

His hands stilled on her back and he sighed. "I hadn't planned on staying the night." He eased her out of his arms and confessed, "Meg... I don't mean to turn you on and off like a faucet."

She could see the play of emotions he was too tired to hide and tried to lighten things up. She was ready to open her arms to him but had a feeling he needed a little more time to work it all out in his head. If only he would open up and talk to her about his past, maybe she could help him get past it. "I love it when you talk plumbing."

When he just stared at her, she said, "I'll still be here when you're ready to take that step back to where we left off."

"It's not you, Meg—" he began, only to shake his head and take a step back from her.

Her body ached in every single spot he'd touched with his hands, his mouth, and his heart. Being noble just might drive her over the deep end. She needed him to understand where she was coming from. "I've been existing for so long that I didn't realize I wasn't fully alive until the other night. Dan, you touched a part of me that I thought had died."

He looked at his feet and then back up to meet her gaze. "I didn't mean to."

"God, I hope you did because I've never felt so wonderful in my life." He lifted his gaze and the flicker of indecision she saw hurt. She was so sure about him. "I want to share what's inside of me with you, Dan, if you'll let me."

A piece of her heart hardened and chipped off when he remained silent. She wouldn't beg for scraps—she wanted it all. "I believe in what we could have enough that I'm willing to give you more time to make up your mind. Just don't take too long deciding that you want it—or me."

"You're making this harder than it has to be."

She waited until his troubled gaze met hers. "That's where you're wrong. I'm making it easy offering you everything."

"Meg, I want you so bad it hurts," he told her. "But I can't afford to make another mistake—you mean too much to me."

With that glimmer of hope, she struggled to smile and found that she could. "You're worth the wait, Dan."

He nodded and turned to go. She closed the door. With her back against it, she waited until she heard the sound of footsteps walking away from her. Footsteps that paused on the stairs.

When his car started, she sank to the floor and let her head rest on her knees. It had taken every bit of her control to keep from jumping into his arms and kissing him senseless. He needed the gift of time, and she was going to give it to him, but that didn't stop her from feeling drained, weak, and sorry for herself.

Wondering if Honey B. might need someone to talk to, she pushed to her feet. Dressed in comfy sweats, she found her phone and dialed her friend's number.

"Hey, Honey B.," she said. "It's me."

"Hey, you. Is everything alright?"

Tears gathered in the corner of her eyes, but she ignored them. "I'm not sure," she confided. "Dan was just here."

"Did he take what he wanted and then leave you all alone?" her friend teased.

"Well," Meg said slowly, "you're right about the second part."

Honey B. was silent for a moment before she asked, "So he's still keeping his distance?"

"Yeah." Meg wished she could do something to push Dan back into her arms where she wanted him. "Is it me?" she finally asked.

"Oh, sweetie," her friend rasped. "Not a chance. You are one in a million. Gorgeous, talented, and wonderful. If he can't see that, he's not the man for you."

Meg laughed as the words she so often told Honey B. were quoted back to her. "You're pretty smart, you know that?"

Honey B. chuckled. "It must've been those powerful vibes you're sending my way that had me whipping up a batch of fudge. How about if I bring some over and we can trash-talk Dan Eagan and Mitch Wallace?"

Gratitude filled Meg. "I'll make the cocoa."

Her friend snickered. "A woman can never have too much chocolate."

"Thanks, Honey B."

"Dig into your collection of chick flicks and pull out a couple of good ones. I'm spending the night."

Chapter 11

DAN SPENT ANOTHER RESTLESS NIGHT ALONE, AND FOR the life of him couldn't remember why it had been so important to keep the distance between himself and the woman he craved. They'd enjoyed dinner and had chatted about a lot of different things, although the main focus had been Honey B. and her date. Still he'd felt the need to keep that space between them.

His hesitation was going to push Meg away—and that's not what he wanted to do. He needed her more than he'd ever needed anyone before. Why couldn't he just go with what his heart was telling him? Why couldn't he trust his gut? What was his problem?

He tried to sort through the morass of feelings inside while he shaved. "Ouch, damn it!" His chin bled where he'd nicked it with the razor.

"I'm an idiot." His reflection grimaced but didn't disagree. "I've got to talk to someone who will understand where I'm coming from." But who? He hadn't been in town long enough to trust anyone's judgment... except for the sheriff. But Wallace had his own problems, mostly centering around the current crop of teenagers gearing up to make the most of their senior year and keeping an eye on Honey B.

He could always go visit with his aunt, but then he'd run the risk of whatever he said circulating through the gossip mill—maybe that wasn't such a bad idea.

Dressed and on his second cup of coffee, he decided not to call his aunt; it would be better if he dropped by the garden center. A quick glance at his watch told him that he had enough time for a short visit before heading to school.

Driving through town, he slowed down to obey the speed limit, but also to get a good look at the town waking up and getting ready to meet the day. The Apple Grove Diner was bustling with early morning customers. He'd have to make it a point to stop in to have a piece of the McCormack sisters' pie. He wondered if their crust tasted different than his grandmother's... maybe he could offer a chance to compare his secret ingredients with theirs.

Honey's Hair Salon was still closed, but there were a couple of cars outside of Murphy's Market. He smiled, remembering the way the guests at the wedding had referred to her as the Widow Murphy and not Mrs. Murphy. He grinned at the sight of the fire-engine red F-350 parked in front of the sheriff's office. The sheriff knew how to make a statement. If you saw that big red pickup in your rearview mirror with the lights flashing, you knew you were in major trouble.

He smiled as he pulled up to the garden center and saw a familiar figure in khaki jodhpurs, crisp white blouse, and Wellingtons standing out front with her back to the road, a pot of flowers in each hand. He slowed down and pulled into her gravel parking lot.

Trudi Philo looked over her shoulder and smiled in welcome and he knew he'd made the right decision coming here this morning. He put it in park and got out. "Morning, Aunt Trudi."

"Daniel." She beamed. "What brings you here today? It's Friday, isn't it? I thought you were coming tomorrow morning." She set the pots down and rearranged the display she must have been working on when he pulled up.

He stuck his hands in his pockets and rocked back on his heels. "I still am and the boys are still coming with me. I, um…" He hesitated for a moment then blurted out, "I need to ask your advice about something."

She stared up at him for a few moments before she answered, "Grab those two pots over there for me please and tell me what's going on with Megan. You didn't give her those flowers, did you?"

"I got distracted and they wilted." He moved a few more pots before she was satisfied. "I don't know what to do about her."

A knowing smile lifted her lips. "Aside from what most young men with their sap on the rise want to do."

He opened his mouth to speak and then ended up shaking his head. "I don't want to hurt her, Aunt Trudi."

His aunt linked her arm through his and patted his hand. "I know you don't, Daniel dear, but by stepping back from what you've already started you already have."

He stopped and looked at her. "How do you know?"

"I have my ways, young man. Now tell me what you're going to do to salvage your relationship with Megan."

"That's just it. Every time I think I'm ready, I remember what happened back home—I don't want that to happen between Meg and me."

"Now, Daniel," she said, tugging on his arm to get him to stop walking. "Have you talked to her about it?"

Miserable with the way things were working out, he

shook his head. She tapped her finger to her lips and finally said, "That's the problem, you know."

Dan tried to replay their conversation in his head so he'd know what the heck she was talking about. He finally had to ask, "What is?"

Her laugh was infectious; soon he was chuckling too without knowing why.

"Land sakes, Daniel, you need to get to work."

He looked at his watch. "I still have time—"

She was shaking her head at him. "I wasn't talking about your job, I was talking about Megan. You need to get to work building your relationship with the girl; otherwise, she'll think you're only interested in one thing—and whether or not that's true at the moment, if you want your relationship to last, you need to build that foundation on solid ground."

Her words sank in and made sense.

"She needs you to give her a reason to trust you."

"Too late."

She hugged him and then smacked him in the back of the head. "It's never too late to trust her with your past, so she can understand why you are acting like a complete idiot right now."

He stared at her, wanting to tell her to mind her own business, but knew he wouldn't because Aunt Trudi was right. "I guess I am."

"And that, my dear, is half the battle. Once you've talked to Megan, come back and I'll tell you what else you need to know about her."

"Why can't you tell me now?"

"If you don't get going, I just might not tell you. Now get to school so I don't have to hear from the Board of Education that my recommendation for their phys ed teacher isn't reliable."

He bent and kissed her on the cheek. "Thanks, Aunt Trudi. See you in the morning!"

He thought about his aunt's words in between classes and before practice. They had an away game tonight against Newark High, so he wouldn't have a chance to have a talk with Meg until after the game. He couldn't afford to be distracted. He owed his team his full concentration, and whenever he started to think about Meg, he simply lost all perspective.

Setting thoughts of the fiery, auburn-haired distraction aside, he focused on getting the team to work together and perfect their skills.

―⁓―

Grace cornered Meg in the shop. "Sooo… spill."

Meg was still jittery from chocolate overload the night before and not in the best of moods. She pretended she had no idea what her sister meant. "About what?"

Her sister flushed, a sure sign that her Irish was up. Grace's next words confirmed Meg's suspicion. "You know what I'm talking about."

Meg pretended not to notice and prodded her sister to lose her temper. "I think we'll need to reorder some pipe dope and some roofing tar—"

Grace's eyes flashed a warning, although her voice remained calm, "Don't be difficult."

"Just following your strict reorder policy, Sis. When I use something up, I'm supposed to tell you about it."

"Damn it, Meg, what's going on with that hunkalicious soccer coach?"

Caitlin walked in and grinned. "Need a referee?"

"We're not fighting," Meg told her.

"We're about to," Grace bit out. "Meg won't talk about Dan."

"Ah," Caitlin said. "The hometown hero."

Meg rolled her eyes. "I'm not having this conversation with you, Grace."

Her sister put her hands on her hips and got in Meg's way. Instead of sinking to Grace's level, she stepped around her younger sister and waved. "I've got to go. Got a dinner date tonight."

"With Dan?" Grace called out.

Meg didn't even bother to turn around. As she got into her dad's truck, she sighed. "There isn't anything new going around about us."

Rather than sink into a depression, she realized that she'd better get a move on if she was going to pick up Honey B. and drive over to the soccer game in Newark. It wasn't that she wanted to see Dan that much—well, OK, she really did want to see him and it was definitely a side benefit, but Honey B. had asked her to double date with Pat Garahan and one of his coworkers from the firehouse the other day before she and Dan has sorted things out. How could she say no when Honey B. was always there for her? Besides, she'd promised that she'd have Honey B.'s back when her friend had decided to do this online dating thing.

Meg switched to hands-free mode and dialed Honey B. When her friend answered, she said, "I'll be there in five."

"Great. I'm wearing my navy blue wrap dress. Want to wear the black one?"

Pat had already seen Honey B. wear the black dress, so

it didn't really matter if Meg wore it tonight. She wasn't out to impress anyone—well, anyone at the restaurant, but maybe afterward, when she got back to Apple Grove, if she could convince Dan to come on over. But that would remain to be seen. She reminded herself that she was going as a favor to Honey B. and concentrated on that. "Only if I can borrow your shoes again."

"One of these days, Meg, I'm dragging you shopping."

Meg laughed. "Many before you have tried."

She pulled up out back and dashed inside. Honey B. was holding out the dress, but when she got a good look at Megan she shrieked. "Oh my God, what happened to you?"

Meg looked down at herself and sighed. She'd forgotten about the rotten gutter that had broken when she was doing a repair on the Peterson's front light. "Long story—"

"Never mind that now. I'll call Pat and tell him we'll be a little late. You go grab a quick shower."

Meg didn't stop to ask questions; she dashed to the far back of Honey B.'s shop and closed the door. She'd stripped and was under the hot spray in the miniscule shower stall when she heard her friend call out, "I left a towel on the toilet seat."

"Be right out."

True to her word, she was washed, dried, and dressed in under ten minutes. "Good thing I don't need any makeup; it'll save time."

Honey B. drew in a breath and huffed, "I'll drive and you'll borrow my mascara, blush, and lip gloss. No way are you going to show up looking like a teenager."

"Jeez, you're bossy."

A half hour later they'd parked next to the field. "They're already playing," Honey B. said as she got out. "Come on."

Meg looked down at her form-fitting black dress and spiky heels and wondered when her friend had lost her mind. She rolled down the window. "I'll wait here."

Honey B. stopped, spun around, and stalked back over to the car. "You are coming with me. I didn't drag you here to let you sit in the car. I'm not entertaining Pat and his friend… whatever his name is by myself." She glared at Meg. "You promised."

Meg sighed. "I hate dresses."

Honey B. opened the door and soothed, "I know you do, but you're doing this for the greater good."

"Yeah," Meg grumbled. "Yours."

"You got that right." Honey B. laughed and waved. "There they are—whoa. Hold on to your hairpins, girlfriend. Tall, dark, and gorgeous at three o'clock."

Meg got out and stood next to Honey B. When Meg's mouth finally closed, she leaned close and whispered, "Holy crap."

Honey B. frowned at her. "For Pete's sake, Meg, remember what I said about first impressions."

"Honey, Megan," Pat said, walking toward them. "You ladies look great!" He grinned and turned to his friend. "Mike, these are the ladies I was telling you about."

Mike was tall and broad; his muscles had muscles. "I'm glad to see that for once Garahan didn't exaggerate." His eyes twinkled as his smile broadened. "You ladies are everything he promised and more."

"Knock it off, Snelling, don't embarrass my new friends." Pat turned toward Honey B. and Meg and sighed. "Mike's got a big mouth but there's not another firefighter I'd rather have watching my back."

They all laughed, and Meg noticed that even though Mike couldn't keep his eyes off of Honey B., her friend was friendly and attentive, as always, but that was it. There was only one man that lit that special spark between himself and Honey B. Whenever Honey B. and the sheriff were within ten feet of one another, those two could start a brush fire with one look. *Dan was right*.

"How's the game going?" she asked.

Pat's face looked serious as he told her, "No score. The teams are evenly matched so far. We'll see how things go once the players start getting tired."

While she and Pat watched the game, Mike kept Honey B. busy talking. Meg didn't mind; she was more interested in the outcome of the soccer game anyway. When the ball shot past them to the other end of the field, she knew Dan had seen her standing on the sidelines, but he ignored her.

As if Honey B. could read her mind, she leaned close and whispered, "He's here as a coach. Don't distract him."

Meg smiled as her friend had intended.

"Whoa, yellow card!" Pat grumbled. "Kid should have known better than to take the Apple Grove player out from behind. Whether he meant to or not is something he and his coach will be talking about later."

Meg didn't know much about soccer; she knew more about baseball. "Is a yellow card bad?"

Pat nodded. "It's a warning from the ref. One more and the player could receive a red card and be out for the rest of this game and all of the next."

"But aren't there enough players to substitute?"

Pat explained, "A red card means you cannot substitute; you play one man down."

"But that would give the other team an advantage," Meg said. "That doesn't sound fair."

"Receiving a yellow or red card means that the player did something that wasn't fair or legal in the first place."

"OK," Meg said. "So number twenty-two will have to be careful not to take anybody else out then."

Mike grinned. "Pretty and smart. Great combination, Pat. Thanks for bringing me."

Meg shook her head and turned back to watch the game, only to see that Dan was frowning in her direction and that the play had moved past her, to the other end of the field again, when the defender cleared the ball. She looked behind her to see if he was looking at someone else. When she looked back, he had turned to follow the play and was shouting encouragement to Apple Grove's offense.

"Maybe I imagined it."

"Imagined what?" Pat asked.

She looked up at him and smiled. "Nothing." Pat didn't look as if he believed her, but that wasn't her problem. *Dan Eagan is*. He was tying her up in knots.

The game ended in a draw. Both teams had played all out, so Meg knew that the team bus ride back to Apple Grove would be a boisterous one. She missed those days. It had been years since she'd played on the field hockey team. With a glance in Honey's direction, she could tell her friend was having similar thoughts. But they weren't kids any longer.

"Hey, Mike," Pat called out. "Wait up. I want to congratulate the coach."

Before she could refuse, Honey B. had her by the hand and was following along behind Pat, who was headed toward the two men standing in the middle of the field. The coaches were talking and smiling. Pat called the other coach by name and the man turned and called out, "Garahan! Glad you could make it today."

"Pat?"

"Hey, Dan. Good game."

Dan's gaze tracked past Pat and got stuck on Meg—had she come here to watch the game with the guy? "Er… thanks, Pat."

"Were you on your way home from the firehouse?" the other coach asked.

Pat shook his head. "Mike and I are off tonight and having dinner with two fine-looking women."

The other coach smiled, but Dan didn't want to hear him agreeing. He knew that Meg was beautiful. Honey was pretty, but she wasn't his concern right now; Meg was. "Could I talk to you for a minute, Meg?"

She looked like she was about to refuse, but Honey B. prodded her toward him. He'd have to thank the woman later. "Did you change your mind?" he bit out.

She shook her head. "Of course not."

"Then why are you dressed to kill and going out to eat with Pat and his friend?"

"I made a promise to Honey B. to watch her back when she began the online dating. I can't back out now."

He scrubbed his hands over his face.

She looked up at him and crossed her arms beneath her breasts. Did she do that on purpose to torment him? *Damn it!*

"Hey, Dan," Pat called out. "My friend Mike here

and a few of the guys are going to drive over to Apple Grove next week. Did you get a group of guys to play us yet?"

The tension left Dan by degrees—and with it, his jealousy. "Yeah," he said, looking from Meg to where the others were still standing. "How's Thursday sound?"

Pat and Mike were smiling at him. "Be ready to lose."

Dan didn't think it was possible, but he laughed. Shaking his head, he looked at Meg. "Can I come over tonight? There's something I want to talk to you about."

"I've got another full day tomorrow. I'm not planning on staying up late."

"It won't take long," he promised. "I've got a couple of things I need to tell you."

Meg leaned in close and whispered, "Are you going to try to talk your way into my bed tonight, Dan?"

He grinned. "Actions speak louder than words, Meg."

She smiled at him. "I should be home around ten o'clock."

"I'll be waiting for you." He reached out and grabbed a hold of her hand and squeezed it. "Thanks, Meg."

"Hungry over here," Pat called out, making Meg laugh.

Dan's guts tied themselves into square knots. He wanted to be the one to make her laugh... and make her sigh. He knew how to do the latter; now he had to learn how to do the former.

The next few hours were the longest of his life—not counting the night he'd spent waiting for his ex to show up, but he tried not to relive that night too often. He'd have to bring it up when he and Meg sat down. A look at his kitchen clock told him he still had some time, but he was restless and needed to do something or he'd lose his mind. Grabbing his keys, he headed for the back door and was in his car heading to town before he could decide whether or not it was a good idea.

"I'll look like a dork waiting outside her apartment for an hour." He had time to kill and no one to spend it with. Needing to do something with his hands, he decided to stop at the diner for a cup of coffee. Now might be as good a time as any to talk to the McCormack sisters about their piecrust.

He opened the door to the diner and smiled. The two ladies in question were behind the counter serving up coffee and pie.

"Well, well, if it isn't the coach," Peggy drawled. "Heard Apple Grove played a good game today. Congratulations."

"Thanks, Peggy. The guys played well."

"What'll it be?" Katie asked, bringing a full pot of what had to be fresh coffee over to where he sat at the counter.

"I'm back for another slice of your pecan pie." When Katie and Peggy smiled, he did too.

"Whipped cream or ice cream?"

Now that was a choice he hadn't considered. "I'll have it plain this time."

Peggy grinned. "Planning on coming back for more, now that's a plan I can get behind."

He added milk and sugar to his coffee, blew across the top of it, and sipped. "Good coffee."

"So we've heard," Katie said, serving up his pie. The sisters stood there waiting while Dan slid his fork into the pie and scooped up a bite. The decadent flavor hit his tongue all at once, so that his taste buds were momentarily stunned.

The pie was the perfect consistency—not runny—and

the pecans were in perfect halves—not chopped. Add in the flaky piecrust and he was in heaven. He savored, chewed, swallowed, and immediately took another bite.

"Get his picture, Katie," Peggy said. "I want to post it on the Internet. It'll be great for business."

Dan swallowed his second mouthful and drank some coffee. "Ladies, that is one amazing pie. I like to cook," he told them. "My grandmother taught me a few things about baking that my mom didn't know. One of them is her super-secret piecrust recipe."

Katie had taken two pictures of him and was busy posting them to the Internet, so Peggy asked, "How does it stand up to ours?"

He shook his head. "Yours is good, but I think my grandmother's recipe is better. From the first bite though, I can tell you it was delicious."

"Why don't we put your pie to the test?" Peggy suggested.

Dan shrugged. "I'm game."

"We always bake the pies for the turkey supper the church puts on every November. Why don't you donate a couple and we'll have a taste testing? I think that would add a nice touch to the supper this year. Rally the town around the local favorites—my sister and me—and the new hometown hero—you."

He smiled and felt his competitive self pumping his fist in the air. "I'd love to. I'll wager my mom's apple pie, my grandmother's buttered pecan pie, and her sweet potato praline."

Peggy held out her hand. "Deal."

Katie smiled and put her hand on top of their joined ones.

No one noticed the group of teenagers standing in the doorway or the fact that their phones were recording the moment for posterity—that and the front page of the *Apple Grove Gazette*.

"Hey, Miss Peggy," one of the girls sang out as she walked inside with her friends.

"Hello, ladies," she answered. "The usual?"

They smiled and nodded. "We'll take it to go, though."

Dan noticed the look of surprise on Peggy's face but got distracted when Katie asked him if he wanted more coffee. He declined.

Fifteen minutes later, he was back in his car and sitting in the driveway waiting for Meg.

The knock on the window startled him; he must have dozed off waiting. He rubbed his eyes and rolled down the window. "Hey."

She smiled. "Hey, yourself. Have you been waiting long?"

"What time is it?"

She shrugged. "I'm not sure; I need a battery for my watch."

He looked at his and frowned. "It's a quarter to eleven." No wonder he'd fallen asleep waiting. "I've been here over an hour."

"Oh… sorry. We got talking and lost track of time. Honey B. and I were talking about it and we think we should introduce Pat and his friend Mike to Caitlin and Grace. What do you think?"

He nodded. "Sounds promising."

He paused and she asked, "Do you still want to talk to me, or would you rather wait until tomorrow?"

He was so tired his eyes were having trouble focusing.

"I'd like to get it over with." As soon as the words left his mouth, he realized that wasn't the best way to put it, but he was tired, damn it.

"Sounds ominous."

When he didn't respond, she motioned for him to follow her. He got out and stretched before heading up the stairs. She already had the coffee brewing by the time he reached the top step.

"Isn't it too late for coffee?"

She grinned. "It's decaf and I needed something warm to drink."

Meg stood on her tiptoes to reach down two mugs. Dan couldn't help but appreciate the subtle curves of her body. He wanted to get his hands on her but knew they had things to sort through first. He had to look away because the temptation was too much.

She filled the cups with the steaming brew and asked, "Milk and two sugars, right?" When he didn't answer right away, she looked over her shoulder. "Are you OK?"

He ran his hands through his hair to hide that fact that they were shaking. "Yeah, just tired I guess. Milk and two sugars is great. Thanks."

She turned around and he couldn't help but get side-tracked by her soft blue eyes.

He'd lost his mind; it wasn't such a short trip after all. "Meg, I'm really tired and can't stay long. Do you mind if I just say it outright?"

She sipped from her mug and nodded.

"I was engaged to be married a couple of years ago." When she didn't do more than raise one eyebrow, he continued, "I guess it was fortunate that I found out she was cheating on me... the unfortunate part was that it was with my best friend."

Meg set her cup down and reached for his hand. Grasping it in her much smaller one, she said, "Dan... I'm so sorry."

"Well, that's part of what has my head in a spin, Meg. I want you so bad it hurts, but I'm not sure I'm ready to get involved again—it's too soon for me. Besides, my grandfather is only just now starting to talk to me."

"I see. Was he very fond of your ex-fiancée?"

"What? Uh... no. It was the Mickey Mantle rookie card."

"My dad mentioned something about a baseball card the other day, but what does a baseball card have to do with your ex?"

He sighed and pulled out a chair for her to sit on and then his own. "I have to sit down for this." When they were seated across from one another he set his cup down and wiped his palms on his thighs. He knew it was a nervous reaction—hell, he could feel the tension ramping up inside him. He had to just spit it out before he lost his nerve.

"I couldn't afford the ring my ex wanted, so I pawned the Mickey Mantle rookie card my great-grandfather had given to me before he died with the understanding that I'd be making payments to the pawnbroker until I could pay to get the card back."

"What does that have to do with your grandfather?"

"I'm getting to that." He drew in a deep breath. "My grandfather wanted that card, but he'd argued with his dad and to spite him, my great-grandfather gave the card to me—not to my father or my grandfather, but to me."

"I guess that caused a bit of a problem at the time."

He sighed. "Yeah, but not as big a problem as when I went back to make the last payment on the card and found out the pawnshop had sold it for more than I'd pawned it for!"

"Oh my God! What did you do?"

"I saw my life flashing before my eyes and knew I was a dead man."

Meg scooted to the edge of her seat. "Don't keep me in suspense. What happened?"

"Because the guy stiffed me, he told me the name of the person who'd purchased my card. I figured I'd go after the guy and try to make a deal to buy the card back." His shoulders slumped forward as the memory of that day swamped him. "It was my ex–best friend—"

"The one who stole your fiancée?"

He swallowed against the lump of emotion clogging his throat. "Yep."

"Did he let you buy it back with the money you got for her ring?"

He snorted. "Hard to do when she flushed the damned ring down the toilet."

Meg's mouth opened and then closed. "She flushed the ring instead of giving it back?"

He sighed. "She figured she should keep the ring. I told her she figured wrong. I guess she showed me."

"I guess you never really know someone until their back is to the wall." She got up and walked over to him and cupped her hands on either side of his face. "The real losers are your ex and your ex-friend." She brushed her lips across his.

He felt the electric charge all the way to his toes. "I'm

hoping he'll see reason if I keep badgering him to buy the card back."

As if she sensed he was done talking about it, she slid onto his lap and wrapped her arms around him and laid her head on his shoulder. "Mean people suck."

He laughed so hard he had to grab Meg to keep her from falling off his lap. "Hey, are you OK?"

"You've got a great laugh," she said. She was staring at him and he had no idea what she expected to see. "There are so many great things about you aside from your laugh."

"Really? My ex only thought about spending my money, until she realized my ex-friend had more. So she drained me dry and made sure it would take me a year or so to recover."

"The bitch."

"Pretty much covers it."

"So you came to Apple Grove to forget her?"

Dan shrugged. "And to start over. I couldn't see myself living in the same town, running into her at the grocery store or the bank—it would be a constant reminder of the way she and my buddy raked me over the coals."

Meg kissed the end of his nose and pressed her cheek against his and sighed. "I'm sorry for the reasons that brought you out here but am so glad you're here."

He eased back and put his hands on her face. "Meg, I want so much from you, but I can't be wrong again—it would destroy me."

She lifted her lips and he took what she offered.

When he came up for air, he had to pull back or else he'd toss her over his shoulder and kidnap her. "You taste amazing."

She hugged him tight. "You're addictive." She drew

in a breath and said, "There's something else you need to know about Jimmy."

He rested his chin on top of her head and waited.

She sighed. "I thought I was going to marry him."

"Weren't you in high school at the time?"

"Yes, but I had lots of friends who got married right out of high school."

"Still… did you really know your heart at sixteen?"

She stiffened in his arms and he thought she wouldn't answer him, but gradually, she relaxed again. "I'd been so in love with him for so long. It took years to get over the fact that he wasn't coming back or going to ask me to marry him."

"It must have been hard."

"No one in town was surprised when the Bengals made him an offer, but they were when he decided he preferred city living. Everybody thought he'd be back during the off-season." She buried her face in his neck and confessed, "So many people were trying to console me that it had the reverse effect—I retreated from the dating scene for a long time."

"I know I don't have the right to ask, but before the other day… how long had it been since you've been involved with anyone?"

She pushed against his chest and glared at him. "How long has it been for you?"

His lips twitched. "Fair enough, Mulcahy."

She stood up and straightened her skirt. "I've got an early morning, Dan, so either come to bed or leave."

Every ounce of spit in his mouth dried up, making it hard to speak. "I… uh… maybe we could—"

"I promise not to jump your bones, unless you beg

me to. Come on." She tugged on his arm and he followed her to her room.

Meg undressed quickly. Standing before him in an
itty-bitty scrap of black lace, he wondered if he'd spon-
taneously combust. But she slipped an ancient T-shirt
over her head and put her hands on her hips. "You're
overdressed and I'm going to bed."

She slid under the covers and watched him. He wasn't
hung up on his body or anything, but having her watch
while he undressed felt weird. "Maybe you could close
your eyes."

"And miss out on the striptease? Not on your life."

He tried not to be charmed by her open appreciation
and failed. "Brace yourself, Megan," he warned right
before he toed off his shoes and drew his shirt over his
head. He let his fingers linger on the button to his jeans
before he worked it through the buttonhole. Her eyes
told him how much she enjoyed the show he was putting
on, so he amped it up, by slowly sliding the zipper down
one half inch at a time.

Meg's eyes widened as he tucked his thumbs in the
waistband and shoved his jeans to the floor.

"Those boxers are seriously sexy the way the hug
your... um... thighs."

He was grinning as he pulled off his socks.

She flipped back the covers. "About that promise..."

He pulled her into his arms and tucked her against
his heart. "I'm holding you to it for the next few hours.
I'm exhausted."

She wrapped her arms around him and sighed.

He pressed his lips beneath her ear and whispered,
"But I might let you change my mind come morning."

"If I have to keep my hands to myself, you have to keep your lips to yourself." She turned around and scooted her backside until it was cuddled in his lap.

"Megan Mulcahy, you are a dangerous woman."

The last sound he heard before sleep claimed him was Meg's lilting laughter.

Chapter 12

MEG OPENED HER EYES AND REACHED OUT TO TRACE the tip of her finger along Dan's jawline. Whiskers darkened his face and were surprisingly rough to the touch.

"Not a dream."

He didn't move, so she gave in to temptation and touched his bottom lip, outlining the shape with her fingertip. She didn't want to wake him just yet... she wanted to revel in the fact that a gorgeous hunk of man had spent the night in her bed and held her—all night.

Easing back just enough to free her other arm, she let her fingers do the walking and lightly followed the broad span of his shoulders.

Unable to resist, she brushed her hands over his pecs, marveling at the strength that she knew he possessed but wasn't obvious while he lay sleeping. She placed her hand over his heart; the strong, steady beat reassured her that he was here... for now.

"Are you going to break my heart?" Meg hoped he wouldn't but knew that one didn't always have a say in matters of the heart. "You'll still be worth it." With a sigh, she leaned forward to kiss him and her world turned upside down as Dan wrapped his arms around her and flipped her onto her back.

She narrowed her gaze at him. "You're not asleep."

"It was torture lying there while you touched me."

"Why did you?"

He leaned down and brushed his lips across her cheek. "It felt amazing to have your hands on me."

She reached up to run her hands over his shoulders and down his back, grabbing a hold of his excellent backside with both hands. "You're so hard—everywhere—I can't keep my hands to myself."

"You go to my head like a double shot of whiskey, Meg." He captured her mouth, teasing and tempting her with his wicked lips, teeth, and tongue. "I'm not sure what to do about you."

She smiled and slid her hands to his hips and kneaded them before slipping one hand between them. He was hot, hard, and more than a handful. "I've got a couple of ideas if you're interested."

He strangled on a breath. "Kiss me back, Meg."

How could she refuse? Their mouths fused and their tongues danced to the rhythm in her head. If she could spend the rest of her life kissing Dan Eagan, she'd be happy—or so she thought until he started to build a fire inside of her with those clever lips. There were a few other things she could do with him too.

She hadn't realized how sensitive her neck or the hollow of her throat was until Dan fanned the flames with the flick of his tongue and press of his lips. She tilted her head back and surrendered to the magic he wove around her.

—⁕—

Meg's beauty hit him in the gut. The soft smile on her face as she silently offered herself to him nicked his heart. He thought he was immune to love, having been vaccinated by his bitch of an ex, but the fiery-haired woman in his arms offered her love, her body, and her trust—all he had to do was to give her his in return. A relationship with Meg would be full of fire—he'd be a fool to back away from her.

He'd been protecting his heart, but with Meg he wanted to open that battered organ to the possibility of love. He leaned on his elbows and asked, "Will you trust me with your heart, Meg?" She slowly smiled. "I might bruise it a little before I figure it all out, but I promise to be careful with it."

"You're worth the risk, Dan." She wrapped her arms around his neck and pulled him back down. "Now shut up and kiss me."

He was laughing as he kissed her. Easing out of her arms, he leaned over the side of the bed but couldn't reach his jeans. "Hold that thought." He got out of bed, grabbed his jeans, and reached into the back pocket.

She giggled as he opened the foil packet with his teeth and covered himself. "Where's the fire?"

He climbed back into bed and nudged her legs apart. "Right here, baby." He suckled her breasts, moving from left to right and back again until she was writhing beneath him, begging him to take her.

"There's no one else, Meg." He waited a heartbeat before he slid home. Bathed in her heat, he withdrew slowly, encouraged by her breathy moans and the strength in the hands that tried to keep him from leaving her tight sheath.

He picked up the pace, slid his hands beneath her curvy backside, and lifted her up as he plunged deep.

"Oh my God—"

He dipped his head and nipped the side of her neck

as he thrust deep into the very heart of her. She moaned and rocked against him. She tightened her inner muscles around him, and he felt the heady rush of heat right before she ground out his name. He thrust into her again and again until the tight knot inside of him burst and he followed her over the edge into madness.

She came back to reality as he pulsed inside of her. "Seriously?" she asked, brushing a lock of hair out of his eyes.

He pinned her to the mattress with one thrust. "I wish we had more time this morning because I'm ready, willing, and able to please you again."

Her heart jolted at his words. "If we take a shower together, we could save time."

The bed shifted as he got up. He held out his hand to her. "Then let's not waste any more time talking."

She grabbed his hand and shrieked in surprise when he tossed her over his shoulder. Laughing, she told him, "It takes a couple of minutes for the water to get hot."

He set her on her feet inside the tub and turned on the taps. "Don't worry, I'll keep you warm."

Meg locked her knees to keep them from buckling as he caressed her body with his soapy hands.

"You're so beautiful."

His words were a balm to her healing heart. No matter what else happened between them, she would always have these stolen moments where they shared their hearts and their bodies.

Taking the soap from him, she worked up a lather and filled her hands with his backside first before working her way up to his shoulders and soaped her way back down to his erection. "No, you are," she teased, letting her hands glide the soap along the length of him.

"You're killing me," he gasped, moving them beneath the hot spray so they could rinse off.

She flicked her tongue across his left nipple and then the right. "But what a way to go."

He groaned and banded his arms around her. "Later. I need to eat or I'll never make it today. My aunt has a lot of work lined up for me."

She sighed, got out, and grabbed a fluffy orange towel. He took the towel from her and dried her off. "I like waking up with you, Meg."

Grabbing another towel, she grinned up at him. "I slept like a baby last night."

Capturing the droplets of water from his face first, she worked her way down his body, but when she reached his hips, he stopped her. "A man can only take so much provocation."

"Really?" She wondered about that but let it go. "How about if I start the coffee while you get dressed?"'

"Deal. I'll scrambled up a mess of eggs if you have them."

"That sounds wonderful. Thanks."

Fifteen minutes later they were sipping coffee and devouring the breakfast he'd made. "I didn't realize I was so hungry."

His smile was just this side of wicked. "We worked up an appetite this morning."

"I could get used to this," she confessed without thinking. "I'm not trying to force you into making a commitment, Dan, just because we've shared my bed."

"No," he said, reaching for her hand. "It's a relief to hear you say that because I feel the same way."

Hope blossomed in her heart, giving her the courage to ask him flat out, "What about taking your time?"

He shook his head. "I really messed up big time." He brought her hand to his lips and brushed a kiss on the back of it. "When I was telling you about everything that happened last night, it was as if a heavy burden was being lifted. It was a relief and everything just felt... right."

"This might be a small town, but not everyone knows that Jimmy and I had an understanding—sort of—and I kept waiting for him to ask that all important question. Until I met you, I hadn't realized how much of my life I was wasting, waiting for him."

"He's a major asshole and a fool." He stood and tugged on the hand he still held, urging Meg to her feet and into his arms. "There is one good thing about him leaving."

He slid his hand down to her backside and pressed her against the heat of his erection. His eyes darkened to charcoal, a sure sign that he was locked and loaded. But a tiny kernel of doubt had her lifting her gaze to his and asking, "Is this all there is between us?"

A bleak and desperate look flashed across his handsome face. "It's hard for me to share what I'm thinking and feeling, Meg," he confessed. "But I'm working on it. Will you give me a chance? I want to spend time with you and learn the things that make you laugh—I already know some of the things that make you cry, and I don't intend to let that happen again."

Tears filled her eyes, but Dan wasn't finished speaking. "You fill my thoughts from the time I open my eyes until the time I go to bed."

This time, the ache in her heart was from opening it up to the promise of love again. "I wasn't looking for a relationship, but then you showed up and I couldn't seem to keep from falling for you. I'm not used to having a man in my life on a regular basis. How do I fit you in? I'm usually at the shop by now and gone most of the day, exhausted by the time I get home. I don't know that I'll be very good company."

"I'm a man on a mission until soccer season is finished. We have a couple of tough weeks ahead working toward the States. Our guys are solid and want to win the championship as badly as I do—for Coach Creed."

"He'll be proud of the team's accomplishments either way."

"I'm not sure what I'll do with my afternoons once the season is over, but I'm open to suggestions."

Meg thought about it and offered one. "The whole town really gets into the holiday spirit once Halloween is over, starting with our church's annual turkey supper. I'm sure they would welcome your help—that you're a good cook is a huge bonus."

He looked surprised by her suggestion. Did he think it was woman's work?

"When Mr. Winter was alive, he helped his wife in the planning stages and in the kitchen. He used to chop a pile of celery and onions and peel a small mountain of potatoes every year."

He smiled. "I'd love to get involved. Do you think they'd mind my input? I'm the newcomer."

"They're a good group, and I know they'd love to have you."

He cradled her against him, holding her against the steady beat of his heart.

"Promise me one thing," she said. "If you are going to leave, tell me before you go."

He crushed her to him and buried his face in her hair. "I'm not going anywhere."

He hadn't promised, and she needed to hear him say the words. She wiggled around to get him to loosen his hold. "That's good to know, but not what I'm asking."

Their eyes met and she knew he was struggling to get the words out. He'd told her it wasn't easy for him, but this was too important to her. "Dan?"

He knew what she was asking and gave it to her. "I promise."

She wrapped her arms around him. "Thank you. Hey, I've got to go or I'll be late for my first job."

"Do you want to have dinner with me?"

She unplugged the coffeemaker and looked over her shoulder. "Are you cooking?"

He smiled. "I could, but I was thinking about taking you out."

She nodded. "I'm tired from trying to keep Honey B. out of trouble. Could I have a rain check on the date but not the meal?"

Dan's smile seemed to come from the inside. His eyes were twinkling when he agreed. "Come on over after work."

She looked down at her carpenter jeans and laughed. "I'm usually way too grubby for that. I'll stop here and get cleaned up, then come over. Is six OK?"

"Six is great. That'll give me time to work for my

aunt, work on the Model A with your dad, and plan something simple but elegant for dinner."

He swept her back into his arms and kissed her until her head spun. "How do you do that?"

He grinned down at her. "Want me to show you again?"

She put a hand to the middle of his chest to stop him. "Save it for later. My sisters get cranky if I don't show up on time—especially Grace."

"But you have a good reason this morning." He pressed his lips to her forehead.

"I know, but—"

"Just one last kiss."

She gave in and was rewarded with a mind-blowing kiss that had her juices flowing and her heart pumping. "You do that really, really well, Eagan."

When he dipped his head again, she pushed out of his arms and laughed. "Later."

He checked the stove and followed her out the door.

"Megan, we need to talk."

Her heart missed a beat. "Is everything all right, Pop?"

The look on his face told her it wasn't. The unwanted memory of the night they'd lost her mom filled her. She had to dig deep to shake free of it.

"I need to ask you a serious question."

Relief speared through her. "I thought you were going to tell me you were sick or something."

He shook his head. "Right as rain."

She double-checked what was in her toolbox against her list of jobs for the day and went back to the shelves looking for the pry bar, just in case. "Ask away." He didn't say anything until she'd grabbed the bar and stowed her toolbox in the truck.

"I think it's time I move on with my life."

Her hand froze on the tailgate. She noticed the way her father was shifting from foot to foot, like he was standing on hot coals—he was nervous and that made her suspicious. "Move on how?"

He tucked his hands in his front pockets and sighed. "You know I loved your mother with my whole heart."

Her throat tightened; she didn't know if she was ready for this, but she remembered the nights she'd followed her father out to the barn and listened to the sound of his fists pounding on the sacks of grain until she wondered if he'd break one of his hands. "I do."

"I've been thinking about it for a while now and I wanted to tell you first."

"So just tell me, Pop. You dancing around what you want to say is making me crazy."

He shook his head. "You're so much like her."

Her belly clenched and she knew she had to say something to lighten his mood. "I know—it's the only reason I'm not still mad at Gracie and Caitlin for growing taller than me."

He smiled. "It's more than your height and the color of your eyes, Meg; it's your spirit."

She reached for his hand and squeezed it. "Thanks, Pop. Did Miss Trudi convince you to put your bio up on one of those dating sites?"

He laughed, a full-bodied sound. "Not on your life. I'm thinking of asking the Widow Murphy to have dinner with me."

Meg liked Mary Murphy and knew that her father had

been spending time with her. She wasn't sure she was ready for her dad to start dating the woman, but it wasn't her call. "Just dinner?"

"You're a grown woman. I'm sure you can figure things out for yourself."

"Jeez, Pop, I don't know if want to think about you and the Widow Murphy doing anything other than eating."

"I'm not that old, you know."

"Kids don't ever want to think of their parents having a sex life."

"Who said anything about sex?"

"Oh, so you're not interested in her that way."

His face turned beet red. "I didn't say that."

"Sorry, Pop, I just couldn't resist teasing you."

"I just wanted to tell you that I've been thinking about it."

She hugged him tight and asked, "When will you tell Gracie and Caitlin?"

"I'll tell them next; you were the toughest of my three little nuts to crack."

She laughed. "Gee thanks." He was halfway to the back door of the shop before she asked, "When are you going to ask her out?"

He frowned. "I'm working up to it."

Studying the fierce look on his face, she knew it hadn't been an easy decision for him, but he'd been alone a long time. "Go for it, Pop."

He flashed her a grin and then said, "There's something different about you."

She laughed to cover up the uneasy feelings rioting inside of her. "I'm the same as I was yesterday."

"I noticed it the other day."

She shook her head. "It's just your imagination."

He stared at her. "I don't think so. You seem just a bit lighter in spirit and you're smiling."

"I've got jobs to see to and I'm running late."

"Not because of me…"

She couldn't help but wonder how this would affect her family dynamic. Maybe the Widow Murphy wasn't interested in more than dinner now and again. Looking at her dad, she tried to see what a woman, and not his daughter, would see.

Broad-shouldered and tall, grays mixed in with the pin-straight auburn hair she inherited from him. He wore his high and tight, military style, from his days in the coast guard before he married her mom.

Cool green eyes watched her from a face she'd loved forever. Her dad had never been movie-star handsome, but with his crooked nose and rugged features, he was her image of the perfect man… well, except for when he was trying to tell her what to do.

"I like Dan, Meg. He's someone I think you'll be able to count on."

She looked at her watch. "Thanks, that means a lot. But I really do have to go. Talk to you later, Pop!" Driving through town, her phone buzzed, but she didn't stop to look at the text message. It could wait until she got to Mrs. Winter's house. When she'd parked outside her friend's home, she read the message and stared at the photo, disbelief and unease sprinting through her system.

"This picture's worth more than a thousand words," she grumbled, staring at the image of Dan shaking hands with Peggy McCormack, with Katie's hand on top of both of theirs. She answered Rhonda's message with a question. Why don't you find out what's going on instead of making it up? You might sell more copies of the paper.

Her friend was quick to text back. Speculation always sells.

He's got a reputation to uphold. Please just ask him first, OK?

Rhonda seemed to have disappeared or gone in search of more information for her story. Before she headed in to see Mrs. Winter and the leaky elbow pipe under her sink, she had to warn Dan about this. She fired off a quick text with the picture, hoping he'd have a chance to look at it before the end of the day.

"Megan, dear," Mrs. Winter greeted her. "It's so good to see you. How are things going with your young man?"

She shook her head; there was no use to denying it. "I guess good news travels fast."

"Well, there was actually talk the day of Edie and Bill's wedding, but that was just the gossip chain gearing up. Why don't you sit down and tell me before you settle down under my sink?"

Meg wondered if there was time; she'd started her day later than she'd intended. "I'm running short of time. If you keep me company while I work, I'll fill you in."

Her friend's smile was answer enough. "Is it as serious as Trudi says it is? I mean, after all, he is her grandnephew, but Miss Trudi does tend to exaggerate at times."

Meg's grip slipped, and she smacked her knuckles hard on the cast-iron elbow pipe. *Damn*. She should pay attention to what she was doing. When blood oozed up from the split, she sighed and shimmied back out from under the cabinet.

"Oh dear," Mrs. Winter exclaimed. "You've cut yourself."

She always carried a few first aid essentials in her toolbox. Mopping the blood with the paper towel Mrs. Winter handed her, she was reaching for the box of bandages when an age-spotted hand stopped her.

"You cannot cover it until you wash it out properly. There's no telling what kind of dirt is under that sink."

She was about to protest, but the look in the older woman's eyes stopped her. She nodded instead and followed Mrs. Winter to the bathroom. "Wash it out good with soap and water first, while I get the peroxide."

"It's nothing really—"

"Have you ever had a deep cut like that fester?"

Just the word conjured up images she'd rather not have whirling around in her tired brain. Now that she'd cleaned it out, she noticed that it was more of a gash than a split. Must have caught it on the edge of the pipe. Blood welled up again and her head felt light. "Uh... not that I can remember."

"Well, Mr. Winter did." The older woman handed Meg the dark brown bottle and a few cotton balls and watched while Meg cleaned the wound. "It was a bad cut from that old combine of his. Lord, that man was always scraping or cutting some part of himself—said the job wasn't finished unless he'd drawn blood."

Meg winced at the thought and stared down at the blood welling up on her knuckles. She washed it out again and was pretty sure the white she was looking at was her knuckle bone. "I uh... think I'd better sit down."

Fast on her feet, Mrs. Winter had Meg by the arm, sitting down on the lid to the toilet, and was shoving

Meg's head between her knees. "Do not move while I call for help."

"I don't need help," she told her. "I just felt light-headed for a minute. I'll be fine."

Mrs. Winter let go of the back of Meg's neck and stood with her arms crossed, frowning. "Put pressure on that cut with this."

Meg stared at the fluffy white towel and shook her head. "Paper towels are fine. I don't want to ruin a good towel."

"Damn the towel, Megan! You put pressure on that cut with this towel while I call Doc Gannon."

Still a little shaky on her pins, Meg decided to listen and pressed the thick towel against her aching hand. It shouldn't hurt that much for just a cut. Should it? She couldn't remember the last time she'd cut herself deep enough to need stitches.

"I don't need to see Doc Gannon." At least she hoped she didn't. Staring down at the towel, her hands started to shake. Funny thing about white, it sure turned crimson fast. Mrs. Winter scurried back into the bathroom and had Meg by the arm again. "Doc's waiting for us, dear. I'll drive your truck."

"Pop doesn't let anyone but me drive Grandpa's truck."

"Special circumstances. Let's go."

A few minutes later, Meg was sitting with her head between her knees again—this time in the front seat of the Mulcahy's pickup with Mrs. Winter throwing the shift into reverse. Meg's head smacked into the dashboard when the woman shifted into second and floored it.

"That's gonna leave a mark."

Mrs. Winter was patting her on the arm. "Not to worry, we'll be there in just a few minutes."

True to her word, they pulled up outside of the white brick building at the opposite end of town from the sheriff's office. "I'm fine," Meg protested as she was pulled out of the truck and up the steps.

"Well, Mrs. Winter, you're right," Doctor Gannon said. "I can see the knuckle bone." He caught Meg as her legs gave out. "Easy, Megan," he soothed. "Just lay down right over here."

Meg hated stitches. "Are you sure you can't just butterfly it? That's what I was going to do."

"Hmmph." Mrs. Winter sniffed. "She wasn't even going to use soap on it."

Meg didn't want to see twin looks of censure, so she kept her eyes closed.

"I'm going to numb your hand."

"OK." The only thing she hated worse than stitches was the needle that came before the skin got sewn back together. She gritted her teeth while he injected the needle into her hand.

"What were you doing when you cut your hand?"

She concentrated on the soothing sound of Doc Gannon's voice. He sounded just like his dad. "Mrs. Winter has a leaky elbow pipe under her sink. I was fixing it."

"You're going to need a tetanus shot."

Meg's eyes shot open. She knew she didn't need one of those today, so she told him, "I'm sure I had one recently."

Mrs. Winter leaned close. "Do you want me to call your father?"

Her gaze collided with that of her friend. "No. He'll just worry." Turning her head to the other side, she watched as the man she'd grown up with tore open a package of sutures. There was a tiny vial on the stainless steel tray along with gauze and some Betadine. He knew what he was doing and had since he'd taken over his father's practice. "You probably checked my chart."

He grinned and it was as if the years since graduation melted away and they were sitting in chemistry class together. "Probably. Come on, Mulcahy, it'll be over before you know it." He reached into his pocket and pulled out a cherry lollipop. "If you're a good girl, you can have this."

She looked from the lollipop to the sutures in his hand and the tray with the syringe. "Can I have one for the stitches and one for the shot?"

He laughed out loud, a warm, rich sound that put her at ease. "Some things never change." While he worked he kept her talking. "Did you know my dad added that to your chart?"

"The part about not liking shots?"

He didn't look up from what he was doing as he answered. "No, the fact that you always bargained for two cherry suckers if you thought you could get an extra one out of him."

"How is your dad?" She had always liked Dr. and Mrs. Gannon and missed them since they had retired to Virginia.

"Playing golf three times a week and bridge the other two."

"Your mother sent the nicest card for my birthday," Mrs. Winter told the doctor.

Before Meg could brace herself, the doctor had finished and had given her the shot. "Hey, not fair. I wasn't ready."

Instead of answering her, the doctor handed her the promised lollipops. "Don't use that hand for a day or two and don't get it wet."

"But I—"

"I want to take another look at it to make sure it's healing properly."

Meg looked down at her gauze-wrapped hand. "How am I going to work today?"

"Let me think." His voice was grave as he considered her options. "You aren't if it involves using that hand. Now, don't forget to have some orange juice with lunch; it'll help with your blood sugar."

"But, Doc—"

He waved her away. "No buts or I'm calling your dad."

"Man, you sound just like your father."

"Thank you." His smile told her just how much he appreciated the comment.

"I didn't mean that the way you took it," she grumbled, hating the way she sounded.

"I'll overlook the fact that you're acting like you did when Sheriff Wallace rescued you from the crow's nest," Doc Gannon told her.

"If you hadn't dared me to climb in the first place—" Meg began only to be interrupted.

"Ah, the melodious sound of my big sister griping because she can't stand needles."

Meg frowned as her youngest sister walked into the examining room. "What are you doing here?"

Grace shrugged. "Mrs. Winter thought one of us

should know, and since you told her not to call Pop, she called me."

Meg turned to glare at Mrs. Winter, but the old woman was already frowning at Meg. "You should be glad there are people who love you and are worried about your welfare, young lady."

"I'm hardly a young lady," she griped. "I'm nearly thirty."

"Half my age," Mrs. Winter reminded her. "Now be a good girl and don't complain. I'll follow you two back to the shop and drop off the truck. Grace can drop you off so you can answer phones while she drives me back to my house."

"Don't I get a vote?" Meg protested.

"No!" The three of them were staring at her as if she'd lost her mind. Maybe she had.

"Who's going to finish my jobs for the day?"

"I'm sure Pop can handle it."

"But then you'll have to tell him what happened."

"Do you think he doesn't already know?"

Meg groaned. "He'll lecture me about not paying attention."

Grace hooked her arm through Meg on one side while Mrs. Winter did the same on the other. "You should be used to it by now, Sis."

She was, but that didn't mean she had to like it. "Perfect." As they were walking through the door, she tugged on them to stop. "I'm sorry to be such a lousy patient, Doc."

Doc Gannon rolled his eyes heavenward. "You're my most difficult patient."

She laughed. "Seriously, thanks, Jack."

He smiled at her. "You're welcome, Meg. Now go rest that hand."

"Sure thing, Doc."

They pulled around to the back of the shop and she hopped out; she didn't want either of them thinking she needed help. She was stronger than that. "I promise to hold the fort down, Gracie."

Her sister sighed. "Just remember to be polite when you answer the phone."

"I'm always polite."

The sound of her sister's laughter followed her into the building.

Sitting down behind the desk felt odd; she hadn't done that since the time she'd nearly taken a header off the water tower. It had been a punishment then to answer the phones and not go out on calls with her father. Grumbling, she flipped through the computer screens to see what Grace had been working on.

There were a few spreadsheets open; she pulled up the one with today's date on it and scrolled through the jobs to see what her sister Caitlin was up to, but she didn't have to bother because two minutes later the phone was ringing.

"Mulcahy's, Meg speaking."

"How many stitches?"

Meg frowned at the sound of her other sister's voice and decided to pretend she had no idea who was calling. "You have reached Mulcahy's, where no job is too small. This is Megan; may I help you?"

"Damn it, Meg," her sister said. "It's me, Cait. Now start talking."

She chuckled. "Hey, no need to get grumpy. You weren't the one who had to get two shots and stitches."

"Jeez, why two shots?"

"One to numb my hand and one in case there was rust in the pipe I hit my hand on."

"I heard Doc Gannon saw bone and you got twenty stitches."

Meg scrolled down the screen. "How did you hear that if you're supposed to be putting that addition on for the Millers?"

"Good news travels fast, and I needed a break."

One of the other phone lines was lit up. "Hey, Cait, hang on. The other line's ringing."

"Mulcahy's, Meg speaking."

"Megan dear, I just wanted to make sure you were all right."

She smiled, recognizing Miss Trudi's voice. "I'm fine, just a little cut. I'll be good as new in no time."

"Young Doctor Gannon does a wonderful job. So much like his father."

The other phone line was still blinking; her sister hadn't hung up on her yet. "I have someone on the other line, Miss Trudi, thank you for calling."

"Just be sure to do what the doctor told you to."

"Yes, ma'am." Meg answered before disconnecting and pushing the other button. "Cait, you still there?"

"Yeah, who was it: Mrs. Winter, Honey B., or Miss Trudi?"

"Miss Trudi. I might have to actually do what the doc says for the next day or so."

"Must have been a deep gash if you had stitches and a tetanus shot."

"Deep enough."

"Did you pass out?"

"Damn, the other line's blinking again. Talk to you later, Sis. Thanks for checking up on me."

Her sister was still grumbling when she disconnected and picked up the incoming call. "Mulcahy's, Meg—"

"I just had a call from Grace."

Meg sighed. "Hi, Pop."

"I'm over at Mrs. Winter's house now under the sink."

"I don't think it's the joint that I sweat a few years ago that's leaking," Meg told him, "but I didn't have a chance to spend much time looking."

"How's the hand?"

"Hurts."

"Did you take anything for it yet?"

"I didn't need to before you called. I guess the first shot's wearing off. I swear I can feel where he stitched the skin back together."

Her father commiserated with her. "Hate shots, hate needles. Take some of that extra-strength pain reliever. Second drawer down on the left-hand side of my desk."

"Thanks, Pop. The other line's ringing; can I put you on hold?"

"Gotta go find the leak. Put the other call on speaker and get the damned pain reliever."

She smiled as she did as her father asked. "Mulcahy's, Meg speaking."

The drawer stuck and she had to yank it to get it open.

"Meg, it's me, Honey B."

Meg grabbed the bottle and walked over to the water cooler and filled a paper cup. "I've got you on speaker. I'm getting some water."

"I heard you passed out twice and Mrs. Winter said it took the Doc twenty-five stitches to close the cut!"

Meg swallowed the capsules and finished the water before answering.

"Meg, are you still there? Should I come over?"

She snickered. "Drinking here. No worries, Honey B. I'm fine, just sore. Hey, the other line's blinking. Call you later."

She sat down before answering the call. An hour later she had had to answer a dozen calls, half of which were her nosy neighbors wanting to know the gory details of how deep the cut was, did she chip the bone, did she crack her head on anything when she passed out... Some of the questions were really imaginative. Especially Mrs. Doyle, who wanted to know if Doc Gannon had really caught Meg in his arms before she fainted.

"Like I'd ever admit to that even if it happened." She sipped her second cup of coffee, relieved that the phones were quiet for the moment.

Her cell phone buzzed. She checked the message and laughed. Don't just answer the phones, there's filing.

"Only you, Gracie." Just to be difficult, she texted back, Hand hurts, don't feel like it.

Two seconds later, her phone buzzed again. Pain relievers in Dad's desk... be back in twenty.

Meg rarely got in a snit over something one of her sisters said, but she decided this was worth getting annoyed over. She'd just had her hand stitched back together and had to put up with two needles, damn it. Besides, her sister had probably stopped to have coffee with Peggy and Katie, to help circulate the news. It had been a slow couple of days in Apple Grove, and Grace never could keep her mouth shut for long.

Grateful for the break, she switched to her father's

desk and relaxed in his comfy chair, swiveling around so she could look out the front window. She could work later; her hand really was starting to ache again. Since it was too early to take anything for the pain, she finished her coffee and closed her eyes.

She heard the door and figured it was Grace coming back, so she didn't turn around.

"'Bout time you showed up, Sis. Oh, and for your information, I didn't do the filing. My hand hurts."

"Meg."

Dan's deep voice flowed over her stiff shoulders like warm syrup on a stack of hotcakes. She swung the chair around and was surprised to see the anxious look on his face.

"Aren't you supposed to be at the garden center helping your aunt?"

He shook his head. "I told Aunt Trudi and the guys that I was running over here to see if you were all right first. They all told me to go for it. Besides, the hay delivery got there and the guys were really a big help setting things up the way my aunt wanted it."

She started to rise, and he pulled her to her feet and stared down at her gauze-wrapped hand.

"Did the wrench slip or your hand?"

"Don't you want to know how many stitches?"

He shook his head and pulled her close. "When I heard you'd been hurt, I didn't know if you'd fallen off a ladder or through somebody's ancient barn roof."

She sighed. "Neither."

"Then I heard from my aunt that you'd cut your hand badly. I had stitches a couple of years ago—I can tell you the particulars later—but I know how hard it is to get things done with one hand. And I started thinking about how we both want to spend more time together and came up with a great idea—how about if you come home with me and I'll take care of you for a few days?"

"That sounds like a more interesting solution than me going back home."

He pressed his lips to the top of her head. "I'd like to tell you that I have no ulterior motives, but I keep getting this image of you in my shower, and me washing your hair... and then the rest of you."

She swallowed before she drooled. The image he painted was now stuck in her head. "Maybe it'd be more fun at your place."

He laughed then grew serious. "Was it really thirty stitches?"

She brushed her lips across his chin to get his attention. "Half that and they'd feel a whole lot better if you'd kiss me before you go."

Desire flashed in the depths of his warm gray eyes a split-second before his lips claimed hers. The soft, tentative touch was filled with sweetness that had her relaxing in his arms.

"Don't pass out on me, Meg."

She laughed and laid her head against his broad chest. It felt good to lean on someone else for a change, nice not to have to be the strong one this time. "Just a little tired and taking advantage of your offer starting right now."

He eased back and the hopeful expression on his face got to her heart. "Can you wait for me here? I forgot, I'm supposed to be working on the Model A with your dad this afternoon. Will you want to leave early or regular time?"

"Regular time is fine. I'll ask Gracie to drive me over

to the apartment and pack a few things. She should be back any minute."

He flashed a wicked smile that disappeared so quickly she wondered if she'd imagined it. Maybe she wasn't ready for this. "Dan, I—"

He brushed the tips of his fingers across her face and tucked her hair behind her ears. "Let me take care of you, Meg." He kissed her forehead and then lifted her injured hand to press his lips to her wrist at the edge of the bandage. "I'll pick you up at five thirty."

He was gone before she could gather her wits enough to tell him she'd be ready. She sat back down and watched him jog over to his car. He turned and waved. She smiled and waved back. It was just for a couple of days… but it was the thought of the nights that had her heart stuttering. The need to tell him how she felt warred with the need to wait until he told her first.

Besides, what could possibly happen?

Chapter 13

DAN PUT THE WORRY OF MEG ON THE BACK BURNER while he waited for her father to arrive. He got to the Mulcahy house before Joe, and since the temptation was too great, he got out and walked over to the barn. To his surprise, it wasn't locked.

"Wow. A vehicle like that and the barn isn't locked." He was about to go in the barn alone but realized it would be better if he waited. A few minutes later, Joe drove up and honked, announcing his arrival.

"I was about to give up and head into the barn without waiting."

Joe grinned. "I was wondering how long you'd wait before you tried the barn door. It isn't locked, you know."

Dan smiled sheepishly. "I tried the door."

Joe's laughter was contagious. "Come on. Now that I've decided to start working on it, I'm anxious to get to it."

Dan wasn't sure how to tell Joe about the plans he and Meg had made, so he simply told him, "I'm picking Meg up after work and taking her back to my place."

Joe paused with his hand on the tarp. He finally nodded and whipped the cover off the truck and popped the hood. "Let's see what we can do with this engine."

Wasn't Joe going to ask his intentions? Dan wondered if he should say anything else. When Joe seemed to be totally focused on the engine, Dan finally asked, "Where do we start?"

Joe put his hands on the front of the truck and stared down at it. "How much time do you have today?"

"'Bout two hours. I don't want Meg to get too tired. I promised I'd pick her up at five thirty."

"Doc Gannon is a good doctor. He took good care of Meg. As long as she takes pain reliever every few hours, she'll get through the worst of it." He let his gaze slide over to stare at Dan. "I think it'll be a good thing for you to take care of Meg. She's taken too long to get over that Van Orden kid, but she's got a big heart and a need to love someone. I think you could be that someone."

Gratitude flowed through him. Joe trusted him with his daughter. "I know I am."

"Good," Joe said, looking back down at the engine. "I think two hours will be just enough time to drain the oil and check all of the gaskets and hoses."

"The plugs?"

"Those too. Then we'll take the battery out of the F1 and see if this baby will turn over."

"Do you have a fire extinguisher?"

Joe laughed and pointed to the front of the barn. "Over there."

Two hours later, they both had nicks on their knuckles and broad grins on their faces. "I can't believe she cranked!" Dan said.

"Solid engine. They don't make them like that anymore."

"But your grandfather took care of it, when he put it away."

Joe agreed. "He loved trucks."

They were cleaning up when Dan looked over at Meg's dad and said, "Thanks for letting me get under the hood with you today, Joe. It's like a dream, working on a truck like that. Wait till I tell my dad!"

Joe nodded. "Hey, if you hadn't been so eager to look at it, I probably would have put it off another five years." He looked at his watch and said, "Hey aren't you supposed to pick up Meg?"

"Damn! Gotta run. Thanks, Joe!"

"See you next Saturday?"

Dan felt like a kid again and pumped his fist in the air. "Count on it. See you then."

Now that he was on the way over to her apartment, the anticipation of having Meg all to himself had him envisioning mornings in the shower, soaping up every glorious inch of her, and nights in bed, sampling the flavor and texture of her amazing body. A tiny little piece of his heart cried out that he needed her to love him. He had to tell her how he felt soon.

He texted that he was on his way, and by the time he pulled into the driveway, she was outside. Something warm and wonderful burst inside of him at the sight of her walking toward him. "Hey, I'll carry that." He reached for her overnight bag, but she shook her head.

"I've got it, thanks," she said, "but you could open the door for me." She held up her injured hand and sighed. "I'm having trouble getting used to the fact that I only have one good hand."

He opened the door, let her stow the bag in the backseat, and then opened the passenger door for her. "How about if we take it easy for starters and see how much you can do with one hand. You could help me make dinner."

She reached for her seat belt and felt the frustration

building; her hand wouldn't fit between the edge of the seat and the inside door panel. It was going to be harder than she thought if she couldn't perform the simplest of tasks on her own. Grabbing the shoulder harness with her left hand she tried to buckle up, missing the first two times.

"Here, let me." Dan brushed her hand aside and fastened her in. "We take so much for granted, having the use of both hands. I'm going to need you to remind me of the things you can't do. OK?"

She blinked the tears away, but Dan must have noticed. He leaned his forehead against hers. "Work with me, Meg. I'm not trying to make it harder for you by having you ask me for help. I just might not notice at first that you're struggling with something."

He kissed the tip of her nose. "Besides, I can always drop you off so your dad and sisters can take care of you."

"You have an evil streak in you, Dan Eagan."

It felt good to laugh. He'd been scared shitless when he'd heard from his aunt that Meg had been hurt on the job. "Busted." He laughed and then said, "I've also got a really great imagination, Meg… if you're feeling up to it later."

He watched her from the corner of his eye, encouraged when she licked her lips and turned toward him.

"If I take more pain reliever with dinner, I'll let you talk me into bed."

For a moment the vision of her tangled in the sheets had him tongue-tied. Finally, he managed, "I, uh… that would… OK."

He pulled in the driveway and unbuckled her before she could ask. He remembered what it had been like to be incapacitated, but for him it hadn't been as difficult; he hadn't injured the hand he used most.

"I'm hungry." She grinned as she reached around him to grab her bag. "What's for dinner?"

Wrapping his arm around her waist, he led her into his house. "I know I promised to fix you a special meal, but I forgot about working with your dad. How do you feel about leftovers?"

"Works for me. I don't expect you to foot the bill to feed me while I'm here, Dan. I can chip in for groceries."

The way she stood, with her shoulders back and her chin tilted toward the ceiling, had him wondering if he'd ever known a woman like Meg before. Proud, bold, and beautiful. "Let's see what I can rustle up while you wash up and—" She was frowning at him. "Hold on," he said. "Let me put my briefcase down and I'll help you wash your hand."

He pulled her toward the sink, unbuttoned her cuff, and rolled up her sleeve. Turning on the taps and waiting for the water to warm up, he squirted soap into his hands and then held their hands under the warm water. He urged her to lean against him while he gently worked up a lather then rinsed it clean.

"The dishes are over there." He pointed to the cabinet above the sink, glanced down at the top of her head, and said, "Hang on. I'll get them down for you."

When he'd set everything they'd need down on the counter, she sighed. "This is going to be harder than I thought. So I'm warning you now that I might get a little crabby."

"Noted." He bit the inside of his cheek to keep from smiling. He opened the fridge and took stock of what was inside. "I've got pasta primavera, meatballs with brown gravy and buttered noodles, or the old standby: breakfast for dinner."

Her eyes lit up. "Can we heat up the primavera and the meatballs, and share?"

How could he say no to the auburn-haired woman looking up at him with hope in her wide blue eyes? "You got it."

He grabbed a bunch of containers and set them on the counter, deciding to heat up the meatballs and gravy first. "Hey, can you make the salad?"

"Only if you wash it for me."

"I prepare a lot of stuff beforehand—saves time when I walk in the door starving. The salad just needs to be put on the plates."

He handed her a couple of bags. "Even I know this isn't lettuce." Meg held up a bag of colorful pepper slices.

He grinned. "And even I know that lettuce alone doesn't qualify as a salad," he said, handing her a bag of romaine broken into tiny pieces, then set out bags of cherry tomatoes, chunks of cheese, and croutons.

"A lot you know," she grumbled. "I don't even use this kind of lettuce."

"Well, romaine is all I have at the moment; we can buy whatever you'd rather have later."

"I'm sorry; I'm just having a hard time adjusting."

He watched as she filled a bowl with lettuce, then the rest of the ingredients he'd given her. "Looks great, Meg." The microwave dinged and he switched out the plate for the one with the egg noodles on it.

"Have a seat." He handed her one of the salads, grabbed the other, and guided her to the table. When she was seated, he set the plate down and walked back to the counter and pulled out a bottle of wine from the rack beneath the middle cabinet. While she watched, he opened the bottle, poured a tiny bit in the bottom of one glass, and handed it to her.

"Swirl it around, sniff it, and then taste it."

She rolled her eyes but did as he suggested. "It's good."

He smiled. "It's one of my favorite Merlots." The microwave shut off again, and he added the plate of pasta. When everything was ready, he carried it over to the table and set it in the middle. Meg was staring down at her salad with a fork in her left hand, but not moving. "Do you need help eating?"

She shook her head. "Nope, just hoping I won't be spilling too much. I hate to waste food."

Scooting around so they were side by side, he let her fork up some salad and didn't say anything when she bobbled the first forkful. When she'd had a few bites, he leaned close and held a fork to her lips. "Try this and tell me what you think."

She opened her mouth but from the way she glared at him, he knew she was going to be difficult, so he waited for the right moment and slipped the pasta in her mouth and told her to chew.

Surprised, she did just that. Her glare softened and he handed her the wineglass. "Now sip."

"I can feed myself," she grumbled.

"But then you're depriving me of the pleasure of feeding you." She sighed and sipped the wine. When she reached for the napkin, he snuck in a kiss and licked his lips. "My pasta tastes great on you."

She was laughing when he covered her mouth again,

this time letting his lips linger. "Mmmm… we'd better keep eating, or else you'll go to bed hungry."

He let her eat more salad before waving the meatballs and gravy in front of her. "Ready for something else?"

She grinned. "I thought you were taking me to bed."

"I've changed my mind. You're going to need every ounce of energy you can get from dinner to keep up with me tonight."

Her cheeks flushed a delightful shade… like a newly ripened peach. He watched as she leaned toward him and nipped the food off his fork. "Mmmm." She chewed and swallowed. "Better than my grandmother's."

"Can I try?"

He thought she wanted to feed herself and was pleasantly surprised when she managed to get a forkful of pasta and then offered it to him. "Try it." She beamed. "It's really good."

They took turns feeding one another, pausing only to sip from their glasses. Neither one seemed to need words, when a look or a touch communicated so much more.

They rose together and he shook his head when she reached for an empty plate. "Leave them. I want to take you upstairs."

"But I think I ate too much."

"That's all right; we can take our time until you've digested dinner. I can think of a few things that'll keep us occupied while we wait."

⚬⚬⚬

Meg nearly swallowed her tongue. The hot looks Dan kept sending her way had her heart galloping at full speed. She didn't know what to say, but she did know what she wanted to do. She let him take her by the hand lead her to the second floor.

She hadn't taken the time to notice much about his bedroom the first time she'd been here, but it had been in the middle of the night and dark. He flipped on the wall switch and the room was bathed in the soft, incandescent glow of the light on his dresser. The mahogany four-poster and matching dresser seemed to fit in with the age of the house.

The black and gray striped comforter was soft to the touch. "Silk?"

He shrugged. "I like soft things."

He reached for her, snagging her shirtfront and tugging her closer. Starting with the one beneath her chin, he slid the buttons free slowly, drawing out the task, making her crazy with want. "Dan, I—"

"Shush. Let me." His mouth pressed against the hollow of her throat made her knees weak. She reached out to keep from falling and smacked her knuckles on his shoulder.

She saw stars and before she could protest was cradled against the warmth of Dan's massive chest. "I've got you," he soothed.

"My fault," she said. "I forgot."

He struggled not to smile and failed. "I'm glad I could make you forget… that's the plan tonight."

He set her on the bed and helped her out of her shirt and unhooked her bra. Tossing it over his shoulder, he urged, "Lie down."

The sight of his big hand in the middle of her chest did funny things to her insides. She shivered and he closed his eyes.

"Not yet," he told her, urging her down. "Don't close your eyes yet, Meg. I want to watch your eyes go soft and cloudy as you come for me." He undid the button and slid the zipper slowly down, pressing his lips to the skin he exposed.

Her insides were on fire. With the flick of his tongue, he added to the heat. Shifting her up, he slid her jeans off and tossed them to the floor. He sat on the bed next to her and let his fingers glide from her shoulder, along her collarbone, to the hollow of her throat. When his fingers slid down her breastbone, she moaned.

"Does that feel good?"

His voice added a new dimension to his sensual foray. "Yes," she hissed.

He stopped. "Did I hurt you?"

"No."

Their gazes collided and she knew she wasn't the only one turned on. When she nodded, he leaned over her and let his tongue trace the path his fingertips had journeyed. He blew on the skin he'd moistened with his tongue, tormenting her.

"Dan... I—"

"Not yet, Meg," he whispered. "Let me show you how I feel about you." His lips claimed hers in a heart-pounding kiss that had her body going limp and her juices flowing to the surface.

One look and she knew he understood. His lips tortured her as they slid along her collarbone to her throat. Molding her in his hands, he played with her breasts until the nipples pearled in his hands and she was writhing beneath him.

He put his mouth on her and she shot up and over

the first peak. When her eyes could focus again, he'd stripped off his shirt and was stepping out of his work pants. "Again," he urged as he straddled her and bent to take her other breast in his mouth.

She grabbed a hold of him with her good hand and gave herself over to the splendor of his lovemaking. When he suckled her deeply into his mouth another orgasm shook her to the bone, and still he didn't pause to take off his tight-knit boxers or her black lace panties.

He swept his hands up her sides and down over her breasts with a feather-light touch, again and again, until her skin was sensitized and her core was weeping for him to fill her.

"I can't wait," she moaned.

"Come just once more for me... please?" He slid his hands inside her panties and slowly inched them down to her knees. His dark and desperate gaze set off a chain reaction. Her heart filled to bursting as her belly fluttered and her head spun. When he slid one finger inside her, she reached for him, but he evaded her. "This first time is all you, Meg."

He slid down next to her on the bed and nipped her shoulder. Sliding his tongue downward, he took her breast in his mouth as he slid a second finger inside of her. Working her with fingers, teeth, lips, and tongue, she screamed out his name as she came apart in his arms.

"You're like a wildfire, burning out of control."

He pulled her beneath him. His hot flesh pulsed against her. *When did he strip out of his briefs?*

He traced the tip of his tongue around the rim of her ear. "Burn for me, Meg."

She moaned as he nipped her earlobe.

His big body stilled, and she felt the tension coming off of him in waves.

She lifted her hips and brushed against his erection, inviting him to take what they both desperately wanted, but he held back as he covered himself with latex. Sheathed, ready to protect her, he paused. "Meg, tell me what you want."

She looked up into his eyes and saw everything she felt reflected back at her. "You, Daniel. I want you."

He slipped the tip of his erection inside of her. "What if you change your mind?"

She lifted her hips again; this time he groaned out her name. "I won't."

He slowly withdrew and then surged into her.

Meg knew the answer in her heart; all she had to do was share it with Dan. She arched her back so he was as deep as he could go. "I love you, Dan."

Her words seemed to break the tight leash he had on his control. He drove into her again and again, coaxing her with whispered words, lips, and tongue to come with him.

She willingly followed, soaring into the heavens with his whispered words filling her heart. "I love you, Meg."

Chapter 14

MEG WOKE TO THE SCENT OF COFFEE. SHE OPENED HER eyes and saw a swirl of steam and a bright red mug. "You made me coffee?" She sat up and shifted so she was sitting with her back against the headboard.

"It was a hardship, but you're worth it." He bent so he could capture her lips in a kiss that had her skin tingling and parts of her ready for another bout of lovemaking.

Instead, he drew back and handed the mug to her. She blew across the surface and sipped. "Your coffee beats Peggy's any day."

He grinned at her. "Speaking of Peggy…" he said slowly.

She frowned. "I wasn't."

He took a step back and held up his hands. She worked hard to concentrate on what he was saying—all those yummy muscles were hard to dismiss.

"I just didn't want you to hear it from anyone else; the pic you sent was from the other night when I was in the diner. It was funny—one bite of pie and we started talking piecrust."

She grinned into her cup and sipped. "I hate it when you talk pastry with another woman."

He laughed. "Well, one thing led to another and we have a contest going."

Her interest piqued, she asked, "What kind of contest?"

"We're both going to bake pie for the turkey supper

and not tell anyone which is which and we'll see at the end of the dinner whose piecrust wins."

"How will you know whose is whose?"

"That is the beauty of the plan—it's like a blind taste-testing, but I'm leaving the judging up to my aunt and Mrs. Winter to decide."

She tucked her legs beneath her and the sheet slid off her shoulder. His eyes widened and his nostrils flared; she loved that she got to him as quickly as he did to her. She'd hate to feel this way alone. It totally sucked being in love alone—been there, survived that.

He closed the distance between them and reached for her mug. "I think we need a shower." He set it on the bedside table and lifted her into his arms. "Let's start with your hair and work our way down."

She shivered at the blatant desire in his eyes. "If we get a baggy and some duct tape, we won't have to worry about my hand getting wet and we could start by washing you."

He changed direction and headed downstairs.

"You didn't have to carry me all the way down here. I could have walked."

He bent slightly and opened the drawer in the corner of the kitchen. "There should be a roll of duct tape there."

She pulled it out and he spun around and asked her to open the cabinet above them. "The Baggies are up there."

"Really, Dan, I can walk—"

"I can't bear to let you go yet, Meg," he confessed. "Humor me."

She laid her head on his shoulder. "I love you, Dan."

"Good."

She pinched his ear.

"Ouch! What was that for?"

"I just told you I loved you, damn it."

"And I just said good."

"And you think that's OK because…"

"I'd hate to be in love alone. I love you, Megan Maureen Mulcahy."

She kissed the ear she'd just pinched. "You're right," she teased. "It is a good thing."

Meg couldn't stop smiling. She was in a good mood and knew she was never going to hear the end of it. Grace knew she hated to work in the office and if Meg was in a good mood, Grace would just badger her until she told Grace why.

Despite that possibility, she was humming when Dan dropped her off Monday morning. It might have been the eye-popping kiss they'd just shared. Whatever the reason, nothing could bring her down today.

Grace stared at her when she opened the door. "You're late."

"Sorry," Meg told her. "I'm not used to office hours, so I wasn't sure what time to get here."

Her sister snorted out a laugh. "Good one, Meg."

To her surprise, her sister went back to whatever she was doing on her computer, ignoring Meg.

They worked in companionable silence for the rest of the morning until Meg made the mistake of looking at the clock and then her sister, saying, "I'm hungry, do you want lunch?"

Grace shot to her feet and said, "OK, tell me. I can't stand it."

Meg shook her head. "Tell you what?"

"Don't pretend you don't know what I'm talking about. Just because you're older than me doesn't mean that I have no idea what you and that gorgeous hunk of soccer coach have been doing together."

"For the record, what business is it of yours?"

Grace put her hands on her hips. "I'm your sister! I should know what's really going on before Peggy finds out and starts spreading rumors that might not be true."

Meg agreed and said, "Dan and I are enjoying spending time with one another."

Grace snorted again.

Meg frowned. "Well, we are."

"Playing canasta, no doubt."

Meg smiled. "Grandpa always loved playing cards when we were kids."

"OK," Grace said. "So if anyone asks, I'm supposed to tell them what for instance?"

Meg shrugged. "Nothing. It's nobody's business what Dan and I happen to be doing."

"For God's sake, Meg, we both grew up in Apple Grove... not in a convent. We both know that anything that goes on in town is fair game as far as the gossips are concerned."

"One of those gossips happens to be Dan's great-aunt."

"All the more reason to tell me first so I can make sure I spread the right story."

"Ah," Meg said slowly. "So you really don't care if I'm happy or not?"

Grace picked up her tape dispenser and threw it at Meg's head.

Meg ducked in time and it hit the wall behind her.

"Of course I care." Grace folded her arms. "I just would prefer hearing it from you than from Miss Trudi or Mrs. Winter."

"Fair enough," Meg said. And it was. "Dan and I are having a mutually satisfying relationship… with all the trimmings."

Grace's eyes rounded. "He has a seriously stellar set of abs."

Meg sighed. "Mmmm."

"I'm not asking you to spill everything—" her sister began.

"Good," Meg interrupted. "Because that's all I'm going to tell you."

"But, Meg—"

The phone rang and Meg reached for it. Better to answer the phone than argue with her youngest sister. "Mulcahy's, Meg speaking."

"Megan!" a deep voice answered. "I wasn't sure if you'd be at the shop."

She frowned; the voice sounded familiar, but she couldn't place the face.

"I just got to town and was visiting with my mom. Will you wait for me?"

"I don't mean to be rude," she said, "but who is this?"

There was a pause before he answered. "It's me, Jimmy."

Meg's world ground to a halt as the past and all of the heartache came crashing back.

When she didn't say anything he said, "I want to see you, Meg."

Suspicion filled her heart. She'd loved him so desperately when they were teenagers, and had been his hometown girlfriend every time he came back, but then he'd left—again—and she realized that she'd been convenient... nothing more than someone to be with so he didn't have to be alone. She'd never been important in Jimmy's life. "Why?"

"What do you mean, why? I always call you when I come home. Doesn't what we have mean anything to you?"

She couldn't believe she was having this conversation over the phone. Needing to get a grip so she didn't say something she'd regret, she quietly told him, "Yes. Our relationship has taught me one thing—you don't always get everything you want in life... but you get exactly what you need."

Before he could respond, she hung up the phone.

"Who was that?"

She shot to her feet and strode to the front door. "Nobody. I'll be back later."

"Wait," her sister called out. "Where are you going?"

"I'm going to talk to Honey B." Meeting Grace's questioning gaze, she finally told her sister, "That was Jimmy on the phone."

"Van Orden?"

Meg nodded and left. The walk in the cool, fresh air cleared her head. By the time she walked into Honey's Hair Salon, she was ready to stand up for herself and blast the hell out of Jimmy Van Orden.

Honey's gaze met hers and then swept the salon. Every head had turned toward Meg. She sighed; may as well begin the way she intended to continue—with the truth. Clearing her throat she announced, "James Van Orden is back in town."

She waited a beat, taking in the expectant looks on the faces of the women in the salon. Before anyone could ask, she crossed her arms and said, "Dan Eagan and I are having a mad, passionate affair."

Honey smiled and asked, "What about Jimmy?"

"I'm convenient. If he felt anything more for me, he would have declared himself years ago and we would have worked out where and how to live. Dan helped me finally figure things out."

"Are you sure?" Honey asked, watching Meg closely.

"Dan is the man I didn't realize I'd been waiting for. I'm in love, Honey B."

Her friend's eyes filled with tears, but her hands were filled with the perm rods she'd been rolling on Mrs. Doyle's head. "Congratulations, Meg."

One by one the ladies in the shop started clapping until Meg realized they weren't trying to make her feel uncomfortable; they were actually applauding the fact that she'd taken a huge step forward getting on with her life.

"He's such a good catch," Mrs. Hawkins told her.

"He really fills out the seat of his jeans," Mrs. Jones said with a grin.

"The boys on his team think the world of him," Mrs. Doyle confided. "It takes a lot of hard work to step in and keep a team together and take them all the way to the state championships."

Meg normally didn't gossip, but she felt she owed it to the ladies who were rallying around her. "I thought I was in love years ago… and then I met Dan and I learned the true value of loving someone and being loved in return."

No one spoke until she added, "He's everything to me."

Honey B. finished putting the rollers in Mrs. Doyle's hair, put the cotton batting around her face, covered the woman's head with a towel, and set the timer. While the other women took turns hugging Meg, Honey B. took off her gloves and washed up.

When it was her turn, she hugged Meg tight and whispered, "Dan's worth it. Jimmy never was."

"Does Dan know that your old flame is back in town?"

Meg looked over at Mrs. Hawkins and shook her head. "I'm not sure. Jimmy called the shop and I hung up on him—I needed to talk to Honey B."

"I'm sure if Grace was in the office at the time, then Peggy and Katie already know," Mrs. Doyle said.

Honey brewed a fresh pot of coffee and the ladies sat down to plan out a strategy.

"Are you're interested in making that young man pay for what he did to you?" Mrs. Jones asked.

A part of Meg wanted to say yes, but deep down, there wasn't any room left in her heart for vengeance. All of those feelings had been replaced by the bone-deep love she felt for one very special man. "Not really."

"Would you mind if a few of us let the word out about how you feel about Dan?" Mrs. Hawkins asked with a glance at Mrs. Doyle. "We do owe the man so much for saving our boys."

As if on cue the door the shop opened and her teen-aged nightmare walked back into her life. "I thought I'd find you here, Meg."

"Jimmy?" She could not believe he'd show up here after the way she'd hung up on him. Did he think he could just keep waltzing back into her life, proving to her and the town just how little he valued her?

Before she could think of a snappy come back that would have the man heading for the hills, he'd grabbed a hold of her hand and pulled her into his arms and bent his lips to kiss her.

"Get your hands off my woman." Dan's deep voice had Meg's head spinning.

"It's not what you think—" she began.

But Dan was focused on his adversary and was too busy staring him down to listen. "I think that someone in town called Van Orden and told him that his childhood sweetheart has finally stopped pining for him."

The anger in Dan's voice had Meg realizing that he wasn't angry with her. "He caught me by surprise." She paused then asked, "Who would do something like that?"

As soon as she asked, her gaze met Jimmy's and she knew—his mother. The woman never did approve of Meg for her son.

The ladies in the shop had been silent up until that point, but Mrs. Doyle agreed. "Just walks right in as if the months of silence in between visits never happened."

"He always had more ego than brains," Mrs. Hawkins added with a smile.

"Now wait just a minute," Van Orden ground out.

"No," Dan said, taking Meg by the hand and tucking her against his side. "You'd better listen because I'm only going to say this once." He brushed his lips against her forehead. "Meg Mulcahy is the best thing that's ever happened to me."

When Van Orden drew in a breath to speak, Dan pulled Meg flush against him and kissed her as if now was the only moment that mattered—the world could end and he wouldn't care as long as he had Meg in his arms. He lifted his head and looked over the top of Meg's head and asked, "Are you still here?"

"She's my girl—"

Dan hugged Meg to his heart and shook his head. "You had your chance over the last few years, but never did anything about it. In my book you forfeited any claim you had to Meg's heart." He dipped down and kissed her; when he came up for air, he heard the sound of the door slamming and the ladies of the salon cheering.

"I love you, Meg."

Meg looked as if she'd been given the sun and the moon. Heart in her eyes, she smiled. "I love you more."

The door to the shop burst open and Dan spun around, fists ready to do serious damage to Van Orden, but it was the sheriff who stalked inside. Without a word he grabbed Honey B. and yanked her close for a kiss that had everyone in the shop hooting and hollering again. "You won't be going out to dinner with anyone else but me, Honey B. Harrington."

Honey B. stared up at the sheriff for a moment before getting her gumption back. "Who are you to tell me what—"

He covered her mouth with his again and this time no one spoke—no one moved. The gentle way the big man held Honey B. spoke volumes. "I'm a man who takes what I want. I'm tired of living in the shadows. I'm taking what I want, Honey B.—you!"

Honey B. squealed as the sheriff bent down, wrapped his arms around her waist, and tossed her over his shoulder. "You've got five minutes to tell me you don't love me."

"Damn it, why the hell *do* I love you?" Honey B. hollered as the sheriff opened the shop door.

"Close enough," he chuckled, stepping through the door with his woman.

Dan touched the tip of his finger to Meg's chin and she realized that her mouth had been hanging open. She glanced around the shop and noticed the ladies all having similar reactions. She shook her head. "Well, I guess he just told Honey B. what."

The looks of surprise changed into smiles as the ladies realized they had two juicy tidbits of gossip to pass on. Mrs. Doyle ran to her purse and pulled out her phone. When she pointed it at Dan and Meg, Meg started laughing.

"I hope you realize we'll be making the headlines of the *Apple Grove Gazette*, Coach."

"I'm thinking that I've been scooped by the sheriff and Honey B."

Mrs. Hawkins was already out the door chasing after the sheriff and his woman, hoping to take a picture before he set Honey B. back on her feet. Two seconds later she ran back into the shop face flushed and holding her phone high in the air. "I got it!"

Everyone gathered around to see the picture of the man who'd been upholding the law for more than a decade hauling his woman off to his bright red pickup with her over his shoulder and his wide-palmed hand on her backside.

Meg smiled up at Dan. "I think you're right, Dan. That picture will make the front page, but that's OK. I'll settle for page two as long as I know that you love me."

He lifted her into his arms and walked to the door amidst the clicking of phones snapping pictures. "Then let's give them something else to talk about." Her laughter filled the shop and his heart. "So you're not sorry that you're no longer available now that he's back in town?" Dan asked, setting her on her feet by his car.

She stood on her toes and nipped his bottom lip. Dan's nostrils flared as passion roared to life between them. Taking advantage of the situation, she wrapped her arms around his neck and tugged until their lips met and their hearts thundered together. "Not a chance. It is too bad you can't take me home, handsome, because I've got plans for you."

He wiggled his eyebrows at her. "Oh yeah? It just so happens that I have a free period and there's an assembly right after lunch."

She trailed the tips of her fingers along the line of his jaw. "This really is my lucky day. Let's not waste any time."

Passion dark and desperate flared in his eyes.

She was laughing when he buckled her in. "Dan, wait! I forgot to lock up the shop."

"Text Grace and let her know you're going home with me."

She shot off the text and then set out to drive him crazy all the way to his house with her quick hands and full heart.

They made it to the kitchen, where he pinned her against the wall and whispered in detail the things he wanted to do to her. But he got so caught up in the image he was painting for her that he was the one who couldn't wait to go upstairs.

She soothed him with kisses on his cheeks and chin before she led him over to the counter, leaned back against it, and struggled to unbutton her jeans. He didn't wait long before offering to help her. His eyes never left hers when she shimmied out of her panties and kicked them to the side.

"Meg, I—"

She shook her head and had her hand inside his jeans before he could finish whatever he wanted to say. His eyes crossed and he groaned out her name when she freed him. She swept her fingertips along the top of his erection and then lightly traced the vein, awed by the power and beauty of the man in her hands.

"You're so beautiful," she cupped him gently, watching his face to see if he felt as much pleasure with her hands on him as she did putting them there.

He covered himself from tip to base and ground out, "Now." He lifted her up. "Put your legs around me, Meg."

She had set the beast loose and it was time to ride him. Heart in her eyes, love in her heart, she held on for dear life and took him in. His hand clamped on her backside as he drove into her again and again. Each time he withdrew she felt a cold chill chasing up her spine.

"Love me, Dan."

"I do, Meg."

They came together in a blinding flash that threatened to incinerate them. "You're going to kill me, Meg."

"I think you're a lot stronger than that." She patted his hand and he let her go. She tugged on his hand and coaxed him up the stairs. "How about a little nap and then you can let me have my way with you?"

"What do you call what we just did?"

Her lips twitched and she slowly smiled. "Foreplay."

—◆◆◆—

Dan watched as Meg slept. The woman in his bed had wormed her way into his heart. He'd been falling in love with the woman from the moment he saw her walking on the fence rails. Since he'd been in Apple Grove a lot of things had changed—most importantly, he had changed.

He brushed a silky strand of hair out of her eyes. It got stuck on her eyelashes, so he carefully plucked it free and brushed it behind her ears. She shifted and mumbled something unintelligible in her sleep. He grinned. They'd exhausted one another by making love off and on all night. But what he wanted in his heart woke him up.

He'd been accepted in town from the first. The people here were open and willing to embrace change—well, some change. It didn't take as long as he'd thought to win the team over, and he'd discovered they weren't just a great group of players; they were great kids too.

He didn't dwell on the incident at the railroad bridge, because he still wasn't certain that a part of it wasn't his fault, even though both boys' mothers tried to convince him it wasn't. Things like this didn't happen back home, but then again, he hadn't lived up in the wilds of Sussex County or in the western or southern part of the state, so who knows if things like that happened in similar sur- roundings. One thing was certain in his mind—teenagers were predictable in their unpredictability.

Meg rolled over and he traced her curves from the top of her shoulders slowly down her side to the dip at her waist and up again along the sweet curve of her hip. He'd been in love before, but not like this. He wasn't sure he could put the all of the feelings rioting inside of him into words—but for Meg's sake he would.

He frowned, thinking about the way her past had rode back into town. He wasn't sure if Meg was right and it was Van Orden's mother who'd been the one to tell Jimmy that Meg was over her infatuation with him, but it didn't matter anymore. Meg was all the mattered—her loving him and him showing her how much he loved her.

He placed his hand low on her belly. In her sleep, she covered his hand with hers. He wondered what it would be like to see Meg grow round with their child. Would it be a boy or a girl? Would their child have auburn hair—straight as a pin—or wavy light brown hair? Freckles or dimples? Tall or short? Either way, he'd love their baby with all his heart—the same way he loved its mother.

Would she want to have children with him? Before he asked that particular question, he needed to hear the answer to one that had him lying awake all night, watching her sleep.

"Wake up, Meg."

She didn't even stir in her sleep. He tried again, this time shaking her shoulder and calling her name.

"Mmmm."

Needing to settle what was in his heart and on his mind, he rolled her onto her back and pinned her hips to the mattress. Her lashes fluttered and she slowly opened her eyes. Soft, beautiful blue eyes looked up at him.

"Hey."

He bent down to capture her lips. "Marry me, Meg."

She stiffened beneath him.

He wasn't deterred; after all, he did just wake her up. "Meg, I'm serious and you're not dreaming. Will you marry me?"

She touched the side of his face with the tips of her fingers and slowly smiled. "Because we're good in bed?"

"That's part of it but not all of it."

"Why do you want to marry me?"

"You're passionate about your work, your life, and making love to me—and you love me."

"That's true, but shouldn't we give it time? We've only been together a little while."

"I heard from a reliable source that a very close friend of yours had a biological clock that was ticking. She's only a little older than you—is yours ticking too?"

"Not a point you want to press if you're trying to convince a woman to marry you, Eagan."

He kissed her furrowed brow and the tip of her nose. "I want to raise a family with you. Do you want kids, Meg?"

She closed her eyes and sighed before opening them again. "Yes. I was thinking eight for starters."

He drew in a breath and held it until she started laughing. "If you could have seen the look of pure panic on your face."

"Not funny, Mulcahy." He pulled her close and rolled over so she was on top. When she put her elbow in the middle of his left pec and rested her head on her hand he knew he hadn't totally blown his proposal—yet. His mind raced for the words that would convince this amazing woman that he wanted to marry her for all of the right reasons. Women were tricky. He prayed for wisdom and enlightenment came.

"When I first came to town, I wasn't really living. I was escaping life—leaving it behind me, rather than picking up the pieces of what was left."

Her expression softened and he knew she was really listening.

"Then I met you and everything seemed to click. You know I was attracted to you from the first, but then I got to know you and liked what was on the inside as much as what was on the outside."

Her lips twitched and one side of her mouth lifted before she caught herself about to smile. "I'm sensing there's an *and* here."

He rolled again so she was beneath him. Leaning all of his weight on his elbows, he cupped her face in his hands and rasped, "There's a hole in my life Meg—only you can fix it."

Tears filled her eyes, magnifying the blue. "Handyman analogies," she sighed. "For a phys ed teacher, you're pretty good with words."

Hope hadn't been something he'd experienced in the last few years and he didn't recognize the emotion at first. His confusion must have shown on his face, because she reached up and placed her good hand over one of his. He had to ask, "Is that a yes?"

"You're not asking just because Jimmy came back to town?"

He couldn't lie to her. "I'll admit I was worried that you might still have a soft spot for the guy, but you have to know that isn't why I asked. I want and need you in my life, Meg. I love you and want the whole town of Apple Grove to know how I feel."

Her smile was blinding. "I happen to know one way to get everyone's attention—it's kind of a tradition around here."

"Then let's do it."

She squeezed his hand before sliding hers around the back of his head. "How do you feel about heights?"

He shrugged. "Not a problem for me."

"How are you with a paintbrush?"

The light went on. "The water tower?"

She grinned. "I'll give you my answer now, provided you ask me again in John Deere green on the Apple Grove water tower."

He leaned across her, reaching for his watch. "It's after midnight. Where can I get a can of that paint?"

She slipped out from under him and got up. "I think we should call the sheriff."

"And wake him up at this hour?"

"He lives the job—that's why he held off for so long staking his claim to Honey B., but that's not the point. He thinks no one knows his secret, but I figured it out years back."

"And this secret has to do with paint?"

"Kind of," she said, pulling her T-shirt back on. "Hey, where are my pants?"

He grinned and got out of bed. "In the kitchen."

She must have figured out what he had in mind because she dodged him and ran out the door. "Come on. We have just enough time to get it up there before Jimmy leaves town."

He caught up with her at the bottom of the steps. "Is it that important to you that he knows?"

Her eyes were serious and her cheeks flushed with embarrassment. "He needs to know that you aren't just a man of action—that you are man of words, and one who will keep his word. He needs to know that I've put the past behind me and maybe, just maybe I want him to suffer a little bit."

He put his hands beneath her arms and swung her in a circle. Dizzy with love for the woman he held, he kissed her on the lips and set her back on her feet. "First we get dressed, then you call the sheriff. By noon tomorrow, I want everyone in town to know that you're going to be mine."

She pulled on her sexy panties and jeans. She tossed his boxers at him and grinned. "They'll know by sunup."

"How? Do the people in town use that water tower as a form of communication?"

Her laughter was music to his heart. "Absolutely." She reached into her pants pocket and pulled out her phone. She hit one number and locked gazes with him. "Hey, Mitch, it's Meg. No, it's not that kind of emergency," she said then laughed. "Tell Honey B. I said hi... and do you have an open can of paint?"

She nodded and listened. "We'll meet you there."

Fifteen minutes later, Dan had climbed to the top of the ladder and pulled himself onto the catwalk. Dan met the man's gaze and noticed something was off. "You don't look so good. Are you all right?"

The sheriff gritted his teeth and said, "Let's just get this done."

Dan realized the sheriff was a braver man than anyone knew. "How long have you been afraid of heights?"

Their gazes met. The sheriff looked away first. "Didn't say I was."

Dan nodded. "Your secret is safe with me. Here, let me." He reached for the can of paint and the brush.

"How do I reach high enough?"

"Well now," the sheriff drawled. "That's the tricky part. See that rope up there?"

Dan groaned and glanced down at Meg. She waved at him and he thought she might be smiling but couldn't really see; the spotlight only illuminated the tower, not the ground.

"You grab a hold of that to steady yourself as you step up on that pipe up there."

Dan drew in a deep breath and let it go. "You must really love the people of Apple Grove."

The sheriff grinned. "You must really love Meg."

Dan laughed. "I do."

"Keep saying those words," the sheriff told him. "It's good practice."

Chapter 15

MEG'S CELL PHONE WOKE HER FROM A DEEP SLEEP. SHE rolled over and reached for it, but it wasn't under her pillow. She started to roll over and smacked into a warm, hard body—Dan.

"What's up?"

"My phone's ringing. Do you remember where I left it?"

He smiled and pulled her into his arms. "They'll call back."

"But it's all part of the process and I've waited a long time for this."

"You mean me?"

She kissed him with all of the giddy excitement sprinting through her heart. "I've waited half my life for you. Now where the heck is my phone?"

He sat up and looked around and then leaned across her. He grabbed her phone off the bedside table, but it stopped ringing.

"Damn. I wanted to answer that first call."

At the buzz, her gaze shot up to meet his before she read the message. "It's from Pop."

"Your dad?"

"He said he's got the coffee on and he'll be waiting for us."

"Why?"

She was busy texting and ignored him, saying instead, "I told him we haven't had breakfast yet."

"Great, so he knows we're still in bed."

"Where else would we be after you slapped paint on the water tower last night?"

"Is he mad?"

She laughed as she read her father's reply. "He says you just might be good enough for me."

"He's right. Tell your dad we're on our way."

"But we didn't get cleaned up yet."

"You go first and make it quick. I'll see if he has anything else to say."

She hopped out of bed and disappeared into the bathroom. He heard her singing but couldn't quite make out the words.

Knowing he'd have to get cleaned up next, he walked over to the bathroom door and heard her singing. "…in letters three foot high, and the whole town said that he should have used red, but it looked good to Charlene in John Deere green…"

He had no idea what song she was singing, but she sure sang it with gusto. "You almost done?"

She laughed. "Yes. Come on in."

He chuckled. "Can't. I just told your dad we were on our way. You know what will happen if I get in there. Hey," he said. "Are you getting your hand wet?"

"Not really wet… just a little damp. Besides, today's the day I change the bandage, check it, clean it, and re-wrap it, and report to Doc Gannon."

She shut off the water, opened the curtain, and smiled. "Next."

"You will pay for teasing me," he ground out. "You do know that, don't you?"

She laughed as she wrapped herself in a towel and started humming.

He hauled her close for a brief kiss and then got in the shower. "Did you know that you hum when you're happy?" He scrubbed himself clean in half the time it usually took. She hadn't answered him, so he figured she was using her phone.

He pushed the curtain aside and reached for the towel she'd left on the toilet seat. It was too quiet. Unease sprinted through his system. Wrapping the towel around his waist he called her. "Meg?"

"In here." She was dressed and sitting Indian-style on the bed. "Pop said he might change his mind about you if you don't ask him properly."

"Ah," he said as he got dressed. "I didn't ask him for your hand."

She got up and walked over to him. "No, you didn't."

He grabbed her hips and yanked her close. "I guess I was distracted." He bent his head and brushed a kiss over her sweet lips. "We have got to go now, or I'm stripping you bare and having my way with you."

"I could text him back."

It sounded good to him, but the need to ask her father for her hand the traditional way had him pulling back on what he wanted to do, going with what he needed to do. He may have done the asking out of order, but he owed it to Meg and her father to do the right thing. "No. Let's go."

―⁓―

"Turn here," she told him.

"But your dad's house is that way."

She nodded. "I just wanted to see the tower in the morning light."

How could he say no? He turned in the opposite direction and drove out of town.

"Here's good. Pull over!" She was out of the car and snapping a picture with her phone.

Dan walked over to where she stood staring up at the tower. "Sorry, it dripped a little."

She spun around and he realized she was crying.

"Hey, I can go back up with paint remover and fix the drips."

"Silly man... these are happy tears."

"So it's OK the way it is?"

She grabbed a hold of his hand and turned back around and read his proposal out loud. "'I love you, Meg. Marry me? Dan.' It's perfect." She tugged and he followed. "Come on."

Her father was waiting for them. One look at Meg and he had to fight to hide his smile. "You had to drive out past the water tower first."

She laughed and flung herself into her father's arms.

"I can read you like a book, Megan."

Dan noticed the catch in her father's voice but didn't say anything. This moment was for Meg and her dad. His would come in a few minutes.

"Come on in. I poured the coffee when I heard your car."

They followed him into the kitchen and Dan was struck by how homey it felt. He'd noticed it that first night and realized it had as much to do with the people in the room as the room itself.

Meg added milk and two sugars to his mug and handed it to him before doctoring hers.

"Thanks."

While they drank, Joe broke a few eggs into a bowl

and started to whisk them with a fork. "So, I take it you two realize what's going to happen now?"

Dan had no idea what he was talking about, but Meg seemed to.

She set her mug down. "I texted a picture of Dan's proposal to Rhonda… just in case the sheriff was too tired to do it last night."

"Good man, Mitch Wallace," he said, pouring the eggs into the pan. "Glad he finally saw the light where Honey B.'s concerned."

Dan agreed. "Wait. Why Rhonda?"

They looked at him as if his question was odd. Then Meg told him, "She'll do the write up in the *Apple Grove Gazette* to spread the word."

"Because?"

"That's how things run around here," her father told him. He turned off the burner and served up the eggs. "I decided to let you two eat before Dan and I take a walk out to the barn."

He choked on that last mouthful of coffee. "There are no witnesses out there."

Her father laughed as he grabbed the toast. "I like your sense of humor."

Meg was vibrating with happiness and Dan was so damned grateful she'd given him the time to sort things out in his head so that he could follow his heart.

They finished eating and her father refilled everyone's mug. "Your sisters should be up soon. Why don't you put on more coffee while Dan and I take a walk?"

"OK, Pop." She followed after them and stopped Dan at the back door. "I love you, Dan Eagan."

Before he could speak, she stood up on her toes and

planted a kiss on him that had his eyes crossing and his heart pumping.

"Give the man a chance to digest, Megan."

She was laughing when she closed the door.

"I love all of my daughters."

Dan didn't think he was expected to say anything, so he nodded.

"Meg's the most like me — she's good with her hands, quick to rile, but honest as the day is long. You won't find a better woman than my oldest daughter — unless of course it was one of her sisters."

"She's got a heart of gold and goes out of her way to help people," Dan added.

Her father paused with his hand on the barn door. "That she does." He opened the door and flicked on the overhead lights. "She suffered for a long time when that idiot up and left town… left my darling girl hanging on a promise that he never intended to keep."

Dan stiffened. "I'm not an idiot. I want to marry your daughter, have kids with her, and grow old with her."

Her dad nodded and started pacing. "Sometimes life doesn't play out the way you want it to."

"If the next six months is all we have together, then we'll make the most of every day."

"What if she makes you mad? She's got a way of getting under a man's skin, and not always in a good way."

Dan laughed. "I know. She can make me mad as hell at her, but I'd never lay a hand on her in anger… she's my life."

Her father stopped and looked over at Dan. "That's what I wanted to hear."

"I've been through the ringer myself and know how

it feels to have your love flushed down the damn toilet, literally, but that only taught me to recognize the real thing when I saw her walking along the top of that damned fence."

Before her father could say anything else, Dan added, "I want to marry your daughter, sir. Do I have your permission?"

Dan watched as moisture filled Joseph Mulcahy's eyes, but the older man let the tears gather and fall. He wiped at his eyes and sniffed. "If she'll have you—and judging by the way she's looking at you this morning, I'm guessing she will—then you have it."

Dan held out his hand and was surprised when Joe grabbed his hand and yanked him in for a hard hug. "Now before we go back in, do you know how much a Mickey Mantle rookie card is worth?"

"Yes, sir," he answered. "I pawned one to buy my ex a ring. The damned pawnbroker sold it out from under me, to my ex–best friend."

"Sounds like the rest of the story will require a couple of beers."

Dan grinned. "It's funny now… it wasn't at the time."

Joe nodded and then opened the barn door. "Let me show you what else I did to the engine after you left."

Dan's face lit up like a kid at Christmas. "There's nothing like a Ford."

His father-in-law-to-be grunted. "Never could abide anyone who drove a Chevy."

—⁂—

Meg watched them disappear and knew that her father would say yes. He'd already told her as much earlier, but she also knew her dad needed to hear Dan tell him how he felt about her.

Her phone buzzed again; this time it was Caitlin. Did you say yes?

She laughed and shot off her reply, adding, Coffee's ready.

Judging from the squeals coming from upstairs, her sisters finally figured out that she was in their kitchen.

"Oh my God, Meg!" Grace ran across the kitchen. "Your name is on the water tower!" She was crying when she hugged Meg.

Meg tried to be strong, but the harder Grace cried the weaker Meg's resolve became. Soon they were both crying.

"What gives?" Caitlin asked, walking into the kitchen. "I thought there was coffee?"

Grace was sniffling when she let go of Meg. "Check out the picture Rhonda posted this morning." She held her phone up so their sister could see.

Caitlin grinned. "I know. Cindy texted me this morning. Seems the sheriff got an early start today."

"I know I shouldn't have disturbed him and Honey B., but they'll have the rest of their lives together, if he follows through and marries her. Besides, I'm betting he'll be making up for lost time every chance he gets."

The sisters all agreed. "If you could have seen him stalking into Honey B.'s shop yesterday afternoon—he was definitely a man on a mission."

"We heard and we saw the picture Mrs. Hawkins took," Grace said.

"Good news certainly travels fast." Meg wiped her eyes and got down two mugs. Pouring their coffee carefully with her left hand, she confessed, "I wasn't sure it would feel the same, seeing Dan's proposal up on the tower, since he wasn't from around here and I asked him to do it for me."

Her sisters drank their coffee while she told them about last night. "I didn't think he understood how much it meant to me, but if you could have seen the look on his face when he was standing at the bottom of the ladder looking up, you'd know how much he loves me."

"Well, the whole town will know pretty soon," Grace said.

"I bet Mrs. Van Orden knows," Caitlin added. "She's probably telling Jimmy right now over breakfast."

The house line rang and the sisters looked at one another and laughed. Caitlin answered the phone and smiled. "He's out in the barn with Pop. I'll tell him you called. We are too." She smiled as she hung up. "That was Dan's aunt; she can't wait to talk to him."

Meg was about to ask why Miss Trudi didn't want to talk to her, when Caitlin added, "She said she can't wait to welcome you into the family, but knows you'd understand that she needs to talk to Dan first."

"I'm hungry," Grace said. "Who wants hotcakes?"

The three of them were laughing and making wedding plans when the men walked back in.

Dan strode across the kitchen and picked Meg up off her feet and hugged her tight. "He said yes." Before she could say anything, his lips were locked on hers and she was kissing him back.

"Get a room, guys," Grace grumbled.

Meg heard Caitlin laughing as her sister said, "She's just jealous that it isn't her name on the water tower."

Dan kept Meg glued to his side while they sat around and gorged themselves on buttermilk pancakes. When he'd cleaned his plate, he leaned close and whispered in Meg's ear, "I didn't think I was still hungry."

Meg giggled and her father frowned at them. "How soon is the wedding?"

Her sisters laughed out loud. "From the looks of things, Pop," Caitlin said, "it'd better be soon."

Dan lifted Meg's hand to his lips. "Where did you want to get married?"

She looked at her dad and then her sisters before turning back to answer, "Here."

He nodded as if he expected that answer. "I figured you'd want to get married in the church in town, but is there somewhere nearby where we could have the reception?"

They all looked at him as if he'd lost his mind. "What? There must be a Legion Hall or something like that. It's too cold to have the wedding or reception outside."

Meg was waiting for him to look at her, when he did, she said, "Pop's got heat in the barn."

He looked from one expectant face to the other. "You want to get married in the barn?"

"It's tradition," Grace told him.

"Our great-grandparents renewed their vows in the barn," Caitlin said.

"My parents got married there," Joe told him.

"And so did our mom and pop," Meg said, laying a hand on her father's arm.

Dan knew then that he'd move heaven and Earth to keep that smile on Meg's face; he hated to see her sad. "I don't want to wait to get married. How about the weekend after Thanksgiving?"

She catapulted up out of her chair and into his arms. "Yes!"

He pulled her onto his lap, so he felt when she stiffened. "What's wrong?"

"Where are we going to get daisies and wild roses this time of year?"

"Is it important?"

"I guess not."

Her father chuckled. "That's Meg-speak for yes."

"Gee thanks, Pop," Meg grumbled. "My own family throwing me under the bus."

"If you don't tell me," Dan said quietly, "I won't know. Promise me to always tell me what's in your heart and on your mind."

Meg cleared her throat. "As long as you do the same."

He drew her close and pressed his lips to hers.

"Wow," Grace sighed. "Do you have any younger brothers?"

Dan chuckled, but before he could answer, Caitlin nudged Meg. "Let Grace and I worry about the flowers, OK?"

Meg sighed. "OK."

Drawing her back against him, Dan asked, "Do you think we can get everything together in two and a half weeks?"

Meg smiled. "Once a Mulcahy makes up her mind, there's no changing it."

Dan grinned. "Then you're in luck, because once an Eagan gives his word, you can count on him to keep it."

Chapter 16

MEG TURNED AROUND TO FACE HER SISTERS AND HER best friend, Honey B. "Do I look all right?" Her mother's dress swirled around her and settled back to fall in soft drapes around her slender form, hugging her curves, accentuating them. Meg couldn't believe that her father had kept it all these years in her mother's cedar chest, hoping Meg would wear it.

"You really should wear dresses more often, Meg," Honey B. told her.

Her sisters laughed and placed a wreath of English Ivy and Baby's Breath on her head. "Now you look perfect," Grace said.

"Dan's eyes are going to pop out of his head when he sees how beautiful you are," Caitlin told her.

The knock on the door had them all going quiet.

"It's Pop, Meg. May I come in?"

"Of course."

The door opened and her father's eyes widened and then he slowly smiled. "You look just like she did the day I married her."

He held out his hand to her. Suspended from his fingers was a Celtic cross dangling from a thin gold chain. "You mother wore this the day we got married. When she was in the hospital—" He paused to clear his throat before continuing. "She took it off and asked me to keep it for you and your sisters to wear on your wedding day."

Meg blinked away the tears that threatened to fall. "Thanks, Pop."

He put the chain around her neck. "Hold your hair out of the way while I fasten it."

Meg lifted her hair off her neck. The physical weight of the chain was slight, but the emotional weight of it felt like a hug from her mother.

"Today, Dan is the luckiest man in Apple Grove." He squeezed her hand. "Are you ready, Meg?"

"Don't I look ready?"

"You look perfect."

"Then I'm ready. Let's not keep him waiting any longer." She followed her sisters and her friend downstairs.

The sun was shining as they walked down the back porch steps. There was a brisk breeze, but she ignored the crisp cold, knowing it would be warm in the barn. Her family and friends had strung white fairy lights entwined with ivy along the roofline. Even in the sunlight the lights twinkled amid the dark green of the ivy.

The doors were flung open and more ivy and lights were draped around the opening, but what caught her eye and held her attention was the bright white satin runner leading from the bottom of the steps to the barn.

"Careful, ladies," her father warned.

"Pop, wait." Meg tugged on his arm to get him to stop.

"What's wrong?"

"I think I have to pee."

He nodded. "Too late now. Besides, it's probably just nerves."

She nodded and the feeling disappeared. "You're right… it's nerves." They reached the back of the barn and her heart started beating faster. "I love him."

"I wouldn't let you marry him if I didn't think you did."

"He loves me too."

"Smart man, that Dan Eagan."

She grinned up at her father. "I love you, Pop."

"I love you back," he rasped.

More lights were twinkling inside the barn, draped from the rafters and hanging amidst garlands of ivy. "It's perfect."

And then she saw Dan, waiting beneath an arbor festooned with ivy and white roses, and her breath snagged in her lungs. He was looking at her as if his next breath depended on her reaching his side. She tugged on her dad's arm and practically ran toward him.

"You're here," Dan whispered.

"Where else would I be?"

He shook his head. "Nightmare. Glad it didn't come true."

Her father put her hand in Dan's. "Always remember the gift I'm giving you today," he told her husband-to-be.

Dan's hand was warm. She shivered at his touch. "Thank you, sir," Dan replied.

Her father chuckled. "Joe will do."

"Dearly beloved," Reverend Smith began.

Dan swore to love, honor, and cherish her. Meg echoed his words, lifting her gaze to meet his. She'd never thought to find love, yet here they stood, before the people that mattered to her most—her neighbors, her friends, and most importantly, her family.

"You may kiss the bride."

Dan bent his head and claimed her lips. Meg felt the wonder of their first kiss as husband and wife and knew that it was fate—maybe her mother—that had nudged her off the top of that fence and into Dan Eagan's arms.

She whispered a silent prayer of thanks as she kissed him back with all of the love in her heart.

A taste of home-cooking from Apple Grove!

Grandma McCormack's Cream Scones

4 tablespoons unsalted butter (½ stick)
1¾ cups all-purpose flour (Hecker's unbleached)
¼ teaspoon salt
5½ tablespoons sugar
1 teaspoon baking soda
2 teaspoons cream of tartar
2 eggs
⅓ cup heavy cream

Using a pastry blender, cut the butter into the flour and salt. Mix until mixture resembles coarse cornmeal. Add the sugar, baking soda, and cream of tartar. Mix well.

Beat the eggs with the cream and add to flour mixture, using a wooden spoon to make a spongy mixture. Place the dough on a well-floured bread board or countertop and pat to ½ inch thickness. Cut the dough into rounds with a biscuit cutter (or large cookie cutter). Flour your hands and place the cut out scones on a nonstick cookie sheet; leave for ten minutes to settle.

Bake in preheated oven at 450 degrees for eight minutes, or until golden brown.

Serve with jam, preserves, or whipped (or clotted) cream.

© 2002 C.H. Admirand

Acknowledgments

A special thank-you to Kim Rocha for dropping everything to read *AWIAG*. You were right; Jimmy did need to meet Dan and fight over Meg! You are THE BEST!

When Deb asked if I would be interested in writing a small-town USA series, I jumped at the opportunity to spread my writing wings. I missed writing about the small towns in my Irish Western series and welcomed the chance to recreate a part of my past and who I am in a contemporary setting.

Growing up on Cedar Hill—a tiny corner of Wayne, New Jersey—our neighborhood was like living in a small town. There were twenty-five homes in our little hamlet of dead-end streets. Unless you lived off Circle Drive, there wasn't any reason to go to Cedar Hill. Tucked away from the rest of the world, we lived in idyllic surroundings—we could run or ride our bikes to our friend's house and still hear when mom rang the dinner bell—a cowbell my dad found when he was a kid living in Colorado, not to be mistaken from the ship's bell suspended between two trees that called our neighbor home—his dad had been in the navy.

My great-aunt and uncle lived right next door and my great-aunt always kept molasses windmill-shaped cookies with the almonds on top in the cookie jar on the end of the counter, right inside the back door. It was always full. She read pirate stories and poems to us on their screen porch on summer nights. I remember waking up to the sound of my great-uncle whistling—he had this six-note call that I'd hear in my sleep. I'd climb out of bed and get dressed but was young enough that I couldn't tie my red plaid sneakers, but I'd put them on—careful not to trip on the stairs, knowing that he'd be waiting to tie them for me.

My grandparents were two houses away, which made it seem like we had three homes instead of just one. My grandmother was a *cheese and crackers* grandma… not the typical *milk and cookies* kind. I'd run up to her house after my homework was done and set their dinner table, nibble on crackers and cheese, watching Merv Griffin or Mike Douglas and the four thirty movie before it was time to go home and set our table and help get dinner ready.

For the last thirty years, we've lived in a small lake community. My husband grew up in one, and from the stories of his childhood, I knew that was the atmosphere we wanted for our kids. It was a mixed community with residents who'd lived there for forty years and those of us who'd just moved in. Five of us were pregnant at the same time and forged a bond that carried over to our kids. They played together, attended preschool together, and graduated from high school together.

One element of both neighborhoods was the core group of women responsible for keeping tabs on everyone and making sure to spread the word, both good and bad; it was like having a town crier.

On Cedar Hill, it was my grandmother, my great-aunt, and both Mrs. Johnsons who kept everyone abreast of the neighborhood goings-on. In Lindy's Lake, it was Honey Baker, Marty Walsh, Ann Ahrens, and Millie Salisbury.

In the fictionalized town of Apple Grove, Ohio, it is Mrs. Winter, Miss Philo, and Honey B. Harrington who are the glue that keeps the town together and in the know.

So brew a cup of tea or grab a cup of coffee, put your feet up and relax, and spend some time getting to know the good people of Apple Grove.

About the Author

C.H. Admirand is an award-winning, multipublished author with novels in mass-market paperback, hardcover, trade paperback, magazine, e-book, and coming soon digital comic and audio book format.

Fate, destiny, and love at first sight will always play a large part in C.H.'s stories because they played a major role in her life. When she saw her husband for the first time, she knew he was the man she was going to spend the rest of her life with. Each and every hero C.H. writes about has a few of Dave's best qualities: his honesty, his integrity, his compassion for those in need, and his killer broad shoulders. She lives with her husband and two of their grown children in the wilds of northern New Jersey and recently welcomed their first grandbaby into the family.

C.H. always uses family names in her books, but this time something truly karmic occurred while she was writing the first book in her new small-town USA series; while tracing her Irish ancestors, she uncovered something wonderful—her great-grandfather was already listed on Ancestry.com with the same picture that sits on her mantelpiece. She had discovered a link to the Mulcahy side of the family; her grandfather's younger sister married a Mulcahy. After sending an email, she was delighted when she received a reply, and even more so when she learned that her connection and her sisters were delighted to be heroines in C.H.'s new series.

She loves to hear from readers! Stop by her website at www.chadmirand.com to catch up on the latest news, excerpts, reviews, blog posts, and links to Facebook and Twitter.

WITHDRAWN
from St. Joseph County Public Library
Excess_____ Damaged _____
Date_____ Initials _____